Born in Detroit, John Shannon grew up in San Pedro, California. He has worked as a journalist and as an English teacher in a secondary school in Africa. He has lived for several years in England. His previous books are *The Orphan* (1972) and *Courage* (1975).

Pluto Crime

Edited by Ronald Segal

'. . . Is there anything inherently illogical with the concept of socialist – or, at least, politically and socially aware – crime fiction? Pluto Press, publishers of serious left wing books, have inaugurated a crime list to prove that the two can mix . . . the first batch of pinko whodunits augurs well for the genre.' *The Times*

'. . . the most innovative publishing experiment of the crime-story year!' *The Guardian*

John Shannon

Broken Codes P

Pluto Press

London   Sydney   Dover New Hampshire

First published in 1986 by Pluto Press Limited,
The Works, 105a Torriano Avenue, London NW5 2RX
and Pluto Press Australia Limited, PO Box 199, Leichhardt,
New South Wales 2040, Australia. Also Pluto Press, 51 Washington
Street, Dover, New Hampshire 03820 USA.

7 6 5 4 3 2 1

89 88 87 86 90

Set by Sunrise Setting, Torquay, Devon
Printed in Great Britain by Cox & Wyman, Reading, Berks.

British Library Cataloguing in Publication Data

Shannon, John
   Broken Codes.
   I. Title
   813′.[F]   PS3569.H336

ISBN 0 7453 0024 3 pbk
      0 7453 0025 1 hbk

For P. G.

We are all cripples, more or less

Dostoyevsky

1

'The Old Man's got his teeth right down to the bone,' Moore said carelessly behind the wheel.

Quarter past eight: a grey Monday in winter, and Ross stared mournfully at the frost patterns on the windshield of the noisy, alien sports car, sitting quite low on the passenger side and trying to avoid the chore of small talk.

'We'll back you up if you think it should be stopped, but none of the rest of us have the . . .'

Has, Ross thought automatically with the pedantry he could never quite relinquish; none of us *has*. The word Moore's perennially fuzzy mind groped toward was probably 'authority', though it might have been 'seniority' or even 'balls'. Jerome Moore III, Yale 1970, Soviet studies and history, was a fifth-generation Du Pont through his mother, and even a tree knew more about the world, Ross thought. Moore guided the whining Ferrari Berlinetta out over the Potomac River, as ominous as slow lava. They arced across the bridge against the flow of commuters, a dreary nose-to-tail procession toward K Street and Pennsylvania Avenue.

'You know what I mean. Jesus, opposing the Old Man is like shoving your arm up a meat grinder. Harv, he was a case officer when I was in short pants; he's been chief of station in places I only dream about. And maybe he's on to something . . . you *do* know what's going on?'

'No,' Ross said grumpily. 'I'll wait for the meeting, thank you.' He wanted Moore to shut up so that he could retrace a particularly elusive drift of argument. He had been struggling with it a half hour earlier: something about defining social class in terms of role and function rather than relationship to the means of production. Poulantzas, it was, chewing up traditional

1

Marxist definitions. Ross woke at four every morning to take a single cup of black coffee and then settle at his desk with obscure journals of European Marxist studies, adding to his voluminous boxes of file cards. What had begun twenty-five years earlier as preparation for editing the left-wing magazine he had been assigned to penetrate had turned into a wagon track across all the changes in his life. The magazine had died after only two years, despite a concealed subsidy, since *Marxist Analysis* had simply outlived its usefulness as a baited snare for radical writers. But even as he had moved on to other deep cover jobs, he had never dropped his reading. It was possible he was drawn by the rigorous purity of the arguments, as others are drawn by crosswords. For a time he accepted his colleagues' estimate that he was simply the champion know-your-enemy buff. But he saw perfectly well that dry scholastics were no one's enemies; no more of a threat than were Brazilian tree frogs. For whatever reason, through bad and worse, Ross had carried on studying his obscure idealogues.

Moore turned north up the Georgetown Turnpike: Langley 2. He pulled out suddenly to pass a slow truck and the acceleration pressed Ross into the hard leather seat like a hand. The habit of study had served him well; it had become Ross's single lifeline out of the wreck of his life after Myra's death. His wife had drowned in a freak sailboat accident fifteen years earlier, going overboard on a nearly windless day and vanishing into the dark Chesapeake Bay, despite his repeated frantic dives. Ross had never gone near his beloved sea again. He had moved out of the Georgetown house, sold off their furniture and possessions, and abandoned their circle of friends. He had never driven a Ford again, never gone to the theatre, and he habitually turned away whenever he saw a dark-haired woman wearing white. But to salvage his tenuous identity, to keep from slipping completely out of space and time, he had returned to his books and journals, to Adorno and the Frankfurt School; then, over the years, to Althusser, Macherey, Lacan, Poulantzas and the rest. He knew what he had become, what he was: a stocky, clumsy, middle-aged man whose cheap suits did not fit and whose intelligence had largely shrivelled to a sterile and tactless fussiness. He carried an immense will to punish, but it was held in check most of the time because he recognized it, and knew how fleeting and double-edged the pleasures of severity were.

Perversely he chose to live in the heart of decaying D.C., in the basement apartment of a building owned by Mrs Hermes Mackinnon, a heavy Jamaican woman who brought him spiced chicken once a week and stamped on the floor whenever he tried to type in the morning. For security he had put a 9 mm Browning in a cigar box by the bed, but he had never needed it and for all he knew the pistol had rusted up in the damp years ago.

'It's his vendetta again, Harvey. Heap warpaint; smoke-um funny leaves, go blooey in the head and make-um marks on floor of teepee: *our* side, *their* side, go get-um quick rip balls off.'

Reluctantly Ross gave Moore's blithering his attention. 'Research?' he asked.

'Who else? You must be the only one in the section so fearsome he has to keep you in the dark. I'll tell you somebody's going to get jerked around good. Hell, wouldn't the Directorate shower him with medals if it worked? Remember Mark Antony, "Would that you had done it first and then told me about it."'

'"Ah, this, thou shouldest have done and not spoken on it,"' Ross corrected tonelessly. 'Don't patronize him, Jerry. He's too good for that. And choose a side. If you back him now, stay with him. If you want a parachute, announce it at the outset.'

Moore grinned. 'None of those clever back-dated memoes in the files: Over my violent objections . . .?'

Vehement, Ross thought automatically. For God's sake, man, learn one language well. 'That's what I mean,' Ross said. 'I won't have double-dealing inside the section.'

'Aye-aye. Down with the ship, sir. Anyway, we can be thankful we're nor working for that miserable little outfit. Research has a shitstorm coming.'

At last Moore fell silent, the turnoff only a half mile ahead. Ross let his eyes drift to the bare trees alongside the parkway, skeletons in the Potomac mist. So, the Old Man was building himself a final monument. He knew he should stop it in its tracks if there were the faintest possibility of backfire, but some elusive loss of will held him back. Perhaps it was just that the Old Man deserved a last shot.

Morning: already Ross could feel the sweat prickling on his

forehead, and he swiped at it with a fraying handkerchief. The best in-house specialists in the Office of Medical Services had been unable to tell him why he woke each morning with a body temperature of 101°F. Nerves, they suggested in the years when that was a popular explanation for everything, which was most years at Langley. But Ross never felt nervous.

'They'll have my car tonight,' Ross said. 'I won't need a lift.'

'Sure thing. No bother, though.' Moore double-declutched and shifted down twice as they slid across the shallow turn that approached the modern fortress, set back in its hundred acres of trees and glen behind double fences.

★

Sloane hesitated a moment on the top step, noting the dark sky low over the terrace houses, then moved on down two further steps and along the cracked twenty-foot walk to Richmond Road. It would drizzle, he guessed, but it wouldn't rain, not rain as he had known it in his childhood. He had lived thirteen years in London without carrying an encumbering umbrella and he wasn't about to start now, no matter what Sarah said. She knew he hated umbrellas, but she had bought one for him anyway – or, perhaps she didn't know after all. Few people in his experience could be quite as unobservant in small personal matters; even after a year of their marriage, she occasionally had to be reminded that he didn't take tea, almost never ate eggs and hated the gamey taste of lamb. He observed their little contretemps shyly and secretly, hoping one day to work out the tortured roadmap of her psychology, for in other ways, at other times, she could be so extravagantly considerate that it took his breath away and turned his legs flaccid with tenderness.

Jeffrey Sloane turned right at the corner and shuffled toward Balls Pond Road, a slight, grey-looking man in his late forties carrying a tattered briefcase. His tired, wary eyes habitually darted around him, not in an exaggerated way but like those of a man who cannot bear even minor checks and disturbances and wishes to be forewarned. A few years earlier – before The Fall, as he might have dated it – this apprehensive manner had been no more than a curious air of gentleness, like a painful hangover, and one of his colleagues in Research's front office had even nicknamed him the Wrath of Grapes. But the drinking had always been secondary; he had known even then that his nerve was beginning to go.

After The Fall – the smashup, the breakdown, whatever people chose to call that horrifying moment in which they were suddenly naked to everyone's eyes and they finally made the choice that was always there, waiting – after taking the choice, the person he had once been was still there inside, like a younger brother, but buried deep under layers of defeat. He was sure he could still run like a scalded rabbit if he had to, but he chose the turtle, the watchful pose, slow music and obscurity. It was the morning after the fever had broken, tenuous as fresh ice on a pond, and he could hardly believe he had manufactured a form of peace with Sarah.

Mrs Granby shambled toward him at his own pace with a string bag full of groceries, and he nodded.

'Filthy weather,' she observed, the formula London greeting.

''Day. Cyril came back from school. He said to tell you he's gone to the clinic up at the grove.'

'That lad!'

She hurried on. Her son Cyril was one of the Richmond Road Apaches – their own name for the club – urban boys who were aging prematurely into quick-witted, cynical, emotionless men under the city's tutelage. Even as he watched, they learned the brash ways of holding off a hostile world or leaving their mark on an indifferent one. He guessed Cyril was actually up in Hackney Downs, prowling the garages and car-breaking yards in the arches under the rail embankment. The young Sloane would have been there too, though in another country far away.

He took his place in the bus queue at Balls Pond Road, behind two old women and a West Indian with a silver-topped cane. The area was miles from a tube station, an island of Victorian squalor bypassed by the northward migration of young professionals. It was a wilderness of lost hopes, with the rents marginally lower.

Drizzle began to prickle on the backs of his hands, the sort of rain that made you damp and uncomfortable without driving you under shelter. He turned his briefcase upside down so that the moisture wouldn't seep through the seam that no longer met properly. The briefcase was a lot like his life, he thought: worn out, but still serviceable, just.

★

The black Lincoln passed through the gateway of the twelve-foot security fences with only a momentary pause for the guard to peer inside. It drew up at the side ramp that led up to the smoked-glass and steel building.

'You'll have to phone the pool tonight, sir,' the driver said. 'I won't be on.'

The driver sat patiently in front, knowing better than to offer help as the Old Man shouldered the back door open. The aluminium crutches emerged, their rubber tips caught on the pavement and then, one after another, his legs kicked out with audible snaps as the leg-braces locked. He levered his body out heavily without a word, tossing back a mane of white hair, and propelled himself up the ramp.

Not in six months had he glanced around at the Operations wing to the right, headquarters of the plum clandestine services. His former office was on the outer corner of the third floor, 1,000 square feet, with a genuine rosewood desk and a straight run to the executive lunchroom with its linen tablecloths and first-rate food prepared by in-house chefs. The victim of two successive Saturday Night Massacres, he had never counted on much of a future and was therefore not inclined to any more bitterness than was his due. He did his duty, whatever he was asked, and did it better than anyone expected, and if he found himself written off from the Big Table it was no more than a doctor whispering in his ear: cancer. There was nothing to be done.

He shouldered his way through the glass door, and the guard stood up behind his Dutch door to peer at the badge on the Old Man's coat pocket. It showed a full-face colour photograph with no name or title, just a frieze of small boxes around the rim, some blank but most of them occupied by single letters. The guard nodded, and the Old Man acknowledged it with the tiniest lift of his snowy eyebrows.

He had been retired from the field in the early 1960s. By the time all the scattered sections had moved into the new Langley building, he was moving up the hierarchy rapidly. He had become deputy area head for Europe – before geographic divisions had been abolished in the first big shakeup. All his life, until the second shakeup, he had been in Operations, the choice directorate that controlled two-thirds of the personnel and three-quarters of the budget; the star of the service that attracted the best and brightest of the new career officers. He had served under all the directors, from the austere and doctrinaire who were doomed by their own blunders, through the persistent but overwhelmed, walking out in disgust when they couldn't rein in the messier cowboys, the pathetically naive who were eaten alive, the stolidly liberal axed by change of administration. Axe after axe. The axes had always been aimed above him, but they were too blunt for delicate organizational surgery, and his career had tumbled and sideslipped with the rest.

Now he found himself in the poor stepchild branch, riding herd over the cul-de-sac Office of Economic Analysis, the Gray Bookkeepers. 'It could be worse,' Tom Berkely had said, with a shudder meant to be consoling. 'Look at Jimmy. He's sent into training, exiled to The Farm. Cliff is marooned in personnel. It could be worse.'

Only two years from mandatory retirement, he refused to be a time-server, and he refused, even now, to join the tendentious games of intrigue and gossip that they called 'office politics' when it referred to themselves but 'power struggle' when it referred to one of their targets. As many of them said, the Old Man was simply too straightforward, too solitary and too coldly proud for his own good.

'Don't stand,' he said crisply.

The half dozen people in the Playpen stirred uncomfortably, but stayed in their seats as the Old Man rowed across the room and unlatched his leg-braces to lower himself into his chair. The overhead clock stuttered and bit off a whole minute to reach nine o'clock. Harvey Ross sipped the last of a bootleg cup of coffee, and Dru Wheat rustled a stack of notes in front of her during the perfunctory greetings. The fluorescents did strange things with the highlights in her gold hair, and, as several of them noticed, her photo badge tugged at her blouse. Dru was the section's token woman career officer. There weren't enough token Blacks to go around. Beside her was a mousy, hard-eyed man who was not from their section at all and who watched the Old Man the way a hawk watches a wounded rabbit.

'You'll have noticed this is a staging meeting. I know you find that unusual, but I hope you're not so sunk in your journals and summaries that you've lost the use of your operational legs, so to speak.'

No one dared move a muscle. 'You have permission to smile,' the Old Man announced. 'I'm a famous cripple, and I'm not sensitive about it.'

A callow junior officer named Francis MacIlvaine tried out a small chortle, but it fluttered to an uneasy silence when no one else took it up.

'I've asked Willy to sit in from our directorate's own modest Ops office in case we need backup. Jerry –' The Old Man pointed at Jerry Moore, sitting brightly across from Dru, but used only his first name as house rules demanded '– will work with him, or "liaise" as some of you insist on putting it, in one of the ugliest back-formations in the English language.'

At this in-joke several of them did smile and glance wisely at Harvey Ross. Tutoring their language errors was normally his office. Ross sat back like a coiled snake.

'Dru will do the background.'

She squirmed in the moulded chair, trying once again to overcome the dismay that a roomful of men, certainly *this* roomful of men, would never put any faith in what a woman said. She flipped over the notes in front of her. 'I'll be brief.'

'Why not stand up?' MacIlvaine suggested lasciviously. 'It adds dimension to your reports.' He was referring to her large breasts, which rose and filled with each breath. He never missed a chance.

She made a point of ignoring him. 'I'll skip the introduction and go straight to the background parts. Foundation. The Civil Overseas Research Organization, known to the press as CORO and to most of us in the community as "Research", was formed in 1920 at the height of the great red scare that followed World War I, when Attorney General Mitchell Palmer thought it would be useful to have an eye in Europe watching for Bolshevik agents trying to board the immigrant ships. That was their primary charge, and they opened offices in most of the major seaports that served the immigrants – Cobh in Ireland, Liverpool, Bremerhaven, Livorno and Naples, as well as major exile centres like Switzerland and London.

'Two. Early History. What there was of American intelligence at the time, mostly ad hoc bodies started by the Army and Navy during the war, was soon disbanded, and in 1929 Secretary of State Stimson closed down even State's Cryptanalysis Section with his infamous dictum that gentlemen did not read each other's mail. It was a singularly ingenuous time.'

'No editorializing,' the Old Man interrupted.

'Sorry, sir. From 1929 until the OSS was formed in 1942, Research was the nearest thing to an intelligence service we had, and understandably its tasks multiplied until there were forty stations overseas and something like 5,000 career employees.

'Three. Wartime and immediate postwar. Research lost three-quarters of their stations during the German advance across Europe, including what had become their operational headquarters in Paris. They retreated offshore, but played no role at all as contact to anti-Nazi groups or partisan guerrillas in the occupied territories. This was only natural since they were exclusively and notoriously an anti-communist organization, and many of the partisan groups were made up of indigenous communists. For the same reason, the OSS shunned Research completely, unwilling to jeopardize their own relations with the partisans, and' – she glanced at the Old Man, the only one of them who might be familiar with the historical irony from personal experience – 'if you will remember, until the spring of 1945, the OSS itself employed several score American communists as field agents and cutouts in the European underground. It was, after all, the era of the Popular Front . . .'

'Yes, yes,' the Old Man said. 'Move on.' Johnny Alsfeld, his second in command in the German operations, had been a *Daily Worker* correspondent from Milwaukee. After setting up brilliantly successful escape routes for downed air crews by contacting his old KPD friends in Germany, Alsfeld had been booted on Truman's orders, only two weeks before the German surrender. Personally he had liked Johnny and his irreverent jokes about Uncle Joe and Uncle Franklin, but the Old Man had not been fool enough to stand in the way of the cold war jugger-naut.

'In 1947, when all civil intelligence was supposedly centralized with us, the Attorney General insisted on keeping what remained of Research separate. For reasons of his own, it remained under his department. Research had only nine stations remaining, with about 300 employees overseas and another 100 or so in Washington. Its duties now largely involved monitoring overt sources – newspapers, journals and the like – and assembling reports, though it still ran quite a few low-grade field men.

'Paragraph four. Recent history. Research's appropriations were cut back several times during the sixties and they have, to say the least, languished in obscurity.'

Moore was taking his own notes, and his pen faltered. 'Dru, it's a well-known law of something or other that a bureaucracy tends to expand without limit. Do we know exactly why they were shrinking?'

'Lack of results, lack of function, the AG diverting resources to more pressing business. Actually the law in play here is the one that says any organizational entity, no matter how useless it has become, will carry on operating indefinitely.' Dru thought she had parried the question rather well, and she poked at her hair in a gesture that seemed meant to underline her competence.

'Barring a major catastrophe,' the Old Man added balefully. Ross, watching him carefully, felt suddenly disturbed. There was no sound in the room but the sighing of the air conditioner. Doom had spoken.

'Actually,' Dru pressed on, 'the last drastic cutback came after a rather embarrassing disaster Research precipitated two years ago. There's no need to go into details, but they lost their Bern and Berlin stations, and the AG cancelled their authority to run active operations. They dropped or pensioned off their contract agents and field personnel. It was back to the books. At the moment they have about 100 employees overall, and just one overseas station, in London, with ten officers. Actually, all they have left is a handful of fossils who clip economic bulletins and assemble a few low-level bulletins of their own that are roughly parallel to some of our own.'

'There's the rub,' the Old Man broke in. He glanced around,

as if Research was a presence there in the room to be confronted and crushed. 'As you know, two months ago I delivered our yearly economics estimate on the Eastern Bloc before the 40 Committee, and last month the National Security Council reviewed our paper on the Soviet oil situation. In both cases, some . . .' He caught himself, apparently thinking better of adding a rude epithet. 'Someone in the panel cited Research reports on the same subjects that countered our conclusions. Our papers were well researched, detailed and thorough; they involved thousands of man-weeks of preparation, and more expensive computer time than I can justify in the budget. Theirs were cut-and-paste jobs from gossip magazines, but they succeeded in confusing the issue.'

'The bad drives out the good,' Moore interjected.

'Or weakens its authority,' the Old Man went on. 'I won't have that any longer. Research is a thorn, and I think everyone in the Directorate will sleep more soundly when it's been torn from the flesh.'

'How literally are we to take that?' Ross put in mildly. It was his first comment of the meeting, and they all grew watchful. Moore leaned forward on a palm, Dru flushed as she chewed a lock of hair, MacIlvaine grinned behind his fist, waiting for the gladiators to engage.

'How literally would you like to take it?'

'Our intervention in the affairs of a sister organization would go far beyond our statutory authority. In fact, an active operation at all – '

'Don't go Jesuitical on me, Harvey,' the Old Man cut in harshly. 'There is a difference between active entrapment and simply floating out bait to see if anyone bites. I mean to exploit that difference.'

To their amazement, Ross subsided with a nod. 'I'll hear it.'

★

'And God as a punishment sent her to the same hairdresser as my wife,' Bolton concluded over the hillock of papers on the tiny desk. He ran three fingers through his styled brown hair and glanced across the cluttered, impossibly narrow office at Phelps-

Hargood, twenty years his senior. The brutal shine of the older man's bald patch under the bare bulb amused him.

'We must all pay for our peccadillos, old boy,' Phelps-Hargood offered in his smug public school voice, as if pinching his nostrils. His hand fluttered slackly above the desktop, signalling some obscure reproach.

'I don't mind paying if I've got value for money, but this Angela creature was only good for a little of the slap and tickle.' Bolton laughed, remembering the walk home from the pub and the coy fluttering of eyelashes, like something learned from a musical comedy. Her eyes beneath had been over made-up, permanently astonished. 'Hardly that even. A peck on the lips.'

'It's the intention that matters. Or so St Paul tells us.'

'If intentions were acts, beggars would be horses.' Bolton laughed again.

'If wishes were horses, beggars would ride,' Phelps-Hargood corrected primly.

The old bugger had no sense of humour at all, Bolton thought. He didn't bother pointing out that there were probably only three people in all the British Isles who couldn't recite the homily perfectly. 'Ah, yes, thank you. Translating all this wog language makes me confuse my English idioms.'

'German is hardly a wog language,' Phelps-Hargood objected.

'The wogs start at Calais. Excepting Brixton, of course.'

There was a bustling at the frosted-glass door, a shadow crossing the reversed Times Roman lettering that said Pentonville Translation Bureau. Finally the door opened. The man outside was still clumsily swapping an old briefcase to his free hand. He shuffled to the counter while Phelps-Hargood ignored him.

'Hello, sport,' Bolton said.

'Good afternoon,' Sloane said. 'I have the Polish travel book.'

'Precisely six days late,' Phelps-Hargood pronounced without looking up.

Sloane opened his case and took out a bound volume and a thick sheaf of manuscript translation. 'I wanted to get it properly.'

Phelps-Hargood finally swivelled in his chair and dipped his head forward to peer at Sloane owlishly over the round spectacles. 'There are at least eight hours a day when the pubs are closed, old boy.'

'I'm not drinking,' Sloane said with a defensive flutter of his hands. 'I'm not.'

Reluctantly Phelps-Hargood stood and gathered up the translation which he stuffed into a rabbit bin under the counter. He turned away as if their business were completed for all time.

'Please,' Sloane said. 'You must have another commission.'

'I rather think we're short of requests at the moment. Perhaps next month.'

'I need the money,' Sloane said doggedly. He looked a sad case, Bolton thought, the face crumpling in earnest entreaty, shoulders hunched down vulnerably under the ill-fitting coat. He wondered where human wrecks tottered off to when the world just didn't want to know.

Phelps-Hargood fingered two stapled documents on his desk. 'A technical manual on the disposition of metallic substrates on integrated circuits. From the German. Or a Polish paper on vitamin therapy. It's only fifty pounds.'

Sloane looked disappointed. 'I'll take them both.'

Phelps-Hargood shook his head. 'One.' He tossed one of the documents carelessly, and Sloane had to slap at it to keep it from slipping off the near edge of the counter.

'Could I have half in advance?'

Phelps-Hargood shook his head again, and Bolton could see him enjoy the petty cruelty like some frosty old schoolmaster. Sod, he thought. 'Upon completion.'

Bolton glanced at Sloane's eyes and was startled: abruptly they took on a fierce depth, just the eyes, with the face still pasty and flat; like one of those trick portraits with the removable eyes in a mad duke's castle, and the mad duke himself glaring through the gaps into the sitting room with murder in his heart. The fire died away as suddenly as it had leapt into life, and Sloane set the papers listlessly into his case.

'Sloane,' Bolton said with a conspiratorial beckoning. 'Not to worry, man. If God hadn't meant us to drink, he wouldn't have put the elbow right in the middle of the arm.'

Sloane's eyes rested on him, and the disturbing trick came again. Bolton drew back physically from the fire, momentarily dismayed.

'No,' Sloane said finally, and his hands stirred gently. 'I'm not drinking.'

'As you wish, sport, as you wish.'

The sterile anger past, Sloane went out, closing the door softly behind him with the smallest tick at the end. He hated the slam of a door. At home he set down plates and cups with the same care, easing them at the last into a silent touch. From time to time this obsession with stealth drove Sarah to complain that he was unnerving her. It was like living with a cat burglar. But he put her off with a smile and a joke. She had her own fears, and he was not sure that she could share his. How could you explain that you chose effacement, that you needed invisibility?

He started down the stairwell that smelled vaguely of mildewed book paper, watching the busy street approach like a Herculean labour that lay between him and the quiet flat. His dull, heavy body had once held another tenant: a brash young man setting out to live on his wits in Europe after an Army discharge in Garmshorst, jumping the MATS flight home and hitch-hiking west into France with his one duffel bag of possessions. Long before The Fall. He knew no one ever changed totally; the old tenant was still there, watching and waiting – not waiting for anything to happen, but just hunching down in the corner, subdued by the new regime and tolerating the new virtues for the peace they brought. From time to time, though, a spark of humour rose up, gently mocking the timid, weary man who now held the lease.

2

'Gold will be the bait,' the Old Man announced. 'Jerry.'

It was Moore's cue, and he dug into his own notes as Dru sagged against her chair, pleased to have acquitted herself well.

'A well-rounded report,' MacIlvaine said with a leer. 'Two points well taken, filled out quite thoroughly, weighty and promising despite a lack of supporting material.' He had evidently composed the double-entendres in his mind with great care.

'Can we skip the rutting ritual?' Dru snapped, and she turned and glared at the Old Man. But not keen himself on women in the service, he offered no assistance. Moore set a graph drawn on stiff card onto the chalk rail behind him.

'I'd better begin. In case you've forgotten, and if any of you have you're unique in the western world, this will refresh your memory on the course of gold's asking price on the open market.' They all glanced at the sawtooth line that stretched beyond the $1,000 an ounce mark.

'Mother of God,' MacIlvaine said. 'It's my blood pressure.'

The Old Man frowned at him, and he subsided.

'Over the past few years, the price of gold has risen again so convulsively that it is now theoretically possible for almost all of the major western nations to metallize their currencies.'

Moore launched into a long-winded summary of the history of gold as a currency standard, from the rigid gold standards of the late nineteenth century, through the unsuccessful manipulations of the gold price by Roosevelt in 1934, the Breton Woods agreement of 1944 that made the freely convertible dollar the lynchpin of the system, the breakdown of Breton Woods in 1967 and the emergence of the two-tier public and private gold markets. Then had come the creation of Special Drawing Rights

15

as an increasingly unsatisfactory substitute for gold; the resurgent strength and then, under mounting deficits, the gathering weakness of the dollar.

Moore reached into a document case by his feet and extracted a slim blue-bound folder. He held it up theatrically, then passed it to MacIlvaine beside him. 'This report we prepared states that the French are rumoured to be making secret purchases of large quantities of gold, very large quantities, from the Russians. The report suggests they are acting in concert with and perhaps on behalf of their EEC partners. Of course, if the Europeans metallized on their own to bring back the gold standard, the unsecured dollar would overnight be in roughly the same class as the Albanian lek.'

The Old Man sat impassively, but Ross thought he sensed a tightening around his eyes and a firming of his jaw. Ross could count off Moore's points well before he reached them and he anticipated what was coming, wondering again if he should try to head it off.

'Late yesterday,' Moore continued, 'we leaked this report to the Research office in Washington. They'll almost certainly jump at the bait and do everything they can to be the first agency to confirm the rumours. They've long been hoping for a gold star – so to speak – from the President.'

Moore seemed to have finished, leaving a silence that slowly grew brittle as the Old Man and Ross watched each other like cats: the one aloof, stern, formidable; the other curious and – Dru across the table saw it best – almost protective.

★

Downstairs, behind the door to the first-floor flat, Mrs Cromer shrilled at someone whose voice was too soft in reply to penetrate to the stairwell. He wondered idly if she was having gentlemen callers again. As usual the button by the entry plopped too soon and the timed light went out as he was on the last flight of steps, past the *minuterie* on the half landing and not quite at the one outside his own door. He had taken one of the fat buttons apart once to see if the delay could be extended, but it was a simple spring-loaded pneumatic cylinder with no adjustments, designed, like so much modern engineering, for the convenience of the engineers.

The Victorian terrace house had been cut into two flats, with the upper, because of its smaller rooms, the cheaper of the two. They had a sitting room facing the street and a bedroom at the back, with a toilet and bathroom up a half flight of internal stairs and a small kitchen and nondescript pantry down a half flight behind a new wall that sealed off what had once been a doorway to the landing. It had been a decade since he had considered accommodation such as this – cramped, squalid and inconvenient: at least half the city lived in similar flats, thankful to have rooms at all. With two cranks of the key he had the Chubb deadbolt open and then he worked at the smaller latch below.

Inside he noticed that some of the comforting disorder on his writing desk had been tidied away, with the portable typewriter sealed up into its black case. He guessed that Sarah had become restless. Then he noticed her standing rigidly erect at the bedroom door, her eyes closed and her face more pale and drawn than usual. Pain made her look almost his own age, though she was more than ten years younger. Her dark hair was limp and uncombed.

'Huh-oh,' he said. 'What is it?'

One finger rose and pointed to a vein in her temple. 'It's the vein. Throbbing. I think a migraine is coming.'

He crossed the room swiftly and touched her shoulder.

'Lie down. I'll make some tea.' He led her into the small bedroom. She sat reluctantly on the edge of the bed, then stretched out full length, her eyes still closed, tugging her skirt smooth. For a moment he said nothing, and her fingers began to dig and knead at her thighs.

'I've been feeling anxious.'

'You've been so well. I was just going to suggest you give yourself a reward and visit Felicity.'

'I can't seem to believe in rewards.' She felt for his hand and squeezed it. 'I looked for work this morning. There didn't seem to be anything suitable. In me, I mean. I do hate trying to sell myself.'

'I only got a small job at the Pentonville shop myself. I'll have to look into some of the others.' The light caught her skin, almost transparent where it was stretched across her high cheeks, the colour of candle wax. 'A few days late with a four-month job and the fool accused me of drinking. I even rang up last week and explained.'

'Did someone there know you? From before, I mean.'

'Maybe. This city is a thousand little worlds overlapping. What he thought he knew was three-quarters a lie of convenience anyway. You know, when you can't tell children the truth, you tell them a story that fits their experience of the way the world works. Oh, hell, I did drink for a time.' He realized Phelps-Hargood's contempt *did* sting: he was justifying himself . . . to whom? Sarah didn't demand it.

'I know we promised there was no world before the hospital, but some day I want to know.'

In a year of marriage she'd only asked three or four times and she was easily put off. The less he told her, the more unreal it all remained, and the more protected she would be.

'Sure,' he offered vaguely. 'Actually, it's a comfort knowing your limits. It's like international frontiers, marked out by searchlights and fences and patrol dogs. You just watch them on the edge of your vision and stay well away and everything keeps its delicate peace.'

'I wish I saw something as orderly,' she whispered forlornly, and he could see the respite was nearly past.

'Calm . . . security. I love you very much.' He bent over and pressed against her, filling with tenderness.

'You say it, but I can't believe it.'

'I know. It's all right.' His hand went out and touched her forehead, once, twice.

'Don't pat. I'm not a dog.'

'Sorry. I'll make the tea.'

He was afraid there would be tears in her eyes, and he stood up quickly and slipped down the steps into the cluttered kitchen. He peered into the electric kettle at the white scale that curled and flaked off the aluminium. He had read a remedy somewhere, but couldn't remember it. And the kettle was no worse than the kitchen wall, where the plaster was crumbling away like cheese around the old square basin and the pine shelf above the basin was mildewing in the damp. He thought: room and tenant, both suffered from being sealed in, cut off from the outside. Even children knew that a wound under a heavy bandage never healed.

But only inside could he protect, he thought. Telling her about the past would be like throwing open the first window, and step by step he would be drawn out into a world that was waiting to devour. Out there, he couldn't even protect her from himself.

★

'The truth is, the report we prepared is a fake.' The Old Man looked around with grim satisfaction. 'I doubt whether the Europeans would dare mount so naked a challenge to the dollar. In fact, it's the President who is considering making the US dollar convertible, though it's a closely guarded secret. He hopes to give the currency speculators a jolt and bring inflation under control in one sharp action. A small team of Chicago economists is studying the question up at Camp David right now, cloaked in the tightest security since Oak Ridge.'

'Known only to a few thousand bureaucrats and the *New York Times*,' Ross said evenly.

'No,' the Old Man retorted. '*You* didn't know, Harvey, did you? Not this time. He's got a team of plumbers guarding the secret *before* it leaks. And I must remind you that we don't know it in this room. There will not be a hint of a clue of a leak from us.'

'How *do* we know?' MacIlvaine asked.

'We *don't*, Francis. Let's leave it at that. If I catch one of you snapping up a few gold coins from your great uncle, I promise a terrible retribution.'

'Research is going to leak the secret,' Ross said softly, his eyes resting on his folded puffy fingers. 'Without knowing it.'

The Old Man nodded once. 'Precisely. When they blunder around Europe following the scent we've offered, babbling away about gold and tripping over their own feet in their inimitable fashion, a lot of people are going to sit up and take notice. And when they queer the President's plans, I would not bet heavily on the Civil Overseas Research Organization surviving the rage they bring down on themselves.'

★

Ralph Cutter sat with his feet up on the desk, reading the racing tables in *The Sporting News*. From time to time he ran a toughened hand across his crew cut, picked a pencil from behind his ear and drew a belligerent circle around a line of agate type. There were nine other desks in the large room, but only two were occupied and the others were so stacked with cardboard cartons and dusty files that they appeared to have been unused for years. A precarious mountain of file boxes stood in the circular alcove, filling the Edwardian turret that overlooked Charing Cross Road thirty feet below. A wall of gauze curtains strained a furtive grey light to meet the bank of shaded bulbs. The only heat came from a pair of kerosene stoves at each end of the room, and when someone despaired enough to light them the office reeked with fumes. Central heating, Cutter had thought bitterly, on first seeing them. In this country, it meant a candle in the centre of the room.

He dropped the pencil onto the floor and contorted his body lazily to pick it up. The sight of the worn green linoleum annoyed and disgusted him – it reminded him of heavy black typewriters, dog-eared file cards and rusted scissors; reminded him in fact of a dusty, unimportant office where papers were pushed from one niche to another in order to kill another day: such was exactly where he found himself. What possible enjoyment could he find in a room cut off from the world of human collision? Even Hoffacker was gone. He missed having an enemy in the building. Enemies were what he liked; proximity of conflict, the spice of rivalry every day. The only senior officer remaining was an unobtrusive little man who worked two desks away, diligently underlining sentences in a copy of the *Far Eastern Economic Review*, and he was no rival at all, a browbeaten wimp. Once Hoffacker had quit, the empire had become his, for what it was worth.

Cutter, too, had considered quitting for a while. But he had finally decided that he might as well ride the fucker until it dropped. Even if the job held none of its old energy and excitement; none of that manipulation of resentful actors out in the field who stretched all your tricks to control them. The confrontations when your mind filled with nothing but the duel of man against man; watching and circling and screwing up the bets until you won inevitably. He loved nothing so much as breaking a man to his will, and he made no pretence to himself that he did it with regret, out of duty. It was what everyone wished they had the power to do.

Cutter straightened a paper clip, bent it over a rubber band and launched it towards Downs's desk. It slapped off the desktop and sailed into the turret room beyond, and Downs glanced around warily.

'Vicky's Prince in the fifth. What do you think of that, shithead? Ought to go like a fucking bomb on the wet. Anything in the *Economic Review* on the fifth at Churchill Downs?'

'I haven't n-n-noticed,' Downs said, careful to say as little as possible and not contradict him.

'Oh, you haven't n-n-noticed, have you?' Impossible not to torment such a worm; he begged for it. The Acolytes downstairs were better company, but they were too stupid to edit the summaries. The whole group had no more IQ than a slab of granite. He needed Downs almost as much as he despised him.

'It's time for the P.O. pickup,' Cutter said. 'Make sure Crabb hasn't fallen into the toilet and flushed himself down, would you?'

Downs laid a card into the crease of the *Review*, closed it and set it square on his desk. He kept his surroundings obsessively tidy, a compensation for the stammer that shredded his confidence and seemed to him to disorder everything around him. He was five-three, with a sad, round face and stubby limbs, so folded into himself that he appeared lost at the cavernous desk. He wasn't entirely helpless in the face of Cutter's taunts, but he saved his more complex counter-stratagems for larger occasions. Downs had a long memory for slights but a mind practical enough not to stand on his dignity when nothing was at stake. He had learned long ago the ways around, the obtuse replies, the empty apologies, the evasions, and most of all the compensations. When he came back upstairs, he decided, he would go by the lockers and fetch the bar of plain chocolate from the lunch Alma had packed for him. He used small things all the time, deferred rewards, to keep out the vacuum, and they worked. Tomorrow night there was a BBC2 programme on one of his favourite subjects, the history of English gothic architecture.

Sometimes he could go a whole day on a promise as substantial as that. Downs wanted more from life, but he was always tempted by less.

He hadn't been out of the room ten seconds when the buzz went off and Cutter snapped up in his chair, his eyes darting around in a momentary panic. Cutter hadn't heard the sound in a year, but when he stood he saw the old green telephone on the lower shelf of the dictionary stand winking its light at him in time to the buzz.

'Jesus fuck . . . *Downs!*'

Cutter slammed through his desk drawers, searching in haste. It wasn't there. He started through the abandoned desks, remembering by the second bank of drawers to open them burglar-fashion from the bottom to the top so he needn't shut one before checking the next. Dust balls, crumpled memoes, old government forms, a pair of dirty socks, scores of unsharpened office pencils with the erasers worn away.

Downs finally came back in, his tiny brown eyes fixing on the shrilling telephone.

'Where'd you put the fucking scrambler?' Cutter bawled.

'I d-d-didn't know we still had one.'

'Help me find it!'

Together they attacked the grey filing cabinets along the wall, cleared of active case files a year earlier and mostly filled with back issues of magazines.

'They haven't used that line in a year,' Cutter complained, as if the buzz was a plot against him.

'I saw it once, I remember. I saw it once.' Downs closed his eyes, trying to picture where, but by then Cutter had found the Sperry Multiphase II scrambler in a cardboard box on the farthest desk. He hauled out what looked like a portable tape recorder with a telephone handset attached and hastily unwound the patch cord lacing it together.

Then he was on his knees in the corner, jamming the phono plug into the insistent telephone. He pressed two keys on the front of the scrambler and the buzz immediately cut off, replaced by a hum.

'London-one,' he said, after yanking the handset out of its recess. Downs could hear the ghastly bray of the scrambled signal from the monitor Cutter hadn't switched to decode. 'If you want faster service, then send us some decent equipment. This damn thing is almost pre-war.'

Downs sat on the corner of his desk, watching Cutter's face curiously. It clouded slowly with resentment and something Downs rarely saw there: caution. Cutter was speaking to someone who outranked him.

'That's crap. Their currencies are all tied to the SDRs like everyone else's. We *already* watch the indicators.'

The honking of the monitor began to annoy him and he pressed another key so that it gave way to plain speech. '. . . You had a man with a contact in the Soviet Trade Mission.'

Downs could hear the withering voice at the other end plainly but he didn't recognize it. It wasn't the Director, but it had to be someone in his office.

'You know we don't have active field men,' Cutter said.

'You have authorization for this one. Mine. Find him and get him back.'

'It isn't possible You can't know what's best out here. We can get fifty others who'd be better –'

'We're racing time on this. Is he dead?'

Cutter paused, his body growing very still. 'Usefully. He went bananas.'

Downs watched with fascination. He knew how Cutter detested excuses, from either end.

'Zip up your banana and put him to work. You ought to be capable of that, right? Cutter, the great agent runner? You won't have trouble touching bottom, will you? If it's too much trouble, of course, we could send someone from here. I mean, if you can't handle it.'

Cutter's eyes were closed, and his knuckles whitened on the handset.

'Just a little grease with the White House and we're out of the woods for good. You know what that means: the AG's blessing for funds, more overseas stations, a real role in the intelligence community again. You might even earn your keep.'

'We'll get right on it,' Cutter said, emphasizing each word with controlled fury. 'Don't call us, we'll call you.'

He hung up, wrenched the plug from the phone and stared at

the plug stupidly for a moment as if trying to decide how best to destroy it. Downs knew better than to speak.

'Our first chance for an op and it has to be that yoyo. What was his name?;'

'Sloane. J-J-Jeffrey.' Downs remembered him well, especially toward the end – a death mask of a face with eyes like bruises on a peach. At first, not long after Downs had come in, Sloane had been an ordinary office employee, useful as a researcher and translator because of his languages and his knowledge of northern Europe. Cutter had begun using him as a courier, and then predictably, had pushed him further and further into active operations. One day Sloane had become a C in the green files, a letter that stood for coercion and ordinarily indicated an agent who was recruited by blackmail. And then he had disappeared from the files altogether, at least from the green ones. That meant he had become a double, and he was working somewhere so sensitive that no details would be passed on to Washington, only results.

Downs remembered the man as proud and unpredictable, despite a guarded manner; sometimes rattling off the information he was asked in a drained, sarcastic chant; sometimes mumbling and slipping in an oblique turn of phrase that sent Cutter into a frenzy, fearing he was being mocked. One astounding time Downs had stood in the Tiergarten in Berlin, backup for what was meant to be a brush contact between Sloane and Cutter. Sloane had come along the path with a fixed, angry look on his face and at the last instant he had snapped open the handbag of an old woman ahead of him, dropped in the film he carried and snapped it shut. He had walked off into the German afternoon, leaving Cutter with only his high school German to sputter apologies and try to wheedle the film away from the woman. That had still been the early Sloane, making Cutter pay in face for every torment. Surreptitiously, Downs had admired the brash resistance, but he had cringed for the man, knowing how foolhardy it was to stand up to Cutter. Sloane had lost big.

'Dig up his file. I'll get the Acolytes downstairs geared up to find him.' He stopped at the door. 'We're not going to screw this up. And he isn't either, or I'll clean his clock for good.'

Downs found a sawtooth padlock key on the ring of retired

keys in his desk. The steel bar lifted through the handles on the single stand of black files that still contained records, and then he was into the masters they had saved from the old active files. His finger flipped idly along the manila folders. It took him a moment to recall Sloane's office name: Carson. The Cs rarely brought in anything nearly as good as the product you got from defectors or walk-ins, but were always out there at work, plugging away, until they broke.

3

They had traced the possible developments – or scenarios, as MacIlvaine persisted brightly, embarrassing them all with the stale drama of the word. They had discussed counter-moves and covers and, in case the earth began to rumble, fallbacks on the leaked report. No one had opposed the plan. Now the meeting was winding down, just in time for lunch.

'Notes in the basket, please,' the Old Man said. 'Dru will take them along to the shredder. The single library file will be in my office.' He paused as Moore's pen pounced on an incriminating doodle and blotted it out cleverly with a row of Xs. 'One thing. Normally, for obvious reasons, we choose code names unrelated to the project in question – those dreadful birds and fish and abstract nouns. If all goes well there will be no record of this project and no further need for action, so I've decided to make an exception.'

From the hall came the shuffle of feet slipping off to the cafeteria. Ross sat as he had been sitting for some time, his hands folded in front of him, listless, like a man waiting to be called as a witness for a hopeless court case. They were all surprised that he hadn't intervened, perhaps the Old Man most of all. At several points Ross had evidently stirred to say something, but then had seemed to make a decision and subside into his deliberate patience.

'Operation Broken Back,' the Old Man said, and there were a few appreciative chuckles. 'When we discover the poor soul they entrust with their little adventure – to us he will be "Lumbago".'

★

Sloane loaded the tray with a teapot under a cosy, a cup and saucer, a bowl of sugar and a few of the overhard cookies he had ultimately learned to call biscuits. He crabbed sideways up the narrow stairs to protect his knuckles from the walls and set the tray on the bed table.

'Tea and sympathy,' he said softly. She looked brighter, and he hoped he had been wrong: maybe it wouldn't be a bad night after all.

'You'll make an excellent housewife. I think I'll marry you,' she said.

She sat half up, tipping the cup with her forefinger to inspect it for the milk, and poured. 'What's the time?'

'Quarter to five. Oh, to be somewhere else now that autumn is here; soon it'll be dark by four. Then those horrible three-hour days in December.'

'You exaggerate.'

'A little. I have to walk over to the shops. We won't have milk for breakfast.'

'I'm sorry,' Sarah said, chagrined. 'I forgot.'

'That's all right.'

'Before you leave, could I have a Nembutal. I think I can nap.'

He touched her knee softly and went to his desk in the sitting room, switching on the lamp in the gloom. He fished a thin chain out of his shirt with a small key on the end and stooped so that the chain around his neck would reach the drawer. The brass latch tongue snapped open and he slid out a drawer containing several pill bottles. Extracting a slim red capsule, he locked up again carefully and took it to the bedroom.

'Thanks, Jeffrey.' She slapped the pill into her mouth from a cupped palm and chased it with tea.

'You nap and we'll eat a light supper later.'

He didn't like the rigid way she held her arms, lying back like a body arranged in a coffin; perhaps it was the fear of pain. At the door he remembered he had only a five-pound note. The Indian woman at the corner shop would glare at him for days if he offered that for a pint of milk. Sarah's purse lay beside the bed, and he slipped back to the bedroom. She was twisted around on the bed, stretched out toward the small bedside table on the far side, with her hand poised over the open drawer. Before his mind was fully engaged, he had leapt across the room and had her wrist locked fast in his grip. He hammered her small closed fist against the lip of the drawer until the fingers uncurled, and he heard the soft tick of the capsule hitting wood. Eight red capsules lay in the drawer like tiny bloodshot eyes.

She hugged his back as he sat heavily. 'It was only insurance,' she sobbed. 'I wasn't planning . . . Honestly. It's just . . . it makes it easier knowing they're there. I wish I could concentrate. I wish I could keep my thoughts together. You don't know what the dread is like.'

'Don't, don't,' he said softly. When he took her hands, he could feel the long scars on her wrists.

★

He remembered dread, though perhaps it was a different kind from hers. He remembered a little glowing worm in a bulb, and bulbs all down the infinite corridor, with darkness pooling at the doorways. A long, long run past them all. 'Steal the papers. Hurry.'

He remembered malevolent cities that lost you in a maze of alleys and canals. 'Take this suitcase. Go, man, hurry.'

He remembered the waspish pleasure of hurting, and only later the discovery that it had been a friend crying out behind the door.

He remembered floorboards that sank under his feet, halls that tipped forward, fierce whispers. He remembered a policeman's eyes studying the bulge under his coat, a voice that couldn't quite speak in the right accent to go unnoticed, indecipherable train schedules on a wall.

He remembered hearing a nasty blubbering for pity in a universe without ears. Were they all dreams?

★

'Don't, don't,' he said softly. When he took her hands, he could feel the long scars on her wrists.

'If you can't give reasons, the doctors treat you like useless baggage. There aren't reasons the way they mean. "An old man in a mac poked his hand up your dress when you were six and,

Bob's your uncle, there's the secret trauma." They watch too much telly.' She pressed the flat of her hand against his cheek. 'Shops. Go on. I'm all right.'

He tore one of the red capsules in two and juggled half the powder into each end, then handed her one of the ends. 'Please. I know you didn't sleep last night.'

'Did I keep you awake? I'm sorry.'

'Every time I stirred I saw your eyes.'

'You never let on.' After placing it on her tongue, she displayed her empty palm, then washed it down with the last of the tea.

'Buy some milk or you'll hate me in the morning.'

★

Crabb drove the American Ford, a gaunt man with a sutured scar across his scalp that was only partially hidden by a few whisps of hair. Downs knew that Crabb had got the wound in a pub brawl, but Crabb occasionally boasted that it had come in the line of duty. Crabb didn't know that no one gave a damn; he didn't know that people only cared about stories if they cared about the people who told them, and Crabb did not have the knack of making people like him.

Downs watched the colour-leached world of Islington flow past outside. London allowed a splash of brightness for the front door, red or marigold, but only a few West Indians had the cheek to wear colour on their bodies. The pedestrians were bundled up into tan, black, navy blue, the brown of dessicated chocolate, and everything around them was a sooty ochre and sooty rust like an autumn forest, the small animals camouflaged against an unknown carnivore who waited to devour the conspicuous. The street reinforced an impression that had been growing on Downs: he lived in a universe in which everyone was damaged in some fundamental way.

The car inched through the permanent traffic snarl at Highbury Corner, and Downs broke off his melancholy reverie and returned to the file in his lap.

'Balls Pond Road,' Cutter said with distaste. 'The dumps I've known.'

Crabb chuckled. 'You want some real shit, I'll tour you through Bethnal Green down that way where Loory lives.' When no one acknowledged him, Crabb twisted the radio knobs, but even Capital Radio drifted off into static and he snapped it off.

The file held a recent sheet Downs hadn't noticed before. 'He's married now,' Downs announced. 'A woman he m-m-met in the hospital.'

'I read it,' Cutter grunted. '*Two* fruitcakes. Fucking wonderful. Fifty former field men and we get to use the one that picks his nose with his elbow.'

Downs gathered himself for a small act of rebellion. 'He was a d-d-decent man.'

'Oh, fuck.' Suddenly Cutter straight-armed the seat ahead of him, jolting Crabb forward. 'To the right.'

Downs had met men more frightening – there was no mystery to Cutter, and without mystery you lacked that edge of worry about what he would do – but he had never met a man more extravagantly savage. No, there was something else setting Cutter apart.

'Why don't you quit?' he'd asked Cutter after Hoffacker had left for a job with a news agency. 'Why go through the motions when the whole b-b-bureau is collapsing?'

'Because I *believe*, you little shit. I believe in defending my country, I believe in the republic for which it stands, invisible for all. I believe in cherry fucking pie and people sleeping sounder at night. So go to hell.'

Cutter didn't believe, Downs was sure of that much. Belief implied the capacity to be touched by something that was not immediately, physically present. He was certain Cutter had lived all his life without noticing anything beyond immediate gratifications. Even the whisky didn't exist until it burned his throat. Cutter had habits, not beliefs.

Yet he bellowed that he believed – the last man in the universe who would defend an empty image of himself with such fierce intensity. That was what distinguished him.

As the car turned off the busy canyon of Balls Pond Road, Downs recalled the French writers of the 1940s that he had been forced to read at Dartmouth, frequently puzzling whether it was his trouble with the language that made them seem so intractable, so elusive. They seemed to write about nothing but those odd, withdrawn, intellectually preoccupied men for whom whole systems of belief had failed – Christianity, Marxism, humane liberalism – and who set out to construct new beliefs wholly within themselves. He could never work out what it was they constructed. The whole conceit had never rung true; it was just so much Gallic rhetoric. People didn't go around saying to each other: The deed precedes the idea, or, One shall make it true through an act of will. And then he had met Cutter: a real existential man. Cutter built a world with his petulant fists: he would keep any idea of himself alive forever simply by booming it out and hammering to death anyone who contradicted him. And there, at the centre, nothing at all existed but Cutter, cold and indifferent, never giving the horror a second thought.

'Park by that car. *There*, in front of the old cunt with the baby carriage.'

Crabb slid in behind a fat, rusting Zodiac, set up on bricks, and shut off the engine.

Cutter sat forward, his chin on his folded hands on the seatback. 'I want a feel for this hole. Know the environment, know the man.'

★

Sloane came down the three steps carrying a canvas shopping bag, and a finger jabbed into his back. 'Hold it, mon.'

He knew the voice and he turned slowly, hiding the gentle smile that he knew would have disappointed them. Johnny FitzGibbon, the twelve-year-old Jamaican boy from across the road, glowered at him, incongruous in a cowboy hat sunk to his ears. Crouched in the hedge, Zenon, an olive-skinned Cypriot boy, covered him fiercely with a water pistol.

'Bossman want you.'

Sloane sighed theatrically. They herded him toward the ragged gap in the hedge that led into the next front yard, no more than a fifteen-foot square of terrazzo with a fallen birdbath, behind which Cyril Granby waited imperiously, hands on hips. Cyril was the chief of the Apaches, hollow cheeks and a short brush cut making him look like a crushed tennis ball.

31

'Move your arse in 'ere.'

Zenon hurried past and Sloane stepped through, raising his arms.

'You scarpered on us. Expline yourself.'

'I had some business down in the West End. Sorry.'

'You try me patience, old man. You tell us 'ow the Wyoming Kid gets out of the trap.'

'I really have to get to the shops before they shut.'

Johnny prodded him in the back again. 'Get ready fe tek some blows!'

'All right,' Sloane gave in, defeated. He thought back, stalling. 'The Wyoming Kid and I were trapped in the bottom of the gulch. The road on to Tombstone was at one end of the gulch and the old Indian trail back to Cheyenne was at the other, but you remember Wyatt and the sheriff were blocking both trails.'

'Shoot it out,' Johnny suggested brightly.

'That's for mugs. The point is to outwit them. I had a plan and I whispered it to Wyoming and pointed back the way we came. Here, say Zenon over there is the sheriff.'

'Piss off,' Cyril snapped. 'I'll be the sheriff.' He shouldered Zenon aside.

'Wyoming crawled toward the sheriff and hid himself behind some sagebrush on the path. Then I started shouting, "Hey, you stupid Eastern dude, come and get us." You know how he hates being called an Eastern dude and I didn't have to shout for long before he was mad as a hornet.

'He got so upset he came running after me and he wasn't looking where he was going. Wyoming stuck out his boot and tripped him up. That 300-pound sheriff slapped down on his nose in the dust and we jumped him and tied him up. We mounted the sheriff's horse, with Wyoming in the saddle and me holding on for dear life behind and we galloped back toward town as fast as we could go. In town Doc Holliday was waiting for us at the stables with a shotgun. That's for tomorrow.'

'Aw, bovver,' Cyril complained.

'Too easy, too easy.'

'I really have to get to the shops. Tomorrow I'll tell you how Doc Holliday gets caught in his own trap and ends up hanging upside down over the saloon.'

If only life were that simple, he thought. But he enjoyed making it that simple in stories – the exotic old man on the street with the funny cowboy accent. He wished he and Sarah could have a child and he could watch it grow up to say, ''Ere's some fings I want for me birfday.' But how could he ever protect a child? Even out in the country it could drown in a stream, or catch whooping cough, or break a leg running away in a tantrum. The responsibility seemed to him overwhelming. Sloane backed out of the yard, drawing the Apaches along behind him like ducklings.

'Tell us about Doc Holliday now. Please,' Zenon begged.

'We ain't got nofink to do.'

'One chapter a day. That's the rule.' He saw the tan Ford waiting up the road, standing out like a battleship. One leg dragged as he concentrated on the car, trying to see inside. The sun had gone, but the long slow twilight evened out the light, erasing shadows, and he thought he could see . . .

'We'll go wif you.'

'Like yestidy.'

The back doors swung open. Even Cutter was astonished by what happened next. One moment Sloane had been standing there in a cluster of street urchins and the next he was gone, vanished like smoke. Two men charged down on the boys, toward the hedge and the side garden that cut through to the next road.

'Hey, Eastern dudes!' Johnny called. 'Hands up!'

Zenon fired his water pistol several times at their backs going over the garden wall.

'Bloody hell,' Cyril said.

The car started and squealed away, wallowing on its soft springs toward the corner.

'Them was Doc 'Olliday and the sheriff,' Cyril stated darkly. ''E's for it now.'

★

The car cut him off at the corner and the men closed the gap from behind. Then they had his arms.

'Leave me alone,' Sloane said miserably as Cutter pressed his head down to clear the car roof going in.

'No fucking way.'

★

Sarah drew the bedroom curtains across without looking out the window. Outside, the day was dying. She wasn't sleepy. She was just exhausted, so short of energy she could hardly move. What would they have for supper? Jeffrey was always hungry before she was. Why wouldn't that woman at Cobham's offer her a position? Her thoughts wouldn't focus and stay put. They scurried back and forth and then darted away like squirrels. She wished she had the knack of promising herself a greener future, but she wouldn't lie to herself. All her life she had insisted on looking square at the worst, particularly about herself. She refused the rationalizations and the comforting half-truths that a large part of her education had seemed designed to teach young girls. No lies: it had seemed an admirable trait amidst all the decorous omissions, but lately she had come to believe that such honesty had no intrinsic merit at all. It was only a code for self-blame and the eerie dismay that slipped in with it. Felicity would laugh at her and cheer her temporarily, but even Felicity grew weary after a time. Jeffrey would too, eventually. He would leave her.

Is it nothing to you, all ye that pass by?

She wanted the same things as other people – to be useful, to do some good in the world, to love. But as desires they were too general and diffuse to do much good. She had tried to want something more accessible, but nothing would fit. A job at least; but the woman at the bureau had been insufferable. 'It appears you're quite overqualified for office work, dear. A university first just wouldn't *do* behind a typewriter, would it? And look at your *vitae*; you're not a stayer, are you?' Frowning haughtily under the make-up, nails rattling aggressively against the glass counter top. 'I'll take anything. I *must* have a position.' Why was Jeffrey taking so long at the shop?

Behold, and see if there be any sorrow like unto my sorrow.

She had tried to do good, to do simple, straightforward charity work – with Oxfam two years ago and at the Women's Institute when she was eighteen – but a voice kept telling her it was vanity. She stood there piously at the jumble sale only to steal a virtue she didn't deserve. The other women were there for the gossip and companionship of women of their class, and for the meretricious little glow of philanthropy, recalled endlessly over dinner tables. But it didn't bother them. Why was she different? Sarah lay down on the bed. She was anxious and restless. She noticed the stains on the wall; the room needed repapering. When she had read history at university, none of it had meant a thing to her. Battles and royalty and great churning events that could as easily have gone one way as another. 'What do you plan to *do*, dear? I don't believe you'd enjoy teaching.'

Is it nothing to you, all ye that pass by?

Now she was thirty-eight. She would probably never have children. Not that she wanted them, but . . . They were like a magic word she had refused to speak aloud, not believing in magic words. 'Children are a joy in the heart, Sar.' Had she and Felicity been a joy to her parents? Like hell. Her father's brow furrowing up, trying hard to understand why one played and the other sat quietly and studied old books, without friends. 'No reason, father.' The only light came from the lamp Jeffrey had left on in the sitting room, and it lay in a yellow spill across the rug. She had promised herself that when she grew up she would be far better and more loving than both her parents put together. She would never sit silently at dinner. But she had never learned how to be better, so she followed the daily horoscopes in the *Evening Standard* with a melancholy intensity, not believing a word.

Behold, and see if there be any sorrow like unto my sorrow.

She had waited. Waited for the sixth form to finish, waited for university to get her away from home. Waited for pointless ceremonies and waited for tragedies that rarely came. Waited eagerly to lose her virginity 'in the right way', waited for the cancer that was bound to strike some day as a twinge in her cervix. She waited to be popular at Sussex University, because after all she was pretty, fairer than Felicity and slimmer. And then a whole year of waiting for Michael to do more than recognize her name, to flirt with her. And then . . . the worst of all had been the waiting – living with Michael – waiting for him to lose interest in her, find her shallow and tedious and walk out. Which he had. It was the worst only because it had been the first; she couldn't even remember clearly now what he looked like. After that she was reconciled to it, knowing it would happen over and over to the end of her life, an end she never imagined standing some hazy distance far ahead, but already a palpable presence inside her. Death: its only surprise would be how it came. Motoring accident, that strange ache in her belly, or possibly . . . She rolled onto her side on the bedcover.

She prayed: If You're out there, all I ask for is a short period of peace and contentment. It's not a lot to ask. I'll carry on like this another thousand years if You'll promise me that at the end. She heard only the water pipes hammering in the walls; Mrs Cromer was washing vegetables downstairs.

★

'I had a bout with drinking once myself,' Cutter said with terrible friendliness, his eyes fixed fiercely on Sloane.

Sloane's own unfocused eyes darted around nervously. The sedan sat in the shadows of a looming warehouse. Ahead of the car, soggy wind-driven rubbish was heaped against the brick building. They were somewhere in the bleak square mile of goods depots and derelict Victorian warehouses that lay like fallen tombstones behind the railway stations of Euston, St Pancras and King's Cross. It was a forsaken landscape Cutter often chose for his conferences, an area known colloquially as the arsehole of London, and nothing alive seemed to have touched the desolation for a century. A fading political poster peeled away from the brick out the window, its message meaningless. Had anyone ever seen it here?

'You're just a cutout really, a go-between. You were his contact before. We can't slot someone new in, you see that.'

Still Sloane seemed not to have heard.

'We didn't drag this turkey back into the kitchen, Sloane, but it's going to be plucked so make up your mind to it.'

'I don't think you understand.'

Sloane's expression was complex. Downs saw the fear there, but something else as well. Then Cutter unleashed the sort of

36

incontinent tirade it was impossible to listen to, except in snatches, without becoming embarrassed, without wanting to join a different race.

'. . . Then picture *this*, Sloane – picture this cunt you live with all by herself beside a telephone that keeps ringing and every time she picks it up a voice, maybe a good imitation of *your* voice, tells her she's a worthless piece of shit, no good to anybody, a failure, a turd in a slop pail, picture a Peeping Tom rapping on her window every night, picture someone following her around with a camera, whatever it takes to send her cuckoo, baby, draw yourself a picture because that's what you get . . .'

Downs sank into a corner of the back seat, trying to dissociate himself from the ghastly malice of Cutter's voice. He tried pinching a tiny fold of skin on his wrist to distract himself. The fit of savagery stirred a deep disenchantment in him that had been gathering for some time. How long could you go on excusing a mad dog by your clever logic? Outside, the buildings seemed black islands sinking into a gloomy sea.

'. . . I remember you, Sloane, you arrogant prick. I remember your tricks and I'll get you too, for all the shit I had to take from you . . .'

Downs tried to think of Alma, and he tried to concentrate on the house they would build in the Vermont woods some day when he had the money. Two interconnected A-frames in the shape of a cross, with a high study under the skylight where the arms met. It would be a lovely retreat.

'You can blackmail me,' Sloane said, with so much lassitude it was difficult to make out the words. 'That's your art. It doesn't mean I can do what you want.'

'You're gonna help us because you're a pain junkie, because you been keeping lame birds in shoe boxes all your life, and if you don't help, I'm gonna jolt your little bird. Just for starters.'

Cutter slammed the front seat and held his hand out to Crabb, who fumbled fearfully in a black briefcase on the floor before finding a paper and passing it back. 'Don't mistake we won't push all the way.'

Cutter stuffed the paper into Sloane's hand like a derisory tip to a waiter. 'Here's his address, but you ought to know it. You go chat up your old buddy and the two of you figure out how to get into the files.'

'Give me a cigarette,' Sloane murmured.

Downs reached into his pocket, eager to offer the small favour. Sloane slid one out of the pack, then he plucked the gas lighter from Downs's hand and lit the cigarette himself. A plume of smoke jetted up toward the padded roof. He didn't return the lighter, but Cutter was speaking again and Downs couldn't bring himself to interrupt.

'You know the file we want. The rest is your lookout, the two of you.'

'I was told once the meek shall inherit the earth,' Sloane said, wry and cautious, not far from rebellion.

Cutter shot him a foul look. 'You were misinformed.'

Abruptly Sloane went into a coughing fit. He doubled over, racking his chest toward his knees. For some reason, Downs didn't believe it was a genuine cough. Perhaps just a nervous mannerism.

Slowly Sloane recovering by taking rapid, shallow breaths. 'Sorry. Haven't smoked in a year.'

'We still got the photos on him. Remember them? He'll piss and moan all he wants to and then he'll do what we say.'

Downs smelled it then, sharp and acrid beneath the pall of cigarette smoke. Sloane's arm lay flat on the seat, beside his leg, and his hand was out of sight over the edge. Downs squirmed.

'Cutter –'

'Shut up. This is nothing gonna strain that precious yellow streak of yours, just a little in and out, maybe a quick bag job. Jannings will be carrying the can.'

Downs was torn between images of Cutter's rage at a further interruption and his rage at not being told what was happening. The dilemma came over him so physically that he was rocking on the seat, gulping air like a fish. A horrible black billow of smoke settled it for him.

'We're on fire!' Downs cried. Suddenly the back seat was all elbows and knees. They piled out in panic, Downs tearing his shirt cuff on the window knob as Sloane shoved heavily at him.

Before they realized what had happened, Sloane was pounding away into the shadows of a warehouse. Crabb recovered first and bolted after him. Cutter was a pace behind.

'This doesn't buy you anything!'

Downs slipped out of his jacket and leaned into the smoke to flail at the lip of the seat, where the fire was already dying out on its own. He brushed tentatively at the fuming hole in the seat cover and felt the plastic give like toffee under his fingers. A string of melted vinyl was drawn from the hole like a fibre in some laboratory experiment and it trailed away into the night.

★

He had scrambled up an embankment through a patch of stinging nettles that had already turned brown and papery and lost their sting, over a low brick wall, and then had dropped into a vast rail yard with the gleam of tracks curling off toward depots and sheds almost half a mile away. A few lamps on high poles showed him the scene dimly, sending futile cones of light into the misty air. The panic had left him back in the car, and he ran with determination now, with no plan beyond getting back to Sarah to protect her from the unimaginable that had risen so suddenly. They would escape together . . . somewhere.

He heard them from behind calling to each other, and he angled across the tracks, running like a man with a long way yet to go. He dodged the twisted shapes of signal boxes that jumped suddenly out of the dark. Cables and piping plucked at his feet, but he kept his balance and hurtled on. A massive whistle shrilled angrily, very close, and he leapt forward just as the wind of the train hit him. The stunned white face of the driver stared down at him from the side window of the cab. He ran alongside the slowing train, not quite keeping pace, and glanced back, just as the last coach trundled past, to see Cutter and Crabb fifty yards back, momentarily thrown off and searching him out. He followed the train toward a brighter spot in the corner of the yard where it was disappearing under a road bridge.

'For Christ sake, man!'

Beginning to gulp for air, he passed under the bridge and saw the tracks bottleneck down toward the high open roof at the back of a station – King's Cross or St Pancras? he wondered. It was a toyland of light in the darkness, with criss-cross girders holding up the glass.

Concrete steps took him up onto the tail of the platform, and then he was running alongside the stopped train, doors opening and banging beside him, the people stepping down and squinting in the sudden light. He recognized it now, King's Cross.

Hurrying, he dodged the pillars and the wire-sided mail trolleys. One quick glance told him Cutter was already up on the platform behind him. Just short of the barrier an old couple in matching tweed were carrying small calf suitcases away from the first class. Without breaking step, Sloane snatched a ticket out of the woman's hand and hurled himself along the side of the queue at the barrier.

'Henry!'

'You there! I say, stop!'

He could hear Cutter only a few paces back. A string bean of a man with a stolid air of authority collected tickets at the barrier. Sloane elbowed a woman mercilessly and pushed through a young couple to slap his ticket into the collector's hand. The man looked up with a scowl as several people complained.

'Don't jump the queue there!'

But Sloane was already past.

'Look here, he's pinched my wife's ticket!'

The ticket collector was turning to go after Sloane when he was confronted by a second problem. Unsettled by the first gate-crasher, he firmed his jaw and blocked Cutter with an arm. 'Go to the back, I say!'

'Get out of my way!'

As Cutter shoved at him and took a step, the collector speared him with a high rugby tackle, ramming Cutter back unexpectedly against a four-foot fence. 'Police!'

Cutter seemed to explode in a windmill of limbs, and the two men toppled into a writhing heap.

A constable had been eyeing the suspicious rush of a seedy-looking man through the waiting room. At the call, he turned and trotted in an ungainly fashion toward the melée on the platform.

Crabb pursed his lips, suppressing a grin, as he squirmed through the circle of awed onlookers. He slipped a leather ID wallet out of his jacket as the policeman approached, his eyes on the strange tableau at his feet. A number of concerned citizens had come to the aid of British Rail, and the barbarous, humping

and bucking American was pinned flat to the concrete.
  'I'll break your fucking necks, every fucking one!'
  'Here now, what's this about?'

4

A girl with a salad-bowl haircut and hard sharp eyes paused beside his seat to speak over her shoulder. 'I don't take a blind bit of notice myself, but he'd do for you.'

The second girl lurched into her as the bus accelerated in its grumbling way. 'Get along with you. He's after a flutter with me Mum.' They both thought this was hilarious, laughing all the way along the aisle to the conductor who cranked their tickets out of the machine slung over his shoulder.

For the moment the fear had subsided, like the false remission of a disease, and Sloane felt an odd objectivity. He was calm enough to stand outside himself and consider what had to be done. He had been lucky enough to hurry out of the station and hop straight on to the rear platform of the 73 bus, a chance in a million with the evening buses. A car was indispensable now, but he'd got rid of his old Anglia long ago. He had never been able to bear driving in London, the constant nerve-edge alertness that was necessary to navigate the maze of cul-de-sacs, and the shattering games of chicken with oncoming trucks for the wider spots on the narrow roads. There had been enough tension in his life already, and he'd sold the car to the first person who asked. That left him at the mercy of the buses, and he wasn't going to drag Sarah back and forth on buses with the banshees at their back.

The bus leaned perilously as it neared the curb, and stepping off, he just avoided a puddle of vomit. Wind swept through gaps in the buildings, driving the damp into his coat. It was after seven, but the traffic was still heavy.

His own road was empty, a wet stage set for a police movie, lighted only by the three streetlamps that hadn't been broken by the Apaches and by a blue glow from the gauze curtains, so faint

42

it hardly picked out the rain. He waited beside a hedge that was two feet taller than he was, watching the dark niches carefully for movement. Then he gave an exaggerated shrug of resignation, the sort of gesture you give when you are alone and edgy. He had to have a car.

'Hands up!'

The voice boomed at him through the hedge, and the shock sent him whirling. His heart thundered away – objectivity going fast – but the ghost of Cutter evaporated as he focused on the small black finger pointing at him through the hedge. Sloane stepped into the gateway, his hands trembling, and picked out the worried face that was almost invisible in the shadows.

'Hey, sorry, mon. I don' suss de scene wit you.'

Johnny slipped out of his observation post and Sloane put his hand tenderly on the tiny bony shoulder.

'Dem men rampage for sure.'

An idea formed swiftly from the kinship he felt for the tiny Outsider; the boy's swagger was both a denial and a witness of terrible vulnerability. I knew you in Flint, Sloane thought. We stood side by side against the boys from Eighth. One of us tripped the cop while the other swiped the traffic lantern.

'Would you help me do something? It's very important to me.'

Johnny straightened. 'You need halp? Look in we eye.' He drew up his chin like a soldier. 'You see me dread boy or no.'

★

'That's it then,' he said, flipping the notebook shut and dumping it into the pocket of his tan Burberry. The plainclothes policeman was Crabb's height, with a firm intelligent face and the moustache affected by young policemen all over the world. 'In future, Special Branch would appreciate advance notice of your more boisterous activities.'

'Sit on it, limey.'

From the bench, Cutter stared straight at the policeman. Uncharacteristically, he had held himself back for half an hour, and Downs expected the explosion at any moment. They hadn't been taken into a discreet office as they had anticipated – just sat down on a bench along the wall and questioned, put in their place with a firm derision so dry and smooth that Cutter had found nothing to grasp and fling straight back.

'We may need to send a babysitter,' he said. 'That's all.'

The older policeman, who up until then had watched with a bored, indolent air, inclined his head toward the station entrance. 'He means you can piss off, gents.'

'You and me . . . some day,' Cutter said with deceptive mildness. Cutter stood and Downs thought: this is it, this is where Cutter punches one of them and we spend the night crawling before the Ambassador.

The younger policeman smiled grimly at him, setting his legs but saying nothing. Downs stepped between them, pretending to stretch his legs, and it was enough to break the eye contact. The two policemen walked away toward the unmarked Rover on the pavement outside.

'Sloane,' Cutter said. His voice quavered. 'We didn't scare the son of a bitch enough.'

★

'Not this one,' Sloane said. 'And not the Vauxhall.'

They waited beside the cars queued up at an intersection in the thin rain, like father and son examining exhibits at a museum. The small side road crossed over with a slight jog to begin again under another name, but none of the traffic crossed with it. The cars all turned left to slide into the stream or edged out fitfully for the difficult right turn. Standing next to him at the corner, Johnny gripped eight inches of green rubber hose with both hands.

'There, the Mini.'

Sloane referred to a battered white Mini-Cooper that sat third in the queue, reflective green tape along the sills and a loose bumper guard shuddering with the rough idle. His hair awry, the young driver glared impatiently at the Vauxhall sedan ahead of him.

'Just do it and run. I'll take care of the rest.'

Johnny grinned. 'We a warriyah.'

The van slid out around the corner and the queue edged forward then stopped as the Vauxhall in front was checked trying

44

to cross the stream when a truck with a covered trailer closed up quickly. The cars behind grew impatient, and one honked, but the woman driving stuck to her resolution and finally spurted across in front of a chivalrous sedan that flashed its lights to her.

Now, he thought. Sloane stepped into the road just as the Mini came to a stop. Johnny scurried out, keeping low. He hammered at the rear bumper with his hose, rocked the car with all his weight and then disappeared into the night. The young man at the wheel whipped around indignantly to glare at the driver of a humpy Morris, who gave an innocent shrug through the windshield and pointed the way Johnny had run. Sloane ambled down the middle of the road with curiosity. After a glance at the rear of the Mini, he shook his head sadly at the imaginary crumpled bodywork.

He heard the driver's door open. The man's feet hit the road with an angry stamp and it was time to move. Sloane backed a step to let the driver pass to inspect his damage. Then Sloane was in the hard seat, ramming the shift lever into first and pouncing into the cross traffic with only a glance, the front-wheel drive wrenching the light car around like a stone skipping on a lake.

'You bloody cunt!'

A truck braked hard and an air-horn complained, but the Cooper engine had him up to 25 almost instantly, matching the flow, and then he cut hard across an oncoming Jaguar into a narrow residential road, leaving the apoplectic owner far behind. The steering wheel was tacky, varnished by years of cigarette smoke, and sloane's leg trembled woozily on the clutch pedal. He caught only a glimpse of the small black boy throwing him a fist of triumph from the curb.

Gradually the thumping of his heart died away as he drove deeper into the wilderness of decaying terraces and quiet streets. Long ago he and his friends had pulled the bumper-banging prank a few times trying to provoke fights. Simple mischief, it had never really worked. He wondered if his father would have approved. He had never been there to say.

Sloane found a ghastly shrunken-head toy on the parcel shelf and tossed it into the back seat. As he drove, memories came to distract him from the fear that had slipped up on him again. He recalled the one image he had of his father, though he had toyed with the picture so many times over the years he no longer had any idea whether it was real or just verbal reconstruction. He couldn't have been more than four or five, tucked into a cardboard box in a corner of the blacked-out storefront window. Peering out of the box, he saw the backs of women's heads, dozens of them, and beyond them an earnest, ascetic-looking man with sandy hair swept straight back, both his arms raised in an exultant V. 'Will you now choose salvation?' It mustn't have been very long after that moment, the only picture he had, that Pastor Alex had drifted on to greener pastures, without his encumbrances. The pastor's woman, married in the eye of the Lord but out of sight of city hall, had struggled by on her own, an obstinate, private woman with – he remembered them clearly – large, practical, mannish hands. He could see them at work as they tugged at balls of reprocessed rag cotton and stuffed them into the bench seats of 4 by 4 Army trucks. That was much later, her wartime job. She had not been a forgiving woman, and Sloane could imagine her silent prayers even years after the abandonment: that Pastor Alex be drafted as expediently as He could manage it and posted somewhere very hot and very uncomfortable in the Asian Theatre of Operations.

He turned and circled back through the bleak no-man's-land of southern Hackney. The passenger-side wiper was broken, a finger of rubber trailing the blade back and forth across the dismal smear. The next war had caught her son, plucked him out of Fisher Body No. 4, and since he had put in for the motor pool the Army in its wisdom had made him an office clerk. But by some other fluke he wasn't sent to Korea at all but to the moribund four-power Control Commission in Berlin, where he stamped and filed police reports – *procès de commissariat* – from the police teams. Bored, he picked up languages easily from the other soldiers and clerks, learning German and French in a year, though Russian took longer because they were less friendly and often absent to protest some indignity. As he learned to move his mouth in new ways, he discovered the disturbing secret of language students: personality was as fluid as words, and new words could build a new personality, from the outside in. His German personality had a tenacious application he had never possessed, and he found himself reading works by Goethe, and

Schiller's historics – a startling change for a young man who had read nothing but pulp westerns in his own language. In French he was more fanciful. He wrote a drawerful of very bad poems and he had an affair with an adventuress from Lyons who really wanted nothing more than his passport. He aped the surfaces of the cultures he touched, and began to question everything about his own, gradually succumbing to the ultimate dishonesty of the uprooted: approving what he liked of each new culture while ignoring the worst because he had no responsibility to it – and rejecting everything of his own because it was all of a piece and could not be separated. Too many worlds opened: he was like a poor boy thrust suddenly into a roomful of expensive toys. It was intoxicating; illusions of opportunity fed the cockiness of an untested young man who had no past to go back to. He was free to try every fantasy: he could be a Bohemian artist, a respected scholar, a businessman lounging on the Riviera, he could go anywhere and do anything.

Sloane winced as he drove past the grim Holly Street estate, two blocks from his flat, and he tried to put the silly young man out of his mind. All he had found after being discharged was a series of dreary office jobs and a growing dissatisfaction that had led him straight into the world's last trap. Hoffacker, clever and avuncular, had taken him onto a hill and offered him the world, or at least offered him adventure, aiming him inexorably toward Cutter. Idiot, he thought, wincing again at his own foolish pride.

He pulled straight in over the curb, the only space left on Richmond Road. Four cats' eyes watched him malevolently from the hedge as he hurried to the door. The television murmured away from Mrs Cromer's flat, and a smell of liver hung in the hall, mixed with the reek of urine that nothing could ever get out of the linoleum on the stairs. What could he say to Sarah? He had put off planning that as long as he could.

She must have heard the key or his footsteps because she was just inside, reaching out for him as he opened the door.

'*Jeffrey*. What happened?'

He held her to avoid speaking, and with his hands on her back he felt the steel she carried under her skin. Was it just the lack of so much as an extra ounce of body fat or was it the tension as well? She was like a greyhound, bred and trained for a race that had never come.

'We've got to get away from here tonight.'

'What's wrong?'

He tried to tug away toward the bedroom, but she clung to him. What could he say? *Sarah, I was a spy. They want me back. You were what?* Whatever he planned broke down when he was faced with a human situation. And he was suddenly frightened in a very primitive way, trapped by the four walls so that he couldn't see what approached. Cutter was at the foot of the stairs. Just outside the door.

'Please,' he said. 'Help me pack. I'll explain when we're in the car.'

'What car?' Her voice rose sharply.

'I borrowed a car. I'll tell you everything when we get out of here.' He hurried to the bedroom, tugged the old suitcase down from the wardrobe and began shovelling in clothing. He felt her standing against the light.

'What's *wrong*, Jeffrey?'

'It'll be all right if only . . .'

'I *insist* you tell me.'

He turned and held her shoulders, as much to calm himself as her, but she backed away testily. Her eyes were round and panicky; she had caught it from him.

'The past has come back. Some people are after me, after both of us. They're not very nice people. Please help me. I can't think about anything but getting away.'

She studied his face curiously, drawing strength from somewhere. Then she pushed past him to the wardrobe. 'You're not half making a jumble. Let me do it.'

'Just enough for a few days,' he said.

'Will you want a jersey?'

'If there's room.'

In the sitting room, he unlocked the desk drawer and dropped several of the pill bottles into his coat pocket. He slid the drawer out another two inches to reveal a flat black box that might have held two packs of paying cards. On the lid it said Walther PPKS. Inside was the demonstration target folded in quarters with its three ragged holes near the centre, the manufacturer's boast of accuracy. He slid the paper aside to reveal the angular little pistol and the spare magazine with a comma of hard-rubber at the bottom.

Collins, the blunt New Englander, had held the box out to him in Research's basement like a failed term paper. All you get, Sloane, a .32, a ladies' gun, good for killing a pat of butter at six inches. If you *have* to have the damn thing, don't ever load it. If you have to load it, don't carry it on you. If you have to carry it for some reason when you're over there, don't ever point it at anyone. And if you *do* point it at someone, don't *ever* pull the trigger because if you hit him he's going to be really angry. But seriously . . .

Sloane pulled the magazine to check and saw the brass nose of a cartridge. He made sure there was nothing in the chamber and snapped the magazine home again. Sloane refused to carry it Collins's 'official' way.

But seriously, this is the only way to keep a pistol, man, ready to use. Let it hang about unloaded, you may as well throw it in the river. Cocked and locked, we'd call it with a Colt or a Browning, but this crazy German safety drops the hammer so you can't properly call it cocked. No matter, it's double action and the first trigger-pull recocks and fires all in one – stiff as a priest's pecker first go, but it works. Go on, work the safety – the wrong way, man, it goes up. It's loaded.

He had jumped back and nearly dropped the pistol. The safety lever did indeed drop the hammer. In theory – and apparently in fact – the inner mechanism locked up the firing pin before the hammer fell, but the sight of the exposed hammer snapping down on a loaded chamber had been so hair raising that Sloane had vowed right there to carry the pistol his own way, with a loaded magazine but no cartridge in the chamber.

'Is it raining out?' Sarah called, and he slid the pistol into his coat pocket opposite the pill bottles, noticing that it still had its spurious magic: he felt safer.

'Of course.' He turned out the room light and parted the curtains to check the street. He had been wrong: the rain had stopped for the moment. An old man limped past along the shiny pavement from the off-licence, carrying a bottle of wine. Nothing else moved. Slates and gables and chimney pots stood out against an ominous orange glow on the underside of the solid bank of cloud. It was an end-of-the-world scene, evil with radioactivity and undefined menace.

'Let's be off.'

He turned and saw her in the half light, wearing the overcoat and lugging the suitcase, and his heart went out to her, reproached by her efficient courage.

'Thanks, Sarah.'

5

He avoided the main roads from a lingering fear that Cutter would be waiting for him there, or that the police were onto the car. Continually distracted as he fought through the labyrinthine alleyways, he told her at first only snatches of his fears and the main outlines of what had happened. They wound south through the narrowest streets of Shoreditch and then across the fairytale folly of Tower Bridge. Still chased by the ghosts, he kept east of the A23, moving parallel to it along residential streets that cut through the flat reaches of Camberwell, Denmark Hill and Selhurst, while she heard enough to subside into an apprehensive silence. Finally, as the centre of the city dropped behind, the pavements widened, the houses grew larger and squatter, and a few trees made their tentative appearance, his terrible claustrophobia receded so that he could concentrate to tell her the rest.

By the time they had emerged from the shiny tangle of Croydon, Sarah knew as much of his story as she needed to know. And she had met the byzantine cast of characters, from the egregious Cutter to the shrewd old Russian at the trade mission whom Sloane had doubled against. Wrapped in her coat, she had listened to it all intently, seeking all the while for some way of connecting this man with the one she had slept beside for more than a year.

On the hilly southern edge of the city, they touched the main highway briefly, and then they pulled east again along the smaller A22 that would curl eventually into Brighton via the eerie Sussex Downs. Outside the city, he began to breathe more deeply, and as soon as they passed the final outflung sentinel of London at Godstone, he turned abruptly onto a lane that trailed away into the Surrey countryside. The weeds beside the lane had been cut back harshly to the bramble hedgerow and he parked on mown stubble. When he killed the lights, the world went out. The seat creaked in the dark as he tried to limber his stiff legs, and neither of them spoke for some time in the startling quiet. Before long he could see a dull square of light from a farmhouse a mile ahead in the broken, rolling country. He had never felt more alien from everything, from her, from his own life; an utter fugitive. He was still not sure how she would react to it all.

Gradually the glow of moon through cloud came up slowly like the lights in a theatre, and he could just make out fallow fields with bare oak hands straining against the sky. As gradually as it had come, the landscape began to fade through the misting windows.

'I can't picture you as a spy,' Sarah said finally. 'Mild-mannered translator. I wonder, did you change in a call box?' He heard her make a sound, perhaps a soft laugh in the darkness.

'You're lying to yourself,' he said, annoyed by the laugh. 'It was all there at the hospital. Remember our Sunday trips? I stole one of the doctors' cars for the afternoon. You knew that.'

'Everything is bizarre at a hospital,' she said. 'You changed after.'

He ran his finger along the damp inside of the windscreen. 'I suppose. Way back at the beginning of time I used to think I was the cat's pyjamas. I could do just about anything. Hoffacker used that to hook me in the first place, but it was Cutter who got me in over my head. Cutter's a rapist,' he said bitterly. 'That just about sums up his relationship to the world. Give him money and he'd give it back so he could break your arm to take it.'

Sloane remembered one debriefing in which Cutter had been unusually lucid about his view of life. Loyalty is shit, he had growled. Ideology is shit. Bribery is shit. *Blackmail* lasts; *blackmail* is certain.

'I knew Cutter was setting me up. I thought I was a step ahead of him and I could stay ahead. I pretended I didn't see what he was doing; that way he had his rape and I was one turn of the screw wiser. I actually looked forward to a bit of . . . "risk" sounds idiotic. Just something adventurous and different. Something to get away from the self-loathing I felt, trapped in empty office jobs. What a *child*.'

He brought his nearly invisible hands together in front of him.

They weren't in fact trembling, but he felt they were. He rummaged for her bag and found a cigarette. With the one in Cutter's car, it would be his second in a year. That dependence would come back, too.

'There's a lighter somewhere in there,' she said.

He fumbled for the lighter he had seen on the dashboard, but it didn't work and she lit the cigarette for him with a burst of blinding flame, and then one for herself.

'I won't say a word about it,' she promised. He assumed she meant the cigarette. 'You've done better than I.'

She had cut down to seven or eight a day, her rock bottom. After The Fall he had fought the smoking along with the drink, and he had won. By giving up everything you wanted and needed, he thought, you built a counterfeit of self-respect.

'It got worse, like dealing with any blackmailer. First to stay in Europe. Cutter threatened to have me sent home. You don't know how much I feared that; it would have been like a death sentence. To keep the job, to stay out of jail. He had proof of everything, of course, and half what I did for him had been illegal. The very worst was making friends with a man I liked . . . and having to blackmail him. I was only the go-between, but still that was the very worst. Morally. I felt like a plague on mankind, and I was.'

He coughed once on the acrid smoke, but already he could feel he was getting used to it again. Her face lit with a rosy glow and he saw a private apprehension that gave way to a sad gentleness as soon as she sensed his eyes on her.

'The rest was just falling off a mountain. By the time he forced me into the double game, there was no question of enjoying it any longer. I just had to survive. I was hustling back and forth between Cutter and Komarovsky, changing my story a little each time and making sure my left hand didn't know what my right hand was doing.'

She touched his arm softly and he closed his eyes for a moment. That man still existed, hidden, deep inside.

'A thousand eyes were watching me, waiting for me to stumble. It would prove some obscure point against me if I stumbled, I don't know what. Maybe that I was just another mediocre human being with no special skill in the world.' Sliding back the window to toss out the cigarette, he felt the blast of frigid air. There was a singing in the power lines above the car: the most forlorn sound imaginable.

'Even the vain young man hadn't liked surprises all that much. But what was left of me . . . I started anticipating and worrying the possibilities all the time, rehearsing what I had to say and planning every step. I was smoking five packs of cigarettes a day and sometimes I'd look at an ashtray and find three going at once. You know how it is when you can't concentrate. I couldn't eat either. I learned it was physically possible to sit down in a chair and make a whole room tremble around you.

'Everything was borrowed time by then. I'd look in their eyes when I brought the latest little time bomb and know they didn't believe a word of what I was saying. Maybe they did, maybe they didn't – I felt the deceit showed. I couldn't even get on a bus without wondering why the other passengers didn't point me out and tell the conductor I didn't belong. In the end I didn't stumble; I just broke open like a ripe plum. Drank and ran, ran and drank.'

Sarah leaned against his arm and her hair brushed his cheek. 'Jeffrey . . .'

It was her first comforting word. Softly he said, 'This time they say they'll hurt you.'

He felt her stiffen. 'You mustn't let them get to you through me.'

He was angry at himself. He had let self-pity break cover, and like a clever child it had tried to shift some of the horror. 'They have a hundred ways to get to me. It doesn't really matter what they choose. I'm going to have to do what they want.' It was the first time he had admitted it to himself.

He kissed the top of her head awkwardly, feeling the grainy hair against his lips. For a while they talked of their brief past, avoiding the present, and he slid her step by step away from the terrible selfish disclosure he had made. At least, he thought, he could protect her from himself.

'Sometimes at night I touch you to make sure I'm not alone,' she confessed. 'It's a different sort of dread. You make mine seem small.'

'I can see my enemies, that's all. If you can see them you can fight them. I had that advantage. I'm going to leave you at Felicity's for a while, a few days.'

'What will you do?'

'I don't know. I'll get some sleep and then I'll think of something.'

'I wish I could help,' she murmured. 'I'd be no help. I won't cling.' And to prove her point, she let go of his arm.

'You don't cling,' he said, and he felt a wash of tenderness and kissed her. She shivered, and he noticed suddenly how chilly it was in the car. He ground the starter for a long time until it caught.

'But what will you do?'

'I'll find something. Some way to do it and make it the end. Cutter's weakness has always been his . . . massive excess. Trying to open Chinese boxes with a hammer.'

Finding an old shirt under the seat, he walked around the car wiping the windows. Mud under the stubble sucked at his feet. Something tiny and nervous scurried away into the hedge. He saw a thin line of smoke that rose and sheared away from the small farmhouse with its glowing window, a postcard sent from a simpler place far away where cruelty and treachery were always defeated by innocence.

★

She was expecting them. They had called from a phone box beside a foul roadhouse, the carpark jammed with shiny Jensens and Rovers, and hearty laughter leaking out of the bottleglass windows. She lived in a Regency terrace not far above the pebble beach in the stuffy half of Brighton that was called Hove, bought long before property values there had begun escalating even faster than London's.

'Don't say a word – you're pregnant,' Felicity greeted them carelessly at the door. He was struck once again by the sight of her: Sarah fleshed out and given colour, the same face but more mobile and confident, carrying an air of aggressive independence. A wool wrap-around skirt clung to her hips as she gestured them in. She was only two years younger, but the difference seemed much greater, set against Sarah's drawn, sad features.

'Actually, no,' Sarah said earnestly. 'You know I wouldn't surprise you. I'm not a surprising person.'

They picked their way through an obstacle course of brass pipes and thin crates stacked in the entry.

'Mind your step, the floorboards are up in here. Another decade or so and the engineers will have the central heating in. This is the last room but one. I hope you brought plenty of jerseys.'

'I won't be staying,' Sloane said, and she seemed to spot the urgency in his eyes despite his resolve to remain light and cheerful.

'For pity's sake, have a sherry at least. The best South Africa has to offer. I've given up the damn boycott. I think I've had it with pointless gestures.'

They followed into the sitting room. The rug was rolled back from one wall where the floorboards had been pried up, and flat, grey-primered radiators, like the plates of a battleship, leaned awkwardly under the bow window.

'I'm down to visit for a few days,' Sarah explained. 'Jeffrey has to get back. He's obliged to return the car.'

And thank you, Sarah, he thought. He couldn't have lied convincingly then, wearied more than he realized by the drive, and by the sudden re-entry into the chaos of the past. He chose the worn end of the old sofa.

Felicity stood indomitably at the mantel, pouring sherry into thin tumblers, and he could see that she suspected something. 'If you're not coming back, mind, you must write to us.'

He laughed falsely. 'I think I'll make it back.'

'I thought that was your fighter-pilot, Battle-of-Britain face. Here.' She distributed the glasses. 'Just tell me you're not having a row and I'm satisfied.'

'We're not,' Sarah said. 'Actually, we don't row.'

'Give it time,' Felicity suggested. 'A year is so short.'

'Can I get you a saucer of milk?' Sarah said in play, but her tone was harsher than Felicity's. 'Leechy, if you carry on with your bitchy academics much longer, ordinary people will start shunning you.'

Felicity settled into the wing chair with a dry smile. 'You've got it wrong. The Poly is hardly a circle of dons fencing wit. They're more pit ponies plodding after their little technical pursuits. Half. The other half are blushing virgins lost in the great forest of Higher Learning. I *am* cruel, aren't I? The most compelling metaphysical question I've heard in a year was whether Brighton and Hove Albion could beat Liverpool and escape relegation to the second division, and that was from the staff, mind. You mustn't romanticize us – *you're* the cosmopolitans down from the Capital.'

It was an immense effort, but he kept up the cocktail talk for a polite half hour. He liked Felicity; there was enough self-parody in her to soften the drawling, plum accent that ordinarily set his teeth on edge. He had always wondered whether Sarah had lost the accent, or Felicity had acquired it, after leaving home. Sarah pitched in and helped him over the obstacles, chatting about her unsuccessful search for work.

'It's all done through friendships, you nunc, absolutely all,' Felicity insisted. 'You'll want to cultivate some of your old friends from Sussex.'

'I had none, except for that peculiar girl who was my room mate at Falmer House, and she's in South Africa.'

'The men, dear, the men.'

'Sods, the lot of them,' Sarah said with feeling.

'The heart is *not* on the mend,' Felicity observed, raising her eyebrows. 'More sherry?'

'No thank you,' Sloane said.

'I don't mean to sound bitter. I suppose I went through university during a bad vintage – the ones I met were only out for a good time to console themselves for not being at Cambridge.'

He sensed that being with Felicity had an effect on her; she was livelier now and more censorious as well, as if slipping into a former big-sister role. He wondered if it would last or taper off after he left, when they began readjusting to each other.

He excused himself finally, and Felicity saw him to the door.

'Ciao, Felicity.'

As he started outside, she touched his arm and held him back. 'Is it going to be all right?'

'It's going to be all right.'

'You must ask for my help, unless you feel it shames you.'

'I will,' he said, ignoring the tiny bite in her words.

It was raining again by the time he entered the patchy woods of northern Sussex, and the wiper still dragged its arm of rubber limply across the windscreen. It felt odd being alone; not expecting to see Sarah in the next few hours; not rehearsing things to say to her and worrying about her. They hadn't been separated in a year. It was a relief in a way, but – also, it felt almost like a death.

★

. . . During the time period May/December, hard currency shipments to BERNCREDIT appear to have fallen off considerably and cannot (to the small enterprise groups in any case) usefully be substantially increased while labour troubles on the state airline prevent direct tourist flights, either to Europe proper or to connecting capitals in the Francophone (CFA franc) states. It may prove interesting to observe the effects of this sudden diminution of outflow on local reinvestment, if any, as the small enterprise groups have traditionally met the appearance of similar situations simply by hoarding rather than elective local development possibilities which, as in so much of the developing world, naturally run at a higher risk level and of lower inherent prestige.

The Old Man frowned at the cumbersome bureaucratic prose that trampled drunkenly across the simplest ideas. In Virginia it was four in the afternoon as he flipped over the third page of the tiresome report that covered secret transfers of currency to Switzerland from a number of West African republics. Even tiny Gambia seemed to have fifty or more dollar-millionaires, and the Old Man wondered idly how long a continent like Africa could go on leaking its wealth through a few holes. Or anywhere, for that matter. He scratched an itch on his hips and readjusted his right leg with his hands.

Like most of his colleagues, he knew exactly whose interests he was charged with defending, but unlike almost all of the career officers, he had not come from one of the old families himself and he did not identify himself as one of them. The others were automatically woven by their birth and education and marriages into a net of loyalty that was far more potent than any ideology; he was not, and they would probably not have understood the shape of his motives, nor trusted them. He sent his reasons sliding down the well-worn groove whenever doubt padded up on him: the people he defended supported the arts, they preserved standards of taste and culture, they formed the only truly international stabilizing community; at home in one another's parlours and schools, they bequeathed the sort of world where the vast majority – at least the vast majority in the metropolis – could ignore the swift passage of history, and only a handful like himself had to concern themselves with questions of stubborn intervention. And if, in the end, it were to become inescapable that their world devoured its future in order to survive the present, if the steady leaks one day emptied the bucket, it would be for his grandchildren – the thought was metaphorical; he had never married – it would be for others to think again. He couldn't see the bottom of the bucket now, and those who wanted to kick it over while it still held water were dangerous fools. He smiled to himself: were *self-styled* revolutionaries, as that prize ass MacIlvaine put it, parroting *Time* magazine, as if there were another kind, appointed by a credentials committee and confirmed by a senate. For now, for the rest of his life certainly, what most of the career officers saw as the natural order carried on, and it was his to defend.

In Gambia, someone named Putney Muwalo (Leeds University, 1965) had made a fortune from a fraudulent government export contract for peanuts, and he had used the money to invest in Anglo-American gold mines and to set up a local distributorship for Land Rovers. Putney Muwalo was a friend of the west and collected impressionist art: a man he could understand. How could he relate to a peasant farmer, uneducated, ragged and now starving because his peanut crop was suddenly worthless? He knew it was a cruel thought, but it was honest: if some odd day he ended up in the Gambia, he would far rather be entertained in Muwalo's home than the peasant's.

There was a discreet knock and he set the report aside.

'Enter.'

Dru stepped in, and as she crossed the office she was preceded by an overwhelming scent of musk. He disliked the rotting odour; it reminded him of hostile, loveless sex on a hot afternoon.

The only kind he had ever known, and he had finally renounced even that.

'Sir, it's about Broken Back,' she said proudly.

'Yes?'

'I think we've got a Lumbago. I managed to snatch this advisory from London Special Branch before it went up to Central Files. It sounds like Research has picked him.' She glanced at the pink paper torn from the teleprinter. 'An old contract agent of theirs. He bolted and they appear to have run around shooting up the city like cowboys. It couldn't be better for us.'

He took the paper and read it through quickly. It told him nothing further except the meaningless name: Jeffrey Sloane. 'Come, let's find Jerry and Harv.'

'I could handle it for you, sir.'

'I know you could, but let's stay a team as long as possible, all right? Before the rivalries begin.'

Unintentionally he found himself brushing clumsily against her as he levered himself up, feeling one breast rise up unhaltered and slip away from his shoulder. He said nothing. One great pleasure of being this age, he thought, was finding that the lifelong worry of sexuality, all the flirtations and turmoils, the whole querulousness, had faded nearly out of existence. He could get on with business, like someone freed of a chronic disease.

Ross and Moore were in the Playpen fanning out bridge hands listlessly beside Willy, their loaner from Ops, and Francis MacIl-vaine, perennial dummy. The Old Man set the advisory on the table and let them read it before speaking.

'I knew Hoffacker, their old head, and I know Cutter's style. Unless I'm pretty far wrong, Lumbago will have worked at the Soviet Trade Mission or been close to someone there. What I want to know is who in the opposition would be interested. Does Dzerzhinsky Street have a resident in the trade mission?'

Covering all bets, Moore had read through the current files on London and the putative KGB heads operating out of the embassy, the trade mission, TASS, Novosti, Radio Moscow, Aeroflot and the odd loner under legal cover as a student or supposed exile. 'The deputy head of the mission, Alexei

Komarovsky. He actually pulls some trade duties, but not enough to convince even a rural bobby that he's a genuine commercial agent. An old war hero, I imagine he's a tough piece of goods.'

Willy's eyes played over them in his annoying, superior way, and the Old Man skewered him with a grave stare as he spoke. 'We don't really care whether Lumbago gets his information or not. We just want him to make a fucking great noise rustling the bushes, don't we? Would you get one of your people to give this Komarovsky a discreet ring?'

Dru worked up an exaggerated grimace for Ross's benefit: he was the only one whose judgment she trusted. 'You want us to blow his cover?'

'Oh, we'll *hint*. We wouldn't want to endanger a fellow American now, would we?'

Jerry Moore smiled. 'Only if it were necessary.'

The Old Man kept his eyes on Willy. 'Give him a day or so to start digging, then drop the pebble. You can sort out something so it doesn't trace back. Nothing too obvious, just whet their interest. And set a watcher on Lumbago, too. I want progress reports.'

Willy nodded impassively. 'Will do.'

'My lead,' Ross said without emotion. He wiped the fever-sweat from his forehead with a stubby finger, as Dru held the door open for the Old Man. When the Old Man had gone, Ross set his cards down and seemed to study Willy. 'Your people happy about this?'

'Section head says assist, I assist.'

'And how many clerks and office boys are whispering about him at coffee break?'

'We don't kiss and tell,' and his tone said: *we* in Operations, *we* in the real world.

Outside they could hear the Old Man's door shut down the hall, and Ross patted his cards tidy then pushed them away from himself into the centre of the table. 'Lord knows, when he came into Economic Analysis, I said to myself, who needs another FDR? Especially a big star who's on the downhill run after the last massacre. But he's a damn good man. He's a legend, a real one.'

'Sure, a regular Lone Ranger,' Willy said amiably.

'I won't have you people paying out rope only to yank it away. If you back him now, tell your section head you're going to keep backing him till he's satisfied. He's going to come through this with flying colours.'

Willy folded his hands behind his head and said nothing.

'To tell the truth, Harv,' Moore said tentatively, 'we all thought you'd disapprove of Broken Back.'

'It stinks to high heaven. But until the Old Man cancels it, we're behind him. Understood?'

'I just hope we're a long way behind,' MacIlvaine offered.

'I'm sorry, Harvey, I feel that way too,' Dru put in doubtfully. 'I think it's going to get someone hurt.'

Ross held them in his gaze one by one, as if gauging the weak links, and then released them. 'We'll try to prevent that. We'll try very hard.'

Willy rose confidently, like a first-stringer finally summoned off the bench. 'Work to do.'

★

In London, it was after midnight, and two empty tumblers chimed together eerily on a small table beside the bed. The tiny hotel room in Paddington where Sloane lay trembled angrily as trains passed below. Outside the window, steady traffic on the Marylebone flyover added its rumble to the clang-clang-clang of freight cars in the shunting yard and the fussy rattle of the grating on the hall lift that never seemed to stop bringing and retrieving guests. Sloane heard none of this consciously. An empty Scotch bottle lay beside him on the musty bed and he was fitfully asleep, dreaming of ominous half-human machines that rose from a flat plain to rumble threateningly toward him. Someone had once told him that every image in a dream is a piece of the dreamer's personality, and a disturbing scrap of that idea stayed with him now in sleep. Each of you is me, he thought desperately. I can stop you, I can make you vanish.

★

Eero Saarinen had designed the building in 1960 to express the exuberant optimism of the New World, and its slatted white facade walled off the west end of Grosvenor Square like a huge bleached waffle topped by a thirty-five-foot golden eagle. The subdued mock-Georgian neighbours along the other sides of the square did not object to the intrusion because most of them, too, belonged to the US State Department. From his plinth in the gardens, Franklin Roosevelt surveyed the northern buildings that had housed Eisenhower's headquarters in 1943, and only toga-wrapped George I out in the middle added a non-American note, but then it had all been his great-grandson's fault.

In the cold early morning, well before sunrise, a tall figure stepped silently from one of the doors on the southern flank of the square. Neither beside the door nor on the fat white pillars that the man passed on his way to the sidewalk was there a brass plaque like so many others around the gardens. This door was one of three in a row that remained anonymous, and the fourth displayed a plaque that had long been a standing joke: *United States of America, Department of State, Records Storage Annexe (All enquiries to Consulate).*

Guy Kohler wore an open-necked blue shirt under his camel blazer. He wore neckties to weddings and funerals, and to the rare official functions he attended; but despite the official fluffing and several imperative memoes, on ordinary days he simply kept one emergency tie rolled up in his Mercury and another in his desk. As he had explained many times, in various tones of voice, his job didn't *exactly* involve meeting the public, did it? And if something came up . . . Here he would produce an old knit tie from a pocket.

He walked westward along Upper Grosvenor Street, over the unmarked spot where Adlai Stevenson had collapsed and died in 1965, and the air was still so cold that whisps of fog lay on the street like a shredded blanket. Kohler disliked overcoats too, and he preferred to shiver a bit and walk briskly rather than wrap himself in one of those long skirt-like garments that he secretly found effeminate. If there was one thing Guy Kohler avoided it was any item of clothing, any gesture, that he found remotely effeminate. Once, in the military academy where he had spent six gruesome years of his youth, a boy had leaned over and whispered maliciously that crossing one knee over another – like *that* – was for fairies. Ever since, if one of his legs grew weary, Kohler would carefully splay it out and rest the ankle on the opposite knee. That was just one trick in a large repertoire acquired over twenty-five years of study: never using two hands on a Zippo lighter, never holding a cigarette between thumb and fingers like a peashooter, never allowing the wrist to break the plane of the forearm, always the proper quick and casual snap that opened a pair of sunglasses. But the predatory eyes in London station were hard on secret vanities. Kohler would have been dismayed to hear a junior career officer drunkenly proposing his epitaph at the last Christmas Party: One thing's for *sure*, folks . . . he was *definitely* butch.

He crossed the double width of Park Lane illegally, scurrying ahead of a pair of black taxis that bore down on him, and strolled into Hyde Park, leaving footprints on the dew-sodden grass. Speakers' Corner, a quarter mile to his right, was empty except for a few browsing pigeons, and only a handful of figures hurried along the paths this early.

A pair of stony eyes among the lime trees followed his progress gravely, like an owl studying an inedible rodent. Before long, the tiny dark man was beside Kohler, as if coming out of nowhere, and Kohler eased back his pace so that the short legs needn't pump so hard to keep up.

'Top of the morning, Sparrow. Sorry we haven't seen much of you recently. Touch and go these days. You've been all right?'

Sparrow rapped once on his left palm with two cocked finger-knuckles of his right hand – a swift little punch that looked as if it could break bricks. Sparrow's full name was Thomas William Jefferson, but he almost never used it. The nickname had been a cruel joke of his platoon sergeant's – he was only five-five and had cheated to enlist – but after seventeen solo long-range reconnaissance patrols into the central highlands, the name Sparrow had acquired a terrible mystique. The word 'patrol' was an Army euphemism for tiny search-and-destroy missions deep into enemy territory: setting booby traps, ambushing supply bearers, assassinating NLF cadres. Never given to speaking very much, Sparrow had gone totally mute after the fifth of his long patrols, one that had lasted three weeks, and he hadn't spoken a word aloud since. No one knew why, and no one had ever been able to force the issue. He made his way in the world with hand signals and a few scribbled notes, but mostly with an air of leaden menace that did not encourage questions.

'What we need is a bit of your pavement artistry. No one better as a solo, we all acknowledge that.' Knowing there would be no reply, Kohler felt a compulsion to rattle on, as if allowing a gap in the one-sided conversation would be some kind of social failing. 'Worth a dozen of the Farm trainees, I've always told them. Sorry we can't pay you the dozen salaries, though. The SOE committee says we're wasting too much money as it is, and this is something of a lateral request, not our own division at all.' The monologue faltered, and Kohler realized there was no reason at all to tell Sparrow so much; bad policy, in fact.

Kohler too had wondered why the tiny man refused to speak aloud, and he had once sent a query back to Langley that had received no satisfactory answer. No one trusted Sparrow enough to offer him regular status, but they used him on contract often enough to keep him eating because his talents were incomparable. A standard find-and-follow with a low priority required two teams of at least four men each, covering exits, moving ahead of the target along likely routes, relieving each other for meals and sleep. But Sparrow did almost as well alone. As conspicuous as a zebra, one would think, he managed to drop out of sight almost at will. And he could wait in some sort of suspended animation, wait forty-eight hours, seventy-two hours, staring at a single, suspect door until it opened. He had lost contact a few times – even full-scale umbrella teams did – but he had always managed to regain it, and he had never let them down when it could be helped. And there was another skill that made Sparrow invaluable, a skill that was discussed only in the most metaphorical terms: measure him, take special action, buy him a ticket.

'Jeffrey Sloane, late forties, American with a residence permit and British wife. Unemployed, but hires out as a translator to the seedier bureaus in Soho and around. Worked for Research once – you know, Cutter's Bowery Boys over in Charing Cross. Lives at 16 Richmond Road, upper, Dalston. Just coattail and report daily.'

He handed across a small photograph, and Sparrow devoured

it quickly with his eyes before handing it back.

'We'll keep in touch in the usual way. Any problems?'

Sparrow rapped twice into his palm, and his eyes narrowed, watching an elderly man in a black overcoat and bowler hat stride past them, swinging his umbrella aggressively.

'Good,' Kohler said. 'Observe him from well back; the Old Man doesn't want anyone to know we're taking an interest in this.'

Sparrow glanced up at the tall man, and Kohler thought: more information he needn't know.

'Yes, the Old Man's baby. Bit odd, but. . . never mind. That's all.'

Without a sign, Sparrow peeled away like a small round fighter plane and banked off toward a row of plane trees, where he managed to disappear in ten seconds flat. Kohler went straight on along the sandy path toward the Serpentine Bridge. He wondered again, irritably, what possessed Sparrow to inconvenience himself so thoroughly in daily life. How did he ask directions? Buy stamps at the post office? How did he complain about shoddy service in a restaurant? How did he complain in the shops? Kohler would have been devastated if he had been denied the ability to complain. That was the way you proved your distinction against the world. Others might accept second rate, but he wouldn't. Politely, but firmly, you showed you were someone who played the game for real, the right way. From the bridge, he could see a little fog clinging to the lake like steam over a pot, and two hardy bathers bobbed and shivered along the south shore at the Lido.

Kohler headed back toward the office along Rotten Row, watching a morning rider canter past. How heavy horses are, he thought. Large-hipped. The man hunched forward in full riding gear, posting up and down and looking so foppish to Kohler that he vowed he would never ride anything but a Western saddle, legs straight and ass down, no matter how sore it left him.

6

Drizzle: dark clouds shrouded the morning streets with the gloom of an eclipse, and his head still buzzed as he climbed out of the tube at Blackfriars. He crossed through the traffic and headed into the angular masses of the City, an island chain of bank headquarters jutting out of the swamp of concrete. He felt the echo of a headache, or a bit more, as the buildings pressed in at him. His stab at moderate drinking the night before had got out of hand and now he vowed the classic drinker's vow: to buy smaller bottles. He knew he would not go off entirely until the job was done. Wet grime covered everything like used motor oil, making walking treacherous, but once he was into the narrow alleyways there was hardly room to fall between the parked delivery vans and the foot traffic of sleek hurrying secretaries. Despite his head, his mood was a bit lighter because he had a plan; a fluctuating hope that he would be able to shift some of the burden.

Inter news was one of the very few press buildings that actually fronted on Fleet Street, but Harry Trebartha met him furtively at the side entrance on a small court. He was a rumpled ageing figure with a fringe of white hair puffing over his ears, tall and large-boned in a brown coat that was a shade or two too flashy for the sober City.

'Long time, Jeffrey.'

'Longer than that.'

They shook hands formally, and Trebartha's was warm and moist. His face was a parchment map of his life, with more red veins than Sloane remembered, and his eyes seemed weary and beaten now, despite a hint of the old irreverent humour.

'We can't go inside. Davis would do me for sure, the beastly man. I know a place along the road.' Nigel Davis – Sloane remembered the complaints from long ago – was head of the rewrite section where Trebartha worked, the sort of Dickensian supervisor who enforced total silence by day and counted the paper clips at night.

It was far too early for the pubs to be open, and as they walked, Trebartha joked about the clever legal conspiracy that set pub hours exclusively at times when you weren't thirsty. He made for an ugly little sandwich bar with orange booths like seamless machine extrusions.

'I hear the sole meunière is very good here.'

Trebartha ordered coffee for them both and Sloane left some change on the counter. A portable radio by the tea pots blared out savage pop music.

We're the rats of the modern city,
And we gnaw at your empty pity.
You think all is lost?
Feed us, feed us, or pay the cost . . .

'What brings you to the centre of the universe?'

'A favour, as I said on the phone.'

'What I have is yours – saving Inland Revenue's own and what's bespoke by Edna for hire-purchase.'

'Not money.' Sloane suddenly felt shabby, looking him up after three years and immediately begging a favour. He held back his own impatience and asked after the old man's life.

'Reduced station,' Trebartha said cheerily, concealing a universe of failed hopes. 'First floor now, doing rewrites on stringer pieces from Germany that'll go into local evening rags, the *Basingstoke Belch* and all its glorious cousins.'

The coffee was thin and bitter, and the large-grain sugar refused to dissolve. Sloane slid his away. Trebartha's breast pocket bulged with pens, and he twisted the buttons on his coat as he talked. 'It's not that I'd complain for myself, really, but it's what it looks like to the wife. Old man a poor scribbler – once an illustrious foreign correspondent, you know? Well, overseas bureau anyway. Now Davis's humble footman, hoping the new computer set-up won't make him redundant altogether. Still, only a few years to retirement, and even Davis wouldn't be so mean that he'd screw me out of that, so it's the best face on it and stiff upper lip and a toast to the foul outfit.'

68

Sloane chatted aimlessly, something about having married recently and working as a translator, while the better half of his mind studied the old man. It was remarkable, he thought, the amount of dignity that pure physical size could salvage. As a smaller man, Trebartha would have been truly pathetic, but his meaty frame made him look like a boxer at the end of a noble career. Maybe it was the size that allowed him to keep up his friendships with the rough crew in the East End as well. Trebartha had done quite a side business for years taking orders for goods that had 'fallen off a lorry' – the trade that Sloane, in his boyhood, had called the 'Midnight Sears'.

'Not working for that spook outfit any more, are you?' Trebartha enquired with false carelessness.

'No. I quit.'

'Jolly good thing. Word is, even your own chappies are ready to write them off. Don't amount to a row of pins any more. Any inside info to sell?'

Sloane shook his head, and Trebartha laughed archly at himself. 'The dream of the big story, buying my way back to the top. A bit stale now. Truth is, even if I caught Princess Anne having it off with Colonel Gaddafi Davis would put me on a dog show and assign one of the bright new boys. They're all university now, you know? No more of our back-door sort, clawing our way in from the grammar schools in the East End. All plum voices and history firsts, even if they come out of redbricks. Good lads, but some are a bit wet.'

Trebartha sat back and closed his eyes. After the pause for meditation, he resumed, 'It was the war, you know. I can sit here and run the newsreel like the bloody News at Ten. Watered beer, the taste of powdered eggs and steri milk, paper so shoddy the books started crumbling before you got them out of the shop, all queues and coupons – it was wonderful. Pulling together and worrying about your neighbours when that bumblebee sound headed your way. Finest hour. You know, I covered that twit Monty in the Netherlands. That was journalism.'

He stared down into his cup. 'Another?'

Sloane shook his head, and Trebartha walked to the counter for a refill. He came back resigned and falsely cheery again. 'The high point. Ever since, my fortunes have rather exactly paralleled the country's. Colonies all walked out, finances collapsed, closing the industries, musing about the green days. To tell the truth, I don't much care for hard work any more either.' He chuckled. 'Let there be anarchy in the schools and punks in every bed. What was it you wanted?'

'Information. Contacts.'

'Ah, yes.'

Sloane had been watching the café carefully. The bored old woman sat in a corner behind the counter with her ear a foot from Radio One. Two postmen read their papers in another booth, but far across the shop. The street noise and the raucous dedications to Vera from Eddie and Charles and all the boys at the engineering works would cover anything he said. 'I need a good second-storey man, and I mean a good one. In and out of a high-security building with no bells ringing.'

Trebartha studied him curiously. 'Not turning bent in our old age, now?'

'I can't tell you, Harry. I'm sorry. It isn't for money.'

'You *are* still a spook. My, my. What makes you think I can help?'

'You grew up with them, you drink with them all the time, so you say.'

'So I say. You could pop into any local in Bow and recruit a bent lad at the drop of a fifty-pee.'

'I need a good one.'

Trebartha considered warily, as if Sloane had asked him to do the job himself. 'I don't know, Jeffrey. I can get ten years for conspiracy just listening to you.' He shifted uneasily on the orange seat. 'I don't know,' he repeated sonorously.

The counter was suddenly teeming with young clerks announcing complicated take-away orders and pestering one another gaily. It must have been break time.

'Look at Fred Astaire then,' a girl said, watching a boy in a coat with velvet lapels do a complicated dance step off by himself.

'Not half,' the boy replied amiably.

'Do you ever miss your youth?' Trebartha asked solemnly.

'Sure, but I wouldn't repeat it. Too much commotion and too little learned from it.'

Trebartha nodded. 'That's an attitude. I understand it, but, no, not for me. I want it over, all of it, only with the advantages the lads have now.'

'It's all that sex you missed,' Sloane said.

'Truthfully, yes. You never had privacy enough to get your end away if you grew up in London. Still, the girls you didn't have were probably a lot like the ones you did, so why be hot and bothered?' He went straight on, without a pause: 'Archway Tavern. Ask for Flegg. He won't do it but he can put you on to someone, if he takes a fancy to you.'

'Will he take a fancy to me?'

'Use my name, but tell him it's nothing to me.'

'Sure.'

'I mean it, Jeffrey. Once you use my name as a calling card, it was two other blokes had coffee here. All I need is a whiff of scandal to have Davis setting me licking envelopes for a year.'

'Thanks,' Sloane said.

'Cheers. Drop round sometime and tell me how it turned out.'

There's so much unhappiness, Sloane thought, watching him plod out of the café. Trebartha tugged his lapels up around his neck before bolting across the street like a gigantic rabbit.

★

The Research office lacked a conference room. They met downstairs around a long pine work-table that was littered with stacks of half-collated reports, an empty stapler, a guillotine paper knife and the general disorder of most common rooms. There was no doubt it was a war conference, with Cutter growling and snorting like a band saw at the head of the table, flanked by Downs and a restless Crabb. Remembering the old days, Downs let his eye wander along the table in a melancholy way across the seven men Cutter acidly called the Acolytes – some of whom had once been substitute case officers, but who were all now reduced to compiling thin background reports on the Satellites that no one anywhere seemed to take seriously. The best have gone, he thought; Thoms, Shapiro, Johnson, then Hoffacker carrying away their soul. Those left at the table varied in appearance from Roy Di Santis by the coffee machine, with the pinched glum pallour of a failed accountant, to fat Howard

Macky wearing a chartreuse bow tie and checked coat, looking like a racetrack tout.

Downs gave up and stared fixedly at a silent teletype against the wall: it wasn't a staff that bore much study. There was no denying how far Research had fallen, not just in numbers and duties, but in the quality of human material. But if he looked too closely he was afraid of spooking his last fugitive hope. Cutter, for all his weaknesses, gave them a focus with the energy and pure stubborn wrath that might prove capable of holding the muddle together and even revitalizing Research as an organization. This one hope was the reason for Downs's – not loyalty, he wouldn't have put it that strongly, just a sort of watchful inertia that kept him from quitting the service, kept him standing by like a quiet page to a grotesque and savage Canute who flailed away at the rising tide. You couldn't always choose your saviour, and Cutter was the only one Research had.

'As of this moment, we're on duty seven days, no sleeping, no eating, not even a quick piss in the alley, till we run him down. It's been a while since any of you went out on foot, but some of you know how, and I'll team you the best I can so you can hold hands.'

Di Santis raised a sulky arm. 'We're *all* going out? Even office services?'

Cutter fixed him with a baleful eye and the silence lengthened intolerably. 'When you reach a certain point in any war, you stop checking limbs and start *counting* them. Anybody with one good limb, one eye, one lobe of their brain is drafted. If you want to eliminate yourself on that basis, Roy, I accept.'

Downs was fascinated. By Cutter standards, the tongue-lashing had been a masterpiece of restrained, ironic wit, with not even a rattle of profanity to punctuate the finish. He wondered whether the new urgency had brought out subtler aspects of Cutter that had lain dormant for years. Then Cutter stubbed out his observation in one scathing downhill run of words.

'Help or get to fuck out! Roy and all of you! I mean it. I'm going to find that son-of-a-bitch and twist his head around so he doesn't know whether to wipe his watch or wind his ass. We're going to teach him fucking terror. Are you following, Roy, or are the words too big for you? Well?'

'Yes, sir,' Di Santis replied feebly.

'Loory, you've done room searches – '

'It was a long time ago . . .'

'That wasn't a question, God dammit! You're our search expert. Go to Sloane's apartment and turn it up as you've never turned a room up.'

'What am I looking for?'

'You're not looking for anything!' Cutter snarled. 'How simple do I have to make this? You're destroying a piano, the way the kids did once. I don't want anything left at his place that won't go through a six-inch hole.'

'If you say so.'

The rest of the orders came down in the same vengeful vein, and Downs's momentary honeymoon with Cutter was over. What was the point of sending them all running amok, Downs thought. Simply to frighten Sloane? *It doesn't mean I can do what you want.*

'Have we heard about the stolen M-m-mini?' Downs asked politely.

Cutter raised a sinewy shoulder in one half of a shrug. 'It was on the British hotsheet this morning, or off-hotsheet or whatever the fuck those bastards call it, found in a parking lot in North London, which means he probably went south . . . or east. Or west. Or nowhere. He's a goddamn corpse. If you trap him in a corner and snap your fingers hard under his nose, he'll disintegrate like sawdust, but you've still got to trap him there. He's a devious bastard and don't underrate that.'

'Can we have a look at the car?' Downs persisted. Tracking down the concrete evidence was the only approach that seemed to him to offer much hope.

'No, we can't. The police won't give us the time of day since our face-off at the station. So fuck 'em. We'll dig him up ourselves. Crabb and me will go after his old friends that we know. Downs and Myerson, you'll check his old haunts in Camden Town. Di Santis and Macky will go for the wife and her relatives.'

'I'll bring the wooden cross and three long nails,' Loory put in as a try at lightening the atmosphere, but Cutter only glared at him.

'Call in tonight if you're still out. I'll be here by nine. That's it, *move*.'

Downs stood up along with the rest, and with the distinct feeling as well that he was about to waste a lot of his time.

★

It was a huge, austere pub in Archway, squatting under a red neon signboard a few feet from the busiest truck route in London. Inside, in the cheerless room, there were dozens of single Irish labourers from the furnished rooms behind Holloway Road, drinking themselves glassy eyed as they talked out their exiled misery. The bartender pointed Flegg out for him, but Sloane might well have guessed: a stocky man who sat with four others in a corner, and who had a half-Pekingese mongrel perched on his lap like something in a tiresome film about English eccentricity. A drift of white dog hair on the linoleum behind the chair suggested that it was Flegg's accustomed spot. Sloane nearly walked out, but Flegg was the only lead he had.

The dog complained once or twice, clamped under an arm, as Flegg followed a ten-pound note outside to the road junction in front, where trucks downshifted roughly one after another to swing uphill toward the Hornsey bridge archway. They talked in a hoarse shout over the noise. Flegg pinched the bridge of his nose and insisted that he knew no one at all who would interest Sloane. Unnoticed, the dog pissed in irritation, aiming his amber stream across the narrow walk. In the end, for the ten pounds Flegg gave him a name, Eoin Hanlon, and an address in Canning Town, the lower reaches of the East End.

Sloane took the tube to West Ham and then walked the rest of the way through a desolation of gasworks and warehouses. What once had been a dense warren of workers' terraces had been aired out ruthlessly by bulldozers, with whole square blocks razed to swamps of rubble and mud. What remained looked like a few teeth in a shattered denture. Pope's Folly Lane was now as bizarre as its name, a single row of decaying two-storey terraces, half of them blinded by brick and corrugated iron stopping their windows. He could see that the other half of the row, away from him, had been broken into and squatted by a company of

London's homeless. Even when new, a century earlier, they must have been grim dwellings; the walk ran directly against the flat doorways, without an inch for porches or flower beds.

Number 23 had lost its doorlatch. But through the hole Sloane could see a contraption of screws and wire serving as a makeshift bolt. He knocked for some time before a grey eye inspected him through the hole.

'Flegg sent me,' Sloane said.

'Looking for someone in particular, are we?' a cool Irish voice prompted.

'A man named Hanlon, about some work.'

The eye withdrew. He heard a laborious rattling, and finally the door opened on a thin man in his middle thirties with bushy flame-tinged hair. He stood there for a full thirty seconds, surveying Sloane shrewdly before stepping aside. 'Come in, then, mate. She's not so poncy but all she wants is a bit of bunging up, God bless her and all who sink in her.'

Sloane followed him into a hall stacked with sharp-edged new bricks; stolen, he guessed, from a building contractor. The banisters had been ripped off the stairs leading up, and everything in the house was peeling, mildewed or simply missing, like all the internal doors. Hanlon indicated an old bus seat in the front room propped against a coal grate that was stuffed with newspapers, and Sloane sat.

The man perched opposite on two packing crates, hiking up one leg of his dark trousers. He had the sunken cheeks and grey complexion Sloane had seen so often on those navvying bricks up wooden ramps outside construction sites. Reaching under him for a bottle of whisky, Hanlon stripped the cap and studied the few inches left against the light.

'Care for a drop? A jar now and then is known to cure the bitter lack of a jar now and then; that's my view, all considered. What do you say?'

He drank from the bottle and handed it across. Sloane took a swallow, wondering if Flegg had been pulling his leg; Hanlon hardly seemed what he had in mind.

'I'm told you're one of the best second-storey men in London.'

'Go on with you now, who would be telling you a thing like that, pray?'

'A dog that looks a bit like a hamster warmed over.'

'It rings a faint bell.'

The hackles on Sloane's neck rose suddenly. It was a faint whimpering – was it human or animal? – from somewhere in the house. He listened hard but heard only his breath and the sullen quiet of the dying building. Hanlon didn't seem to have noticed the sound.

'American, aren't we?' he observed. 'A lovely gorgeous bloody land that is. It eliminates certain possibilities in regard to the London Constabulary and bloody CID, doesn't it? Mind, on the other hand, I lived in Chicago once. Jaysus, what a glorious country of opportunity. I mean, one wonders if by any chance someone in Chicago would be interested in my return to help the police with their enquiries. Know anything about that, do we?'

'Why don't you call Flegg?'

'Never heard of him,' he said, surveying the whisky bottle. 'It appears I'm going to require another bottle before the night is finished. If you'll stop here a moment or two I'll just nip over to the local offy before they roll up the shutters. Don't go away now.'

He walked out of the room with a hint of a roll in his step, like a sailor or an acrobat. He's going to call, Sloane thought, and after a moment he stood up to inspect the room. Despite the suggestion of furniture and the mess, it didn't look lived in; there were no signs of personality, no books or magazines, no pictures, television, not even an ashtray. The kitchen at the back had been systematically sabotaged by an owner fighting illegal tenants: the water pipes had been ripped out, the gas sealed off and the old stove bashed in with a large hammer. Looping over from the next house, an electric cord entered through a cracked window, and makeshift extensions spidered out from a crude junction box, up through a hole in the ceiling, to a bare hanging bulb, to a hotplate by the sink, and along the floor into the front room. A few dirty plates and cups lay on the draining board, and a cardboard carton on the floor held what food there was: half a loaf of bread, jam, some canned goods, a box of tea and a square of cheese in plastic. A bucket of water stood in the corner. He grew less and less hopeful about Hanlon's possibilities. If the man were as good as Flegg had suggested, he'd have bought himself a house in

Hampstead ten times over.

Then he remembered the whimpering. He had seen all of the downstairs, and he went curiously, cautiously, to the hall and then up the broken staircase. At the head of the stairs there was an open doorway. An expensive-looking carpet rose into view, and then a chest and the corner of an elegant bed, everything here in much better condition than the rest of the house. A toilet and bathroom stood open, largely demolished. Sloane's eyes were drawn to the one other room on the landing. It still had its door, sealed by a bronze padlock the size of a fist.

Sloane was bending over to peer through the keyhole when he heard a noise behind him, a long, luxurious sigh with a tiny throat-rattle at the end. With cold foreboding he made his way slowly toward an open doorway. The chest floated into sight, supporting an antique brass lamp and two empty Guinness bottles. An electric heater glowed on the rug, aimed at the bed, and in its beam a small bare foot poked up from the end of the bed, then a motionless leg, long and slim and feminine. She lay splayed out on her back, staring blankly at the ceiling, and for an instant he thought she was dead, stripped and tidied for the embalmer, but then she moved, wriggling her shoulders and making the whimpering sound he remembered.

Hastily he took the emaciated wrist and felt for the pulse. At first a narrow, selfish thought rose in him: he was being set up to be found with a dying woman. An elaborate plot of Cutter's . . . Then he felt the throbbing, slow and even, quite strong. She was alive and she was disturbingly beautiful, so grave and vulnerable in her coma that her body admonished anyone who was upright and alert. A tangle of blonde hair like a white Brillo pad unravelled from her pinkish scalp, and her breasts flattened back of their own weight like melted candle wax. He waggled his fingers over her face, but she continued to stare upward with milky eyes. He was frightened for her. The heater began to singe the back of his trousers and he leaned closer.

'Are you all right? Can you hear me?'

She stirred ponderously. Between his fingernails, he caught a tiny flap of skin from her wrist and squeezed. Immediately he felt the resistance as life came into her arm and she tried to tug away. Her eyes rolled toward him, half focusing.

'Are you all right?' he repeated, pinching again.

'Bloody hell.' She yanked her arm away. Consciousness seemed to drift up into her eyes from somewhere deep inside. She smiled lazily at him. 'You can take me home if you like. If you give me a nice present.'

'You are home. What's the matter?'

'Scrub, scrub, use Persil soap powder.'

'Are you sick?'

'I feel fab, darling.' She closed her eyes and hummed for a moment, holding the tune then losing it with a puzzled wrinkle forming across her forehead. Sloane plucked up a corner of the bedspread and pulled it across her. He had finally noticed the needle tracks on her leg.

There on the bed table was the syringe, a length of amber surgical hose and a little glass ampule, empty. He felt sick to his stomach: the idea of something alien inside his body controlling him had always filled him with loathing. What were you supposed to do for an overdose? Walk them, as they did in the movies? Liquids? From somewhere the idea came to him: give them liquids. It was better than inaction.

Drifting away again, she gave a sing-song lilt that might have meant anything. He had no idea whether liquids were the right thing, but he hurried downstairs, obsessed by the idea of doing something for her. It suddenly seemed terribly important to save her.

He grabbed the bucket of water and a stained cup from the draining board. The bucket sloshed on the stairs, but very little spilled.

'Drink this,' he ordered harshly. Her stillness terrified him, even now that he knew she was alive. 'Concentrate. Wake up. Dammit, *wake up*.'

He sat on the bed beside her, sinking startlingly into the soft mattress, and patted water onto her forehead.

'Geroff,' she complained wearily. A car started noisily outside and then rasped down the road without a muffler, setting something in the house rattling. The sound covered a few words that she spoke.

'What was that? Come on, drink this.' Sloane forced a little water into her mouth, and she turned her head and let it dribble out. He was shamed by his inability to do anything for her, and he was hit suddenly by the idea that this woman, Sarah, even his mother thirty years earlier were all the same woman, all lying helpless on a bed in front of him, suffering. Over and over he dithered and made pointless consoling gestures while someone drifted away from him. Why did some people always know the right thing to do?

'Keep your eyes open,' he begged, and he could feel the note of panic in his voice. 'Water is good for you. I promise.' She was too young and frail; some things were beyond the ordinary run of injustice. *If you give me a nice present.* He tried not to imagine what her life was like. 'Look at me. Open your eyes.'

Then he started: a hand rested heavily on his shoulder. He turned to see Hanlon's angry eyes on his.

'We've got to get her to a doctor,' Sloane demanded.

'Samantha? Don't mind her, mate. Just another junkie.' He tried to sound callous, but there was something deeply pained in his voice. He pushed past Sloane and took her chin in his hand. With his thin, nicotine-stained fingers he pried open her eyelids to peer into her eyes. For a moment, his whole body had the tension of a surgeon.

'Hannee,' she moaned from far away.

'Shut up, Sam,' he said softly. He closed her eyelids, and when he spoke again, much of the hardness had gone out of him. 'Right as rain in a couple of hours. Right as rain. Oh, Jaysus. Have to pinch her clothes over the peak to keep her from wandering.' He shook his head sadly. 'Thanks for troubling though.'

'Your wife?'

'When she was a whole woman. A bloody misery to me, to tell the truth. One gorgeous day I'll catch up with the bloke who did it to her, and Mary and Joseph my witness, he'll cop it soon after.'

The intensity of his voice left Sloane in no doubt that he meant it. Hanlon walked to the window and stared out at the ochre smoke from an illegal coal fire rising into the rain clouds.

'It doesn't do to leave anything so fine unprotected in this world. Nor even when you're had up on a little holiday and can't help it. You can bloody quote me on that.'

The melancholy anxiety hadn't left Sloane. 'Sometimes . . . sometimes you want to blow the whole world away,' he heard himself murmur. He realized that for the first time in two days he had thought about something other than his own problems.

'What was that prevented God doing it – three just men?' Hanlon said. 'He'd have a flaming great search these days, isn't it a fact?'

He leaned back on the windowsill and folded his arms. His eyes turned cool, and he gave an iron bar of a smile to re-establish his strength. 'You say you've got a spot of work. You're not completely over the hump, mind, but certain sources advise that you're not a copper. Is that a fact, now?'

'How do I know you're any good?' Sloane said.

Hanlon's smile broadened, but without warmth. 'We're put off a mite by the sodding accommodation, aren't we now? Love, it sometimes doesn't do to have a landlady eyeing what the van drops off at night. Many factors argue against. And there's the social advantages to a squat, like the coppers not having your house number down in their little book, for one. Come with me.'

'You're sure she'll be all right?' Sloane asked, taking a last glance at the tiny fingers working at the edge of the bedspread.

'Sure and give it a rest, man,' Hanlon said irritably. 'I take care of my own. Mind your step out here. Town Council buggered the landing to keep out filthy squatters, don't you know. Seem to think the poor folk should all go off and rent bloody great luxury flats in Mayfair.'

He opened the padlock and did something with a loop of wire protruding from the doorframe, then led Sloane inside. Stacked two high along one wall were console television sets, no two alike, and the rest of the room was a storehouse of typewriters, stereo equipment, cameras and unopened crates. Hanlon raised the lid of a tea chest to show off the gleam of silver plates and candelabras.

'My credentials, now, don't you know. The secret these dark days is slow turnover, cooling it off and flogging it later when the poor buggers get tired of checking back in the records. Like a Nikon F – not the newest model, mind, but in excellent nick? Fifty quid to you.'

Hanlon pointed to the camera and Sloane shook his head.

'What I'm after is a lot simpler and more portable.'

Hanlon took up his favourite stool-posture on a television

console. 'The time has come to talk of cabbages and the like. What wants pinching, and where?'

'Papers. Only papers. From a filing cabinet. I need a quiet in and out. Photographing them would be best.'

Hanlon frowned and scratched his ear. 'Sound like an insurance vetting. Worked for one of the big firms once myself on contract. You a private copper?'

'Something like that. The problem's going to be a combination code lock on the door, one of the new electronic ones with the pushbuttons.'

'Don't I know. Mostly they keep in the big government research digs, but even some of the picture galleries over in Mayfair have got them now. Made by Imperial Security up in Leeds.'

'This one won't be. Is there a way through them?'

Hanlon foraged in his shirt pocket without looking down. 'Mate, there's damn precious few trade secrets in the profession. Not one chappie in the history of deadly sins ever sandpapered his fingers to open a strongbox. The way in is buying the combination from a bent housemother or drilling and blasting. Full stop. No magic fingers and nor the cute little stethoscopes to listen for the pins dropping. I'll tell you that for nothing. The way into your code-box is the same: learn the code, or cut the power to the alarms and kick in the door.' His tone changed abruptly. 'Tell us now, love, why you're so certain this beauty isn't from Imperial.'

Sloane hesitated.

'You could grass on me on the evidence of your eyes, man, and turn me over for twenty years. I figure you've got all the edge you'll want.'

'The second floor of the Soviet Trade Mission in Holborn,' Sloane confessed finally.

Hanlon cocked his head like a labrador puzzling over an unfamiliar command, and then he laughed. 'Sorry, mate, I mean, I thought you spooks had your own bloody legmen.'

'I'm private.'

'Sure you are, aren't you. Flying back home on the Concorde, there you sit, never heard my name, and I'm bunged up for the rest of my natural in Brixton with the cockroaches. It doesn't matter if you're risen like Lazarus, man, I wouldn't do a dip establishment if you threw in the Queen's bloody diamond hat.'

'It could be worth a lot of money.'

'Invest it. A power of good your money would do me after fouling the nest. Weren't you around when the Provos were blowing up half London? You pull a political and you've got the regular coppers, Special Branch, the CID, the Special Patrol Group and even those bastard SAS commandos coming for you. I don't know how many times I was had up and questioned back then just on account of the accident of me birth and me quaint Gaelic name. The Provie boyos had the network to scarper off, but me, I plan a long quiet life right here.'

It sounded about as definite as it could be, and Sloane nodded solemnly, resigned to the disappointment. Deep inside, he had only half expected to find help.

Hanlon now spoke in slow, exaggerated Irish, deliberately emphasizing the gulf between them: 'You won't find any laddies at all, not in all London town, willing to bung through the Bolshies, that's my considered view. You'd best bring over your own boys.'

'I told you I'm private,' Sloane snapped. 'For what it's worth . . . ' Use it, he thought. Think of Sarah; use anything, crawl, plead. 'For what it's worth, I'm being blackmailed. They threaten to do something like *that* to my wife.' *That* was his thumb aimed carelessly at the bedroom and the drug-shattered girl. 'I don't expect you to believe me.'

Hanlon's eyes searched Sloane's face for something he didn't seem to find. He became more deliberate. 'Yes, well, normally that story and two bob would buy you a cup of tea most shops . . . but hold on, don't bugger off mad. You did come to me the approved route.' Hanlon sucked at his teeth with concern, considering, and guardedly he said, 'Come down and share a jar with me. Just two gents of the twilight world, waiting for the sun to go.'

Hanlon slid a loop of wire out from the doorframe as he locked up, then he looked in on the slight figure of his wife. She seemed to be asleep, snoring softly and evenly, and he nudged the heater closer to the bed with his toe and tugged another cover over her shoulders. For a moment he contemplated the woman, then he glanced at Sloane as if comparing something in the two of them. Slipping his arm through Sloane's in a surprising gesture of affection, Hanlon led him downstairs and pressed another drink on him.

'Gorgeous pair of men, aren't we? Don't want to get too sentimental now, do we? World will roll right over us and never bloody well look back. I'll tell you one more thing for free. A little fable it is, and, mind, I'm breaking all the rules and taking you for a deserving gent.'

Suddenly something dropped to the floor overhead, the weight of a book or a shoe. They both glanced up at the damp-consumed ceiling, but there was no further sound.

'Okay, then. Here's the fable. A mate of mine has a mate who has a mate and so on, you know what I mean, works up at Imperial Security. Now he tells me there's a flaming great hush-hush flap up there and has been for some time. It seems someone developed a thing called an inductance circuit reader that can have a peep at any electronic whatsis and suss out what's inside. Stereo, telly, radar – even locks, don't you know. I mean, this gent says Imperial's catching rockets left and right from the military for talking them into going over to electronic locks in the first place – the general rule being someone can always build a cleverer bit of electronics – and very quietly they're going back to mechanical locks, "passive devices", he calls 'em. They're all in a lather in case someone like yourself gets himself one of those circuit readers and takes a saunter through Porton some night to pinch himself a bottle of nerve gas.'

Hanlon sat back on the crate in the sitting room, linking his hands over one knee. 'That's the fable. Now, I expect he was prattling a lot of old rope, myself. Still, if you *do* have friends in the right place, your boyos ought to be able to tell you all about it. Can't be so far behind the Brits, right, love? You're not going to let them have the Concorde, the hovercraft *and* the circuit reader to boot. I mean, no justice in that, none at all. You can ask, right?'

'I can ask,' Sloane murmured dubiously. If such a thing existed, it didn't seem likely that Cutter would be able to get his hands on it. 'I can't pay you anything right now for the information – '

Hanlon waved away the suggestion. 'Jaysus, we're not all mercenary bastards now. I tell you, it may all be prattle. Anyway, I gave you the little fable for her sake, know what I mean? But if you should be wanting a television or a stereo . . . pistol, perhaps. Good Smith and Wesson revolver. Revolver won't jam on you.'

'I'm fine,' Sloane said, feeling the angular lump of the Walther like a secret companion against his hip.

'Or, still, if you had a mind to sell the one in your coat . . .'

A needle of ice pressed against his spine. 'It's that obvious?'

'Not to a nanny taking the air in St James's Park. The wee lad in the pram might miss it too, but there's an eye or two around the town, don't you know.'

Sloane nodded ruefully and thanked him. 'Take care of her and good luck.'

'I do, friend. Good luck to you.'

He walked away from the stale air of the house as twilight gathered, carrying no more than a glimmer of what he'd hoped for. He had little faith in electronic gadgetry.

Miraculously it wasn't raining, but a chill cut down through the Lea Marshes and made him hug his coat around him. There would be no sidestepping the job, no handing it over to an outsider – he had learned that much. If it had to be done, he and Jannings were stuck with it. Uneasiness rode in the pit of his stomach like an undigested meal.

He stopped at a chemist's and bought a long roll of adhesive tape. In the morning he would strap the pistol into his armpit. Not elegant, not handy, but out of sight to an eye or two.

7

A pigeon that had somehow lost one of its legs hopped across the pavement, desperate to keep up with its comrades' surge toward the crust of bread. Its balance was remarkably good, but the bird simply wasn't quick enough and it lost out, stopping with a little practised dip and nod to stay upright. Sloane waited until the other birds were eating, then interposed himself gently and dropped a tiny circle of salt beef to the one-legged pigeon. For two days he had lived on takeaway kebabs and takeaway Chinese, and now he was eating a remarkable indulgence, a corned beef on rye – salt beef in the idiom – from Bloom's in Whitechapel. The bird pecked up the meat greedily, gathered itself downward like a spring and then hurled its plump grey body into the air with a flurry of feathers. It soared and wheeled toward a ledge; on the wing it was as agile as any of the others. He couldn't help watching the doomed bird; it was remarkable how pure determination could almost make up for a lost leg. A little object lesson from a prankster god, Sloane thought wrily as he walked on.

A trick of mood, he thought. A dead calm had come over him as he woke, like floating on a flat grey sea that stretched to the horizon. Mood, or perhaps the numbness of nerve endings that had fired off all the anxiety they contained. Back before The Fall there had been a few anomalous mornings like this. He had opened his eyes, oddly serene under the fuzz and nicotine taste of walking, and then he had thought: it's over, I've conquered fear. But each time, walking up a gravel path on the Heath to savour the sensation, smiling pleasantly at children playing on Richmond Road, or just enjoying the morning newspaper, he had felt ugly worries creeping back. And each time he had fought them off, denied them to himself, clinging to the peace and insisting that he was still calm and confident even as his hands began to tremble.

It was much worse when it came back like that: even the memory of peace then was a bitter delusion. Dread had no sense of time, and if he felt it at that moment, he must have felt it always and always would.

He discarded the thin paper from the sandwich and walked up Middlesex Street, which was called Petticoat Lane on Sunday mornings, against the main flow of the crowd. Half the city seemed to have wedged itself into the constricting canyon to finger racks of blouses, trousers, Indian dresses with a hum of voices. One fawn-like girl caught his eye, hovering between two racks to admire a red pullover she held against her chest. She looked as innocent as the girl in Hanlon's bed, and he wondered what doom she secretly carried around with her. He heard American voices, quacking smugly at a tree of leather coats, and he saw the party of tourists turning up the price tags and raising their eyebrows to one another. A solid East End voice called out a warning, and a rolling rack of T-shirts came through the crowd like a motorboat with a human bow wave.

'Jenny's run ahead, dear. Would you catch her up . . .'

'Maybe at twelve quid, Sandra, not in heaven fifteen . . .'

A tiny old woman in black trod on the heels ahead of her and swore impatiently. At the curb, a woman on crutches sold canned soft drinks from a washtub, and the abandoned cans were everywhere, on window ledges, piled in doorways, flattened under foot.

He was two-thirds of the way to the top of the lane and he hadn't sighted Jannings. He had called that morning from a public phone box, using his most nondescript voice, and Karn had answered. He had recognized her voice immediately with the twangy East Saxon pressures under her English, but she didn't know his. She had told the Mr Jones, an old acquaintance of Jannings's, that her husband would be down in Petticoat Lane for the morning, hunting for a special kind of child's coat. Perhaps Mr Jones would come for tea later? Yes, perhaps.

An old man eying the breasts of the young girls who passed caught Sloane watching him and scowled over a ring of pastel scarves. Sloane walked on. He should really have waited in one spot and let the crowd drift past him, but he couldn't risk Jannings coming in at the top, stumbling onto something remotely like what he wanted right off, and hurrying away. Jannings could be like that – a plodding rigour in the large things, but impulsive haste at detail. He was anticipating again, he thought sombrely, worrying life like a nursemaid with a perennially sniffling child. Already the false sense of well-being was drawing away.

A man who smelled of public-lavatory soap brushed past in the crush, and Sloane kept his arm tight over the pistol. In his head he thanked Hanlon again for the tip. Brushing through this crowd, fifty people might have noticed something in his coat pocket, and one or two might actually have tried to dip out the prize. A Walther might bring £200 in London. Abruptly a weary rant caught his ear:

'None of the uncorrupted blood of England flowing in their sooty veins, none of the loyalty and decency known to every English boy from birth . . . !'

It came from among a circle of Union Jacks on spiked poles, a crop-headed flushed face above the crowd chewing the words like a mouthful of gristle. Above that straining face in a clenched hand was a newspaper with the banner headline: WOGS OUT NOW! Edgy embarrassment was palpable in the shoppers who approached, as was the slackening of relief when they passed beyond the small circle of malice.

The nearest of the guard looked seventeen or eighteen, with hump-toed boots, tight pants and a baggy white shirt. His eyes darted left and right belligerently. Sloane saw that the other flagbearers were just as young, haggard and sulky-looking, like children kept after school. Only the speaker was past twisted innocence: paunchy and middle aged in an unbuttoned black coat, like an aging grocer dressed for church.

'Pakis and Niggers – Pakis and Niggers taking our homes and jobs and fouling our streets with their smells . . . !'

The folding table of yellow pamphlets appeared not to have been touched for years, and as he watched Sloane found with surprise that he couldn't hate them convincingly, not even the leader. They were despicable enough, and they were certainly a danger to a lone Pakistani caught out at night, but they weren't the danger the Brownshirts had been in another era, with a society collapsing and the clever money slipping in the back door to shoot them forward. They were as irrelevant as spats. History wasn't so crude that it mimicked itself like a failing clown.

Was that the real reason he couldn't hate them? Sloane asked himself. Or was it some lack in himself, a growing inwardness that was denying him empathy with the victims – and Johnny FitzGibbon of Richmond Road would certainly be one? He tried on hatred again, watching the speaker's bulging eyes, but nothing came. Mostly he felt a fatiguing pity for anyone so twisted that he would throw away his own possibilities for peace in such a storm of hostility. Is that enough to feel? He wondered if he were reaching the point where he would sell out the rest of the world, sell his closest friend, for some desert island away from fear and pain. You did it to Jannings, he reproached himself. And again soon.

'Load them on the ships with the Irish scum and the poofs and Trots . . .'

Then Sloane saw the still figure who faced the neo-Nazis across the narrow road: square and squat in a banker's three-piece suit, with something sly and powerful in his features. The man's eyes followed the speaker with a personal rage so intense that for a moment Sloane was afraid he would launch himself through the shoppers to grab the stormtrooper by the throat. The man's concentration was broken at last by a craggy old stallkeeper ferrying an armload of skirts down the lane from a van at the curb. The stallkeeper noticed the direction of Jannings's glare and came to a stop beside him momentarily, glancing across at the speaker himself. Sloane could just hear his hoarse, brisk voice: 'We done 'em before, squire. They bloody ran at Alamein and they'll run again.' He nodded and moved on, though Jannings hadn't said a word. Jannings turned away abruptly and walked into the crowd.

On some impulse, Sloane faded back into an open doorway and let him pass, tugging at the impeccable faintly striped coat. He followed a few steps behind, delaying; he realized now that he had no idea of what to say. He had been no more than the cut-out, the unimportant middleman between Jannings and Cutter; he hadn't arranged the blackmail and he hadn't drafted the instructions – but it had been a betrayal nonetheless.

If you are my friend, tell me tales of faraway places where the roses grow all year round. I cannot, everything has changed forever.

Jannings stopped at a pipe rack of children's clothing. The apprehension building intolerably inside him, Sloane finally stepped to the opposite side of the rack, brushing against T-shirts no larger than handkerchiefs that evoked a vulnerability so powerful it tore at old wounds. Get it over, start it now. Jannings's blue eyes found him, and the stocky man stood immobile, a bear caught in the hunter's sights.

'I don't like it any more than you,' Sloane began.

Jannings's eyes closed and his chin drooped, his body deflating slightly. '*Scheisse.* They said I was through. They gave me the negatives.'

'Don't be naive. Anyone can duplicate negatives.'

'Go away.' Jannings turned and walked blindly into the crowd, and Sloane saw that the reflex was identical to his own hopeless impulse to run from Cutter – but this time he, Sloane, was the bearer of despair. And he would have to follow, implacably. Jannings came to a stop in front of a display of postcards, Beefeaters at the Tower, a St Paul's white as ice, cards halved and quartered with tiny sunny scenes given the lie by the solid cloud overhead. He touched Jannings's arm and felt the smooth worn wool.

'We were both had, Werner. They were told to shut down actives, that's all. You can see what they did: they let you think you were buying your way out, but they were just raking in a little last-minute product.'

Jannings glanced around with an air of disdain. 'So?'

'Let's go talk.'

★

Vlad Stepanovich Blok leaned back in the uncomfortable typist's chair, his feet up on the switchboard as he read a copy of *The Lay of the Host of Igor*, though one translated into modern Russian. He found it excruciatingly boring, and only by bringing no other books with him on Sunday duty could he force himself to read it. And for all the effort, he knew that the recourse to a translation rather than the Old Slavonic original might well be taken as further indicating that 'lack of a thorough mental discipline' which the Writer's Union had cited in rejecting his satiric novella. Still, he told himself that reading the dry old work at all showed some worthy dedication. How to convince them? A writer, he yet remained a minor trade clerk given Sunday phone duty. He would much rather have been out prowling one of those areas of London that gave him such delight when he recognized a brick workshop or an entire street lifted bodily out of one of the English novels he had read in university; mostly brooding Victorian stories about amazingly good and amazingly bad people who collided head on. He sometimes wondered if the Englishmen out there were like that still.

Anna was sure the rejection had something to do with his last name, but Blok doubted it. It was true that his paternal grandfather had been a practising Jew, but whose hadn't been? Everyone knew Judaism meant no more to him than the secret ikon-worship of Anna's parents. He would redraft *The New Bust of the Mayor* and submit it again. He refused to go the clandestine *samizdat* route. That was only playing at writing. He wanted real readers, lots of them. It would be official publication or nothing.

The phone buzzed at his elbow. Without moving his legs, he reached over and lifted it off its cradle. 'Soviet Trade Mission.'

'Could I speak to someone in your payroll department?'

The voice did not quite sound British to Blok, but he knew he was no expert. In response, he tried to sound as British as he could. 'This is Sunday. Certainly you understand that we do not work on Sunday.' For an instant he wondered if he should have used the plural, *on Sundays* – English could be so damnably ambiguous on small matters, with nothing like the certain precision of good Russian. 'You can speak to me,' Blok added warily.

'Very well. This is Mr Smith of Inland Revenue. We're backed up and working weekends for a time. I meant to ring you Friday afternoon. We're preparing a retrospective tax audit on a gentleman who appears to have done some contract work as a translator for your mission a few years ago.'

'The trade mission is exempt from PAYE withholding.'

'Of course it is, but the gentleman in question is not. We only wish to know his total earnings and the dates of his contracts, as we're entitled by the consular treaty of 1931. The name is Jeffrey

Sloane and we list his address as 16 Richmond Road, Upper Dalston.'

Blok did not bother taking notes because he knew it would all be on the tape. 'We will ring you Monday morning. You're in the London office, yes? Your name again?'

'Smith. Mr John Smith.' The man rang off.

John Smith, Blok thought, and the name sounded to him suspiciously like Ivan Ivanov, the befuddled ordinary citizen of all those jokes in *Krokodil*. Did they really work on Sunday – Sundays? Their day of worship? Blok had strict instructions to inform the assistant head of mission, not the head or anyone else, if something the least suspicious happened while he was on duty. He hesitated, because it was always easiest to do nothing, to avoid upsetting the even flow of routine. They would check the tapes Monday morning automatically; wouldn't that be soon enough, no matter what it was? No, he thought, best to take no chances. He slid open the mahogany panel and ran the tape back, then reached for the slim black directory to look up the number.

★

The fashionable three-storey house on Isis Grove in Hampstead was only a two-minute walk from the Parliament Hill end of the Heath, as fine a location as the embassy's agents could find in North London. It had been built from a durable brick that had retained its cherry red for more than a century, and the bright turrets and stepped gables of number 23 seemed trowelled into place only yesterday. In some moods Alexei Alexeivich Komarovsky found the finicky mock-gothic Victoriana just too oppressively sentimental for words, but not on Sunday mornings; not squatting in the front garden to tend the small bed of cyclamen sent through the diplomatic pouch that reminded him of home in the late Ural spring. On Sunday mornings, the house smiled happily above him, even under a dark sky; its smugness become the robust confidence of a younger world, and its suggestion of lazy conspicuous wealth only warm-hearted whimsy.

He was happy. In the afternoon he would take Irina to his own discovery – the blue tile high over Holford Square with Lenin's stern profile. He smiled at his own childish delight when first seeing the house and imagining the wiry intense man slamming the door to hurry toward an exiles' meeting somewhere. Astounding, Komarovsky thought, that he would have missed running into Marx on the street by only thirty years and a few miles. He wondered if Lenin, too, had made his pilgrimage to desk G-7 at the British Museum reading room, but it wasn't like the practical Lenin who had never written a word or taken a step that wasn't directed toward some present end. It was an odd country, he thought, to have harboured so many revolutionaries, yet to ignore them so thoroughly.

'Alexei Alexeivitch,' Irina called from the door. 'Breakfast is nearly with us.' She was proud of her English and tried to use it as much as possible.

He stabbed the trowel into the earth, and as he stood he prodded the bottle-thick spectacles up his nose. He could see only outlines of light and shadow without them.

Inside he saw immediately that Irina and the maid had overdressed the breakfast room again for her late Sunday morning meal, the samovar moved in from the sitting room and real silver on the long table.

'I did not know you had invited the tsar,' Komarovsky teased formally.

'Alexei Alexeivitch, don't be a goose. It is only for your Sunday.' He watched her tenderly, her face as brown and wrinkled as a walnut. Or as his own. Their faces meant a great deal to him. If there were still tsars, he thought quite often, these would be the faces of serfs. We would be property to be owned and traded along with the land, and one day a landlord would come to take his pleasure from my daughter, and I would have to stand aside in shame – or kill him and bring retribution on the whole village. At best, after the false emancipation, we would be debt slaves, subject to cleverer forms of the same bondage.

Already a young soldier in 1941, he had joined the Party the day after the Germans marched across the border. June 23 1941. The Motherland Levy, as their mass intake was called. A group of them had taken vows that day with fierce resolution. They had all sworn to sweep away the world of greed and corruption encroaching from the west, but only he and Sevin had gone on to continue the fight after the war. And now, unable to keep from picturing the burned and looted villages they had liberated (though not his own; he had refused to enter it and had stood on Goat Hill with his back turned), the mass graves of executed Russian prisoners; unable to forget the bitter, necessary shooting of the collaborators at Ozarichi; luxury like silver and lace always made him uncomfortable. He had never quite seen the difference between a Mercedes limousine owned by a parasitic banker and a Zim limousine 'in the service of the whole people'.

'Sunday is the day for religion,' he rumbled. 'A high official with a secretly religious wife is very dangerous; I shall have to report this to the KGB.'

She knew very well who her husband worked for and she smiled. 'I will tell them everything. That my husband is a man who searches out old monuments. A sentimentalist with a dangerous fixation on the past.'

'You mustn't,' he said with a peasant's wry cynicism that she knew did not go very deep. 'They would likely promote me.'

Almost on cue as he sat, the telephone rang. Komarovsky glanced over his shoulder and saw dimly through the glare on his spectacles that it wasn't the ordinary London telephone, but the yellow one that connected directly with the mission. It winked a tiny light at him. His chair scraped on the parquetry.

'Komarovsky,' he announced.

His wife watched his face go puzzled, then frowning and secretive, his back stiffening.

'Play it.'

The silence carried on for so long that she thought he was lost in thought, and she said, 'Alexei Alexeivitch, could you – ?'

He waved brusquely for her to be quiet and she looked down at the linen cloth, hurt. She realized now that it was an important call and she went to the kitchen dutifully to make sure the maid didn't come in.

'Extraordinary,' Komarovsky said. 'Of course there is no such person at Inland Revenue. I will be in the office by noon.'

There went the afternoon with Irina, he thought irritably, and ahead of him he could see a tedious day of going over the files on this Sloane he hadn't seen in over a year and the dismal query-and-response cables that would pass back and forth to

Dzerzhinsky Street marked 'decode yourself'. All that methodical ciphering work that he loathed.

He found Irina in the hallway and laid his plump hands on her shoulders. 'Forgive me, Irina Kirilovna. I did not mean to be rude. My dove.' He kissed her forehead softly.

★

'The organization is still the same?' Jannings said.

'I imagine.'

'Cutter upstairs. The Acolytes below, and poor Downs running up and down like a chihuahua.'

Jannings's voice was acid with resentment as he sat heavily on the bench. There might once have been a church on the corner of the weedy lot; the next building along ended abruptly in a large X-brace to hold up the wall. Fissures wandered the concrete between the old benches, and half the rubbish of Whitechapel lay abandoned in windswept drifts across the derelict churchyard. Some distance away, in a Brechtian burlesque on the middle classes at their leisure in St James's Park, a dozen winos sat in a sociable circle among the weeds, handing around bottles, and an old woman backed away tipsily, dropped her underpants and squatted to piss al fresco. A fitting place to conduct a betrayal, Sloane thought.

'What makes them think – ?' They heard a squeaking, and Jannings broke off as one of the city's homeless pushed a rusting stroller across the yard, his belongings in a black rubbish bag tied to the frame with string.

'How dare they come to me again,' Jannings protested. 'Cutter! The spiritual kin to those Nazis.'

'Don't be absurd,' Sloane said. 'Cutter's just a gangster. Maybe a gangster who missed his calling. I shouldn't think he knows the word ideology.'

But Jannings was lost in his own thoughts, staring blindly away toward where Petticoat Lane emptied onto the bleak high street. A few shoppers drifted out toward the tube station with purchases draped over their arms. 'I am a thirty-year member of the Socialist Unity Party of the Deutsche Demokratische Republik . . . not some whining ballerina who sells herself for the bright lights and Coca-Cola. This is intolerable.'

'You passed trade papers to the west. I am not sure Komarovsky would appreciate the difference,' Sloane said drily.

The massive head rotated deliberately toward Sloane, like an owl's. 'I copied a few innocuous current papers, under duress. I have never taken unauthorized material from the files. Never.'

Sadly Sloane thought: the fictions we maintain with fine distinctions. The child who hadn't stolen the money from his mother because he intended to return it in a few hours. The man who wasn't the direct blackmailer, only the intermediary.

'Cutter is mad. All right, I am German and all Germans are ambivalent to some degree about the Russians, but I am not ambivalent about what they did for us. They sheltered my father and defeated the Great Beast, almost alone. Write a six on a piece of paper and write six noughts after it and you have the number of Russian soldiers who died for all of us. Change the six to a seven and you have the number of dead Russian civilians. They defeated over 300 divisions of the Beast. Do you know what they suffered for that? And the remembrance they get in the west? Just now an old Englishman mentions El Alamein to me.' He gave a characteristically German hiss of contempt, like steam rocking the lid of a pot. 'This tiny country pulls out all its stops to defeat three German divisions in North Africa, and still they can think they won the war. Absurd.'

Sloane stretched his legs, stiff and aching. He let Jannings run on, knowing the man would wind down on his own.

'And *your* country – you had 250,000 dead. Yugoslavia lost more; there is hardly a medium-sized city anywhere in Russia that did not lose more. Oh, *scheisse*.' His hands, about to gesture, fell like two shot birds, and he waited as if for Sloane to supply his next line, but Sloane was still silent. 'You know perfectly well that all non-Russians are confined to the first floor of the mission. I couldn't get near the files.'

'Arguing with me is no good, Werner. If you won't do it, I suggest you tell Karn about your "bit on the side" in Brixton so Cutter can't use his photographs.' *His* photographs, Sloane thought with a taste of self-reproach. Not *mine*, not *ours*. 'I have a feeling he's ready to push all the way.'

Jannings made a rumbling noise in his throat, like distant

thunder, then slumped forward. 'Jeffrey . . . she'd leave, she'd take the children. I can't have that, I couldn't bear it. This is impossible, believe me.'

'Of course it is. I can't tell you what to do.'

'Damn!' Jannings kicked with the side of his foot at a mound of rubbish in front of the bench and managed to strew rotting paper and empty bottles a few feet across the cement. 'Look at this filth! They can spend a fortune to hand-rub motorcars for the rich but they can't waste a penny for public services for the poor. *That* is what I wanted to fight as a boy.'

'*Christ*, Werner . . .' He had known that Jannings would slide away at least once more into politics, like turning his back and stalking away helplessly in Petticoat Lane.

Jannings pushed his toe through the rubbish again, as if he might turn up the man responsible for such waste. 'You know what this is?' he asked sourly. 'No, this is not capitalism. Capitalism is over in the fine offices, in the City. The Bank of England is one tube stop away, you know? This is the *leavings*. All of this, all of these people. I wanted to fight a system that had leavings.' His fierce expression gradually seemed to yield, and shadows formed on the face that had once been handsome. 'We were friends, and you made me into a shabby little file-pincher against my own people.'

'The only thing that ruins the high note of tragedy,' Sloane said evenly, 'is the love nest down in Brixton.'

'Thank you for that,' Jannings said icily. 'I am back to reality.'

'Werner, I don't give a fuck whether we get the gold files or not. If you can think of some way out of this, instead of talking about the forward march of humanity, please tell me.'

Jannings rested his chin on a palm. 'I could work late perhaps, with some excuse, but I still couldn't get through the stairwell door into registry.'

'I might be able to take care of that. If I can get you through the door, are you willing to do it?'

The abandoned churchyard filled with the man's stillness, a furious repressed silence. 'I suppose I no longer care. I suppose that is what I could say.'

'The fate of the world doesn't turn on this rotten little job.'

'I will go in next week and look at the door and decide what to do. I'll meet you here next weekend.'

Sloane shook his head. 'Monday evening, seven o'clock. We can't stall. *I* can't.'

8

Sarah lay on the pine bed in the spare room, trying to wriggle into a comfortable solidity against the restlessness she felt. The modern bed clashed with the fluted plaster moulding above her, the floral wallpaper, the cast-iron sconce light by the door. Except for this room, Felicity had modernized the house to the current fashion, with tongue-and-grove panelling, stainless steel basins, cork kitchen floor and built-in cupboards everywhere. Sarah wondered if it was the teaching that kept her interested enough to bother, the pressure of younger minds tugging at her – and then maybe this was the room she used as a retreat when she wanted to escape callow cheer and be melancholy over the past.

The framed portrait of their parents on the chest could hardly have been any less oppressive to Felicity than it was to her. Even lying down she could see her mother's martyr face, accepting and grave over the high collar, a black ribbon and cameo at her neck – one cameo wearing another. The feeling rose inevitably: a sort of bleached-out guilt. Elizabeth St Jores had been a difficult woman to love, yet any child who did not love its mother unreservedly was an evil child. She had sat primly at the funeral, moved for the most part by what she sensed she ought to feel. Her father had dabbed a discreet tear off his cheek, and Felicity on his other arm had sobbed inconsolably. But in her, honesty and convention had fought a war that would have dismayed any fourteen-year-old. She felt the loss, more or less as she was expected to do, but when she tested it she found the sense of abandonment utterly personal and selfish. Conventional images of her mother: sitting stoically at dinner, brushing their hair in bed with long firm strokes, lying ill in white nylon. Later Felicity had said, 'Illness was the only form of self-expression she was ever taught.' These images would never be repeated, and Sarah had felt the absence from her own future of something like a consoling presence, even though her mother had never been very much of a consoling presence in reality. Her own future. How honest was it for a fourteen-year-old girl to cry over her own loss? Especially when her mother was happier now. Two months – six? – earlier, she had tip-toed into the sitting room to see her mother, obviously believing herself alone, touch an oil painting of her own mother, stern Grandmother Gower. The odd thing she had said so evenly: 'You stayed the course, but I can't find any confirmation of myself anywhere.' Sarah knew the adults in the church would have been deeply shocked by her thoughts, but she had stared fiercely at the polished coffin and offered it godspeed rather than a plea to return. It was a sincere act of charity. That was clear to part of her mind. Unfortunately, enough of the conventional had remained to torment her later – as if the thought had been a wish, an act of murder.

'Excuse me, have I caught you in the middle of an overdose or something?' Felicity drifted into the room smoothly, her head cocked ironically.

Sarah tried to smile for her benefit. 'I always envied your humour. Could it be the name? Mother should have called me Joy.'

'Yes, I can see you at a party. "Hello, I'm Joy." Like something out of Faust: "Hello, I'm Avarice." "*Pleased*, I'm Gluttony."'

'Sarah is such a dreary name, like something in a damp cave.'

'Stop being morbid. You know I have no patience with it.' Felicity sat beside her on the bed and ran a finger through Sarah's long dark hair. 'Will you be eating, or should I just ring the doctor for transfusions?'

'You won't be with your young friend?'

'Meow. How did you know about him?'

'I heard last night.'

She seemed amused. 'How dreadful for you. I'm sorry. I broke two rules over Jean-Pierre. He's my student at the Poly, and he's a Frog. Wretched lovers if the truth were known. *Three* rules, I suppose. Having him home. In *Hove* . . . shocking, really. I'm certain there's a town by-law against it.' Her fingers clutched at Sarah's hair momentarily. 'Sometimes you just have to find a new lover or the whole world will die.'

'You're not seamless after all,' Sarah observed.

'Prick me, do I not bleed? When Arthur left, I was so alone some nights, I . . .' She gazed off into the middle distance.

'You're making fun of me.'

'You silly goose, you always loaded all the virtues on to me and assumed you had the corner on suffering. Don't you realize I always envied you? You were the worldly one, the bright one, the one who saw all the things my silly eyes missed.'

Sarah pushed herself up in startled protest. 'That's simply ridiculous. I envied *you*, you were gay and clever. You were so vital. You couldn't have envied me, except because I was older. That's nothing.'

'It matters. When I was sixteen and unkissed, you were eighteen and strong and silent and wise. I know I slid through adolescence in utter naivety, while you were the cause of many a sigh in young men at our gate.'

Sarah laughed in self-mockery and pressed her forehead against her sister. 'I only threw myself at them because I was so desperate to be liked. You know what they wanted.'

'They didn't get it, did they?'

'There was that much of mother in both of us.'

'Listen, I've always wondered. Can you imagine mother and father having it off? It's impossible.' Felicity chuckled. 'I almost said "inconceivable". I'm certain they never undressed completely and the bedroom was utterly dark. It must have been arranged like a business tax, paid quarterly and very reluctantly but with a high sense of duty.'

'With no interest,' Sarah added, and Felicity laughed.

'Point. It's as far out of the question as their arguing,' Felicity said.

'There you're wrong. They argued all the time.'

'Nonsense, they hardly spoke.'

'Don't you remember that Ophelia voice mother used at table? And father gravely addressing the coal grate? With the proper knife we could have carved the venom in that room.'

'I'd have preferred screaming.'

Sarah agreed. She saw that they were talking as they hadn't talked in years. They had entered that delicate region and both of them tested it gingerly. She longed to take another step and ask: Felicity, how did you forgive them? How did you care for them? But saying it aloud carried such an aura of danger that she let the moment pass.

Perhaps Felicity sensed the danger too, because she turned to the present and began probing for Sarah's sorrow. 'You don't want to talk about it?'

'It's just my life running down,' Sarah said evasively. 'There's no energy left in it. Jeffrey has such a need for order. I didn't know at all why until very recently, but I felt it and I couldn't offer it and . . . Christ forgive me – sometimes I resented him for it. I think if he could have glued my mouth into a smile, it would have been enough for him. He would have been satisfied. He so desperately needed to make me happy that it was like another burden. My God, it's bad enough being sad without being made to feel guilty about it. I *do* love him, but it hasn't changed anything in me.'

It was past four and dark crept into the room like a gas, pooling in the corners, under the chest, along Felicity's hip where the foam mattress sagged.

'That's not why you're here, is it?' Felicity enquired softly.

'No.' Sarah rolled onto her side, her legs cramping. 'I'm so restless. I'm talking about myself to keep away from it. Last week . . . something happened. I can't tell you about it, but his past caught up with him, and I think he's in real danger. It's odd. It's changed him. Did you see it?'

Felicity nodded. 'He was frightened to death.'

'More than that. It's brought someone different to the surface, someone he had pushed deep down inside. Actually, I think I like this new person. He's afraid, he's lost his defences, but he won't back up a step. I'm quite sure he stole that car. Can you imagine Jeffrey stealing a car?'

Felicity glanced at the lace curtains over the window, and Sarah saw that her face had clouded. 'I don't want to alarm you, but perhaps you'd best see this.'

Felicity went to the window, standing to the side so she couldn't be seen from outside. Sarah followed and allowed herself to be held back from the curtain by Felicity's arm. There was no question what she was meant to see: a dark brown

American sedan was parked at the end of the road. The cloud bank above the chimney pots obscured the street and left the interior of the car murky, but in silhouette she could make out two figures slumped down in front, waiting.

'They've been there since noon,' Felicity said. 'Is it Jeffrey they're after?'

Sarah felt her breath quicken, and she dug her fingertips into her fleshless thighs, pressing until it hurt. 'They can use me to get to him. Will you lend me your car?'

'It's just there.' Felicity inclined her head toward the street, and Sarah saw the red Triumph three cars ahead of the sedan.

'You go out alone and drive it off,' Sarah said. 'If they stop there, I'll go over the garden wall and meet you on the next road.'

'My, this is getting exciting.' Felicity pressed against her, a scent of some indefinable flower in her hair, and then a flash of lightning lit the street like a flare. The figures stirred in the car as the rumble echoed between the buildings.

'I'll do anything you want, Sar. You know that.'

★

Gusts of chilly rain fled before the wind, and gray cloud flowed ponderously above the canyon of the road like a mirror-image of the Thames three miles away. A blue placard was fixed to the brick wall: *GEOFFREY DOUNT JUNIOR SCHOOL, R. G. Nuss, BA(Hons.) Headmaster.* Roofed gates at either end of the wall led into the schoolground and a century of weather had almost effaced the letters carved into the brick above them: *BOYS* here and *GIRLS* along the road. In between was an old poster for a circus at Highbury Fields, plus the usual graffiti: *Arsenal Rule*, *Up Provos* and *NF*, to which another hand had added: *ARE CUNTS*. A large trash can stepped him onto the wall over the poster, and he hung by his hands for a moment on the far side, flinching for the drop. His weak ankles survived the momentary dismaying skid on the rain-slick asphalt. Stealthily he moved along the shadow of the outer wall, climbed a wire backnet behind the soccer goal and then launched himself onto the back wall, tearing the skin of his wrist.

From there it was easy; down cautiously to the roof of the

garden shed so that it didn't cave in under him, then into his own back yard, a tangle of weeds and untended flower beds. Sloane let himself in by the back door with a key from the empty flowerpot on the step and before going up, checked the mail lying on the bench by the front door. The names were vaguely familiar to him, like the names under an old class photograph; some were old tenants and some were people who seemed to use Mrs Cromer's flat as a mail drop: P. D. Wall-Henshaw, Esq., Mrs R. Gajraj, and one On Her Majesty's Service buff envelope for H. Gold. A typed notice was taped to the wall above the bench:

> All tenants will please to observe, owing to rise in rates, that as of the 1st prox., rent will regretfully become £32.50 upper and £35.50 lower/week. (Mrs) F. R. Vanbrugh.

Absurdly, he worried for a moment about paying the increase. He went up quietly and listened at his door for more than a minute. There was no noise in the room, and when he set his ear directly against the wood there was only the rumble and drone of London carried up through the walls. No noise at all, not even the burring mantel clock that he thought he should hear. The room beyond seemed ominously empty, and opening the door, he saw with a chill what it was that he had not heard. He stood with his back heavily against the door. He was frightened: suddenly he couldn't keep his mind away from it any more. The flat looked like the result of some terrible experiment with wild animals. The sofa had been skinned and stripped and the wood frame pointlessly torn apart so that parts lay splayed and limp like a carcass after the meat had been taken. His papers were spread in disorder, the small desk was broken up, and the floor lamp lay on its side bent into a shallow U. He moved dumbly through the rubble of his life, squatting to touch the shattered clock, staring with a special chill at Sarah's knitting basket, the wool yanked into a tangle and slashed. Flaps of wallpaper hung where they had been ripped from the plaster. For a year, this had been guarded space, his sanctuary against disorder, and now it had been invaded with someone's sinister intuition for the greatest shock. It was too brutal, too malicious and pointless to be a search. *Someone.* It could only have been Cutter – repayment with his own giddy, usurious interest. And a warning.

The bedroom was no better, except for one jarring detail: in the midst of the debris a small clawfoot table stood upright, exactly centred between the door and the shredded curtains. A postcard sat on the table and he stared at it for some time, as if it might be booby-trapped, before picking his way through the torn bedclothes to look closer. Beach chairs, sun, and gay flags suspended from the Edwardian light poles along the front. Red letters were burned into the sky to spell out FESTIVE BRIGHTON AND HOVE. Sloane turned the card over as if it might snap at him, and read the neat block printing on the back: *OR ELSE*.

Panic fought with a new anger in him. His heart raced, his legs felt heavy and stiff, and though the room was much warmer than the street outside, sweat made a cold hand on his back. A dark crevasse opened. What had he brought down on Sarah? If they so much as . . . He knew this was the way it came – half of him fighting the other half, plans skimming far ahead, missing stages. He clutched the pistol under his arm for comfort and it brought him part-way back. If they went after Sarah, he would do one thing with single-minded intensity, damn all consequences. He would let them know that.

★

Komarovsky reached down to the graph paper with his fingernails and plucked off a shred of tobacco that threatened to turn a 1 into a 7. He already had the message in grade four commercial code, and now figure by figure he was working across the one-time pad with its rows and tiers of five digits, transposing the coded message into cipher, that second level of security that drove him mad with frustration. It was all such tiresome nonsense. He would just as soon have dialed someone at the big grey six-storey building on Dzerzhinsky Street and said, 'Look here, we have an unexpected callback on that questionable double who disappeared last year. Have I permission to look into it?'

It should have been an axiom: the more regulations they put between a case officer and his work the more they compartmentalized and removed authority, the less efficient the whole business of security became. One day everyone would be busy thumbing through the rule books, while some wretched idiot sauntered through the Kremlin and walked off with the First Secretary's briefcase.

He locked his office carefully and hammered the message onto the teletype with his stubby fingers. If they approved he would have to commandeer some help from the Embassy over in Kensington Palace Gardens or from Novosti or TASS. All he had in the trade mission was a driver. He would need a leg, a backup, maybe a hammer. For the moment, though, all he needed was a pair of eyes to help him sift seventy collateral files for references to Jeffrey Sloane.

★

Blok's feet snapped down off the switchboard as Komarovsky came in, and a book whisked out of sight under the counter.

'Come, what is it, Blok? *Cancer Ward*? *The Master and Margherita*?'

'Oh, no, sir.' Hesitantly Blok drew out the volume of *The Lay of the Host of Igor*, and Komarovsky flipped through the yellow pages.

'This is dry as the Party protocols. How do you read it?'

Blok shrugged diffidently. 'There are some who would despise reading a modernized version.'

'Pedants are always with us. Most people would find it astonishing that you read this sort of thing at all. You write satire, don't you?'

Blok tried to swallow his fear. 'This is part of my general education, sir. I must learn to write better.'

Komarovsky hiked up his trousers and sat on the table of London directories in an avuncular way. 'I read *The New Bust for the Mayor*. Many can begin satire, but few can sustain it to the end. That is the secret, don't you think? In the last two decades they seem to have lost the art in the west. Everything is too broad and the targets keep shifting; they're like children throwing rocks at anything that moves. While you are in London, you should pick up an old copy of *Animal Farm*. It's quite good.'

Blok said nothing. It was as if he had just been told to buy a gun and shoot a policeman.

'Oh, I'm not saying those toadies of the Writers' Union would publish something that sharp today. Maybe in twenty years, if this regrettable cold war will only thaw again. We'll need a generation of writers to help sweep out the cobwebs.'

'Did you really read *The New Bust*?'

'I cleared you for overseas duty, Blok. Yes, I read the draft. It showed promise. I laughed aloud in that scene where the sculptor strikes his match on the nose. I think you described the mayor's reaction beautifully.'

Blok ventured a smile. 'I thought that was the best part myself.'

'When you get depressed, remember one thing: in the west you can publish any damn silly thing and no one cares, no one even notices. The question of censorship, for all the excesses, shows that your country honours literature and believes it matters. It's your duty to push it as far as you can.'

'If you say so, sir.'

Komarovsky laughed in a friendly way. He took out a cigarette and lit it with a tubular Czech lighter, a process that seemed to take up all his attention. 'Last year the First Secretary brought his old mother in from her village to visit,' he began in a musing tone. 'She was of course a peasant, like my own mother, with legs as thick as oak trees and masses of grey hair wrapped in a shawl. With great pride he showed her his private office in the Kremlin with its new steel desk and his own bar. "Do you like it?" he asked, but she just hung back in a corner and nodded with fear, like you. He couldn't understand what was wrong and he took her down to the garage to show her the fleet of limousines, hoping they would stir a little admiration. But again she huddled in a corner. "Oh, yes, very fine, my son."

'Now he was getting upset, and he drove her to his luxurious flat, and he had to push her through the seven rooms. She nodded dully at everything, hardly seeing it. Finally he drove her out to the beautiful dacha. "Isn't it superb, mama?" he said. She stood to one side and refused to touch anything at all, not the hand-rubbed mahogany nor the silk wall coverings. "Don't you like it?" he said with complete exasperation. "Oh, it is very nice," she said finally, but with doubt, and then she looked at him with concern. "But, son, what if the Reds come back?"'

106

Komarovsky roared laughing, his voice hammering back and forth in the confined room, as Blok sat holding his breath, paralyzed with fright.

'Blok, I am not going to arrest you for laughing at my joke.' Komarovsky wiped away a tear of laughter. 'You must stop grovelling if you truly want to be a satirist. Now I want you to give me a hand. I have to scan at least seventy files before an answer to my cable comes in.'

'I don't believe I'm cleared to see your material, sir.' Blok sat stiffly in the secretary chair.

'You are now. If you help me, I'll give you my own personal copy of *Catch-22*.'

★

Downs ruffled his hands through his damp hair, then threw on a clean shirt, another white one with the small-point collar so Cutter wouldn't guess he had been home. He and Myerson had made the bargain: they were supposed to be methodically checking every place Sloane might hide in Camden Town, but since the job was pointless and they both lived nearby, they had taken an hour out to go home themselves. He had dropped Myerson in Tufnell Park and driven on to his own Kentish Town flat.

He heard Alma's footsteps enter the bedroom, the distinctive scrape-rap of her foot, and he tensed for the excuses he would have to make. In the mirror he saw her long blonde hair, so pale it was transparent where it fell over the quilted pink robe that always suggested illness and sorrow. She tucked a chicken sandwich into his coat where it hung over the chair. There was a chugging sound in the taps as he rinsed the comb, and she wrapped her hands around him from behind with a dependent clinging. She was two inches taller and on her neck he smelled a perfume she hadn't been wearing a half hour earlier; he wondered if she thought there was another woman. The thought was like a pain in his heart, and he pressed back against her, wanting to tell her that he loved her and needed her and there couldn't possibly be someone else, but he knew it would let loose too much for him to handle just then.

'Where will you be?' she asked querulously.

'Just Camden Town, then probably back at the office.'

'What's happening?'

'You know I'm not supposed to t-t-talk about it.'

'You *like* to keep secrets.'

'That's not true. We're looking for someone who used to work for us, that's all. It's important, for the first time in years. A real job.'

She had been a bright and independent woman when he married her, and almost unaware of the deformity. She still read a dozen books a week and watched all the cultural shows, but quitting her secretarial job to become a housewife had somehow made her increasingly childish. He wondered if it was his own fault, something in him feeding on her dependence and encouraging it.

'I hope you're not counting on your Big Recovery,' she jeered gently.

'It might be. I don't know.'

'Please tell me when you'll be home.'

'I can't say. *Honest*, Alma. I'll c-c-call you when I can. I've got to pick up Wayne again and stay on duty till this thing is over.'

'You do too much for that Cutter. He takes advantage of you.'

'Can you still tie a tie?' he asked with a vulnerable optimism, remembering all the silly games of their first years. From behind him, her thin fingers deployed the ends of the tie on his chest and set to work. 'You have nice fingers,' he said.

'I want you,' she whispered, and her hand slid quickly under his trousers.

'That's cheating. We haven't got time.' He pulled free. 'Why don't you stay with Joan until this is over? She'll be alone, too.'

'I bore her,' she murmured, and things were suddenly dangerously close to the surface.

'If anything, she's the b-b-boring one.' He was tense as a whip now. He slipped into the coat, and saw with amazement and gratitude that she was gathering her strength. It might have gone either way.

'You men are so footloose,' she said. 'I'll just embroider my – what was it Penelope worked on?'

'A shroud I think but she k-k-kept unravelling it at night so she wouldn't have to marry one of the suitors.'

'Don't take too long or I'll stop unravelling.'

He smiled and kissed her. She followed him along the hall, and he had to slow up as her clubfoot forced her to descend the stairs crabwise. 'I'll c-call by ten, for sure. You really should go see Joan.'

She nodded vaguely, but he knew she wouldn't.

Outside, all Caversham Road was a mist, washed down to an ugly yellow by the sodium lights; even his old Ford Escort double parked by the curb had turned from pale green to orange. He kissed her cheek and hurried desperately to the car. Looking back, he saw her watching him, an orange phantom clinging sadly to the front door.

'You'll be all right?' he called.

'Come back to me.'

She meant *now*, he thought, for another embrace. But he took it in another sense; he nodded and waved and drove away. He circled northward through the residential streets, knowing that she would be crying because he hadn't gone back to kiss her, and he stared fixedly at the narrow passage between the parked cars, drawing him forward like a vacuum. If this operation didn't salvage Research, he would quit. That was all there was to it. He would take her home, build them the house in Vermont.

Then something cold and hard pressed alarmingly against his neck.

'Pull over,' a voice demanded. 'On the left there.'

His heart thudding with panic, he stopped even sooner than the voice had demanded, the car riding up on a sandpile in front of a half-demolished house.

'Sloane?' Downs guessed with trepidation.

'It's me. You can turn around.'

Downs eyed the blue-black Walther beside his head. It looked almost like a toy, but it wasn't. 'What d-do you want?'

'I'm sending a message to the golem. I'll haul the garbage, tell Cutter that. To get you off my back and off Jannings's back, I'll do it. Don't come to me, don't try to find me, don't go near Sarah. Is that clear enough?'

Sloane was doing his best to appear intimidatingly cool, but Downs could see anxiety winking beneath the surface. The gunbarrel described a small wobbly arc. Downs nodded. 'It's not my fault.'

'I'm hanging pretty near the edge of a cliff. Whoever wrecked my flat did a good job. If he pushes me again, he's going over with me. If he fools with my wife. Do you understand? I know where Cutter lives, too. Tell him.'

'It's not a g-good idea threatening him. He's got too short a fuse.' Remembering Alma for some reason, Downs rediscovered his affection for this unsteady man; he found he wanted to help Sloane if he could.

'Tell me how else to get the bastard. His hide is so thick nothing penetrates. If he hurts Sarah, I'll kill him, I swear it. I want that message transmitted. Don't soften it.'

Downs knew it wouldn't work, but Sloane was right – nothing else would work either. Cutter's forward march was as implacable as a glacier.

'Will you tell him?'

'If you insist.'

Sloane slipped the pistol into his pocket. 'We need something to get through a code-lock in the mission. I'm told there's a device called an inductance circuit reader; you won't have it, but you ought to be able to borrow it from your buddies across town. You get me that for the door or it's no job. Monday at noon have it in a white flight bag and walk the length of Oxford Street.'

'Monday noon?'

'That gives you all Monday morning. I want this over with, and I don't want Cutter with time to dream up embellishments. Walk the south side of the street starting at Tottenham Court tube. I'll find you.'

'I put in a word for you,' Downs said mournfully. 'I t-told him you'd had enough.'

'Jesus, you want a medal? You keep terrible company, Downs. Monday noon.'

Sloane opened the door and slid out of the car into the mist. He looked back and saw Downs's terrier eyes following him before the night swallowed them both. He had never understood how Downs had ended up working for Cutter, or working in an intelligence organization at all. Downs should have been a teacher at a junior high school in some small Midwest city, something of a legend among the students for his embarrassing stutter and his clumsy hangdog stabs at decency in a world that continually overwhelmed him.

★

Two of the three telephones in the Kentish Town tube station were out of order, one smashed to junk by vandals and the second, maddeningly, refusing to swallow his coin no matter how desperately he pressed as Felicity shouted 'Hello, Hello!' over the shrill pay tone. In the third booth, the bar under the coin slot slid away easily and the shrieking pips died.

'Felicity, let me speak to Sarah.' There was so much static on the line it was like calling the moon.

'Is this the Jeffrey with the bright blue eyes?'

'No, grey-green,' he replied, pleased by her caution.

'Someone was watching the house, Jeff. A big brown American car like a shark. We didn't know if they were after you or her, but she decided to slip away.'

His back felt exposed suddenly, and he turned quickly in the booth to glance around the busy station. If they could find her . . . A thin man with a face like a rat waited just outside the booth, but Sloane glared fiercely at him and the man checked his watch with disgust and hurried off. 'Is the shark still there?'

'Yes. I think she's away clean. She took my Triumph – actually I drove it round the back and gave it to her there so they wouldn't see.'

'Good work.'

'She said to tell you the fish are laughing at noon. Does that mean something to you?'

He puzzled for an instant and then smiled to himself. 'It tells me she's clever as a fox. I'm sorry for the bother, Felicity. I didn't think it was important enough for them to trace as far as your house.'

'I know enough not to ask anything right now, but can I help in any way?'

'Not now,' he said. 'If anything happens to me, please take care of Sarah.'

'You may find she's a lot tougher than we think. Good-bye,

Jeff. Mind your back.'

'Thanks.'

He waited in the booth half a minute longer, watching the commuters hurrying into the station, shaking umbrellas and straightening their hunched-down necks. No one waited for the telephone, no one lingered at the newspaper kiosk. He rested his forehead against the chilly glass, wanting a drink. Was it just a watching post outside Felicity's? A full-scale attempt to grab her? Would they keep after Sarah once Downs delivered his message? Stepping out, he caught a glimpse of his ghostly face in the smeared glass, exhausted and fretful. Not for the first time, he had the sense of fading away to nothing like a phantom in someone else's world. The cold damp air outside woke him like a slap, and he decided to take the bus.

★

Behind Sloane a short, dark figure slid from the passage between the elevators, stepped into the street and walked briskly into a stand-up sandwich shop. By pointing with his stubby finger he managed to order a dry cheese sandwich which he took to the window and chewed slowly. Through the glass, Sparrow could just see Sloane standing morosely at the bus queue. He noticed that the mist had grown heavier and the gray sky pressed down on the road like a hand. All it meant to him was an easier tail, with more dark corners and bustling umbrellas to shield him.

★

He was home. *Home*, he thought dully; it was now as little as a seedy hotel room with fading roses on the wallpaper, offering the vague security of two-days' familiarity. But that was more than anything else offered any longer. A tack in the ceiling held the pinkish remnant of a crepe streamer, and he wondered who on earth had chosen that dreary room for a celebration. A celebration of what? He wadded up the last of the cold takeaway kebab in its damp wrapper and deposited it on the night table, then he lay back, immensely tired. And lonely. Sarah, where are you now? Home throbbed like an earthquake as an outbound train trundled past. I hope you're safe and warm somewhere.

For a year he had clung to the tenuous image of a future that was more orderly and manageable than the past, lit by the tenderness he felt for Sarah, secure in the little he knew he could earn as a translator. At moments he had been tempted by more, but he had been content to shore up the walls around them and venture out only when every footstep had been planned in advance. He knew that some day, together, they might choose to try something new, move somewhere and start again, but until that day came there had been a timeless comfort in knowing that he did not have to leave the walls. That security lay shattered in the disorder of his flat. Now he could picture no future at all, and the loss was terrible to him, a deep, cold sickness of the heart. Self-pity caught up with him. You just dropped your guard for a moment, he thought, and some bastard smashed your world to pieces.

He poured more Scotch into the streaky tooth-glass and swallowed it all at once. He heard the door in the next room slap closed, its vibration like a blow against the thin wall, and a giggle came through clearly.

'Slow down, ducks. What would you like? A little of this?' A woman's voice, throaty and calculatedly teasing.

Something hit the floor and a bedspring creaked. 'Righto. That, too,' a man cried gaily.

The woman laughed, intolerably loud, and Sloane covered his ears and rolled onto his side in the failing light.

9

Kohler stared at the steam rising lazily off the coffee cup, still too hot to touch. It was the cheaper kind of Nescafe, not the Gold, that the pool secretary bought for the coffee room to save a few pennies, but it was better than no coffee at all. He leaned sideways to fart comfortably and cradled his chin blearily on his hands. Last night, the caretaker of his Chelsea flat had announced blandly that the toilet had, after all, packed it in for good and they would have to have a builder in with a new one. By the ordinary standard of efficiency, that would be two months of using the Orb and Sceptre down the road, and when the pub was closed he would have to choose one of the other tenants to visit. He couldn't bear any of the stuffy civil servants who inhabited the luxury building, nor their frumpy wives, and the thought of having to ask to use one of their loos left him sour and irritable.

In fact, Kohler didn't much like anything about London. It was cold, cramped, inconvenient, inefficient, unfriendly, dirty and utterly indifferent to his style of casual masculine elegance. Not a soul here could distinguish Ivy League from bowling league. One day he would put on his madras jacket and stand grinning outside the building as they filed home in their dreadful, uptight, three-piece pinstripes and the silly derby hats that they insisted on calling bowlers. Like Incas at a funeral. That would show them. Yes, indeed. Perhaps, he thought, they didn't worry about fixing toilets because they only shit every six months. Or, was it *shat*? They held it back for special occasions. Perhaps it was indelicate to shit at all, and they took some medication that broke wastes straight down to flatulence.

Rusty, irascible thoughts at 6.30 a.m. in a dim inner office without a window for reasons of security and without a personal secretary for reasons of economy. Waiting for a phone call that would come at 6.41, or if delayed, at 7.11 or 7.41. 'Never make appointments for the hour or half hour,' they taught out at the Farm in Virginia. 'Too predictable and too noticeable.'

He sipped the coffee, still far too hot, and ended up with a furry throbbing tongue that would irk him the rest of the morning. Angry, he pushed the cup aside and glanced through the papers in the in-basket: FYI memoes, a query on Irish gun-running, the duty officer schedule to fill in and initial (only the worst slots remaining open), a long report on a new technique of laundering money through an international advertising agency that looked intolerably boring, plus a cable from Intelligence-side: the Old Man wanted an update on Lumbago. He doodled on the cable with a felt pen, tight balanced whorls that turned into a row of flying saucers with little feet.

At 6.41 the telephone rang and startled him into jostling the coffee cup and spilling a few drops across the blotter. The pay pips tore through his sinuses and then he heard a regular rapping noise.

'Sparrow?'

There was one thump in reply. Why-oh-why wouldn't he speak? Kohler found it profoundly exasperating at this time in the morning to have to conduct a twenty-questions interview. Sparrow, is it animal, vegetable or mineral?

'You've got him in sight?'

Yes, Sparrow had him in sight.

'Does he act like he's on a job?'

Yes, he acted like he was on a job. Now what? *How* is he acting like he's on a job? Is he skulking in dark corners? Turning up the collar of his trench coat?

'Stay with him. Do you need assistance?'

No, Sparrow did not need assistance. Anything else to report? No, nothing else to report.

Kohler hung up, knowing he would be crabby and miserable for the rest of the morning. He had come in at six for this. He started nodding sardonically at himself, and it took a long time to make himself stop. What could he wire the Old Man? *Lumbago exists? Lumbago looks like he's on a job?* Jesus, they'd swamp him with sarcastic demands for information. It wasn't fair really; it was Webber who had told him to use Sparrow and no one else.

Why had Webber insisted on a one-man job? Was it just economy, or was something else in the air? He would write: *Lumbago has seized Westminster and threatens to throw out the head of one MP every hour until we free the Samoan Islands.* Yes, that would just about do the nut.

★

It looked like the innards of a pocket radio – a rust-coloured circuit board knobby with resistors and capacitors. Cutter fussed with a wire loop attached loosely to one end and peered aimlessly at the underside. Was that little black can a transistor? On the side was a row of nixie tubes that could display tiny numbers. 'We'll pay an arm and a leg for this,' he said sourly. 'What did they say?'

Crabb prowled the room like a caged cat, always uneasy out of his tiny office downstairs or away from a car. Downs wished he would sit down. 'They're all creeps,' Crabb said. 'They grinned like a mule with a pole up his arse and said we'd get a bill you wouldn't believe.'

'You didn't tell them why you wanted it?'

'Naw, course not. They tried a lot of lame bullshit, supposing this and supposing that, but I didn't say nothing. They're a bunch of overpaid fairies, if you ask me.'

'I didn't.'

Cutter wound the wire around the device, slipped a page of instructions under the wire and set the circuit reader into the bottom of the white Pan Am bag Downs had bought that morning at the ticket office on Piccadilly. Next to it he nestled a motorized Nikon, the only working camera they had in the office. Cutter's eyes swept the room and came to rest on Downs, who sat swivelled around in his desk chair, watching.

'He actually threatened me?' Cutter enquired incredulously.

'I think it was just t-talk.'

'With a PPK stuck in your neck. *Our* missing PPK. The son of a bitch.'

'He agreed to do the job. He seems to have it all arranged with Jannings.'

'Crabb . . . *stop pacing*, man. You look like four virgins at the

116

altar. Is Di Santis still on station with the wife?'

'Sort of,' Crabb said forlornly. 'He thinks she slipped out of the house. The sister came back on foot but the car never did.'

'Get down there again.' He started speaking very slowly. 'Tell them to find her. Pick her up. Stash her somewhere. Would you like me to *number* the steps?' he added sarcastically.

'No, sir.'

Downs cleared his throat apprehensively. He had a premonition it was all going to turn out badly. 'I don't think it's a good idea to – ' Downs began.

'Don't think. Don't even try. Nobody *ever* jerks me around. Let's keep that little rule in our sights.'

Cutter stood up with the flight bag, wearing a large primitive scowl. 'I'll deliver this.'

'He wanted me to,' Downs said softly.

'He needs some shouting at.'

★

A single lozenge of blue sky winked out as if someone had zipped up a tear in the cloud just as Cutter stepped out of the car at the corner. The drizzle came down gently, turning the long prospect of Oxford Street into a black and white etching, huge department stores fading off like fortresses into the distance, and the strange Martian light poles marching away down the middle. The Research office was only 500 yards down Charing Cross, but Cutter had insisted Crabb drive him to the top of Oxford Street. He slammed the car door and walked grimly into the shopping crowd, dodging the occasional umbrella point aimed at his eyes. A blast of angry music hit him as he passed an open door. He swapped the flight bag into his left hand so as to keep it from banging approaching shoppers. They even walk on the wrong goddamn side, he thought.

Sloane had better approach him soon. It was over a mile to Marble Arch and he wasn't about to go a mile in the rain. Mistrust of Sloane tumbled through his mind, alternating with a sweet anticipation of the tongue-lashing he was preparing and a gratifying image of Sloane shrinking in the blast. 'So you thought the worm could turn, you worm . . .'

This was what he lived for, he reminded himself, this was why he had spent the last two years sitting at a numbing desk, paying his dues. Deep inside he had known he would get a chance to go active again, and he had hung on, waiting for just this day, for the exhilaration of the process: not just the threats, but the whole cunning business of moulding an enforced loyalty, patiently building up a landscape of menace, interrupting, deriding, hanging in wait, then pouncing to undercut even an accustomed level of danger with worse, hunting that last hard particle of resistance and then flicking it out with a scalpel. This was what life was all about, forcing your will on a reluctant world.

★

In the chromium bustle of Marks and Spencer, Sloane clung to a table of ski sweaters, his mind drifting with the tension and his hand resting idly on the lambswool at his waist. Six glass doors in a row and a corner of one of the display windows offered a capsule view of thirty feet of sepia Oxford Street. A parade of overcoats, strollers, umbrellas, pinched faces, rubber overshoes – they moved past like a rolling diorama, with buses and taxis on a second scrim in the background. It could almost have been the same fifty people circling across his screen over and over. Even the same three black taxis and a single bright red double-decker hoisted into the air once it was out of his sight and set down to run past again. One of the newer coloured taxis pulled to the curb and broke the illusion as an Arab woman in purdah lugged a bag of parcels past the doors. Now and again a blurry figure detached itself from the stream and pushed in through one of the doors with a momentary gust of noise and chill.

Sloane noticed once again how his mind stretched faces to meet expectations. This was the third rather short man plodding across the glass to give him a momentary jolt and send a wayward motor impulse to his leg. What time was it? He guessed it was roughly ten past, but he didn't look at his watch for fear of missing Downs in the street. He felt glum and, in some very deep place, empty. Nothing, not even thinking of Sarah, would give him a lift, and his life seemed to make no sense. What was the point? Even fighting for safety – for what came after safety? He would protect Sarah; that was absolute. But would they ever be able to make a life again? It had all been so precarious.

At the right edge of the stage he caught a glimpse of white at knee level, winking between the legs. Recognition didn't gel for a moment as he watched a heavy wrestler's body beside the flight bag. A stiff crew cut with a touch of grey, a blue nylon jacket. His eyes saw details, but it was hard for his mind to take in more than the air of taut, checked violence that the man emanated.

Sloane was alarmed, then angry. He had told Downs to bring it. Once again he touched the pistol in his armpit for comfort, and then he turned on his heel and walked straight out of the back of the store into a shabby alley. He would phone Research and tell them to forget the whole thing until they got it right. Sloane came to a halt beside a cat that eyed him out of a window with neurotic eyes, like a fury. He wouldn't call it off. Sooner or later Cutter had to be beaten in his own court.

He hurried along the narrow road, and then cut up toward Oxford Street, past a handful of children playing desultory soccer, nudging a tied-up bundle of rags along the wet pavement. A fruit stall hunched under an awning near the corner, and he just had time to duck behind it as the flight bag appeared, swinging out from the sooty limestone. Cutter stepped into the road, glancing back along Oxford Street, belligerent and irritable. A man badly wounded in his manhood, Sloane thought. Only the pleasure of something primitive like revenge would cure it – but the cure would never come.

Sloane had half a mind to let him walk all the way to Park Lane, but he slipped cautiously to the corner and eyed the crowd. There was no one he recognized, and he was fairly certain he would know Research's people. An old woman in a plastic raincoat ran into him with a gasp, apologized obsequiously and hurried on. He considered for a moment longer, then gave in to the mad plan and bought the largest, hardest apple he could find on the stall.

★

He was even more ill-tempered by the time he had passed the sixth block without a hint of a contact. By God, if Sloane had sent him on a wild goose chase while he took off for some hideaway in the Midlands, he'd drag him all the way back by the balls. He'd drop him straight into the trade mission from a helicopter at 5,000 feet. Without a parachute. For an instant, Cutter could actually see the tiny tumbling body. He came to a stop and his eyes skipped along the pedestrians on both sides of the street, then for no particular reason, flashed up to the ornate window ledges above, as if he expected to find Sloane on his belly, watching through binoculars. He was genuinely disturbed now, increasingly certain that he was the butt of a joke. One fist opened and clenched compulsively. He started again, but Marble Arch ahead was the limit. That was the outer margin of the joke; he wouldn't have it whispered, repeated, gleefully acknowledged, that Ralph Cutter had walked a mile and a half in the rain and then ridden the tube back, damp and humiliated, with the flight bag on his lap.

Cutter knocked away a small hand that tugged at his coat. Another street urchin, begging or picking pockets or launching one of those sophisticated lost-child con games that they learned so young in London.

'Sir, Mr Cutter, sir.'

Cutter turned abruptly. *Mis-uh Cuh-uh*, it had been pronounced, just close enough for recognition. He saw a boy of about ten, short brown hair beaded with water, and that universal chalky complexion like something that had been dead for some time. The boy's fingers tugged nervously at a limp green parka, overwhelmed by Cutter's glare.

''E says come along wif me.'

'Who says?'

'The gent what you want. Come strite, sir.'

Cutter followed him over a curbing and down steps into a narrow passage that ran crookedly behind the department stores. At each turning, the man's eyes swivelled toward the shadows for an ambush. The boy moved ahead uneasily, glancing back to make sure the huge, hostile man was following, and finally reassured, slowed up and walked alongside.

'Filfy wevva, innit?' the boy said in his mysterious language, and Cutter glared stonily.

Cutter endured the indignity of walking the full length of

120

tinselly Carnaby Street. Finally they came out onto a quiet, deserted square, surrounded by tall limestone offices.

The boy pointed across toward two telephone booths that stood in a setback near a garage entrance. ''E says you'll find a piper in the back callbox wif a number on.' Cutter lunged to grab him and demand when, exactly, he had talked to Sloane, but the boy was already darting back up James Street.

Cutter set the bag down under the telephone and found a slip of folded paper tucked into the ten-pence slot. Scrawled in pencil was a 226 number and he recognized the exchange as somewhere in North London. He cursed as he dug for change. He was going to be led through two or three drop points before Sloane was assured that he was alone.

★

Sloane waited in the garage entrance under a hand-lettered sign saying: *Polite Notice – No Parking Please*. As soon as he heard the door shut, he lifted the heavy plastic milk crates and edged out to the nearest callbox.

'I don't care who the fuck *you* are, I want Sloane!' he heard Cutter bellowing.

All in one movement, Sloane dived forward and wedged the bright red crates between the telephone booths, jamming shut the swing-out door of Cutter's. Cutter's shoulder was already heaving against the door, his eyes wide with sudden rage, but the sides of the crates just flexed and the heavy door merely bounced open an inch and slammed shut. He rocked the door with both hands like a madman as Sloane pointed gravely to the bag inside.

'Not a fucking chance!'

'Is the circuit reader in there?'

Cutter said nothing, breathing heavily.

'If it's in there, I'll get your file,' Sloane said woodenly. 'It's all arranged with Jannings. You stay away from him and away from Sarah and we'll do it this week and bring it to you.' He drew out the PPK, shielding it from the road with his body. 'If you harm Sarah, if you so much as go near her again, I'll dump the file and you're dead.'

'Don't make me laugh,' Cutter snarled, his eyes contemptu-

121

ously on the pistol.

He had known it would probably come to this. If only Cutter had been half a human being . . . He gripped the vertical grooves at the rear of the receiver, pulled back against the heavy spring and let go, snicking the first round into the breach. The hammer was up now and he was careful with the pistol; cocked, it took only a half-ounce of trigger-pull to fire. With his left hand he took the apple out of his pocket and rotated it to locate the small hole he had dug. A dense new potato would have been better – that's what Collins had told him to use long ago in the Research basement – but the fruit vendor hadn't sold potatoes. An inch of stubby gunbarrel disappeared into the apple and he pressed the makeshift silencer against the glass just above his waist.

His thoughts slowed to a ponderous crawl. For a moment it was difficult to believe he was standing outside a telephone booth with a pistol, about to loose such violence on an orderly London square. It seemed easier to stand there forever, to levitate, to die than to make a scene like this. He was threatening a man who surely deserved everything that could happen to him. Those who live by the threat . . . Time folded in on him. There was so great a separation between complaint and retribution, it couldn't be happening. Here it was, all set out the way it should be in some pure and magical world – poetic justice, from the hand of the aggrieved.

Cutter shifted his feet, his bravado gradually filling the booth and making it all easier. 'Don't be an asshole. You can't intimidate me with some schoolboy trick.'

The sudden coughing sound reminded Sloane of the thump of knuckles on a watermelon, though quite a bit louder and overlaid by a frivolous sound of breaking glass. There had been a flash where the bullet apparently had buried itself in the grey steel telephone, and Cutter was now turned away, pressed into the far corner of the booth. His arms were up against a second hellish assault of glass splinters. It took only an instant to remove the crate, extract the flight bag and seal the door shut again. The last thing Sloane saw was Cutter staring incredulously at blood on his hand and then the hand diving into his pocket for a handkerchief.

★

On the north side of the square, a dark figure stood at a wire rack of colour brochures propped in the window of St James Travel Bureau. *Bahama Wonderland* fell back into its slot as Sparrow watched Cutter hurl down the useless receiver and ram his shoulder into the door. Sparrow slipped quickly out of the shop. He could hear a hammering and an incoherent raving voice behind him as he hurried along James Street after the receding Sloane, who was carrying the white bag now and moving with quick effortless steps.

★

On the frosted glass of the bow window a Victorian designer had fossilized the outline of a large fish-that-never-was. It was vaguely salmon-like and bent nearly double, its mouth open in an impossibly large cheery grin. The sign hanging by the narrow lane explained the etched window: The Laughing Fish. Once, long ago, she had wondered whether the name was a reference to the joy of catching trout in the Ouse River a quarter mile away, or was it, more logically, a reference to not catching them, from the viewpoint of the trout? But that had been one of the rare moments when something as trivial as the name of a country pub caught her attention. She knew how rigidly her mind focused and how much escaped her notice when the gloom was upon her. One time she had walked a half mile past her road agonizing over a slight from a former lover – the offence not even fresh, but years gone.

The pub lay on the edge of the village of Isfield, across an abandoned rail line from the A26, lost in the shallow valley of central Sussex, and Sarah sat alone in the garden at the side. The cast metal bench had the false dampness of the chill, but it hadn't rained since the night before, and she loved the garden with a desperate, protective melancholy because it reminded her of her first illicit meetings with Jeffrey, slipping away from the hospital in one of the wardens' cars that he had hot-wired so carelessly. What was the word for small pleasures that arrived when least expected? Maybe there was no such word, she thought. Or maybe her vocabulary for any sort of pleasure had atrophied. But those few startlingly happy afternoons with Jeffrey might have saved her life. The Forbidden Excursions, she had called them, though he had once left her a note: *Meet me by the north gate at 11. The Big Breakout.* It was true: he had seemed much stronger to her then – more like he was now than at any time over the past year – and at this very pub, their favourite, she had watched him deny himself any refreshment stronger than lemonade.

She found herself so sunk in memories that she was about to weep. To stop the flood, she turned her attention to the centre of the garden; the largest he-goat she had ever seen was staked out in the middle of the grass. From the trimmed patch it had browsed a wide circle of the spiky lawn, but had wound itself up on the cord and was now confined to three or four feet of space, tugging in perplexity at the tall peg. You will find no symbolism in that, she told herself. No, not in a large dumb animal that is driven to circle round pointlessly until it draws nearer some dead centre where activity is no longer possible and the universe comes to an end. We are not sent signs. All the same, she got up to unwind the goat's cord and give the universe a little more time. As she squatted on the lawn she felt a prod in the arm from the animal. She stroked the bristly head once, and it skittered away to the end of the loosed tether and reared with a playfulness that choked her with affection.

Checking her watch – 12.35 – she drank the last of her beer in something like a toast. 'Bite that cord,' she said aloud. 'Escape.'

She returned the glass to the ruddy-faced pubkeeper wiping tables inside and walked to the Triumph parked in the lane. He would come. Tomorrow or the next day. And she would be there every noon until he showed up, strong again, tender, intent, and patient.

★

An hour earlier in real time, but five meridians earlier in Langley, Kohler's cable worked its way through several interconnected machines. One, years obsolescent, punched tiny holes into a paper tape, and another read the holes with electric eyes and fed binary impulses into a CDC Bytestore/14, the only rapid-access storage device with the capacity to hold a quasi-random cipher key, then out at an IBM 560/30 tape printer that squirted

124

the letters of the plaintext in black ink onto pink gummed tape that was automatically cut into lengths and stuck to a yellow backing (Grade 2 Secret; source privileged). The cable entered human hands finally in Dispatch, and Ross intercepted it on the way to the Old Man. With a blast of intimidating scorn, he managed to pry it away from the nervous messenger. Retiring to his office, Ross slit the brown envelope and then the inner black one to find the briefest return advisory he had ever seen.

F: L96R T: DIR-OER-INTEL LANG RE-BROKEN YOUR 1-3 LUMBAGO MAKING CONTACTS DOT KEEPING NEW HOME DOT ON THE JOB DOT DOT UNDER EYES ENDM

The fluorescent lamp started its buzzing again, and he slapped at it once in vain. Ross's forehead ran with sweat. He would look up 96R, but it had to be that vain, preening idiot Kohler. *What* contacts? he wanted to shout; new home *where*?; what does 'on the job' *mean*? He wondered if someone was purposely under-cutting the Old Man by laying on a half-assed job. He had to make a decision on his own now, and he had to make it quickly. Go there himself to supervise? He had enough contacts in London to handle it easily, calling in past debts. But on the other hand he could stay here and set up the contacts from this end for anyone in the section. He could trust several of the others to watchdog asinine Kohler, but to keep vigil here . . . ? He imagined Jerry Moore trying to run the gauntlet of Langley politics: it was sending a sheep to catch wolves. No, he would have to be the one to stay in Langley and plug any dikes that broke upstairs.

Ross picked up the telephone and dialed Moore's in-house number. 'Jerry, this is Harv. Whatever you're doing, file it. Order yourself a ticket for London and come over here.'

He hung up, giving Moore no time to whine, then wiped his face on a dampened sleeve. Soon he was going to be frying eggs on his forehead. His phone rang, and he was about to chew Moore out for arguing when he heard the Old Man's voice rumble down the line.

'Harv, any word yet on Lumbago from the watcher?'

Ross glanced at the three meagre lines of pink taped glued to the paper. 'I haven't seen anything. I'll check.'

'Call me back.'

Ross set the phone down gently. If the Old Man saw this bit of work, he'd be over on Willy in Liaison, shouting so you could hear him all over the building, and that wouldn't be wise, not if they needed some ungrudging overtime from their operational group to bail out Broken Back. Unless – and Ross's brown eyes swung toward the window and came to rest thoughtfully on the east wing – unless their own Ops people were already in league with the Old Man's former colleagues across the way. Were they setting him up for a fall, just as the Old Man was setting up Research, running out the rope . . . ? A fantastic vision of treachery presented itself vividly: the director and his two adjutants stepping out of a doorway to ambush the Old Man in the corridor, kicking out his crutches with schoolboy sadism and stamping his braces into twisted scrap metal as he lay howling on the carpet. 'Is it our fault you took so long to fade away?' one of them sneered. Ross hurried forward in righteous outrage, dragging his old service .45 from the shoulder holster he hadn't worn in years. He managed to shoot down two of the three, as the director himself fled in fear along the grey hallway. Well . . . not quite like that, then. What is this passion for justice? he wondered. Why was he bringing these austere, youthful demands to the adult who had grown soft and tired? But he could not deny it: he did have a passion for justice, at least for others who had earned it. Yet here in Langley a .45 would do him no good as an avenger. Here people were mugged by deceit and calculation.

He remembered the odd little tête-à-tête earlier in the week. Deputy Director Mulhauser himself had sat down beside him unexpectedly in the ordinary cafeteria, not the high-tea room for supergrades where Mulhauser always ate.

'Hello there, Harvey. I've been meaning to have a family chat with you ever since we dragged you in from the field.' Gray at the temples; with rimless glasses, a tweed coat with elbow patches; like a musty New England professor, except for the sly, watchful tilt of his head. On the plastic tray he had brought only an apple on a single tiny plate, and he didn't touch that. Ross had the odd sense that the tray was just cover for the conversation. But why? 'You're one of our best people, we have the highest regard for

126

you, all of us. How are you getting along down in Economics?'

'All right, thanks.'

'I realize economics isn't exactly your field, but we thought we'd give you a bit of a vacation. Especially after all that unpleasantness, losing a whole network . . .'

He had spoken as if the entire disaster, the rolling up of Blackcurrant and the public hanging of his four Maronite Lebanese agents in Syria had all happened a few weeks ago, instead of four years. Ross had recognized the butter, and he kept waiting for the butterknife.

'The Directorate is high on economics right now. We feel it offers some of the most crucial indicators of new developments at this point in time. An important place to have good men, for the moment, anyway. That's why we put the Old Man in charge too, you see. Of course it isn't like Operations, but we love each of our children in his own way, don't we, eh?

'I've always argued we could make better use of you across the way, but there just hasn't been an opening. I'll go on putting in a good word. Just keep your nose clean.' He had laughed, as if the admonition had no real weight to it; just a reminder not to plough too many of the secretaries and keep out of the petty cash.

'How's the wife?'

'She died 15 years ago.'

'Excuse me, Harvey. Sorry, really. I don't keep up with private lives. The big picture, you know, like all that marvellous work you did for us in Berlin and London. Keep up the good work, Harvey. I've got to run.'

Ross had watched Mulhauser walk away, trailing his vague, disturbing omens; not quite sure whether he had just been offered the point or the hilt of the knife. The apple had been untouched. He wondered now whether keeping his nose clean might not include standing aside and letting the Old Man's last act play itself out to his ruin. If it were true, there was probably little he could do about it. You needed a damn long spoon to sup with Mulhauser's crowd, let alone buck them.

10

Jannings peered into the flight bag. 'This is the magic machine,' he muttered acidly.

'Complete with instructions.'

The last of the homebound commuter traffic lunged and hooted anxiously on the high street, hurrying to catch the lights, and from where they sat the buildings of the East End were a patchwork of empty skulls, stained with moss and decay, hollow black eyes looking down on them with final gravity. Even the streetlamps seemed half dead, throwing only a feeble light onto the damp road, and all the cars ran on their sidelights. Why use only sidelights? Sloane had often wondered. On the theory that keeping the main lights off saved money somehow? He had never seen anywhere so fantastically self-denying as England: tearing up the *Mirror* for loo paper, buying food in cans the size of match-boxes, stoking winter fires no larger than a candle flame. Acceptance of things as they were; petty sins and tiny satisfactions. There were times when all this comforted him like some catholic form of thrift; economy of things, of emotions, of ideas, of energy. At other times it suggested atrophy of the spirit, an anticipated death. And recognition would make him wince inwardly. A few pedestrians cut through the derelict churchyard past them, tugging coats around themselves, but none lingered, and a prowling black dog whined miserably and nosed into the rubbish, its tail curled up behind like a question mark.

'And this camera – I'm supposed to photograph the gold file?'

'I've heard a rumour to that effect.'

Jannings made his Germanic hiss of contempt and zipped the bag shut brutally. He closed his eyes for a moment, sitting as heavily as a bull awaiting the final knife. 'Jeffrey, they came to me. *To my pub*. That is too near by far. They waved that photograph like a salesman's tract, Cutter and the one with the scar.'

'Crabb,' Sloane said. 'I said Cutter was a gangster.'

'There were, of course, threats. My heart became cold. I had to send Karn and the children away for a week. I don't know how to describe it: I sat there in front of the television. I put my hand to my face and it came away wet and cold, as if I was already dead. My stomach is water. I am not sleeping. It sounds like nothing but it makes life a terror all through. Werner Jannings is unmasked as imperialist agent, traitor to his fatherland . . .'

He glanced up, but Sloane said nothing.

'Get them off my back. *For God's sake.*'

'Do what they want,' Sloane said. 'I'll find some way to make certain this is the last job. I'm sorry it has to be you.'

'You are not as sorry as I am.'

'Do you think you can do it?'

'No,' Jannings said angrily, and he added quickly, 'I do not want to meet here again. This place makes me ill. I want to be near my home.'

'I understand,' Sloane said, and he did understand what even the simple proximity of the familiar could mean if everything else was disintegrating. Whatever happened, he couldn't face going back to Rochester Road again now, tidying up the death of the familiar. They would have to rebuild somewhere else.

'I will try to do what you want tomorrow. Come to Notting Hill, to Ladbroke Grove Gardens. At this time.'

Jannings seemed to stir, as if wanting to leave but not finding the right moment. He subsided again and tucked in his legs, toe and heel together with military precision. He was far away somewhere. 'Can you remember the day your father died?'

'He ran off when I was four. He may still be alive out there somewhere.'

'You didn't tell me that. Perhaps you will not understand this. My father was an important man in the Party in Dresden. He was an organizer of the League of Red Front Fighters. That was the red guard the Party formed to protect workers' meetings. This was 1930. Of course the League did not take the offensive until it was too late. They had terrible advice from above. But they did fight. All 1931 and 1932 the streets were a terrible warground between us and the SA. Any notice of a meeting would bring out both sides – to guard it and to stop it. We were stronger than the Brownshirts almost everywhere, and with the Socialists we could have stopped them easily, but we never acted in concert with the Sozis, never. It was a terrible mistake. I cannot think how terrible it was, and I did not see it. At the terrible black end in 1934, when all his comrades were dead or in concentration camps or hiding under other names, my father escaped to Moscow. That is where I was born, in the Lux Hotel with the refugees speaking fifty languages.'

Brakes squealed shrilly on the high street, went on for an intolerably long time, to die off in the tension of anticlimax. Sloane glanced up to see nothing unusual, but Jannings merely sat and tore a loose thread off a button of his overcoat before going on with a shrug. 'My father worked in the Comintern, in the Praesidium. At first he was as you might say a political apprentice at the large profession and then a master tradesman. He learned Russian, though German was still the official language of the Comintern, but still he dreamed only one dream. He was high enough in the Party to receive special permissions, and in 1941 he entreated his permission to join the Red Army. He fought the Nazis again, all the way back from Minsk to the edge of Moscow and then forward again across the burned world to Berlin. He became an *oberst* – I think you would say a colonel, perhaps a high major. He was a remarkable man. He resigned the Red Army in 1945 and worked for the Party again, the German Party. He died only a year ago at seventy-four.'

Jannings faltered and fell silent for a moment. 'He was a quiet man, serious and honest but not warm. He was not proud of me. My life has gone into a dreary cul-de-sac – he could see it as I could. I would not accept help from above, but I could not do very much by myself.' Once again he made his wheeze of deep, quiet contempt. 'It isn't a great thing. One can make contributions in any small way, and he did not reject me or blame me, but he was not proud. That is all. Last year I found out a terrible thing: when your father dies, you are not yourself any longer. You are much smaller and alone.' He stirred heavily, avoiding Sloane's eyes. 'My career fades down to rubbish and dies. Life is like one of your capitalist banks: when it starts to rain, they take away your rubber shoes.'

Sloane could see how close to despair he was. He was hunched over, dried out, grey as cooked meat. Everyone broke in a different way, Sloane thought. Jannings's shoulders rocked slowly in the darkness.

'My father is a hero many times over; the son now a traitor. A filthy anecdote to tell the young Party cadets.'

'Hold on, man.'

Jannings stood up, clutching the strap of the flight bag with both hands. 'We will meet again in hell.'

He rushed away into the night, a stocky figure in a dark overcoat that flapped around his ankles, a cry of pain fleeing into an empty world.

★

Cutter stood with his back to the office, glaring out into the mist at a pitted statue of a medieval knight that gathered grime between the third-storey windows of a Victorian building across the road. The point of the broadsword had dug into the ledge at the knight's feet like a jackhammer, palms resting on the hilt, a purist chipping away the gratuitous ornamentation.

Cutter's hands were clasped in the small of his back. When he spoke it was in the soft dangerous voice that Downs had to strain to hear.

'Tell the Acolytes to locate the woman. *Locate*, but not pick her up yet.'

'You t-take his threat seriously then?' Downs asked.

He turned, his eyes burning with malice, and Downs could see the stained gauze bandage on his cheek. 'I t-t-take him seriously,' Cutter mimicked cruelly. 'He'll probably check with her tomorrow somehow. She had better feel unthreatened when he docs. Afterward, we can pick her up and stash her.'

Downs closed the stapled draft report he had been rewriting – another botched job from Di Santis downstairs, written in a language that suggested a translation of the Latin Mass sent by telegram. Even after the garbled syntax was repaired, Downs had the sense of a mind drowning in a sea of lectures from the Kansas Chamber of Commerce, gulping down quarts of a Penny Saved, Personal Initiative, and modest balanced budgets that lead to heaven – maxims with as much relevance to the world of big business and big government as to medieval romance.

'Is that necessary? He promised . . .'

'You don't back down with a man like Sloane. He's gotten away with far too much already. I'm going to run a rat up his leg.'

It was all getting too much to bear: Di Santis's earnest befuddled prose day in and day out, and now Cutter's brutality on the loose. Downs watched Cutter stare across the room toward the blank wall, and he could almost see the mind spinning out its byzantine plots. How strange to be locked inside there, Downs thought, and peering fiercely out of those eyes at a universe so convoluted with secret design that every path around you hid either a threat or an opportunity for mocking triumph. It wouldn't be a comfortable universe, he decided; even when you won, a future defeat laughed cruelly in the darkness, and the most ordinary greeting from a colleague had to be studied intensely until it revealed its sinister purpose. The worst of it would be the constant sense of being lost, of a world that held no pattern except conspiracy, where nothing could be indifferent to you, yet you could not quite penetrate the mystery. He shuddered slightly at the thought.

'I l-liked Sloane,' Downs announced with a tiny thrill of defiance.

Cutter glared at him as if he were mad.

★

The clouds had thinned out to the south, and the sun's disk hung low and cool above the trees like a china plate seen through gauze. A hint of tree shadow blurred across the perfect circle of close-cropped grass and, the peg relocated, the goat now grazed on the outer margin of the garden where table legs had left matted yellow imprints in the green. Sarah smoothed the cotton skirt over her knees and rested her hands on the chipped white paint of the table. Despite the cold air that rose up her skirt, she tried to pretend somewhere deep inside that it was summer. The mist would disappear soon. A summer outing, a drive through the Sussex countryside, then a stop for a bite at a garden pub. Other people seemed to enjoy weekend outings; suddenly she promised with great intensity that she would too, if only things worked out for Jeffrey. She made this arrangement with the God of Bargains she had known so long ago: I will give up sweets for Lent and You will let me pass the 11-plus; just make Sandi stop teasing and I will be kind to mother forever. Just let Jeffrey get through this, she thought now, and I will be happy and make him happy. It's only a trick, turning up the corners of your mouth, caring about small things. Why did the feelings attached to things keep changing? she demanded. A child's laugh outside the house in the morning brought calm and a sense of gaiety; in the afternoon, anxiety and dread. Things had no fixed centre.

He came down the steps from the pub carrying a metal tray with two drinks. She had watched him intently ever since he had walked in from the bus stop beyond the disused train station, making a great effort to be cheerful and not altogether succeeding.

'Lager and lime,' he said. 'Old times.'

She took a glass from the tray and watched him through the amber summer drink. 'Your breezy mood is a trifle precarious,' she said carelessly. She hadn't meant to say it; she knew she risked throwing them into gloom, but some demon had always forced her to voice her observations, as if, kept hidden, they would be revealed against her will to embarrass her. *Your death honesty*, Felicity had called it.

'A bit,' he said, his voice guarded. He sat. 'How's your mood doing?'

'Adrenalin is a new experience for me.' She took his hand, as if to apologize. 'It's odd. I find sometimes it focuses me. I'm not saying I enjoy it,' she added quickly.

'I hope I put them off you. You and Felicity managed a hell of a getaway. I'm impressed. Where are you staying now?'

In his broken way, he was guiding her off into concrete detail, diverting her thoughts, trying to be light and smooth again. She acquiesced in it. 'The Black Boy Inn near Cuckfield.'

'Isn't that just down the road from the hospital?'

Their eyes met in a shared memory. 'This pub isn't so far either, is it?' she said.

'Two unhappy people sneaking away . . . to be unhappy together.' He smiled gently.

'I was quite impressed with you, you know. I don't know how I forgot all that. My American Sam Spade who knew how to open locked gates with a hairpin. At first I thought you were one of the doctors and your attentions were all a subtle part of my therapy: letting poor Sarah believe someone cared for her so she'd snap out of her agonizing. You always seemed too tough to be . . . in there.'

'But later you knew better,' he suggested.

'I never learned much about you, did I?'

'You didn't ask much,' he said.

Sipping her drink, she nodded sadly. 'And I imagine my eyes glazed over when you talked about yourself. I'm sorry. It wasn't by choice, please understand. My thoughts just wheeled round and round, obsessed with me. It's this . . . it's rather a paralysis of pride, always watching myself through others' eyes and not being able to see what's truly there: I'm not likeable, I *am* likeable.'

'I understand.'

She took his hand in both of hers. 'I love you, Jeffrey. *You*, not some false image of you. You mustn't try to be what you can't be. We'll make it come out right. I know we can.'

'We will.'

'But will you be able to do what you have to?'

'It's all arranged,' he said, and he was suddenly far away from her somewhere, his calm fraying. 'It should only be a day or two now. There's really no danger.'

'How can I ring you in London if I have to? The house never answers.'

'I'm staying somewhere else, just a hotel, but I can't give you a number.'

She could see that there was something he wasn't telling her. Quite abruptly he had become more deliberate, the way he always did when he was preparing a polite evasion of something unpleasant. She wondered how he had ever lied to professional spies. The change had come at the mention of the house, and she wondered if there was another woman staying there. (And all to the good if he had found someone for a time – she knew she had been a poor companion lately.) She rejected the suspicion as unworthy. All the same, there was something hidden.

'We'll do this,' he said. 'Do you remember the mynah bird in Clissold Park?'

'My favourite animal in all London.'

'I'm sorry to make it so complicated, but I think it's best. If you need to reach me, tie a piece of string to the fence outside his cage. I'll check the fence every day. If I find your string, we'll meet at eight that night. Outside the big umbrella shop. You know, the one in New Oxford Street.'

'You really are frightened, aren't you?'

'A little. It'll be over in a few days. Over for good. Drink up. You can drop me at the station in Hayward's Heath. There's a 1.15 to London.'

'You don't usually talk in fragments,' she said, giving his hand another squeeze.

★

'Mother of God, my ass is sore. *And* I'm hungry. *And* I'm cold as a brass tit.' By heaving his paunch from left to right, Howard Mackey managed to resettle himself in the passenger seat.

The Chevrolet was backed up a small farm lane between hedgerows of dry blackberry vine that hung sparsely on the rusted metal grate of the fencing. Across ploughed fields to the B road, they could see the mock Tudor front of the Black Boy Inn against maple skeletons, silent as a grazing cow in the afternoon. Mackey fussed with the radio, tuning away from the 'My Word' game show on Radio 4.

'*And* this intellectual crap makes me want to puke. You'd think a whole country could crank up one decent radio station.'

Di Santis wasn't quite sure what Mackey considered a decent radio station; perhaps one that broadcast a steady run of track results and Dixieland music. Di Santis himself had been enjoying the sophisticated word play and those remarkable ad lib anecdotes that always circled back so glibly to strange set phrases. It dismayed him that someone somewhere had that easy a command of the language, and he wished he had some of it himself. Downs's blue pencil work on his summaries continually shamed him, particularly since he had to admit to himself, despite all his protesting, that the reports were improved.

'You're a hun, Howie. This is the homeland of our culture.'

'Fuck *that*. You know what Goering said about that? "When I hear the word *culture* I reach for my pistol." There was a dude who knew a thing or two. Just had some bad friends.'

Mackey undoubtedly didn't like country inns either, but Di Santis knew just what this one would look like inside with its dark beams low overhead, decorated with odd pieces of brass horse tackle, and he pined secretly for all the history his own young country had denied him. Some day soon he would bring Carol and the children down here for the weekend.

'That's it! That's it!' Mackey cried suddenly, jabbing his fat finger against the windscreen. A red Triumph had pulled off the road below them, parking at the neat border of whitewashed stones under the windows. 'J reg, just like Crabb said,' Mackey added, his eyes now pressed hard to the binoculars.

'Then it must be her,' Di Santis said. Across the field, he could see a slim pale woman unfold herself from the small car. 'Long dark hair – she look about thirty-five?'

'Could be. Not much tit.'

'When we're sure she's staying, go down and phone the office.'

'You want *me* to walk down there?' Mackey protested.

'We can't take a chance on her seeing the car. An Impala doesn't exactly blend into the landscape.'

'It must be a fucking mile.'

'If it's over 300 yards . . .' Di Santis couldn't think of a quip anywhere near as clever as the ones the radio contestants had tossed off so casually, and the sentence hung dismally until he killed it of. 'The walk won't bite you.'

★

It was what they called a stopping train, and he sat heavily through the halts at the dreamlike country stations with their tidy brick waiting rooms: Balcombe, Salfords. As the empty rolling downs that separated him from London gradually fell away, the ancient folly of peace *out there*, in unspoiled nature, began to withdraw before the anxious gloom of the city that he knew rolled toward him, massively unseen, like fate. Another part of him had become alert to a sharper danger that crept close . . . very close, but he made no move that would have acknowledged its presence.

Finally London began its stealthy approach, first its outlying pickets of stucco estates at road lay-bys, then the aloof grey houses of the outer suburbs that spread up shallow hills trailing their gardens like ragged trains. The buildings huddled closer and closer together, spreading over the earth like magma until they were solid islands of terraced cliffs, and trees were only hinted on a distant rise.

The train squealed to a stop at the long Croydon platform and a half dozen passengers stepped off. It was only a short run now to Victoria. He couldn't remember for certain, but he thought there were three more stops. A shrill hand-whistle sounded down the platform and an old man in blue walked the length of the train, slamming doors one after another. The danger was there, breathing on him, as the carriage lurched and started forward. Not yet, he thought. He hadn't stirred for some time, and he slumped back on the plaid seat, only his eyes alive. Not yet. The nearest window drew alongside a young woman walking on the platform, paced her, and gradually pulled ahead. Not yet. Pulled faster. Almost . . .

Sloane leapt to his feet and slammed down the window, fumbling with the latch that was placed absurdly on the outside of the door. The door snapped open against the train's momentum, and he jumped. He kept his balance with a short run along the platform and came to a stop, watching the train pass.

'Here sir! You mustn't alight like that!' An old rail guard bustled officiously toward him, wagging a long finger, but Sloane's eyes were fixed on the accelerating train. In one of the coach windows he saw the face of a small dark man, staring expressionlessly back at him.

★

Ross was bustled forward by the crush leaving Customs into the funneling barriers of the arrivals room, and his old suitcase prodded the tweed skirt of a woman ahead of him. A lot of tight wavy hair flashed across his vision and he heard, 'I *beg* your pardon', in a voice that could have frozen the Bahamas.

'Nothing personal,' he murmured, driven by weariness to an edge of sarcasm.

The hair swirled away again, and he was pressed forward, skirting the bored men holding their cardboard signs – *Mattis Coach Tours, Mr L. B. Holmes, Excursion des filles catholiques romaines* – past embracing families and children on tip-toe. It should have been Jerry Moore making his way out of Heathrow, but they had argued it out bitterly and Moore had won in the end; Moore had a family, Moore had a cast-iron appointment for his yearly CI debriefing, and Moore had no experience at all overseas. So Ross had given in, and God help the Old Man if the scheme blew up and someone tried to sandbag him at the Langley end.

'Harvey Ross, I'll be damned. I'll be double-damned.' Kohler detached himself from the wall and raised one arm, almost a fascist salute over the crowd. An open-necked blue shirt under a camel coat, neatly creased khaki slacks; it made Ross feel seedy in his tired brown Sears suit, but he would never have challenged Kohler to a preppy contest.

'I was expecting an exalted personage named Jerome Moore III. Not a new office name by any chance?'

'*Shut up*, man.'

Kohler rattled on amiably. 'I haven't seen you since – hell, it was the great tunnel caper in Berlin, wasn't it?'

'Guy, for Christ sake – '

Kohler just laughed. 'This is the free world, man, not Langley. No microphones hidden in the olives. Relax. I've got a car.'

Ross followed him out to a dark blue Lincoln with CD plates, waiting on the no-parking stripes with a chauffeur in front. Everything but flags on the fenders to attract attention, Ross thought irritably, and he glanced around with automatic caution, though he knew there was no way he could have recognized danger. In the game he played now, danger would come in a smile and a handshake. As like as not, he would be riding next to it in the back seat.

'Back to the office,' Kohler ordered as they climbed in. 'Unless our headhunter wants the grand tour?'

'No thank you.'

'The office then. I've set you up a room near mine, desk, phones, sharing a secretary – though if there really isn't a Jerome Moore III, I'm going to take back my Daumier prints. I thought a real aristocrat might appreciate them.'

'You can take it all back.'

'What does that mean?'

'I won't be sitting around in Mayfair.'

'Bite the grindstone and nose to the bullet. Sounds like the fur is going to fly in our cloak and dagger world.'

The car slid noiselessly up the tunnel that passed under the north runway and headed along the feeder road to the M4. 'The first thing I want to do is speak to Sparrow,' Ross said with studied calm. 'In person. I want to know exactly what Lumbago is doing.'

'Huh-oh. Sharpen your hatchet, Jerome – you don't mind if I call you Jerome? Good for security, you know. Sparrow lost the man about three hours ago in Croydon.'

'Wonderful,' Ross said drily. West London fanned out as they rose onto the motorway, and he could see a plume of smoke where something burned far away, like a signal of cold greeting from someone who would rather he were elsewhere. The Abortionist has arrived, Ross thought. That was what he was now. The seed had taken, and it had grown into God knows what deformity while the local doctors wrung their hands and paced. They would lead him to the victim and stand aside, clumsy, puzzled, malicious, while the Abortionist did the cutting.

11

By evening a chilly fog had closed in on London, and navigating on foot became a nightmare: the road names were fixed to the sides of buildings fifteen feet in the air, up where a nineteenth-century coachman sitting on his hansom could read them easily, but far less convenient for a six-foot-one pedestrian in a dense fog who did not know Notting Hill very well and had to leave the tube station, find the correct road angling away to the left, of the three that angled away to the left, and then count off two cross streets before turning. Miraculously Sloane found his way to the gardens with only a short detour, and he continued slowly along the black railings, watching the iron arrowpoints take shape ahead of him, one after another, and touching the wet metal now and again to remind himself there was physical substance in the world. He was in a stationary cave in the fog, and it was London that turned under his feet to carry the fenceposts and a hint or two of trees past him. The city was silent beyond the cave; it might have been abandoned for centuries.

They hadn't agreed on a side of the gardens, and for a moment, in his mind's eye, Sloane saw the two of them circling the long rectangle for hours, keeping to opposite sides, always out of sight of each other. They had already missed two fallback times, and it was a minute or two past the third. He was about to turn and try a circuit counter-clockwise when he noticed the slight thickening ahead.

'*Guten abend*,' Sloane called softly.

'*Ja, ja*,' came back out of the fog. The voice had no energy, no spark of emotion. Jannings slowly gathered shape moving toward him. He turned and leaned forward against the railing, oblivious to the condensation he was pressing against his coat. 'I must tell you directly. I did not do it, I couldn't do it. Not today.'

His thumbs rubbed the spearpoints, then the hands gripped like hams.

'Tomorrow then.'

'Tomorrow,' he said; it sounded almost like a question. 'It is not a simple thing to arrange to work late. I had to pretend I had lost my draft of a technical manual we need badly. Tomorrow, I thought, when I have not finished rewriting it, they will not think it odd that I stay.'

'That sounds good.'

'Tonight I must take something to sleep. I must sleep. I cannot go any further without sleep. Nor have I the strength to go down to see Rosemary. I owe her at least a telephone call, but I cannot do it. Ah, *scheisse*.'

'And Karn?'

'Fine, thank you. With a friend at Cambridge.'

There was so little life in him that Sloane wondered if he was going to be able to do it at all. 'I promise it'll be over, Werner. I'll see to it. No more demands, for either of us.'

'Jeffrey . . .' Jannings started to speak from his own world, far away, then shook his head heavily. 'Tomorrow night, here, same arrangement.'

'What were you going to say?'

'It doesn't matter.'

'We were friends once. What is it?'

Jannings looked upward as if he could see something hovering overhead. There was nothing there but the air grown dense, with what light there was so evenly diffused that they might have been standing at the bottom of a fouled aquarium. 'Karn was raised near Eisleben, which is Luther's birthplace. The East is Luther's country, you know? The first obstinate Bolshevik of them all. I read his journals after the war to practise my exile's German. Luther said, "Be a sinner and strong in your sins, but be stronger in your faith." I don't think anyone could accuse my life of having been strong in either.'

Sloane was momentarily alarmed to hear Jannings talk of himself in the past tense. Or was it just a quirk of his English?

'I should not see Rosemary again. Would you give her this for me, or send it . . . when this is all over.' He handed Sloane an envelope. 'It is just money and a feeble apology. She is a sweet girl. But I must be clean of this mistake of mine, as clean as possible. The letter is an apology for not being stronger in my sins. It is more difficult to apologize to my faith.'

'Did Cutter's gorillas come to see you?' Sloane asked.

'In a way, yes. There was an envelope marked *personal* pushed through the letter box. What on earth makes them think Karn would not have opened it? It was another remembrance, of course.'

'A photograph?'

Jannings didn't acknowledge the question. 'One other thing . . .' Sloane saw the death mask turn toward him, and then it enlivened with the fierce determination to be understood. 'I think Komarovsky is watching. You never told him about me?'

'Never. Not a hint.'

'Today he walks slowly through the office and watches me strangely. Perhaps not just me, but I am in his eyes for certain. I think he knows something. I don't know what. Watch over yourself.'

'Thanks.' Sloane had a feeling that he had to speak now or the opportunity would never come again. 'Werner . . .' he began and faltered. There were no words adequate to what had been done to the man. *Had been done*, Sloane thought with contempt. If he began to lie to himself through forms of speech, where would it end? *There were no words adequate to what I did to him*. He had to plunge on. 'I didn't arrange for those pictures. I was scared to death back then, and I would have done a lot of things without a second thought, but I wouldn't have done that to you. If I hadn't been the go-between, he'd have sent one of the gorillas. I think that might have been worse . . . if it could have been worse.' But how did he know he wouldn't have done it? Liar, he thought. To save yourself, to get free . . . There was nothing noble in him. *Noble* was for saints and children.

Jannings turned and began to fade.

'Tomorrow night,' Sloane called after him, and it was like shooting him in the back.

'Oh, yes . . . tomorrow night,' Jannings echoed softly, as if he had forgotten. Then the fog swallowed him completely.

It was the classic whine, he thought: *someone else would have*. Even the guards who turned on the gas in the showers said it. For a moment he wished he could trade places with Jannings and be the innocent party, be free at least of the weight of guilt, but immediately he recalled the dismaying inert eyes and the sluggish movements drifting out of the mist. Jannings was responding to the pressure in almost the exact opposite of the way he had, but somehow Jannings's bearing reminded him strongly of those last few hellish months before The Fall. Sloane realized he had just touched the fixed walls he had raised at the borders of his sympathy, so very gingerly, and he had drawn back. No, he would not trade places, not to save his soul.

He passed the tube station and walked dully along Notting Hill Gate, half listening for cars edging into the intersections. But none came. The street would become Bayswater Road and carry him eventually near his hotel a mile away. He shivered. The sodium lights cut small purgatories into the night, and there wasn't another living thing in the universe.

★

'Would you prefer a more comfortable chair, sir?' the young policeman enquired. He was like a boy trying to ingratiate himself with a friend of his grown-up brother. 'We could liberate one from the next office.'

'This one's fine,' Ross said, glancing indifferently at the straight chair facing the upright machine on the table.

'Anything else you'll be wanting, please ring the number we've left on the blotter.'

'That'll be all, Mellish,' Macon said curtly.

'Yes, sir,' the policeman replied, glancing curiously at big brother's friend one last time before leaving the barren little office.

Still wearing his heavy topcoat, Macon strode to the tape recorder and bent stiffly to peer at the manufacturer's name. 'Phillips,' he read drily. 'There goes the balance of payments. I must send a minute to the chaps in procurement. GEC make perfectly adequate equipment in Birmingham.' He was a lanky scarecrow lost in the tweed coat, and a good foot taller than Ross, with the quiet, assured air of a man who could sleep standing up, like a horse, and still notice everything that went on around him.

As he turned, the vertical creases in his cheeks accentuated a cadaverous face, and even the tidy moustache could not rescue the face from drabness.

'It starts up automatically, voice-activated by the phones across the road once they hook in down below and run the tie. I hope that will suit you.'

'Thank you, Peter.' Ross wiped his forehead. Even here, freezing his ass off in the unheated office that they had commandeered, his sweat glands wouldn't call it quits. 'I know it wasn't the simplest request.'

Macon offered a thin smile. 'You might say. Indeed. I've gone this far in the light of old friendship, *and* because I knew you'd have a flutter on your own if I didn't do so. I'll be wanting a full report. I may put the superintendent into the picture, I may not.'

Now Macon prowled to the window. The fog was thinner up at the third floor, and even ten feet from the windows Ross could make out the glow of a bank of windows on the other side of Charing Cross. The tiny room where Macon and Ross stood, borrowed from Plymouth Union Assurance, Ltd., was lit by a single fluorescent outside in the hall.

It was remarkable how quickly the insurance company had moved one of their top managers out of his office, Ross thought. He wished they had that sort of co-operation at home. Peter Macon was Deputy Superintendent of Special Branch, technically a section of the London Police but in fact Britain's civil counterintelligence service. In theory, each regional and city police department and each local Special Branch was a separate entity, and Macon's office on the Broadway side of New Scotland Yard was simply a unit of the London Metropolitan Police. But then in theory, Britain was a monarchy, and the Queen appointed the prime minister. One of the great advantages, Ross thought, of having an unwritten constitution. That could be bent to serve. In reality, Peter Macon's computer registry stored information on more than a quarter of the adult population of the United Kingdom – excepting only Northern Ireland, which was watched by an even more awesome computer system run by the Army at Lisburn. Ross had briefly been counterintelligence officer, London, in the early seventies, and Macon had been his 'opposite number', as he would have put it.

144

'In other circumstances,' the dark figure murmured, 'I think I should be inclined to offer you the hint of an explanation. If the roles were reversed, that is, you see.'

The oblique request was so characteristic of the man that Ross smiled. 'I'm sure your boys downstairs are hooking their own tap onto this tap.'

Macon chuckled without turning away from the window. 'That wouldn't necessarily put us in the picture, the entire picture, would it? After all, the Branch has beavered around quite a bit to accommodate you.'

'Or you have, privately.'

'Let's say "officially, but off the record", shall we? If this comes a cropper, I'm not terribly keen to be out there all alone. *And* in the dark. Do you follow me?'

'I do pretty well on the short words.'

'Let me surmise. The Civil Overseas Research Organization, a branch of the United States Attorney General's Office and once a large and reasonably efficient intelligence organization, but now . . . let us say a stagnant pool, with no official authorization to conduct even a surveillance, has slipped the lead and decided for whatever reason to get up to some mischief here in London. Am I warm, Harvey? You could just stamp your foot if you like.'

Ross laughed. 'Yes, no, and maybe.'

'The question is, who is their target and why? And why does it worry you so?'

'We're not sure,' Ross lied. 'It might be the Chinese Mission up on Portland Place.'

Now Macon turned and watched him. 'Bit of freelance aggro against the Chinese? That won't wash. If you really suspected that, you'd be having us throw an armed cordon around the mission to protect them. You and the People's Republic are quite chummy these days, aren't you?' He sighed. 'Of course, we don't even know whether you want to stop Research or want them to succeed.'

'I'm watching. I don't plan to intervene. I imagine you will be watching, too. I promise a complete report as soon as I've tied it all up.'

'I thought the expression was "doctored it all up". I never can keep up with American colloquialisms, you see.'

'You do all right, old boy,' Ross said.

'I'll be out of your hair. Anything we can do, any little service, be sure and give us a ring.'

'I'll just speak into the table leg,' Ross said, but Macon was no longer amused, and he marched stiffly out of the office.

When he had gone, Ross studied the machinery he had been provided with, a large open-reel tape recorder wired to a telephone. Plus a second, normal telephone – or relatively normal. As he traced the wires back to the receptacle at the base of the wall, he heard a brief false ring on one of the telephones and a click as the reel jerked forward an inch and stopped; he guessed they had just completed the tap into the Research line. Tomorrow, if he decided Kohler could be trusted, he would ask for a relief man. But tonight, after his brief seven-hour day crossing the Atlantic, his body told him it was still early and he could probably make it to morning. It was odd, he thought, that the only man he dared trust in all London wasn't even one of his countrymen. And even Macon would be a doubtful commodity once he learned what was happening.

★

Off the main road and away from the lights, the fog darkened, and he felt he was plunging forward through the foliage of a phantom jungle that melted and reformed around him, never touching him with anything but its clammy breath. Only a distant hee-haw siren reminded him that there was a city out there somewhere, a few feet away. He stumbled against a traffic bollard with its light out, and at last he saw the entrance of the Orsett Guest House. Through the glass door, the small lobby was like the cabin of a liner, bright and safe. He had been planning to change hotels, but on a night like this no one could possibly have tailed him, and he knew he could slip in and out at will.

The old porter bobbed up and glanced at him as he came in, one of those wizened Englishmen broken by a lifetime of servility. He had wrapped himself in a dark afghan against the cold. 'Sir, thank you, sir; your key, sir.' The porter slid the key and paddle across the counter before settling back to sleep.

Sloane picked up the key, but sat in a fraying armchair facing the blank television rather than going up immediately. Something felt unfinished. The lobby was unheated, and a sinister wisp of fog curled along the rust-coloured rug from the foot of the bay window. He closed his eyes, weary of suppressed rage, of guilt, of so much caution and deception. He missed Sarah terribly. In a day or two, he reminded himself, it would be over and they could rebuild. If only he knew what to rebuild. Which Sloane would appear out of the far end of the madness this time? The whole passive and retiring persona had been so precarious that a single gust had blown it away.

Perhaps he would emerge seamless this time, cunning and corrupt like so many of them, a cool user. But as he considered it, he found it impossible, at some level, not to believe in people. Jannings, Sarah, even poor Downs were redeemed for him by the integrity of their weaknesses. Strange, he thought, that his own weaknesses still reproached him; but then, not strange, since he knew how cruel and dishonest they were. He longed for a simple stammer and a genuine lifelong timidity, even a helpless, preoccupied depression. They did no damage to others.

He took Jannings's envelope out of his coat. It was a standard brown envelope, neatly lettered to Rosemary Beccles with her house number on Effra Parade, Brixton. Sloane had never met her, but he had certainly seen her photograph, taken through the front window of what must have been a basement flat. And he had seen her twice in the flesh, but at a distance, when he had been told to follow Jannings and oversee a brush contact: once near the panda enclosure at the zoo, and again in Kew Gardens. Outdoors and fully clothed, though still pale, she had seemed almost matronly, not at all the fragile girl with the arched bony back who grappled in that unappealing way with Jannings on the sofa.

Something thick was wadded up inside. With a finger he tore free the weak glue on the end flap. He knew he had to open it: it was a concern he did not articulate, not even deep inside himself, the possibility skittering away shyly before he could name it and in some superstitious way bring it about. He shook out a bundle of large reddish-brown ten-pound notes, folded once over. There were seventy of them. Seven hundred pounds was quite a lot on Jannings's salary, with a family to support; it was probably all of his savings. The letter was a single page, handwritten in the same careful round hand as the address.

Dear liebchen,

No, I must call you Rosemary now and not draw upon our store of happy memories. You know I have too blunt a personality to try to make this flowery and – (A word was scratched out zealously, and *less harsh* written above it.) *It is finished now. We both knew from the beginning that it would not have a long future, but I hoped and hoped that some miracle would prolong the happiest times of my life, even if they came only in moments we took like thieves. This is too artificial now and becomes dishonest. We enjoyed each other, but now some men know about us and have made it impossible to go on. You often complained that there were some things I said that you did not understand. It was concerning these men that I spoke, they are my enemies.*

This is the simple truth. I am not bravely saving you pain or rediscovering loyalty to Karn. I am sick to death for myself and by the time you read this I will have gone home. (Gone home? Sloane thought. What did he mean?) *I feel two hundred years old, like one of those old spectators-of-life in the corners of the pubs that you laughed about. It is the way it must be; I can do no other.*

Sloane heard the echoes of Luther in the phrase. And he remembered: 'Be a sinner and strong in your sins, but be stronger in your faith.'

I am sorry about sending money, or if you choose, about sending so little, but please believe it is only a form of a wish from me to aim you toward a life that can be better for you and more permanent. I can't go on – (Here the ink changed quality and Sloane guessed a pen had died and Jannings had begun again with another.) *– writing any longer. I will miss you, and will never dare look at spring irises again. You made me very happy.*

– Werni

Sloane refolded the letter and slipped it back into its envelope with the money. He sat for a long time staring at the dead television screen, and though Jannings's words haunted him it was not primarily because of what they said. He could not quite find it in his heart to see high tragedy in the end of a love affair that had been doomed from the first. (Have you grown so callous, he thought. Suppose this were you, writing to Sarah? But it

148

wasn't, couldn't have been.) It was something else that he had suspected for some time: deep down, the affair was a counterfeit of something else for Jannings. Not that Jannings didn't genuinely care for the young seamstress he had met by accident on Brighton Pier. Sloane was sure he did, but he was sure, too, that she had come to represent something far larger than Jannings may even have acknowledged to himself. On her own, frightened by the world, an early school-leaver without prospects, clutching her sentimental toys and scrimping pennies to buy sugar for her tea – some part of Jannings must certainly have been looking at all the world's poor, at the decent, put-upon working class, even at the brave street fighters against the Nazis and the long battle march from Moscow to Berlin; one poor girl's needs and affection forced to stand in for a whole life of service and self-respect that Jannings had been unable to build so as to mirror his father's. Sloane could sense the larger loss in the letter. By leaving her, he was *settling* – the way dregs settle in a coffee cup – slamming the door on his last emotional comfort, no matter how spurious. That was what worried him: the dry, washed-out tone of the letter and what it meant in terms of Jannings's doom-heavy soul.

I will have gone home. What could he mean? The trade mission certainly wouldn't let him go so suddenly. Perhaps he was giving her the comfort and finality of a definite break, something she couldn't challenge; keeping her from telephoning or coming to find him. Or did *home* have a special meaning for them? Emotional poverty, that place where we both grew up and where we both belong?

Sloane found he was more tired than he thought. Straining on his arms, he pushed himself heavily out of the chair. The porter snored, half out of his afghan, and somewhere in the building a radio played an old dance tune that he recognized but couldn't name. Threadbare carpet left the lobby and ran up the middle of the steps like a long, limp tongue that crumpled under the carpet rods, and the floral wallpaper on the landings, peeled back at the skirting board, thick as steel plate with dozens of layers. The second 3 of the 33 on his door was loose and hung askew.

Inside he checked his watch and sat on the bed wearily, rolling his neck with the tension. The action took his eyes to the bedside table, and what he saw there made him stiffen. An unopened bottle of Russian vodka sat pushed against the wall; not one of the export bottles that you could buy in the fancier off-licences, but with a label entirely in Cyrillic lettering. A tag hung off the neck of the bottle, and Sloane reached out for it in the dim light.

Been missing you
Write more often
K

He stared at the note for a long time with apprehension, and then rose and hurried downstairs to the pay phone on the first landing.

12

As the ringing sounded on the line, he imagined the echoes making their way through the four rooms of the Notting Hill flat. He had only been to the flat once, and his imagination simplified the layout of the rooms, transforming them surreptitiously into his childhood apartment 4,000 miles away in Flint. His mind saw a green plastic kitchenette in a left-hand ell instead of an alcove with its Danish china cupboard, a door opening on the long wall of the front room rather than a narrow vista back to the kitchen. He tried to imagine where Jannings sat or lay in those rooms and why he chose not to answer. Certainly not out, not even to the pub on a night like this. He had said he needed to take something to sleep, and perhaps he was fast asleep across the bed, or on the low sofa. But another possibility rose again as a foreboding without taking on form. A full minute later Sloane hung up.

The desk porter was still snoring as he hurried through the lobby. Outside, the fog had begun to break up, ribbons slicing apart on a building scaffold across the road, as the whole mass flowed past like a syrup sliding downhill. He felt the west wind that was driving the fog bank down the Thames basin toward the Straits of Dover. A clearing wind would simplify finding the pistol, he thought.

A day earlier the boarded-up row of houses on Gloucester Terrace had at first suggested a secure enough cache, but in his mood of anxiety on the way to visit The Laughing Fish he had wanted triple guarantees. Sloane slipped through the narrow break between the houses, picking his way carefully over what once must have been a treasured side garden but was now a heap of rotting wood and discarded pipe from the house, with fingers of weed fighting up through it all. A railway embankment rose at the back of the derelict garden, a tangle of shadow, and a family of hedgehogs scurried away at his approach. With his toe, he scattered the pile of broken brick to disclose the black plastic bag. When he tore the plastic and unwound the rag, he found that the pistol was damp with condensation. The trick of security had grown weaker, but it was still there. After drying the pistol on his shirt, he slid it into his coat pocket where it had begun its journey . . . how long ago? Only four days, he calculated with surprise. He realized for the first time that Cutter's house-breakers would certainly have found the empty black box when they tore his desk to pieces. Either they hadn't taken the trouble to investigate what it was or they had forgotten to warn their boss. He hoped he wouldn't have to fire it again.

A metal sign outside the Royal Oak tube station rattled with the wind, and the dim ramp inside rang with a departing train. At the turning, two bleak figures passed him coming out, an old woman carrying too many packages and a boy with his arm in a plaster cast that was in turn wrapped in a plastic bag against the rain. By some miracle, Sloane soon caught another train, and he sat anxiously – delay had always made him anxious – among a handful of shift workers who read folded *Standards* through bleary eyes or slept with their heads on valises in their laps. He wished fervently that he could join them, come home to Sarah after a day at a boring job, toss his coat onto the sofa, hear her voice calling from the back of the house . . . In three stops he got off, circled past the walled-off gypsy encampment under the flyover and headed into the dense Notting Hill streets.

The fog was gone this far west, and the wind fretted a single plane tree, stripping off the last of its leaves so that they chased past horizontally. High cloud was driven across the moon, alternately obscuring and revealing the half disk to send shadows playing against the gloomy, watchful houses. He knew his way now: the four-storey brick estate bulked up ahead like something in a Gothic romance, old and sinister despite the streamlined planes of its walkways. Sloane thought he saw a glow in the window at the end of the third-floor walkway, and he hurried up the black stairwell, trailed by the sweet odour of garbage. He's asleep on the sofa, Sloane decided. He hasn't even undressed.

He moved past brick walls chalked *QPR Rule* and *Arsenal Wankers*, stepping over a toppled tricycle. He's tucked into bed, he thought. He won't hear my knock. A television played softly somewhere. He had been right: there was a faint illumination from Jannings's window, but even with the curtain closed he could see it was too weak to come from a light in the front room. He knocked, hoping against hope to hear the grouchy, accented voice call out from within. The door felt odd, weak and yielding under his knock; and pressing his opened fingers against the wood, he felt it give. The door had been left on the latch. For Karn to return? Simple carelessness? With a single peevish whine the door opened further, and he stepped up the pressure until the warmth of the room assaulted him. A light was on in the back study.

'Werner,' he called with a guarded voice. 'Werner, it's Jeffrey.'

His palm brushed the pistol for comfort and he stepped inside, shutting the door. The sitting room was tidy and ascetic as a ship's cabin with its bleached teak furniture – Karn's taste – and there wasn't a sound from anywhere in the flat. The study door stood wide open and Sloane sighed in relief when he saw Jannings slumped forward asleep across the small desk. Now he could admit to himself the forebodings.

'Werner, damn, I had a stupid fright.'

Sloane went in and touched his shoulder gently.

Something terrible and mystifying happened to the next few minutes of his life. Much later, trying to separate what had been real from the rest, Sloane could remember for certain only the gritty feel of brushing back a lock of Jannings's dark hair from the ear, fumbling desperately for the man's carotid artery beside his Adam's apple, leaning forward heavily on both his arms as darkness swept into his mind. Later, Sloane had discovered the single sheet of notepaper crumpled into his pocket, and the paper raised the faintest recollection of wrenching it from under an arm collapsed heavily across it. One word was on the paper, *Forgive* – and no one would ever know whether it had been a request, a demand, or the start of a forlorn prayer. And then a memory of the crackling of breaking plastic; his own weight crushing an empty pill vial that had lain beside the stiff hand.

All that, he could fix his mind on with some sense of actuality. The rest was more uncertain. He had been assailed by a vision of faces gathering around him, arms gesticulating weakly to demand help. One stocky figure was more reticent than the others, almost motionless, only his eyes pleading. There were sounds too, a moan, accusing cries, they might have been wind. Sloane's heart had begun to pound erratically in the study. He set his back against the wall and sank slowly with vertigo, until he was crushed down on his heels. How long had that been? A minute? Ten? The over-hasty admission came back to haunt him: he couldn't retrieve the words . . . *I had a stupid fright*. He had anticipated this all along . . . and done nothing. Even two days earlier in Whitechapel – but certainly in the fog-dense square earlier in the evening; even more certainly in the hotel lobby reading the letter. Hindsight foresight, dimly – but surely he had known. He remembered the sentence beginning 'I can't go on' before the ink had changed. The pen hadn't run out after all; he had *known* the pen hadn't run out. Unable to stop himself, Jannings had been confessing his terminal despair, and some time later he had taken up the letter again and added the phrase that hid his intention from the girl: '. . . writing this letter'. But it couldn't hide anything from his friend, not after seeing that death mask in the fog. His own comforting words had been as empty as the night around them: *Hang on, man, it's almost over.* He had never properly gauged the depth of Jannings's remorse at treason – perhaps, he thought dully, because nothing had ever meant enough to him; he had no idea what loss of honour meant.

He was as culpable as Cutter; he had shied away from guilty knowledge, hoping as people hope in the instant before a grinding collision that everything would turn out all right. Hoping that Jannings would hurry and complete the job. Run the risk, old man, just do it quickly and save my skin.

Even now, slumped beside the body, Sloane found he carried a particle of resentment that Jannings had not photographed the file first. What difference would honour make to a dead man? And what would Cutter try to force now? Some insane midnight burglary? Grief chased the callous thoughts away. Rest in peace, Werner, he thought giddily, and I'll take care of the living. Perhaps he had been strong in his sin after all.

Abruptly the light was taken from his closed eyelids. Was it too much to hope that Jannings had come back to life and risen in his chair: a little practical joke . . . ? Sloane delayed opening his eyes, as if the longer he waited the greater the chance of a miracle. Finally, he looked. Thick spectacles glittered in the light, and a wrinkled leathery face peered down on him with harsh curiosity.

'The manner of one's sitting reveals very much about character.' Komarovsky canted his head, speaking softly to someone behind him. 'I have seen men sprawl out in insolence, their bodies open to tell you they are invulnerable. Others fidget with their nerves, or they hold themselves rigid with internal self-discipline. I have never, until tonight, seen such eloquence of self-reproach.'

'Bastards,' Sloane said, not knowing to whom it was directed.

'This? You don't believe for a minute I caused this. I do not send poor broken men to fight my wars.'

The old Russian seated himself on the edge of a leather ottoman, bulking over Sloane. Sloane noticed the second man across the room, waiting alertly near the door in a dark, badly cut overcoat, an ageless figure with a face as hard and self-contained as a professional soldier's. There was a third as well, little older than a boy. The third felt his pockets restlessly, looking lost and frightened. Wordlessly, Komarovsky held up a photograph for Sloane: a photograph he had seen more times than he wanted, and he hardly glanced at the girl who wrestled awkwardly against the man. He knew the man was caught in the act of saying something light and teasing, his brows playful as Sloane had never seen them in life. *In life*.

'It is a remarkable coincidence that you two should know each other. I believe you are familiar with this piece of indecency as well.' He flipped it over to look at it himself. 'Not so very much by the decadent standards of Gerrard Street, but I believe it could be valuable to the right person. I suspect it has already proven quite valuable.'

Komarovsky gestured. The soldier glided forward to feel in Sloane's pockets. He dug out the pistol with a low whistle.

'We have a regular George Smiley here,' Komarovsky said, craning his neck to look at the pistol. 'A Walther,' he murmured, as if cataloguing the find. 'Expensive, but too complicated to be truly reliable, like so many German machines, and with an imbecile indicator pin and a safety that causes more heart attacks

155

than the cold war. Where would you obtain such a thing, I wonder.'

The soldier dropped the pistol into his overcoat and retreated.

'Shall we discuss this problem we have?' Komarovsky prompted. 'You have been disappeared a long time.'

'You and Cutter should discuss it,' Sloane said without emotion. 'I carried his papers to you and your papers to him. You both knew that you both knew. Who got cheated is your business.'

Komarovsky's face livened with a faint smile. 'And discredit to him who is the least clever master. Yes, that is a risk of double games, but then you never told me that this poor comrade was also a player. A Negro in the woodpile, is that the idiom?'

The old Russian held the photo out at arm's length, apparently unable to focus up close. 'This blurred line to the side must be a curtain. Remarkable how small an opening one needs for a photograph. Did you arrange for this?'

'No!' Sloane said vehemently.

'Such indignation. I suppose it is not your style, but that is plainly irrelevant. You westerners have quaint ideas of responsibility.' He canted his head again. 'Lev Davidovich, I want you to listen to this,' and to Sloane: 'The young comrade is our commissar of moral issues. Listen to me now. A long time ago, we crushed the German tank Army at Kursk. It was the greatest tank battle ever in history and the true turn of the war. I was there, leading seven T-34s so new they had no paint, but there were thousands of other tanks and millions of us soldiers. It was a moment of greatness for all of us.

'Afterward, we captured many. There were common soldiers, intelligence officers, *panzerjagers*, cooks, Gestapo torturers, even regular Army chaplains. Some of the prisoners we took were SS, but most were regular Army. If I asked you, you would say that the Gestapo and perhaps the SS were truly guilty and the others should be spared, but you did not witness Novosti before or after. Or many other places they had been. Their regime shot every member of the Communist Party they captured, they looted villages and set up a terrible empire in the occupied territory where all Russians were made a sort of slave. In the division of work, the cook and chaplain and the private soldier made the torturer possible, and where was the responsibility? Even the Gestapo was made of stupid little men. The whole group machine did these things. Who is guilty?

'Oh, yes, we executed the torturers without compunction and we spared the others, especially the foot soldiers who were ordinary workers. We too still carry some of your quaint values. But we knew that did not settle the matter.' Now Komarovsky's voice was burning, though Sloane was hardly listening. He desperately needed to get away from the persistent voice, to some place where he could think clearly.

'There was a question of *causes*, not guilt, and when we got to Berlin we tried to set up a system that could not again give rise to such a group machine. We tried, perhaps we made mistakes, but that attempt is the point. To prevent – to find a historical force that is responsible and destroy it for all time. To punish individuals is merely indulging your petty revenge.'

He turned to the boy who fidgeted in the doorway. 'Lev Davidovich, tell me, do you think there is a difference between a man who takes this picture and a man who makes use of it? Come, your satire deals with questions of moral truth.'

The boy studied the old man with a wary earnestness. 'I don't think so, sir. Fundamentally. There may be a small difference if the user is being blackmailed himself.'

Sloane was unable to find much difference himself – his heated disavowal had left a bad taste in his mouth – but he was not thinking of abstract questions now. He needed to find a way to get away from Komarovsky, to make some kind of peace with Cutter and save Sarah and himself from the madness.

'You see, even we will sometimes think this way. By all means, retain your sense of innocence if you wish.'

Komarovsky signed with his finger, and the soldier picked up the flight bag from a chair and handed it to the old man. He reached in and dug out the circuit reader, trussed up in its wire yoke. 'How long has your friend had this?'

'He didn't use it,' Sloane said quickly. 'I don't think he would have. He wanted desperately not to betray.'

'I asked, how long has he had it?'

'Two days.'

'Not two years?'

'I think it's just been developed. You can check that.'

'We will. Come, we will go somewhere peaceful for a longer discussion.'

Komarovsky stood. Sloane felt himself lifted by the soldier, who made a more thorough examination of his pockets. The brown envelope was lifted out of his inner coat pocket.

'Don't take that!' Sloane cried out.

Komarovsky walked with it to the desk lamp, and read the address on the envelope, then slid out the money and the letter. His bushy eyebrows rose slightly as he counted the notes and he read the letter twice without a sign of emotion.

Where Sloane stood, he could not help looking at Jannings, tumbled forward across the writing surface like a rag doll beside the Russian. Already forgotten, he thought, already so little beside the consequences of his living acts – his letter, Komarovsky's memory of his lies about overtime, a girl's anachronistic love, not even aware yet . . . Before the vertigo could take hold again, Sloane turned away from the desk.

'Please,' he said. 'He meant it for her. She has nothing to do with this. She's just a seamstress in a sweatshop, and I don't think he ever told her where he works.'

Komarovsky tucked the envelope into his pocket with a frown. 'So why did *you* open it?'

It was a question he couldn't answer, not even to himself, without admitting too much to explain, too much to bear. He had done nothing to prevent it. Sloane shrugged.

'Come with us,' Komarovsky said, and when Sloane held back: 'We will not hurt you. Your comic books have exaggerated ideas of our methods. It is your people who export torture machines to Chile.'

'That's not Research,' Sloane said dully.

'Only for lack of funds. CIA are half-wits; Research are impoverished quarter-wits.'

He felt a hand circle his arm above the elbow, like an iron manacle, and they walked out of the flat and down the steps, three silent crows with a fledgling hopping behind. The moonlight was startling as they emerged from the stairway, and the wind tore at them. With the cloud cover gone, the meagre stored warmth of the earth had escaped into the atmosphere, and it was bitterly cold. A dark Mercedes waited in the access lane. A sudden gust ripped the back door out of the boy's hand.

★

'I'm sure she's inside the inn,' the petulant voice insisted. 'Her light went out half an hour ago.'

'Stay there.'

'It's cold and cramped. Let us get a room somewhere.'

'Stay there, you idiot. Sleep in shifts in the back seat. The Impala is large enough for ten of you. Or two of *you*.' Here there was a sarcastic belly laugh.

The phone clicked off and Ross ran the tape forward another few inches before switching the machine back on to automatic. It had been his second replay of the brief call that had come in just after midnight, and he was almost certain now that the blustery hostile voice was Cutter's, carrying just a hint of that nondescript Southern accent so universal in the military. He had heard the voice a few times, many years earlier, a contentious bray requesting – no – demanding liaison for some crackpot scheme he had proposed, while Research was still riding high enough to think of itself as a sister service. Ancient history.

The other voice, simpering down the line, didn't matter. It would be one of Cutter's interchangeable minions, off on a tailing assignment. Tailing whom, Ross wondered. *She*. Did *she* relate to Broken Back? It had to be. If only Kohler had put on a regular team of watchers instead of the single, cut-rate Sparrow. Without information he could do nothing. Nothing. He sat in frustration, fiddling with the cable he had begun drafting, then shoved it aside. He was in the same spot as Kohler now: there was nothing to report.

He pulled the outside phone toward him and dialled Kohler's home number. He was pleased when Kohler answered by announcing the telephone number – it would take Macon that much longer to find out who he had called.

'Don't say my name,' Ross put in quickly. 'Or yours. Tomorrow I want every scrap of information you have on Lumbago and also his target. Send it with my relief.' Let Special Branch figure that out.

'Okay, boss. Anything else we can do for you? Booze, girls . . . boys?'

'Come along yourself and bring an electric cattle prod,' Ross said sharply and hung up. Insufferable man, Ross thought. Kohler had that terrible, empty facetiousness that substituted for a sense of wit, and that way of leaning into you when he spoke as if offering you the privilege of taking him in with all your senses, his smell of leathery cologne, his blocky face filling your vision, even a touch on your arm. For an instant there, Ross could have strangled him out of pure vexation, but his irritation gradually subsided to its accustomed impersonal form. He could not hope to strangle the entire world.

He went back to the window and took up his post in the chair he had set up like a throne, each leg on a volume of the London telephone directory so that he could see comfortably over the sill. A bead of sweat ran down his nose, tickling him, and he ignored it with pointless stoic discipline until it dropped of onto his loosened tie. He saw a head move in the turret room across the street, and before long the light behind the thin curtains went out, plunging the building into a depthless gloom. Only the ledges stood out, faintly blue under the moon. No one came out or went in.

At about four in the morning Ross craned his neck upward to watch the leaden overcast rolling over the city again. Soon it would snuff out the light from the half moon, and day would gather furtively above it.

13

'The time you flew to Hamburg?'

'Nothing. A legitimate courier trip. Research still had an outstation there, its last one. I didn't even know you had people in Hamburg.'

'Of course we have people in Hamburg.' Komarovsky scowled and left the room again. It was a two-storey house in dull Kennington not far from the vast sprawl of Lambeth Hospital, undoubtedly a safe house of some sort kept by Komarovsky's people. For most of the night they had questioned him, and he had given them everything he knew about the past, everything he could remember of the innumerable meetings and exchanges and thefts. Much of it Komarovsky knew in general, since Sloane had ostensibly been his double, but in many of the incidents there was a new wrinkle to add to the record: a hint of planted misinformation or a section of a document omitted. The old Russian had an eagle eye for tiny discrepancies, and each seemingly mundane variation from the facts recorded on his files raised another dozen questions. Sloane gave him everything – or almost everything – in the hope of making a deal. There was just one vital point that he held back.

Around dawn they had let him sleep for a few hours on a cot upstairs, and it had taken him a while to drop off despite his weariness. The house played acoustical tricks, with pipes chugging behind the walls and a weird moan rising out of the old coal grate. Surrounded by alien whimpers and rasps and moans, he lay worrying about Sarah and what she would think about the delay.

The boy came in and woke him with a tray of food, the whole spread of the classic English breakfast that he had never been able to face – runny fried eggs, toast, tough rindy bacon, a thin grey slab of smoked fish and two over-fried little tomatoes. With his mind as fuzzy as his tongue, he ate the toast and drank the insipid milk tea as the grey light gathered over South London. Then he slept again.

'We are nearly up to the present,' Komarovsky said, quite kindly. 'You are helpful to here. You maintain that between the time you left the hospital and five days ago you had no contact at all with Cutter?'

'I didn't think he even knew my address.'

'This is Europe, not Southeast Asia. With a little effort and help from the authorities, it is not difficult to find someone.'

Sloane shrugged. 'Okay, he didn't want to find me. They had no authorization for field personnel any more, and he wasn't about to look me up to offer me a pension. Any more than you were.'

'But suddenly he's interested again, and his cowboys grab you off the street. Why do they do this?'

'That's easy enough. Somebody in Washington smelled a prize.'

'No surmise,' Komarovsky insisted. 'Tell me what you know, what they said to you.'

'They said exactly the same things I told you eight hours ago. Cutter was hot and bothered, and he wanted me to arrange a bag job on your files.'

'*My* files?'

'No . . . I'm sleepy. The trade mission files, somewhere in the trade mission files.'

'They pick you up outside your flat and take you near the St Pancras goods yard to talk,' Komarovsky insisted patiently.

'Yeah, sure, dot all the Ts. Sure. I'm not going to tell you what they wanted. It's the only credit I have with you.' Sloane decided to try a moment's irritation. 'Make me an offer or give it up.'

Komarovsky settled back in his wooden chair, his hands flat on his knees, and stared darkly at Sloane for a long time. It was presumably meant to unnerve him, but Sloane saw only a rumpled, greying old man, himself tired and unshaven. 'I believe you feel you can be insolent to me only because I have never frightened you and never lied to you, never shouted and threatened like your friend Cutter. I believe you are in some ways 'very much a moral coward, Jeffrey Sloane.'

'I'm any kind of coward you like.'

'It saddens me that you would repay honourable treatment in this manner.'

Sloane actually felt a momentary twinge of remorse. He liked the old man, and, yes, Komarovsky had always played square with him. And, yes, he held out now because Komarovsky did not truly frighten him. He was tired, but not so tired that he fell into the trap of admitting he saw Komarovsky's line of logic. 'Ask Cutter how I repaid dishonourable treatment the last time I saw him.'

'You shot at him and threatened his life, I know. You did that because he was so abominably self-centred in his raving, like a mad barking dog. You only shot to get his attention so you could agree to do what he wanted. You won't do what I want when I ask politely.'

'I've told you everything but that one hole card. That's not for giving away.'

Komarovsky raised himself from the chair. 'I am going to take a nap because my mind is not working efficiently. We will talk some more later.'

Sloane rested on the cot, trying to work out various schemes to use Komarovsky against Cutter. None seemed very promising. He got up and peered out of the window as a gang of Irish labourers unloaded bricks from a van across the road and piled them neatly along the walk. Fraying Sunday-best trousers demoted to work pants; thin, dull-coloured jerseys; suitcoats held together by safety pins – the uniform of Irish labour. The window latch turned slightly under his fingers. He could leap to the false balcony over the bay window below and escape fairly easily. But what good would it do him? He'd never get into the files, never satisfy Cutter. His best chance was still to bargain in some way. And if there was still no bargain to be had – he considered escaping again and realized he was just too tired to make the effort.

He ate another meal, takeaway Chinese in soggy paper tubs, and as he ate he tried to talk to the young Russian who watched as if he had never seen food before. Perhaps the boy would show him a chink in Komarovsky's armour. The boy's cheeks had gone yellow and he appeared both agitated and faint from something or other, ready either to tear his hair out or collapse in a heap, or both, one after another. He spoke excitedly of the nineteenth-century novels of George Gissing, which Sloane not only had never read but never heard of. He asked Sloane obscure questions about Victorian London – the location of Marshalsea Prison and something called 'St Ghastly Grim' Church – and Sloane made up plausible-sounding answers to keep him talking. But after a few minutes, the soldier called him out, and the boy scurried away sheepishly.

Because there was no ready solution, his thoughts kept circling pointlessly back to himself, and he made himself stop it. He concentrated entirely on Sarah, as if the effort could somehow throw them together in safety. Like a sculptor with his eyes closed, trying to work by inspiration, he wanted to conjure a miracle solution out of his subconscious. And as he concentrated on her, her physical presence, the way she had of grinding her teeth when she thought no one was watching, an intense vacancy she had in a group of people, like a loner eating in a cafeteria, the dreams that caused her to whimper at night – a new category of dread rose slowly in him. No doubt they had needed each other at the hospital, fed each other and carried each other along. But after . . . had he been recreating the hospital for the past year – simply to keep her dependent? Unconsciously feeding her weaknesses as a claim on her? He had no idea what anyone could see in him to love. People can love anything firm, he thought, even vanity, arrogance, probably even brutality (Hitler had had a mistress) – assertion, self-assurance, fixed active traits. Yet there was nothing firm and certain in him. Who could love an emptiness so complete that it had put on personalities like Salvation Army clothes, copies of some lost model? Never truly at home in any of them. He saw that he was back to himself again.

He chased the self-consciousness away, but nothing else would come. The only idea that offered the slightest hope was a bargain of some sort with Komarovsky. He wondered if he had enough to sell.

In the evening a refreshed Komarovsky made another try at interrogation, teasing Sloane nearer and nearer his object from various directions. 'He mentioned the START talks then?' *No*, *no, never*. 'The oil negotiations with Libya?' *No*. Eventually Sloane tired of the game and stopped talking altogether, merely grunting and shrugging in reply.

'I suppose we have reached a Georgian standoff,' Komarovsky said finally, as Sloane sat stolidly on the edge of the wooden cot. He shuffled his papers together and put them on the floor. 'This Cutter is such a rabid wolf. What is it you believe in at heart to join with this monstrosity against nature?'

'I won't argue politics with you.'

'All life is politics.'

'Let's not talk in bumper stickers,' Sloane said wearily.

'Come, tell me.'

'For God's sake . . .'

'I insist on your motives. Afterward, perhaps we can strike a bargain. Not your motives *then* if you wish. Now. Perhaps I can learn from your high ethics.'

Sloane held back for a moment, but weariness won. 'I believe in people leaving me alone. I want peace and calm for me and my wife. That's all. I don't propose it as a universal moral standard, but it's all I can think of.'

'Very well, I will give it to you,' the Russian said evenly, as if the statement had no special significance.

Sloane's eyes lifted cautiously from the greying pine floorboards. Komarovsky smiled affectionately. 'Seriously. In a way you have won. Come with me to the office and photograph what you want.'

Smiling, he took the camera out of the bag he had brought with him, like a magician producing a rabbit. It was a battered old Nikon F with a motor drive and a macro copying lens. He set the camera tenderly in Sloane's lap, and answered the unasked question. 'How important could it be? It is only a trade mission, after all. What you want is not inside my private office?'

'No.'

'In the commercial files?'

'Yes.'

'A through K?' Komarovsky tried facetiously.

'In the commercial files,' Sloane repeated, curious at the merriment that seemed to have come over the old man.

'The commercial files are nothing. The only importance is

knowing what your people think is important. We will make the trade you wish. You photograph what you want and I discover what it is. You could even use the office photocopier.' He grinned. 'No, that is too much, isn't it?'

'You spoke of honour. Give me your word.'

Komarovsky put his hand to his breast. 'Upon my revolutionary honour, upon my faith in the historical mission of the proletariat, you may take a look at what you wish, photograph it and go in peace.' He raised an eyebrow and smiled ironically. 'You trust such oaths?'

'No, but at least I'll see if you believe in revolutionary honour. I have another card to play.'

'But of course. Come, let us be James Bonds.'

He stood. Sloane wasn't sure what the promise was worth, but he couldn't imagine getting a better one in the situation.

'Kaverin,' the old Russian called softly. 'Bring the car. And wake your young comrade.'

★

Ross dismissed the gangly code clerk Kohler had loaned him and took over for the night watch. The man had kept two conscientious logs on legal pads, one labelled 'telephone' and the other, 'in and out.' Ross read them over quickly.

    9.07 Scarhead departs, N. on foot

    9.23 Scarhead returns from N., with paper bag (food?)

  10.10 Small man met by green Ford sedan in front, drive N. (can't see driver)

  10.37 Crewcut man steps out, looks around, goes back inside

  10.44 Crewcut out again. Possible brush contact with old man in raincoat(?) Back inside.

  11.51 Small man returns on foot, from W. via Bear St.

There was more of the same, but nothing told him very much. The telephone log seemed little more informative.

  8.50–52 In. Anxious woman asking for Downs. Downs will come home when 'it's over'.

    8.59 Out. To Speaking Clock (That's Brit for the Time Lady)

    9.35 In. Male voice. Wrong number. (Or prearranged code?)

  10.33–41 Out. Male voice, identified as Ralph Cutter. Chews

> *out caretaker of flat at length, something about stopping*
> *milk delivery. Nasty stuff.*

1.07–18 p.m. Out. Scrambled.

One detailed entry from the evening caught his attention:

> *8.42–46 In (pay phone). Male voice, identified as Macky*
> *(Macki?), apparently reporting on surveillance, some*
> *woman went for a walk and is back inside somewhere.*
> *Reedy voice replies to call back after 10. Some decision*
> *is 'making its way through the sausage grinder'.*
> *Sounded amused.*

Ross set the pad down, already stained by the perspiration from his hand. He found the 8.42 conversation on the tape and listened to it three times without learning anything more. The stand-in had kept excellent notes. It was after ten now and he turned on the monitor, hoping to catch the call live.

That afternoon Ross had met Sparrow on the bridge over the Serpentine in Hyde Park and dragged out of him what he could. Sparrow thought he had caught up with Lumbago again the night before, but he had lost him in the fog near Paddington. Lumbago's wife was hiding out somewhere in Sussex, and they had met once at a country pub north of Lewes. It sounded likely that she was the woman the surveillance team was watching, but there was no direct evidence. Twice, in the East End, Lumbago had met a heavy-set man with an accent, and the second time he had handed over a white airplane bag he had taken from Cutter in a bizarre scene off Regent Street. Lumbago had apparently threatened Cutter and taken a shot at him. Ross wondered what on earth it all meant.

All he had learned from Kohler's papers so far was that Lumbago was a former Research employee and former asylum patient, voluntarily hospitalized for almost a year after a nervous breakdown. He wondered if Lumbago was running wild on Cutter. That would be just about perfect from the Old Man's end, with enough stumbling and shooting to announce the whole operation on the late news.

On no firmer ground than a hunch, Ross assumed that Research had targeted the Russian Trade Mission, fishing for records of recent gold sales. It was possible that the 'heavy-set man with an accent' was an employee of the trade mission, but again he had no direct evidence, since the surveillance Ross had set on the trade mission had so far shown no results. Even the KGB resident hadn't been in for two days.

The tape reels snapped taut and began to run in the quiet room, causing a flutter in his heart, and over the monitor he heard the sudden hum of the connection.

'Give me Cutter,' said the petulant voice he remembered from the night before. 'Hurry, I'm freezing my ass off.'

There was a harsh buzz as the call was transferred and then Cutter's voice, 'Mackey, she still in sight?'

'Snug as a bug in a rug.'

'The son of a bitch has skipped on us; we haven't heard from him in two days. Pick her up and bring her in here. He'll love hearing her over the phone when he calls.'

Mackey's voice was worried. 'Boss, that's a serious thing you're asking us to do.'

'Listen, you dumb Polack,' Cutter growled. 'The rats won't get a meal out of what's left of you if I have to repeat myself.'

'Yes sir, sure,' Mackey succumbed.

Immediately after the phone clicked off, Ross saw a figure rise against the light across the street, and now he knew the location of Cutter's desk. Apparently things were beginning to move. Ross settled into his throne-chair to watch the heads drift along the window. The Abortionist drew nearer the surgery.

★

'Those strikers ought to be put up against the wall and shot,' Major Danby protested. 'A rotten lot.' He was a trim little man in several layers of brown tweed, somewhere in his sixties. Thinning hair was swept straight back from his forehead, and a shaky, blue-spotted hand grasped his cocktail glass with a tremor of rhetorical fury. Across the small oak table Sarah listened politely, sitting beside Mrs Danby, who wore a froth of silvery Greek curls over kindly quick brown eyes. Their glasses were empty, and Sarah wondered if she should offer to get the next round.

'Where's their sense of responsibility to the nation, eh? Inflation at twenty pence in the pound and all they think of is themselves, selfish lot of shirkers off on a holiday while their leaders hold the country to ransom.'

The brass hunting horn on the beam over his head caught red flashes from the imitation fireplace across the room, a gas heater with a device inside that simulated dancing flames. Even thirty feet from the fire, the rippled window by the table was steamed with its heat.

'Did you see what that bolshy little man said in the newspaper, eh?'

His voice lunged to a halt on more of a rising note than usual. The silence lengthened, and Sarah realized it must have been a genuine question. 'I find it difficult to read the papers,' she replied.

'And well you should, my dear, the way they go on these days, pandering to the bad elements.'

'Owen, would you fetch us another round, please?' Mrs Danby asked gently.

He blustered suddenly, making noises like a balky motorscooter, all of him straining toward action. 'Of course, dear, puh, puh. Certainly. Silly of me. Of course.' When the engine was warm, he rose with awkward haste and went to the bar.

Sarah gave the woman a tense smile. She knew the waiting had not done her very much good. There was almost nothing to do in the tile-hung village that lay grey and ochre a quarter mile up the road, older than the inn, older than the road itself. For two days she had read a long novel desultorily, taken meals at the inn, wandered along the tranquil headwaters of the Adur River . . . and worried. By her guess, something had gone wrong. He should have called or visited by now.

'I do find it difficult,' she said softly to Mrs Danby. 'I try to read the newspapers, and it evaporates like smoke as I read. But that woman . . .' She inclined her head, and Mrs Danby didn't need to turn around: an old woman with her hair awry sat alone in the corner clutching a Siamese cat and sipping sherry, apparently a permanent fixture of the inn. Once or twice an evening she would address a momentary, unintelligible harangue to the room, expecting no answer. 'I feel I have to know everything about that woman. I don't mean I'll . . .' Sarah shrugged, and she felt again how tense her shoulders had become. 'I just want to know. It's a pointless compulsion.'

'The human heart can only focus on the particular.'

In an evening of banalities, one intelligent comment brought her up short like an unexpected gate. Freed of her husband, this was a real person after all, pressing her lips together in a friendly smile, and Sarah gave her an honest reply. 'That's just an excuse people like me use. You see, I won't actually speak to her. I'm frightened of the obligation it would create, sitting and listening, caring. Who knows what else? It's idleness, not a wish to save anyone.' Sarah smiled, feeling its rueful character. 'I might even have the wish to help, but I know I won't make the effort. I think it's a form of madness.'

'Now, dear . . .' Mrs Danby began.

'No, listen. Your husband's generalities are quite sane, really. Coal strikes and trade unions – they lead him back to his own beliefs and experiences. But my focusing on that woman takes me utterly away from myself, away from the human world. It's *too* particular, don't you see? Everything becomes separate, atoms cut off and moving apart.'

The woman pressed one veined finger on the back of Sarah's hand, firm enough to create a pale valley. 'What a very morbid thought. Why should you take an instance of perfectly human sympathy and consider it so . . . poisoned?'

The red-faced barman called to the room, 'Last orders, please. Last orders.' As his arm fumbled over his head, Sarah could see how drunk he was; a lifetime's practice had hidden the fact for hours in the accustomed actions of drawing beer and making change. He finally found the cord and rang a coach bell.

'Because I care very much,' Sarah said. 'But I can never seem to do anything sensible about it.'

Her husband carried a tray of shuddering drinks back toward them, and Mrs Danby brought her whole hand down on Sarah's affectionately. With a little of the beer slopping over the rims of the glasses, he managed to set the tray down just in time.

'Here we are, ladies. I say, I had no idea it was so late, what?' Sitting by cautious stages, he added, 'Time leaps the fences without a fault at our age, eh?' He looked up at his wife, immensely pleased at his metaphor, and Mrs Danby patted his hand as she had done with Sarah.

'Aren't you the cleverboots, dear.'

'Puh, puh, nothing especially to – ' Embarrassed now, he covered his chagrin with a fit of coughing.

'Careful of your stitches, dear.'

'Thank you, major,' Sarah said. 'You really must let me pay for this round.'

'No, certainly not. It's been our pleasure. Our privilege, what? We don't often have a chance to chat with young people, eh? Connect up with the future . . . take the lie of the land, so to speak . . . eh? I believe the world is safe in your hands.'

What on earth could he mean, Sarah wondered, but she smiled. 'I hope you don't hold me responsible.'

Mrs Danby laughed softly. 'That's the first time this evening you've truly smiled. You have a lovely smile, dear.'

Sarah sipped her beer. She found it hard to follow the major's next tirade – against the decline of quality in things, or was it the rising cost of things? – her mind slipping back to her own worries. Making a great effort, she small-talked with them for another few minutes and then excused herself. 'I must be off to bed. I hope I'll see you tomorrow.'

'We won't be away until mid-day,' Mrs Danby said. 'Good evening.'

'Always rushing, you young people, eh? Good night, my dear.' He half rose, was defeated by the angle of the table, and settled for a bow.

'Good night, major. Thank you again.'

She went out through a rustic door held together by long wrought-iron hinges into the dim corridor of the inn. A limp rose stalk scratched angrily on the glass of the french doors at the far end of the corridor as it danced in the wind, and she hunted in her handbag for the room key on its leather fob. Taking out the key, she heard a noise from the room – a footstep or a drawer closing – and she froze. For a full minute she stood listening and heard only the urgent rose bush, the moaning of wind and a distant clatter from the bar. 'Time, gentlemen,' the barman called faintly, and the bell clanged twice, twice again. Nothing short of a deadly fire at her back could force her in through that door.

She tip-toed along the faded carpet to the french doors. Bolts at the top and bottom finally broke loose from the crusted paint and slid under her fingers, and she stepped out into the freezing wind. Gingerly she pushed the rose whip aside and made her way along the bare rose bushes and forsythia to the front of the inn; then, abruptly returning to the chilly glass of the french door, she counted doors along the hall and discovered that her own window would be third along. There it was beside a small gnarled may bush shedding its last leaves. A whitewashed borderstone shifted under her foot and she caught her balance hastily and peeked in through a crack in the curtain. Her shoulders gave a terrible shudder. Part of the reaction was the cold plucking at her neck, but part too was from the sudden touch of one of her most primitive and fantastic fears. Two men stood beside her door in the darkness, one flattened to the wall and the other opposite, fat as Falstaff, hovering between the door frame and the wardrobe. As she watched, they glanced at one another, miming puzzlement, and the smaller man shrugged.

In the car park a large American sedan sat beside her Triumph, aimed out toward the road with both front doors ajar as if it had been abandoned in an air raid. No one staying at the inn or drinking in the pub owned that car.

In the pub, the barman was wiping tables with a benign, inward smile, collecting too many glasses in one practised hand. His eyes were glazed and far away as she walked past. Sipping the last of their drinks, the Danbys glanced up in surprise at her.

'My dear, you're as pale as a ghost.'

'Major, I think there's someone in my room. I heard a noise clearly from the hall. Would you please check for me?' She set her key on the table, trying unsuccessfully to control the tremor in her hand.

'Puh-puh . . . of course. Certainly. What bounder – ' He pushed himself up and took the barman by the arm. 'Proprietor, come with me straightaway! This is monstrous, *monstrous*!'

The barman struggled to bring the major into focus, and after a moment followed docilely toward the hall. Sarah slipped out of the front door. At the Triumph she hurriedly unlatched the steering-wheel lock, a contraption of telescoping steel rods with hooks that passed over the clutch pedal and steering-wheel rim. Felicity told her she had bought it because of the car's soft top

and its popularity with teenagers for the sport the police called
TDA – taking and driving away.

★

Inside the small bedroom, Di Santis sucked in a breath as he
heard a key scratch against the lock. He gestured, and Mackey
stepped nearer the door in order to grab her from behind and clap
his hand over her mouth. Di Santis would pinion her arms from
the front. The first thing that happened after Major Danby flung
open the door was a ghastly shriek from Mackey as the straight
doorhandle caught him just below the belt. Meanwhile, Di
Santis, who had leapt forward to enfold her with his arms, found
himself clinging to the back of a huge round man, almost as large
as Mackey himself. Totally disoriented, Di Santis held on in
tenacious panic as the fat man stumbled across the room and
twisted around blindly to pile-drive his burden against the hand
basin in the corner. The porcelain basin caught Di Santis sharply
in the kidneys, and he let out a howl almost as agonized as
Mackey's.

'*What's the meaning of this outrage?*' a dapper old man bellowed
into Di Santis's pained and bewildered face.

★

Trembling with haste, Sarah slid the upper hook over the
steering wheel and telescoped the device together, with the
bottom hook caught on the curving leg that held the wide brake
pedal. She would have preferred a clutch pedal, but the sedan
was an automatic. She heard the lock snap into one of its grooves
and she ran for her own car against the gusting wind, her shoes
slipping maddeningly on the gravel.

★

Mackey had recovered enough to grab the tweedy little man from
behind and shake him. In a petulant fit, he flung the man across the
room onto a single bed that clattered violently under the
impact. Di Santis, still gulping for air like a fish, spun the big

173

man around by his shoulder. His eyes were so glazed and his face so stupid that he had to be dead drunk. Still, the terrible, solid, breathless pain that filled Di Santis's lower abdomen so enraged him that he punched the fat stomach as hard as he could. Something wet, viscous and sour-smelling instantly drenched Di Santis. Oh, lord, *no*, he thought. If there was one thing he hated –

'*Shit!*'

Mackey managed a crass laugh as they bustled out of the door, Di Santis brushing at himself with loathing.

'Stop, you hooligans! I say there!' trailed after them.

They rushed through the pub room, some furious old woman hammering at Di Santis's head with a patent-leather handbag, and emerged into the chilling night air just as the Triumph squealed out of the car park and away to the east. Leaping into the Chevy, Di Santis cracked his knee against the unseen locking device.

'Oh, fuck,' he moaned, resting his forehead for an instant on the wheel.

Then he hopped out and wrenched one of the whitewashed stones from the border of the rose garden. With all his remaining strength, he flailed at the steering wheel until the lower quadrant caved in. A handful of people straggled out of the ancient inn as Di Santis hurled the locking device out of the car door and took off after the Triumph. Thank God, he thought, that he had covered the licence plate with a bit of cloth. He had done one thing right.

'How will we ever explain this?' he shouted at Mackey, who was either laughing or still fighting his pain, pounding the dashboard with both fists.

★

With her lights out, Sarah took a turning into a tiny side lane and pulled off onto what there was of a verge. she swiveled in the seat, breathless with fear, and watched the big car flash past on the main road. Only then did she collapse against the seat and begin to weep.

14

The Thames was a slow, leaden canal far beneath them as the Mercedes purred north across Waterloo Bridge. The tunnel mouth for the Aldwich underpass was locked for the night and they had to go the long way around the crescent. Komarovsky offered Sloane a small, odd bottle of schnapps, white ceramic with drindled maidens dancing around it. Sloane realized how much he wanted the drink, and he took a long swallow and sucked in air to cut the strange aromatic taste of mossy earth.

'The English call it Dutch courage, I believe,' Komarovsky observed. His air of merry affection still lingered. 'I find these nation-chauvinist expressions of yours amusing . . . in a crude and stupid way. The French call condoms English caps and the English call condoms French letters. As if any people had a special claim on sex . . . or cowardice. Cowardice travels very well, I am told.'

'The joke is stale.'

'Research comes to you,' Komarovsky went on as if Sloane hadn't spoken. 'After more than a year of nothing. It is curious, isn't it? Cutter and Downs, one mad like a wounded bear and the other a field mouse with perhaps half a brain, to rush in and clear up where the bear shits itself. Mad bear and field mouse. Which do you think needs the other more?'

'I won't spoil it. You have it all prepared.'

Komarovsky nodded, contented, meditative, self-contained. 'The Russian peasants have a saying – I will try to translate freely for you because you will not know the dialect even if you remember some of your Russian: "You show me a Cutter pissing into the snow and I will show you a Downs holding his cock."' Komarovsky laughed, and he was joined for a moment by the boy riding in front.

'It's a cruel saying,' Sloane objected dully.

'Cruel?' Komarovsky mused. 'An employee of mine died yesterday. Morally one could consider it murder if one wished to think in moral terms. He was the son of a true hero of the Great Patriotic War, and at one time, long ago, he was a good socialist, lacklustre but steady and honest and believing in the triumph of small men over the world of wealth, as some of us do.' Sloane noticed again that his English grew more cumbersome, the cadences more unnatural, when his emotions were aroused. 'You people entrap him, photograph him, turn him against himself until he can stand it no longer. This is not a small thing to be ignored – or to speak of his enemies with delicacy. You understand me?'

'He was my friend,' Sloane said.

'Men like you should have no friends. You hurt them.' And just like that, the affectionate teasing had been withdrawn, and a door closed between them.

The car headed into the quiet precincts of Kingsway, the flats and offices ranked behind their Edwardian railings like bored head waiters. Sloane rested his eyes on the tan leather of the seats to prepare himself for the battle of wits that lay ahead. Komarovsky was probably right about him, he thought: a moral coward who could not shelter his own friends against his weaknesses. It was as good a judgment as any, and Sloane was prepared to entertain almost any plausible judgment someone made about himself, though he felt, he hoped, it was too pure and too final. It was only in books that people could be skewered with a single aphorism for all time: he is X, he is not Y. Enough. He took a breath silently and tried to push the self-reproach aside. Jannings was dead. The future of those still living depended on the next half hour.

The trade mission was on a business street, its door between a small electronics shop with a bright wired window and a darker shop that sold medical implements. It had been a book store in his day. The shopfronts all had that look of London money: discreet signs, drab colours, a solid tidiness. They left the car up on the curb, conspicuous as a battleship, and Komarovsky bent down painfully beside the door to switch off the alarm with a cylindrical key.

'You see, this spy business is easy,' he said as he held the glass door open, an acid edge to his jests now.

A reception desk in the tiny lobby was surrounded by tall, overbearing marble walls like boasts of grandeur from a small man. The soldier led them up a glass and steel staircase to the main office. The upstairs was subdivided by a lattice of waist-high partitions like an oversize display case for *Clerks: Various Species* emptied for the night. Desks, file cabinets, and the stale cigarette and musty paper smells common to offices the world over. A swing-gate led into the main work area, but their short parade passed the gate and stopped in front of a steel door with a sign in Russian and English: *Registry Files. Restricted Entry.* Sloane remembered that Jannings had once joked ruefully that the Russian version said, *Queue here to join the Party* – a guarantee to keep away the new cynical generation of Russians. The door was featureless, and beside it, where a latch tongue might have entered the jamb, there was a square metal box with buttons like a digital telephone.

The boy cradled the flight bag protectively, shifting from foot to foot as he waited timidly at the side. Komarovsky zipped the bag open and tossed the camera to Sloane who just managed to catch the strap and keep it from hitting the scuffed brown linoleum. Komarovsky dipped in again and came out with the circuit reader.

'Shall we try your toy? I cannot believe it will work.'

Sloane said nothing.

Sliding a list of instructions from under the wrapping of wire, Komarovsky puzzled over them for a moment. '. . . Pulses inducing an infinitesimal current to flow through the target circuitry and, on alternate pulses, monitoring faint variations in the lines of magnetic flux,' he read to himself. 'It sounds like something that predicts your sex life.' He unwound the wire, revealing the naked jewel box of resistors and capacitors and the finned heat sinks of a pair of metal transistor cases. At the end of the cord was a loop of stiffer wire about six inches in diameter that had become crushed out of shape. He patted it back into a circle and held it around the code box on the door.

'Place the sensor ring . . . so, and depress "on" button.'

Digital nixie tubes on the end of the device glowed green and

177

then flicked rapidly through the numerals until a small red bulb lit. The counters froze and Komarovsky read them off with amusement. 'Nine-two-eight-one-one-four. Amazing, this machine.'

He tossed his keys to the soldier who waited implacably at the stairs, blocking any sudden flight Sloane might attempt, and pointed to a switch plate in the corner of the room. Komarovsky wound the wire up again and set the circuit reader on the gleaming water fountain, nodding with apparent admiration. The soldier inserted a cylindrical key into the plate Komarovsky had indicated.

'No, don't shut it off yet. Let's try this machine, shall we?'

He bent over stiffly and tapped the buttons beside the door, repeating the numbers aloud. A moment after the last tap, there was a buzzing from the lock like a trapped insect. Then an alarm went off overhead, an ululating shriek that would have unnerved any burglar. The soldier hurriedly cranked the alarm off, and Komarovsky turned to pat the boy's shoulder.

'Lev Davidovich, will you please go inform the duty officer that everything is all right. No one is here except James Bond.'

The boy hurried out to the stairs.

As Komarovsky punched the number in again carelessly, he said with contempt, 'Of course there are mechanical check digits that the machine cannot know. We have had them from the first. Still, a half-good try, from the sort of half-smart fools who rely always on technique.'

The door buzzed and this time snapped open an inch, and the three of them climbed the short gloomy flight of rubber-tread stairs, petitioners ascending the last Vatican steps. Facing walls in the room were solid with filing cabinets, grey and uniform like cadets at attention. The far wall was all utility shelving crammed with books, pebble-grain ledgers and boxes of loose papers, and at the door there were three sturdier black cabinets with combination locks. Barren work tables sat in the centre, and when Komarovsky switched on the fluorescents the men were washed by a pallid light that made them look weary and ill.

'Three imperialist spies undermining the socialist world. Where do you wish to dig?'

Sloane looked around him, still unsure. It was the last card.

'You do not trust me,' Komarovsky continued with a watery smile. 'Dealing with men like Cutter, I cannot blame you. I give you my word of revolutionary honour, on the mausoleum of Lenin in the east wall of the Kremlin. You may take your pictures and go.'

Sloane nearly laughed, not so much because he doubted the pledge – in fact, he hoped desperately that he could trust it – but because Komarovsky had made it sound so absurd and self-mocking, like the rude sexual boast of an invalid.

He improvised quickly: 'I want the overall trade balance for two days in June, the 15th and 16th.'

'That is simple. Not even in the cabinets.'

Komarovsky's gnarled finger ran along the row of black ledgers, tenderly pressing on the plastic letter tapes that curled off the binding. He found one and opened it flat on a work table. 'We are so backward. We do not even convert to microfiche here,' he apologized with more of his gentle self-mockery. 'We must send a full year to Moscow at once. Perhaps it is the same for Cutter?'

No one wanted Cutter's records at all, Sloane thought. He focused carefully on the page, the split image coming together on a Cyrillic Π. He felt the shutter trip and then the motor-wind buzzed automatically to the next frame. Through the finder he saw Komarovsky's hand turn the page and he steadied himself and shot again. Across the room, the soldier wrote in a small leather notebook.

'The import figures for iron ore for last month,' Sloane said.

'We import no iron ore from Britain.'

'From the Ruhr. Surely you have facsimiles of all your European accounts.'

Komarovsky stooped over, leaning back like a far-sighted dentist, to read the labels on the grey cabinets. What he wanted seemed to be in the third tier. 'Should I break the lock? No, why bother? I have a sophisticated magic device to open it.' He gestured, and the soldier lobbed across the dense ring of keys. The drawer grated open to reveal, surprisingly, only three manila folders lying inside.

Komarovsky set a yellow teleprinter sheet on the table. As Sloane twisted the lens into focus, he read enough of the document to be sure it was what he had requested. For the next few minutes Komarovsky retrieved a wide range of documents of little interest to anyone, least of all to Sloane; there were exports of chrome ore to the US for an arbitrary month, exports of consumer products to Bulgaria, Comecon oil allotments from the Soviet Union to Eastern Europe, plus others that he forgot as soon as he chose them. The only sounds in the room were the nervous hum of the lights, the trundling of the file cabinets and the fussy ratcheting of the camera. Half-way through, the boy returned with a diffident nod to Komarovsky and stood patiently beside the door.

Finally Sloane decided to make his run, resetting his feet and holding his voice firmly in neutral. 'Exports of gold to Western Europe, this year to the present.'

Komarovsky hunted it down as he had the others and laid a single sheet of figures on the table without comment. Sloane took no more care focusing than he had before, and, for good measure, he added a request on the import of car parts for the Lada.

'Have you covered yourself sufficiently?' Komarovsky enquired. 'Or should I pick some files at random to help you?'

'I'll tell you the one when I'm out of here.'

'Of course.' The old Russian checked to make sure the drawers were locked securely, giving little testing tugs. 'Conspiracy, conspiracy, it's such a tedium. If only we could all enroll clair-voyants, but they are such a lot of wretched fakers.'

As they descended the steps, Komarovsky clamped his fist onto the camera strap that hung from Sloane's neck. 'Soon there will come a moment when we must trust each other, no? No matter what the safeguards, life is ultimately a question of trust, is it not? Even for the man of broken courage.'

They passed through the dingy pomp of the lobby and gathered before the window of the electronics shop, where bright lights picked out in urgent red cards: *Sale! Sale!* The traffic noise was far away, on another planet, muffled by the canyon of buildings and the low ochre cloud. Still grasping the strap, Komarovsky said firmly, 'Wind the film back, please. Almost to the end.'

When Sloane glanced dubiously along the street, Komarovsky raised his free hand in a reassuring sign. 'It is all right. Our agreement is good, if your side is fulfilled. This will be my guarantee.'

Sloane pried up the tiny crank and rewound the film, knowing now exactly what the Russian intended to do. His last card withdrew, taking with it the spurious comfort of the ruse and leaving him with a sensation like another death. He stopped when he felt the film pull free of the ratchets but before the tail could disappear into its cannister. With the back open, he saw that Komarovsky had marked the precise start point with a scratch on the celluloid, and he knew that the Russian had anticipated his covering ploy all along.

'Now I rethread to the mark,' Sloane suggested woodenly.

'Exactly. The mark is to coincide with the right edge of this small piece here.'

Sloane rethreaded and closed the back, and the camera was lifted gently out of his hands. Komarovsky opened the diaphram all the way and set the shutter speed to a half-second before placing the lens against the bright window, the strap pulling Sloane's neck toward the glass like a bond of mistrust between them.

'You will stop me when you must. I believe you understand what I am doing. The time of trust approaches.' His eyes caught Sloane's – heavy, sleepy lids behind the thick glasses. 'Is it the 15th of June that you want?' After an interval, when there was no response, Komarovsky tripped the shutter, washing out the first frame with the glare. 'The 16th then? Let us hope my memory is accurate,' he said drily, but his soldier nodded with dark concentration, carefully ticking off a note in his book. Sloane thought of stopping him sooner, pretending he wanted one of the irrelevant frames, but he could see that crying wolf would do no good. The old soldier was thorough; he would simply go on to the next and the next and discover it eventually, or wipe it out.

Sloane ended the charade. 'It's the gold accounts,' he said dully. 'Eighteenth frame. Now you have it.'

'Ah, the magic metal. Research is interested in the large sales recently, no doubt. But let us make certain.'

He destroyed the other frames as Sloane watched, saving only the eighteenth with a palm over the lens, and then they were all left standing in the street, silent and rather embarrassed, like a party of mourners who had missed the wake. The camera dropped against Sloane's chest, Komarovsky still holding tight to the strap, and an ambulance rushed past somewhere nearby, clanging its bell. What now? Sloane thought. The boy, standing apart, blinked his watery eyes like a small dazed animal transfixed by the tableau.

'Gold,' Komarovsky said, fixing the moment on the word like a bayonet. 'The capitalist world trembles before its high altar. I know all. *Now* what will the evil Russian fanatic do? Will he take back the camera? Will he kill you? Will he try to blackmail you and threaten your wife? Perhaps he will starve your family and use electronic torture machines.'

Komarovsky released the camera strap with a flourish, then dug into his overcoat and took out the brown envelope that held Jannings's last letter. This he tucked into Sloane's coat. 'You and I are finished. Go.'

Sloane backed a step, watching all three of them intently for signs of a sudden rush. But Komarovsky only studied his own reflection curiously in the shop window, for some reason mugging a scowl, while the soldier and the boy drifted toward the Mercedes.

'Thank you, colonel,' Sloane said.

The old man shook his head without looking around. 'Such a world, when a simple promise kept is cause for thanks.' Then he walked to the car door that the boy held open, giving the boy a friendly intimate thump on the arm. It was a gesture that excluded Sloane; somehow banished him forever from their company.

★

A single-deck night bus grumbled past him, its bright eyes sweeping the vacant streets until it turned the corner, and the silence hurried in behind. Sloane was happy. By a bizarre turn of its own, fate had completed his labour and given him what Cutter wanted. He and Sarah would be free to start again. He could try for a steady job somewhere in a small town away from the grim resonance of London. He had always been dismayed by the city's air of controlled, irreversible dilapidation, and its wounded, besieged people perpetually waiting for catastrophe. They would go someplace where they could stretch out both arms and not touch damp brick with either hand, someplace where people met your eyes on the street and smiled. A small house, order, routine, but without that deadly sense of futility that had grown like lichen on Richmond Road. His personality would never see a major alteration – that was all illusion. He would probably never again be adventurous, or high-spirited. He would go gentle, and hoe a small garden in peace, with Sarah. It was enough.

A single policeman stamped his feet in the chill, and he found a phone box at last beside a dark pub in Bloomsbury. Enquiries gave him the number of the inn and he dialed for what seemed ages, a seven-digit number preceded by the five-digit rural phone code. It rang and rang as he waited with his coin at the slot, and at last someone answered, a woman admonishing sleepily, 'The inn is asleep from 12 o'clock.'

'I'm sorry, this is an emergency. Could I speak to Sarah Sloane, please?'

'Mrs Sloane left suddenly tonight. There was some row with men in her room. She's still owing for – '

'*Is she all right? What happened?*'

But there was a fit of distant coughing, and the woman was speaking off the phone: 'It's all right, dear. I'm getting it.' She came back shrilly. 'I don't know where she's gone, the police couldn't say. Who is this?'

He hung up, the daydream of peace collapsing around him like a burst tent. His world of peace, which had lasted all of fifteen minutes, now rocked on its axis. A fierce anger rose in place of the hopes, focusing itself on the grey telephone. He cursed Komarovsky for not giving him back the pistol. As he reached out to dial again, the first large raindrops plopped on the glass to meander downward like tears.

★

It was a nightmare he knew so well that often a small part of his consciousness remained teasingly aware that he was asleep, reminding him over and over that he was only dreaming, only dreaming – without in any way diminishing the helpless terror.

The floor shuddered as something rumbled out of the dark toward Alma, who stood pale and vulnerable on a rickety chair, trying to hold her nightgown closed at the throat. (He had found her that way once, over a bright potato bug in the kitchen.) All he had to do was shout one clear word of warning, but of course nothing would come out but the endless, impotent stammer fluttering like a moth pierced by a single consonant. The menace became a huge cab-over truck with a single bloodshot eye for a grill. It bore relentlessly toward the chair, honking at her with an insistent double ring.

Then he was in the half world, trying to prod his mind the rest of the way by questioning details with dogged logic: an eye? The truck couldn't have been real. Nonsense. And trucks didn't ring like a –

Downs sat up on the cot with a thudding heart and groped in the dark for the cord. The feeling of panicky failure still hung over him as he found the cord, traced it to the telephone and repeated the office number into the mouthpiece. Not a stammer.

'Keep quiet and listen,' Sloane's voice snapped. 'You bastards got Jannings killed, and now you've messed with Sarah. I *told* you not to go near Sarah.'

'No, it's all right – ' Downs wailed feebly.

'*Shut up*,' Sloane bawled. 'Nothing is all right. I have the film you want, and I'd have given it to you tonight if Cutter weren't such an asshole. You have one more chance, just one. I'll wait to see Sarah safe, and when we're safe and together I'll give you the film. I'll call. Don't – do – a thing,' he concluded, emphasizing each word.

'Sloane, Sloane – '

The line was dead and Downs hung up gently, trying to clear his mind by repeating the conversation to himself word for word. He snapped on the light and groped hastily for paper to write down the words before they faded. This would be the end, he thought. When the next bulletin was completed, he'd turn in his resignation. He could go on rationalizing his doubts for years, but Cutter simply couldn't be trusted to lead Research out of the wilderness. He had known it for so long that he was surprised he hadn't acted on it sooner.

His pencil point caught in his haste and tore through the

paper, and he stared, startled, at what he had written: . . . *got Jannings killed* . . .

★

Across the street in a small chilly office, the Abortionist made a note of the time on his pad and reached for the ordinary telephone to dial the long international code for Langley. The details would go into a coded cable, but he wanted to pass on a simple message: Lumbago has scored and is on his way home.

15

Bright signs taped to the shopfronts hawked Afro wigs, fresh mangos and the latest reggae records, *Jomo in Trench Town*, *Heed Jah I Say*. Along Railton Road, life still stirred at 2 a.m. as nowhere in London, a darting figure in the rain, a heavy drumbeat thudding away in an upstairs flat, furtive children under the misty halo of a streetlamp. Here and there an ordinary newsagent or ironmonger's stood out as a sign that many of the whites had not yet fled, unlike an American ghetto. Brixton was the heart of the largest Jamaican neighbourhood in Britain, an outpost of tropical anarchy standing off grim and orderly Europe. A knot of dark figures drifted out of a cottage gate into the mist, laughing with elaborate leavetaking, and drove away, the car pressing dull stripes onto the wet street.

At Brixton Station the surly taxi driver had demanded most of the money he had left, refusing to take him any deeper into the tropics. He knew it was much too late to visit her. Bad news was unwelcome at any hour, but 2 a.m. . . . . rudeness on top of grief. Yet he owed the visit, and he needed the next day free.

As he skirted a heap of trash bags, he took a melancholy inventory of himself. Two hours past midnight: he had no home; his only money was little more than a pound's worth of loose change that chimed under his fingers; his worldly possessions were now a stolen film in one pocket and a suicide letter in another. (The money in the letter did not count: that was a debt of honour that would be paid.) Walking the dark alien street, giddy with loneliness, he felt an outlaw, banished to somewhere at the edge of the known world where they sent all those who had failed in some fundamental trust. *Men like you . . .*

During a prolonged drought, he had read, wild animals eat their newborn. That was only conservation, relentlessly logical.

But what wild animal betrayed a friend? Ran from a bully and traded a life for nothing more than a thin illusion of safety? What animal refused to hear a cry for help? *You hurt them.*

He could find no escape from the nagging voice. He had let the arid inertia run on far too long; there was the fault. Like a clam, he had closed up and burrowed deep into a continuous present tense, watching each moment slip past and then reappear exactly the same; safe, undisturbing. In a year he had never once forced himself against the grain. He had told himself he was recuperating and gathering a new confidence behind the walls. He would test himself when it was time. Lies. He had been content to hide, anaesthetized by the idea that he could lock the door forever if he wished. It was this desperate clinging to the vacuum that had left him so defenceless against Cutter – left him a walking time bomb. He had grown so unused to resisting, so fainthearted, that he would ignore a friend's death agony in order to buy a moment's peace. *Men like you.*

In front of a shuttered off-licence, bottles glinting weakly behind the metal grill, he tried to stop tormenting himself. There was a future. Somewhere he would sleep deeply tonight, past the dawn. When he woke, it would be nearly over and he could leave the numbed old shell behind. He could find some way to neutralize Cutter and carry Sarah away to the new life.

No lights were on, but he hadn't expected any. The stripped and rusting hulk of a motor scooter was chained to an iron fence, and the basement entry under the steps gave off the inevitable faint smell of decay. He pushed the doorbell, but heard nothing inside the flat and presumed that it wasn't working, like so much else. He rapped loudly on the frosted pane in the door, waited, then rapped again, and again, until a light went on somewhere deep in the flat.

There was no sound of footsteps, but abruptly the door opened six inches on a chain. A plain, round face was tilted sideways in the gap to hide her body behind the door. The face was pale, and blue-grey eyes watched him fearfully from under a tangle of bleached hair.

'I'm a friend of Werner's,' he said.

'Who?'

For a sickening instant he thought of checking the house

number again. But this was the face he knew. He repeated the name, pronouncing it this time with an English 'W', and added the last name.

''Ow do I know?''

Sloane held up the letter so that she could read her own name in Jannings's handwriting. 'He couldn't ring you. He asked me to talk to you.'

'Just a mo ,' the door closed, the chain clicked free, and as the door came open again he saw her hurrying away across a dark sitting room with a thin pink nightgown flapping at the backs of her knees. 'I'll put somefing on.'

This was how he had last seen Jannings, hurrying away from Whitechapel with his overcoat flapping at his knees. No, the last time but one.

'I'm sorry to wake you.'

A light went on in the back room; the door open a diffident inch, as if to suggest she wouldn't forget him and go back to sleep. He switched on a standing lamp and looked for a place to sit. He was very tired, sleepy and morally wrung out as well, and his knees ached as if he had been doing squat exercises all day. A canvas deckchair with the beginning of a tear looked as if it would rip through under his weight. Another deckchair, folded, leaned against a fireplace that was boarded up with plywood. At last he settled for a mattress against the wall. It was covered by an Indian cloth and backed by two large pillows, and the patterned cloth felt damp against his hands in the chill of the room. Water began to run noisily somewhere in the back, and he surveyed her possessions with a grim curiosity. The overstuffed sofa that he knew from the photograph was gone, but it was the same room: a cheaply framed print of shaggy Highland cattle, a small television on the floor, a table with a ruffled cover holding three used teacups and a Watney's ashtray. The built-in shelves in the corner displayed a row of framed photographs, a stocky man and woman, a boy so like her that they might have been twins. A Coronation plate, a Toby mug, a small plastic sports trophy, and three worn paperbacks lying toppled, *How to Read Your Stars* and *Love is the Flame* hiding the third.

A door opened. He heard her bare feet slap on the bedroom floor, then a rustle of material and the unmistakable whisk of a hairbrush. What would he say to her?

'You ain't English,' her voice came through the opening, alert now. 'You sound American, I think.'

'I've been here a long time,' he said defensively.

'You're his mate, are you?'

'Yes. Jeffrey Sloane.'

She poked her head into the room with a surprised smile. 'Jeffrey!' 'E thinks the world of you! Used to talk about you all the time, 'e did, but 'e 'asn't done recently.'

Liveliness made her face attractive suddenly, and a trusting grin drew his smile in reply. 'I was away.'

'One more second. I want to be presentable for you. I never meet Werni's mates on account of 'e's married and it would get back to the wife, I guess.' He didn't hear any resentment in her voice.

She ducked back into the bedroom. 'Of course, you know about all that. Do you know Karen?'

'I've met her. She was older than he was.' As if that explained something. Karn was also much tougher, as only a very pretty woman could be, implacably ambitious and disappointed in him. Just a hair stiffer with him, and Sloane would have called her domineering. 'Every supper,' someone had said, 'the wife and two veg. What a handful. Pity the bloody man.' With a shock, he realized he had used the past tense aloud about Jannings. But she didn't seem to have noticed.

'Oh, but she's gorgeous. I saw 'er snap.'

'You're a lot more . . . alive,' he said.

She laughed; it was an easy music with a promise of play in it, and Sloane saw how Jannings had fallen in so deep. That stolid crusader with so much pent-up sense of duty – it must have been like fireworks inside him the very first time he had drawn that sunny laugh in reply to one of his laboured questions. Soon he was going to crush the cheer out of her.

'I know we 'aven't got much in common,' she said in a confiding voice, 'but we has our fun. When 'e's shirty and grumpy it's a lark taking the piss out of 'im. Do you work at the same place as 'im?'

'I used to. We w . . . are both translators.'

'*Guten abend*,' she called, and for a moment he didn't

recognize the words drowning in the strange London vowels.

He laughed softly, despite himself. Then guilt padded up. He was dragging it out too long. '*Komm, sitz mal her und ich werde Dich kläglich machen.*'

'What's that, then?'

'I said, stop fussing. I have to speak to you.'

'Go on wif you, you didn't say nufing like that.' Sensing a new solemnity in his voice, she peeked into the room with a subdued air. Her hair was brushed and her eyes made up heavily with blue shadow, and a second or perhaps third layer of filmy pink covered her squared off, stocky body. The fuzzy slippers plopped across the rug, and, as if incapable of gravity for very long, her face lit up infectiously. 'You was 'aving me on, but I don't know what it was. Got a fag?'

He offered her one of the four he had left, and she plucked it gingerly out of the box Komarovsky had given him, like something very delicate. He caught a whiff of cheap cosmetics. 'Rosemary. May I call you Rosemary? Please sit down.'

'It's cold as the grave in 'ere.'

She lit the cigarette and stooped to slide an old heater from under the table. She swapped plugs on an extension cord, pulling out the clumsy television plug, then rapped on the dish until the coil started to glow around its ceramic beak. She aimed the fire politely between them, and neither of them would feel its warmth.

'You have the heat. I'm dressed.'

'I'll be all right, love.'

She sat and faced him in a mocking caricature of expectation, tugging the layers of pink around her. He took the envelope from his pocket and tapped it on his knee. It had seemed easy on the way – or at least straightforward. He's dead, Rosemary. This is his last letter to you. But he couldn't find any words at all, and finally he just crouched forward to hand the letter to her. Returning to the mattress, he nudged the heater around toward her legs. For a moment he watched her reading, moving her lips with the difficult handwriting, the hurt gathering in her eyes. He realized suddenly that she wouldn't understand it as a suicide letter, but only as a dismissal. There was a faint rustle and he saw the wad of money drop onto her knees and hang precariously for a moment before tumbling to the floor and scattering like unwanted handbills.

'I guess we 'ad our flutter, you know,' she said in a slack voice.

'Don't be too hard on him, Rosemary.' He had to tell her now. 'He's dead.'

Her eyes narrowed instantly on him. 'Who done 'im?'

'That's a suicide letter. I didn't know it when he gave it to me. It was last night.' The words came now in a rush, as he piled them up in a race against some threatened flood. 'He sent Karn and his children away this week and took sleeping pills. It wasn't because of you, you mustn't think that. He was under terrible pressure at work and he was being forced to do something he couldn't do and go on living with himself. You know he believed deeply in a lot of things, and he never felt he'd done enough for what he believed. Some men were making him go against his belief, and it just built up to where he saw no other way out. He did the only thing he could see to do. To save his conscience.' The words sputtered and ran out as suddenly as they had come.

She read the letter again, reinterpreting in terms of the simpler but more terrible pain. Two fingers tugged idly at her nightgown. 'Would you 'ave somefing to drink?'

She walked straight back to the kitchen. The light went on, and he heard no sound at all for some time. Then she came back quickly, swung past him without a glance and slammed into the bedroom. Bedsprings creaked, and he heard a wail rise behind the closed door. He sat for a long time, running his eyes over the room as the cry keened through him like a primeval sound from some hideous past, the shriek of the sabre-toothed tiger, broke off, burst out again. To avoid acting (but what could he do?), his eyes roamed the room, trying to add up the curios into a life. It wasn't necessary to resist patronizing her: he envied the surety of the Coronation plate and the Toby mug, and he admired the happy, decent life built up out of so little. Finally he gathered up the letter and money and set them on the table. He unplugged the heater and walked toward the front door. *Men like you*. He had to turn away from her pain. The wail rose and fell behind him. He was the one person in her universe who had known Werner, he thought, the one person who could follow the things she had to say now. But he had his own problems. He couldn't do her any good. *You hurt them.*

There was only a single kitchen cupboard nailed up over the stone sink; he could find nothing at all to drink. A teabox lay ravaged and empty on the draining board. Peering into the waist-high fridge, he found two tall Bulmer's bottles on their side, and he poured the alcoholic cider into glasses with tiny blue cornflowers around the rim.

Knocking lightly with his elbow, he let himself into the bedroom. She lay on her stomach across the rumpled bed, hugging a pillow, and when she turned her head he saw mascara and eye shadow streaked and blotted down her cheeks, making her look haggard and ugly.

'What do you want then?'

'I think you should talk about it. It's easier if you talk.'

She took the glass he held out and sat up, holding it primly in her lap. ''Oo says?' she challenged, and started sobbing again. 'You can all get stuffed. Bloody men bugger everything with their bloody *honour*.'

'You wouldn't have liked Werner if he weren't like that.'

'Oh yes, I would 'ave done. I liked 'im alive, even if it meant it was on the never-never.'

He sat some distance from her on the bed, and it began spilling out of her. She told him about their too-infrequent evenings, the precious whole weekends they had spent together, goofy things he had done under her teasing, ridiculously complicated practical jokes he had set up to get back at her and then denied with a long, straight face until she hammered the truth out of him in a rapid, giggling thump of her fists. Once, with Karn gone home for a week, he had hired a narrowboat and taken her up the Grand Union Canal as far as Milton Keynes. She had lain on the deck in her two-piece bathing suit watching the cows graze the banks. It had been the happiest four days of her life. Tears interrupted, and he fetched the bottle of cider, and later the second bottle.

''E was sort of a boffin, but nice, you know. Didn't lord it over you, even when 'e talked fings you didn't 'ardly know. Bit of a Bolshevik I guess.'

'That's all right if you come from East Germany.'

'Oh, I don't mind. Me dad used to go round to the Communist

meetings and later the Labour clubs. A lot of old cobbler, 'e told me and Tom; they'd vote through a sensible motion in the club and some toffee-nose would go off and sell 'is vote for a lot of letters after 'is name. With Werni it was different, all serious and . . . kind of like the Methodists.' She smiled for an instant, the vulnerable warmth fighting its way up through all the smeared greasepaint. 'You know, 'e was so earnest, with knobs on. A good world tomorrow somewhere. But 'e could be funny when we 'ad a night out on the dine and you loosened 'im up.' She hugged herself. ''E said 'e loved me bum,' she added, out of nowhere, and started crying. 'And it's so fat and soft.'

Then the cider bottles were empty.

'I 'ad 'is child in me, you know. Right inside me and growing like a seed. I didn't tell 'im and got rid of it. I wish I 'adn't done, I wish. I want to be a mum.'

Once, Sloane glanced at his own face in the tall mirror leaning against the dark wallpaper and he saw bruises around his eyes. He didn't have much strength in reserve.

'Funny old bugger sometimes. 'E made me get rid of my old sofa one night. Came tearing in 'ere fit to be tied. Said it reminded 'im of somefing, and we 'ad to drag it out in the street in the middle of the night. I thought 'e'd done 'is nut for sure. Went round pinning the curtains shut too, afraid of the Brixton peeping Tom, 'e was.'

She pummelled her thighs until he grabbed her wrists to make her stop.

'I never rang 'im up, just like 'e said. Never went looking for 'is flat. I wouldn't embarrass 'im in any way, I ain't no 'ome-wrecker. I just loved 'im like a crazy puppy. 'E was so sodding good to me.'

★

He woke with a start to find Rosemary lying with her arms around him, wheezing softly into his chest. Grey light stained the room from the window, covering the skin on her arm in a fine layer of ash. Her mouth was open, but sleep didn't deepen her innocence by much, it merely smoothed away the sorrow, leaving her features more placid. She was very hot, almost steaming against him, and he found he was fully dressed, with a quilted coverlet over them both. He guessed he had just passed out from exhaustion. The touch of her body made him want Sarah desperately.

He pulled gently away from her, trying to guess her age. Her round face, still puffy from the crying, suggested she was in her mid twenties, but something reflective he had heard once or twice in her voice added a few years to that.

His head throbbed from the cider and his eyes felt swollen. His arms and legs ached. Only his hearing seemed unimpaired: soft rain played rhythm games on the bare earth outside the high half-basement window.

She stirred as he sat up and her hand reached out for him. A bloodshot eye blinked open, and he watched memory drain back slowly, turning her body heavy. The eye closed. 'Werni,' she said, but she knew it wasn't.

'I'm sorry, Rosemary.'

'We didn't do nufing. I just wanted to be by someone.'

'So did I. It's all right.'

He splashed his face with freezing water in the tiny washroom, and combed his hair roughly with his fingers. The bruises were still around his eyes. The girl will survive, he thought, looking at his drawn, old reflection in the spotty mirror, and you, you have a future to put together.

'I could make you breakfast,' she said from the next room. 'There's two eggs. Tea's finished though.'

'I have to go.'

'Be shut of me,' she said softly.

When he came out she was in the sitting room, a blanket wrapped around her, staring down at the letter like an enemy.

'Trust me,' he said. 'You'll have trouble the next few days. Get dressed and walk through your normal life. Listen to music, go to a movie, watch television, meet your friends, buy some food and cook a lot. Keep moving. Pretty soon living without him will become a habit.' He didn't say: and then there'll be someone else. There would be, but no one ever appreciated hearing it.

'Will you come talk to be again?'

During the long, long walk to the front door, he said nothing. He opened the door, the sound of the rain suddenly sharper, gaining a smell. *Men like you.* 'Rosemary . . . I didn't mean to, but I helped kill Werner.'

You hurt them. On the street, grey figures bent forward in the rain as they hurried toward shelter that lay somewhere impossibly far ahead, and before Sloane reached Brixton Station he was soaked to the skin.

16

Moore and MacIlvaine sat in the Playpen, waiting for the Old Man, Moore drawing languidly on the table top with the faint grease from his fingertip. With Ross gone, the two of them were like a tiny den of scouts with the scoutmaster on holiday – confident at the merit tests they had passed but secretly uneasy about the ones to come. Moore slumped disconsolately as MacIlvaine tried to catch his eye, preface to some dreadful small-talk. If only he weren't so reminiscent of that cousin from Iowa his mother had made him play with as a child. Even now Moore winced at the memory of having to introduce – what was his name? Anthony, Anthony Banks – to his Groton classmates and subtly try to stop Anthony Banks from asking things like where they bought those 'great tan pants'.

Dru wasn't there. She had grown more and more annoyed at the sexual banter, without Ross to moderate, and her hair-trigger moral sense was even more offended by the transparent poses of expertise and worldly wisdom. She was malingering down in the communications section rather than obeying the morning summons. She leaned against a bank of plastic-silenced teletypes, chatting with the clerks and secretaries on break. Nearly all the women in the building were shunted into these dead-end positions, and women were so thick down here that the communications and office services sections were known snidely as the Geranium Farm. (The women in office services had been given three of the four bathrooms, and having no particular use for the urinals in what had once been a men's, someone had planted geraniums in them.)

'. . . But you know we're forbidden to go outside, and the house shrink is such a pig. So she's trying to deal with it by herself.'

'Sorry, but I've never seen a woman make a lasting change in her life. We're just too emotional.'

'More of your nonsense, Cyn. Just because you can't break it off with that two-timer . . .'

Dru let the women's voices wash over her comfortably. She would have had a tooth pulled, would have let scorpions crawl over her flesh, anything, rather than sit through another meeting in a stifled rage.

'My TWA is up a point,' MacIlvaine announced finally, still unable to catch Moore's eye. 'I've been thinking of taking a chance on some of the electronics cats and dogs. You can loose a bit on the chancier ones, but if one of them takes off . . . zoom.' His hand swept up in an insouciant arc. 'You retire to Bermuda at forty.'

'I suppose so,' Moore said. The people in his circle didn't talk about their investments. As his father had said, it ultimately came down either to boasting or public weeping, both of which were characteristic of Californians and upstart Jews.

'I've got this pal – he's been knocking back corporate reports for some really big boys for a long time. Really big boys, believe me. He told me the bull stock of the next few years is going to come from some of the new bio companies, all those ex-doctors ferreting around with DNA.'

Moore sat forward in relief as the Old Man finally backed his way into the room, a handful of papers mangled against the handle of his crutch. He unlatched his leg braces and sat with a satisfied air that they had not seen for a long time.

'Lumbago shook the bushes with a vengeance,' he said without a greeting, and he spread out the crumpled papers, rubbing them flat. Moore saw that they were the morning's overseas cables, at least a dozen of them. Ross had certainly been busy. The Old Man shuffled the papers around like game tiles, apparently putting them in chronological order.

'One man seems to be dead, an old contact of Lumbago's in the trade mission, or so Ross thinks. He isn't sure yet, but the Russian resident is snorting fire.'

'It sounds like the Mother Lode,' Moore ventured. He should already have read the cables in duplicate, and he craned his neck, trying to read enough of them upside down to get a footing.

The Old Man sketched the time scale of Lumbago's actions, what they knew for sure and what they could reasonably infer. He might as well have been musing aloud for all the attention he gave the other two. 'It's spreading ripples now. The Russian trade mission people have – '

Dru threw open the door. She stood there clutching her clipboard with all the agitated awe of a researcher who had just dropped a tray of live virus.

'Sir . . .'

The Old Man held up a hand as he plodded on, refusing to look up, and Moore slumped back; the Old Man was notorious about interruptions. MacIlvaine gave Dru a leer.

'Someone in the trade mission just shot off a long cable to Moscow, straight to Dzerzhinsky Street. I have a colleague in Crosswords who's having a go at it.' He meant the low-level code-breaking unit that the directorate kept in the building to work on material too trivial, or too sensitive, to send to the National Security Agency's huge facility at Fort Meade. 'So far he's certain it says something about gold. If he's got that far, one of our European cousins is bound to tumble to it within a few hours. If they haven't already.'

'*Sir*,' Dru put in recklessly. 'You'd better see this.'

'Drusilla! When I'm finished.'

She slid the paper in front of him and backed a step before he could bite. Ignoring the paper, he went on implacably. 'Tomorrow we can inform the President that some moron is running around Europe prying into gold dealings. We won't tell him immediately who the moron belongs to. *That* we can save until he sizzles for a while.'

Dru was truly desperate now, her fingers fretting against the clipboard she held over her chest, and her mouth opening and closing with false starts like a seal come up for air. 'Sir, the Geneva report! You *have* to read it before you go on!'

The Old Man stared at her for a moment, as if trying to choose a particular form of torture, then slid her paper coldly toward him. Moore used the opportunity to inch the morning cables discreetly toward himself. There was a startled snort, and they all watched with fascination as the blood drained from the Old Man's face.

'This is a trick.'

'No, sir,' Dru said. 'It's straight from our Geneva station. I worked in Europe-ops before the changes and I know their signature. I have some collateral material here as well . . .'

But he had taken off his reading glasses, and he swiveled the chair to face the window.

MacIlvaine was mad with curiosity. 'Dru, are we at war or what?'

'May I, sir?'

The Old Man waved a hand, as if dismissing all responsibility. Dru started off in the official meeting sing-song that usually drove them all to distraction. 'Geneva reports that in a few days France will request an extraordinary session of the IMF at Rome. The session will probably be called for the middle of next month. They also report rumours of heavy gold buying by the French from South Africa and other sources. The French *government*, not the usual private hoarders. Their private citizens have something like 11 per cent of the world's gold, but the government itself – '

'My God,' Moore broke in, 'could they be going onto a gold standard?'

'What's wrong with that?' MacIlvaine asked plaintively, looking from one to the next. Moore wondered when the penny would drop for him. Perhaps he was too busy adding up what a battle of gold standards would do for his electronics stock. Gloomily Moore contemplated all the cables that he could now ignore. All Ross's quick footwork in vain.

When the Old Man swiveled back, his eyes were like frosted glass, and he seemed to have aged ten years. 'Who was it said irony has no place in history? History moves by logic, sometimes by accident, but never, never by malice. You invent a story out of whole cloth. It's just on the edge of plausibility, as any good story must be if it's tailored for deception . . .' He tailed off and sat forward with his jutting chin resting on his hands, looking drained and weary.

'Oh, Christ, it's not fair,' MacIlvaine said, the penny finally dropping.

Moore looked at the Old Man, but what he saw was his career sinking rapidly in the west, tied to a broken old man and his last crazy scheme for revenge. A perfect boomerang. Ten years of writing research reports on the diplomatic relations between Montenegro and the Hohenzollern Empire, another ten feeding the check protectors in payroll, and then out to pasture – never having eaten in the linen-and-silver lunchroom, never having run a section, never having flirted with his own private secretary. Damn right it wasn't fair.

'We've handed Research a minor espionage triumph,' the Old Man said woodenly. 'When the President sees their material, it's bound to show heavy gold buying. Those wretched idiots will be funded for another generation.'

'Couldn't we beat them to the punch?' MacIlvaine suggested. 'We could tell the President ourselves, immediately.'

'What do we have? Suppositions and rumours,' the Old Man said. 'They'll have the hard evidence. We'd look worse, upstaged in a matter of hours by ever-vigilant Research. Better we seem to know nothing.'

Then Moore found it. It was one of the first papers, covering a short phone call from Ross, the crucial phrase right at the end. 'Sir, it says here Lumbago hasn't delivered his material yet.'

There was a hasty pawing battle as they all tried to read the memo at once, and then a scrambling for other papers as they tried to find out if the delivery had come later.

'Here,' Moore said. 'Lumbago is refusing to deliver until he knows his wife is safe. They must have burned him with some pretty nasty blackmail.'

'Evidently,' the Old Man said coldly and snatched the cable from Moore. He read the full transcript from the telephone tap aloud, plus Ross's commentary on it, still curiously emotionless. Ross had once insisted that the Old Man had been one of the best. Was this all that was left, Moore thought. 'Get on to London, to Ross, even to Kohler.'

'We had a watcher on him, didn't we?' MacIlvaine volunteered. 'He was told to stay back,' Dru put in, 'and he lost him two days ago.'

'Bad luck, but we can't sit here crying over it. Lumbago mustn't be allowed to deliver. We'll make up some cock-and-bull and get everyone we can on to it. Have them call in Special Branch for help. Hell, we'll get the Air Force if we can. Tell them it's most urgent. Security of the Free World.'

'It's not going to look good,' Moore said.

'It'll look a damn sight better than standing here with our thumbs up our backsides while the President hands Research a medal. Who was the watcher?' he added suddenly.

'Someone called Sparrow. He's a contract man that –'

'I know who Sparrow is. He's deniable. He's also not playing with a full deck, but he's useful. All right, let's use Sparrow. Tell him to find Lumbago and stop him. Write him a ticket.'

'*Sir*?' Moore and Dru protested together.

'I said, Sparrow should write him a ticket, squash him. It's deniable.' He shrugged as if he had lost interest in the whole operation. 'Give him some latitude if you insist. If he can snatch Lumbago's treasure with safety, fine; if not, he's to make damn sure it isn't delivered.'

Moore sat in shock, seeing not just the end of a promising career, but a battery of microphones and a hostile Congressional committee. There were plenty of situations in which the directorate would accept a hit, okay it after the fact, cover it, but this certainly wouldn't be one of them. Ross, Ross, Moore thought, where are you now that we need you? He repented his weasling out of the London trip; Langley had turned out to be the hot end after all. He looked around and saw that MacIlvaine had retreated behind a passive smirk, pleased to see others wrangling and too unimaginative to guess the consequences. Dru's knuckles had gone white on her clipboard.

'Gentlemen, you set out on a tiger hunt in the safety of your station wagon, planning to use your humane tranquilliser darts, and suddenly it turns nasty and the tiger's bearing down on some picnickers. You don't shrug and give up because the only safe shot is up his balls with a rifle. You do what you have to.'

He's gone clean over the edge, Moore thought. 'I don't believe the analogy is quite appropriate, sir,' he objected politely. 'Lumbago is an American citizen, and he's done nothing against us that we know – against his country, I mean. We can't justify it by extreme circumstances or national security.'

'Oh yes we can and will. Jerry . . .' He paused, and seemed to drag himself slowly up from some remote depth. 'There are thousands of faceless Chileans digging up copper thousands of miles away. Say it'll raise your family's metal portfolio one point if just three of those miners die. Just cease to exist as far as anyone is concerned. Erased. Agreed? I'll raise you two points for six of them. Ten points for thirty dead faceless miners. It won't hurt a bit. Where do you want me to stop? You draw the line, and don't tell me you care about individual miners. Your grandfather and father have been ordering them killed for a century. I'll promote you section head for fifty dead miners. Your own staff, private office with a window.'

'They're not Americans.'

Slowly the Old Man smiled, a cruel, ruthless smile without a trace of humour. 'What a fine point of morality. Forgive me for not appreciating who I was dealing with.'

Dru broke the silence that had settled leadenly. 'Sir, I'd like to request reassignment to another section.'

'*Or?*' the Old Man said.

'Pardon?'

'There was an "or" tone, Drusilla. What will you do? Go over my head? Go to the press? Write a goddamn book? Denied.'

She looked at her watch and spoke the time and the date. 'As of this moment, I'm filing an IPS-92 for a transfer. I'll have it typed up and – '

'Go fuck yourself,' the Old Man said. 'I never wanted women in the department. Jerry, send my instructions.'

★

The sign said WOMEN'S INSTITUTE JUMBLE SALE – ADMISSION 10P, but the rain had obviously kept away most of the bargain hunters. An anonymous middle-aged woman sat listlessly at a folding table behind a saucer that held only five or six coins. The hall inside was a dim cavern, with a handful of people wandering the tables of used tangled clothing set out in a ring like a flotilla of dismasted yachts.

He was sopping wet, his trousers clinging to his legs and his shoes squelching as he walked. He was also strangely light-headed, with the horrible tension and anguish of the basement flat behind him. His duty to the girl and to Jannings was now done, and he had a sense of moving forward for the first time in ages. He wished his moods weren't so mercurial; even when he felt relatively tranquil there was that apprehension about how long it would last and what would come next.

By the door a small boy pried with all his might at the plastic lid of a pinball table. He strained and hissed at the toy until a heavy-set woman rushed at him and slapped his hand away. 'Leave off, Jimmy. You'll bloody brike it.' As he was dragged away, the boy's eyes clung fiercely to the toy counter.

It's second chances, Sloane thought, watching the set of the boy's jaw. That boy knew there weren't any, and he was hell-bent on examining the toy. *Now.* For a year Sloane had lived in a universe that was the direct opposite of the boy's. There had seemed an infinite number of second chances – stretching infinitely ahead. It had been a buffer against any movement at all, destroying the uniqueness of each moment; a refuge against having to act. He knew that had all been a lie, but he had the great privilege now: this was it, this instant, this day, a second chance for his entire life.

He strode to a likely table of men's clothing, picking through until he found a pair of grey trousers that seemed the right size, and a heavy brown pullover. He'd end up looking like a tramp, but he had to get dry.

'Something for the rain?' he asked.

An impassive-looking woman in a thick woollen sweater pointed her bony finger toward a rack of coats across the room, where a tall vicar fussed with tags on sleeves. 'I think he's put out some macs. Forty pence, the two.'

He paid and went across to the long pipe trestle where he fingered the threadbare suitcoats that smelled musty and sour like old books, parkas that had lost their stuffing, a fake fur going bald in patches. One end of the pipe held longer coats and he spread the hangers, hunting for waterproofs.

'Bless you,' a dry voice said.

'Pardon?'

The vicar's pinched face appeared furtively through the coats. 'I said, "Bless you." Didn't I hear a sneeze?'

'That was the hangers squealing.'

'Ah, well . . . I suppose you have a blessing for free, then. Mustn't turn down something for free these days, eh? Good value

203

for money, you might say . . .' He considered his statement, puzzling, like a lonely man used to questioning and contradicting his own words simply for the illusion of two-way discourse. 'Except, of course, strictly speaking, there's no money involved. Peculiar expression, rather – value implying money, of course – a bit redundant, isn't it?'

'Like vicars,' Sloane suggested. He didn't know why he had said it, except that he felt elated, almost drunk, and the blanched, faintly ridiculous face framed by the coats seemed to have made it inevitable.

'Oh, dear, one is an unbeliever. How *unusual*,' he added with good-natured irony.

'Forgive me. It wasn't called for.'

'Mustn't apologize. Lost our faith, have we? Or never had it, more likely. That's the usual thing these days. Most of the young people grow up believing in nothing but pop stars and their own physical desires.'

'I'm not very young.'

'A manner of speaking. Still, it's a bit Orwellian, that world, isn't it? All those children putting their faith in self-gratifications. Really, they end up quite unhappy, going hammer and tongs at each other to get their share of the pleasures supposed to be there.'

'I wouldn't know.' He half wanted to slink away as quickly as possible and half to laugh aloud at the preposterous discussion that clung to him like an unwanted guest. He could see that the vicar had said all this a hundred times before, and he'd nudged the lever that set off the tape.

The vicar straightened and gave a warm smile. 'Surely you want to be loved.'

'Actually, I want a raincoat. I mean a mac.'

The man chuckled and squatted at a number of cardboard cartons. 'I think I have something for you.' He clucked like an old peasant examining his yard animals, studying one bundle after another and piling folded towels and shirts to one side. 'You're certainly old enough to know love isn't just a quick grope behind the pub. I admit all this emphasis on spirituality can be terribly destructive of the daily world, but if you get caught up in that world, well, I find it's all just muddy pools, eh? I mean, caught up exclusively. Here we are. I thought I saw one.'

A tightly rolled blue bundle shook out into a long nylon raincoat, the kind that folded into a pocket pouch.

'That's fine.' Sloane slid his arms into the coat and tested the pockets.

'Not that I'm puritanical, mind, I just find artificial religion so frightfully sad, and that's what people seem to be driven to these days. Flirting with all those eccentric psychologies or with politics. I've got nothing against real politics, you understand. I'm from Yorkshire originally, and I saw politics that meant something real to families that hadn't got their next meal, but you can't tell me the lads in the streets these days are fighting to feed their families.'

'Didn't God have a little extra feeling for the ones who believed without shoving their hands in the wounds?'

The kindly old face seemed disconcerted. 'Oh dear, I suppose you have a point, if you grant they have genuine sympathy for the poor. Dear, dear. Yes, I suppose if they're sincere, they have every right.'

'Some are sincere, I'm sure,' Sloane said, realizing now that he was defending Jannings. 'Don't take me too seriously, father.'

'Technically, you shouldn't call me father. You're not C of E.'

'How much?'

'Excuse me.'

'The coat.'

'Oh, please have it.' He regained some of his humour. 'It may help you through the muddy pools.'

Sloane pressed a fifty-pence piece into the dry palm.

'Are you married?' the old men enquired suddenly, as if reluctant to lose the company.

Sloane nodded. 'We do our best to love each other.'

'You're a fortunate man. Bless you again.'

'Thanks.'

He drifted away through the dim room, with the vicar's guileless cheer trailing feebly after him. What was sad, he thought, was not that the world was a moral vacuum, but that what goodness did exist was so impotent. Look around, he thought, catching the old man's habits of conversation. Malice, petty self-interest, hypocrisy, outright cruelty were as hardy

Cutter's ham fist brought down on a table. Goodness was crippled, broken like a dotty old vicar. He dodged a sniffling woman who carried an immense string bag of clothing thrust ahead of her, and he sensed a new energy in his quickened movements. Good and evil weren't his problem; survival was, and he was determined to be a survivor. He bought a cloth cap and tried it on jauntily. Today he would meet Sarah; today a new future would begin, a concrete future.

At the door the little boy shoved his fingers through a cardboard doll's house, and the woman came running. 'You've mide ruddy great owls in it!'

Sloane leaned toward the woman and said quietly, 'Tell him about sex. It's what he wants to know.'

She was still squawking after him as he stepped out of the hall into the mist. One delivery and it was over.

He changed in a urinal behind a pub and discarded his old clothes, making certain that the film cannister was safe in his new pocket. Only his shoes still sucked against his feet, the toes ruined and curling up, as he headed for the tube entrance. A wizened gypsy woman in black tried to sell him a sprig of dry heather tied with a ribbon, but he had only a few coins left and he had to risk the bad luck.

17

'This is Macon, Special Branch. I want the Permanent Secretary. Well, disturb him, man,' he said impatiently into the telephone. 'Take a pew, Harvey.'

'I'll stand.' Ross brought out one of the half dozen new linen handkerchiefs he had bought that afternoon and wiped his forehead, beginning the process of wearing it to its inevitable tatters. Other people lost handkerchiefs, he thought dismally, as he felt the heat build up behind his forehead; other people stained them with wine and threw them away. He wore them out. He had awakened at one, which was 8 a.m. in the Eastern Standard Time that still claimed his sleepcycle. Ross missed his morning ration of reading; he hardly felt awake without it. But he had found a half dozen new cables from Langley in his temporary box beside Kohler's dingy cubicle at Grosvenor Square. A particularly hysterical cable from Dru had spoken of the Old Man on a killing rampage. The other cables had already set in motion a vast British manhunt for Lumbago under the veiled suggestion that he was a terrorist working for the Irish National Liberation Army.

'No, tell him I want the orders in writing, and I want to speak to him.' Macon hooked the telephone over his shoulder and hit a key on the boxy intercom on his desk.

Ross could live with the over-elaborate manhunt, just barely, but a more drastic order seemed to have gone out through Kohler. He would have intercepted it if he had seen it in time, but Kohler had met Sparrow at dawn, just as Ross was settling back in his chilly bed-and-breakfast room for a few hours' sleep. He had given Kohler strict instructions to countermand the order if Sparrow called in, but if he didn't call . . .

Ross didn't want to think about it; the Old Man was on soft

ground as it was, and it was going to be hard enough to clean up after the massive drag-net, without anything worse.

A blonde woman came in stiffly, wheeling a trolley of teacups and a teapot under a knitted blue cosy that said, 'I love coppers', in pink. 'Ask Mellish to step in, would you please?'

'Yes, sir.'

'Help yourself, Harvey. If you'd prefer coffee, you'll have to pop over to the canteen.'

'No thanks.'

'You wouldn't happen to know – ?' Macon began, but he tilted the phone quickly to his ear. 'There we are. I'm sorry about that, sir. I understand, but I must have written confirmation. We're already putting our chaps everywhere on your verbal instruction. The whole Met, as well. If the balloon goes up over this, I don't want to be standing here with a silly grin on my face.'

Ross saw him wince and he would have given a lot to hear the voice on the other end. The final telegram in his box had told him what it was about: Broken Back was a fiasco. Through some black irony the French were, indeed, manoeuvring to launch a gold standard with their European partners, or so the indicators said, and if Lumbago actually had stolen the file on Russian gold sales it would probably contain the first certain evidence of the French plan. The President would accelerate his own timetable, and not long after would stand the whole research organization on a podium and salute them through the Star-Spangled Banner. Whatever happened now, the Old Man's plan to discredit Research was down the drain. The best they could hope for was to prevent the unearned credit. Ross tried to peer into the Old Man's mind: this one failure wasn't the end of the world, but he was nearing retirement and Broken Back had undoubtedly represented his last brave operation, his gift to posterity. He was going to extraordinary lengths, possibly catastrophic lengths, to keep the plan from backfiring. Ross could see precisely why Dru had flown off the handle, though he didn't condone it, and wrily he imagined the turmoil that ambitious Jerry Moore was going through. He wasn't sure himself if loyalty to the Old Man wasn't taking him too far.

'Still, it's a bit unusual, all this, isn't it?' Macon said. 'All stops out, and we've got no bloody reason worth a pin.'

The door opened, and the young bearded assistant came in. Macon greeted him with his eyebrows and waved a hand toward the tea trolley.

'Hello, Ross,' Mellish said softly, as he stripped off the cosy and poured out two cups, one of which he handed across to Macon. 'The vultures gather.'

'Did you enjoy my tapes?' Ross asked. Mellish replied with a thin smile.

Ross noted the thick Donegal tweed he wore, with its brown and black flecks, making his own shiny Sears suit feel shabbier and shabbier. Mellish sipped his cup, made a face. 'She's still making it with condensed milk. I can taste the sweetness.'

Mellish was the sort of assistant he would like to have had, bright and resourceful, with a gentle, observant sense of humour. Instead he had Moore and the insufferable MacIlvaine. Dru was the only one with much promise, but she was usually preoccupied with her own private wars.

'Indeed we will, you can be sure. Keep a weather eye out yourself, sir. Ta.'

Macon hung up gently with a hand on either end of the receiver.

'Bloody Sir Cecil?' Mellish enquired.

'Ours is not to reason why, and all that. Yet he'll send an ambiguous written minute within the hour. The best that can be done. For small favours.'

'Shall we set up the mobile command post?'

'Yes, the whole show. Anything that's hanging fire, go to it.' Macon turned to Ross, who hovered in the corner with his bland, unreadable frown. 'Things seem to have crystallized somewhat. Your people are now saying this Sloane stole something from the Russians that could touch off a new cold war if it isn't returned.'

'I thought we already had one.'

'A new hot war then. Quite a change from an urban terrorist, eh? Smells rather of groping doesn't it?'

'Well, actually, he *has* taken something from the Russians.'

'You wouldn't want to tell us what it is?' Mellish suggested.

'I'm not here,' Ross said. 'I'm not in London at all. You've monitored the same calls I have.'

Macon folded his hands. 'Get on with you, Mellish. Press the buttons.'

'Sir.'

When he was gone, Macon watched Ross reflectively and started to fill his pipe from a battered leather pouch. 'All right, you're protecting someone, you're babysitting something gone sour. You don't like it much. And I don't like it at all. A flat-out manhunt is expensive, it's troublesome, someone could get hurt, and I may well come out looking a fool. I'll tell you this, if it isn't atomic secrets at the least, whoever laid on this show is for it.'

'Do you remember the OSS?' Ross said.

'Not personally, but, yes, of course I remember them. The grand old days against the Hun. Shoulder to shoulder with our own spy boys for freedom.'

'There aren't many of them left now, not many at all, but they were genuine heroes as far as I'm concerned. There's one little band called the Aylesham group who did night drops into Belgium and France and even Germany toward the end. They had almost 80 per cent casualties. We both owe them a lot, and any of them left deserve a break.'

Macon took a long time lighting the pipe, going through two wooden matches and a lot of signalling with his fingers over the bowl. 'That narrows it roughly to one,' Macon said. 'Long in the tooth, but still active.'

'I suppose it does.'

'It doesn't tell me what Sloane is carrying and what the whole bloody show is called.'

'It wasn't meant to,' Ross said carefully. 'It tells you why I'll go down with the ship if I have to.'

★

The cloth workman's cap with its peak sewn to the bill was a bit better than nothing and, miraculously, the drab tweed seemed to absorb more of the drizzle than it let through. Only his feet were really uncomfortable in the damp socks as he cut across behind the shops on Blackstock Road. It was only afternoon but so dark that half the cars in North London had switched on their running lights, and schoolchildren in blue blazers migrated home in sullen shoals. A black dog with a bright red collar cocked its head

210

at him as he passed and trotted after him for two blocks before ducking away on a mission of its own.

With unnerving speed, the cheery confidence seemed to have fled and anxiety was taking its place. He reminded himself: you're home free, man. One meeting, one delivery, and it would be over. He wondered how it was possible for so many people to inhabit one body, but he knew that waiting had always torn at the wounds. At one time, just standing in a bus queue would drive him to distraction.

He scurried across Green Lanes at a break in the traffic, and as he reached the gate into Clissold Park he glanced back at the sound. Two police cars brayed past, their blue lights flaring off the windows of the grey houses. He couldn't remember ever seeing two police cars together in London.

The huge chestnut tree that he loved was nearly bare now, with a few shriveled brown survivors arrayed almost symmetrically across its boughs like Christmas ornaments. As he watched, one of the leaves came free and drifted, tumbled and swooped toward the asphalt path, plummeting the last few feet as if finally, truly dead. The haphazard animal pens were mostly empty. A few brown rabbits huddled in a shelter, and one spotted deer browsed the dying grass. Where the geese had been was only a trapezoidal stretch of grass and leaves, with a bit of fluff caught in the chain-link fence as a memorial. The crude wooden bird house was quiet, and most of the songbirds appeared to have retreated into the inner enclosure for the duration. The mynah had been stationed at an inner angle of the building, where the path jutted out into an apron, and when he turned off he was surprised to see the bird still on its perch, rapping its orange beak sharply in complaint. Carefully he searched the length of the fence by the cage: no string, no message.

'Rotten weather, eh?' Sloane said.

The bird responded, preposterously, with a sound of tearing cloth that seemed to come from nowhere.

'My feeling exactly. I don't know about you, but I'm going to get some shelter.'

'Bloody cock! Bloody cock!'

Sloane turned up the skimpy collar of the raincoat and made for an empty bandshell across the grass. She would come today, he was certain. They had chased her from the inn the night before and she had spent the night somewhere, hidden, and would come soon now. If she didn't . . . He contented himself across the damp grass with various fantasies of kicking down the door at the Research office and throttling Cutter, pummelling him, bashing his head against the wall. He smiled at himself: if it came to that he would need three others backing him up. Cutter weighed at least 220 pounds and would probably be a handful for a professional wrestler.

★

In the corridors and anterooms of 132 police stations spread across the vast urban continent of London, in the low-slung building crouching by Westminster Bridge, in the small post inside Wellington Arch at Hyde Park Corner, in the dark and seedy stations at Bow Road and Albany Street and St Ann's Road, and in the Edwardian brick station on Blackstock Road that lay only 500 yards as the crow flies from Clissold Park, evening constables were coming lazily on duty. As they did, they fingered small passport photographs of a plain-looking, dark haired man in his late forties, no distinguishing marks apparent, only a vague air of discomfort too mild to be called anxiety.

'They aren't terribly concrete – the story wants detail still. First they said a possible terrorist, and now something else, something that interests Special Branch in particular.'

'Another flaming political,' a new man put in wearily.

'Precisely. We don't know the whole picture but it's top drawer, so you can take this seriously or pack it in. All of you.'

There was a muttering of agreement, like a Sunday cricket crowd after a well-struck six.

'Duffryn, you'll leave one with the ticket seller at the tube station. The rest of you have a look round the pubs as you go.'

'Is the Special Patrol Group on this as well?'

'I believe so.'

'Then we'd better nick this villain quick, hadn't we? Before our bloody little heroes bloody clout him to death.'

'No more of that talk now.'

18

'All present and correct, Inspector.'

'Take your two to the top of the road, by Foyles.'

'Is this going to go on all night?'

'Fancy a nice lie-in in the morning, do you? All night for you. Especially for you. *Geroff.*'

In the last weary light of evening, Ross watched the detachments deploy haphazardly along the road. The beige panel van, parked up on the curb of Charing Cross and ostentatiously ignored by half a dozen men rocking on shiny black shoes, looked about as subtle to Ross as a missile pad. He leaned back against the bolted doorway of the sandwich shop and wondered how many shopkeepers had peeped apprehensively out of their windows before locking up, expecting some Irish mischief. Even the satellite command post, a yellow Telecom van parked up the road beyond Research, seemed obvious to him, and he wondered if Cutter's Acolytes were peering down from their windows, muttering to themselves. At least the plainclothesmen weren't particularly conspicuous yet, or not from a distance, since they were screened by the commuters who gathered from all directions into solid masses that descended in lockstep through the tube gates. In an hour, though, the whole force would stand out like flags on a desert.

The rain had softened to a mist, hanging suspended as much as falling, drifting horizontally to form beads on every surface. Ross had put his handkerchief into temporary retirement, since the pedestrians all came past now with damp foreheads and stringy hair. A car drove up the road with headlights on to set off a startling display of jewels stuck to the railings, awning poles and ornate cornices. Ross watched with a faint memory of lust as a girl immediately in front of him dabbed at her pink revealed bosom where a rivulet off the awning had gone exploring. How did some of the girls stay so healthy-looking in this climate? Sun lamps? Holidays in Morocco? But, looking across the road, he saw that many of them hadn't. Chalky, grainy, washed-out and stoic, they clutched dark coats around them as they hurried toward the tube or huddled with their satchels under the bus shelter.

Ross hadn't been with a woman in – how long? – more than three years, he thought. Since the misbegotten weekend he'd promised Meg O'Dwyer, the queen bee of the typing pool, after he'd got drunk at the office party. He missed it, not so much the sex but the comfort of being with someone he loved, exchanging observations, doing small favours out of genuine affection. (He missed Myra, but he never allowed himself to think that name openly.) Meg hadn't been comfortable at all. She'd turned out just as he'd expected, shrill and demanding, as abruptly senti-mental as a teenager, excruciatingly boring after the first few minutes of shop talk. Now, the idea of being with someone new gave him a primitive sense of terror. Waking next to a woman he disliked was as depressing as anything he knew.

And he wasn't much of a catch either. Overweight, self-centred, too solemn to offer much fun – and for all its suppres-sion, with an anger inside as cruel as it had been in those days after he had piloted the boat home alone. 'Stop mourning her, you fat clown,' Fischetti had urged after a year. 'There's one or two still out there who'd pick up your spirits.' But there weren't.

Macon walked stiffly back from the satellite van, hugging the shopfronts against the ragged counterflow of pedestrians. He wore a belted, fawn-coloured trench coat that made him look astonishingly like what he was, reconfirmed by an abrupt military toss of his arm to shoot his sleeve to check his watch. He passed Ross and rapped on the rear doors of the van. A young head and shoulders appeared, showing a few inches of blue uniform.

'It's all in place, sir, but we're having trouble tying in. Another few minutes.'

'Step lively.'

'Yes, sir.'

Macon turned crisply in place and, with a look of shared frust-

214

ration, joined Ross in the doorway. 'Have you any idea which way he'll come?'

'I don't know he'll come. But it's either him to them, or them to him. I imagine you've got them pretty thoroughly spooked by now. The log says they're all inside.'

'We've had an intercept on their post. Nothing has arrived that way. Mind, this Sloane chap might have sent it by pigeon. If it's small enough, of course . . .'

He was digging. 'Or by goldfish through the sewers up into their toilet, sure. I don't know if it's small enough, Henry. I expect it's bigger than a needle and probably a little smaller than Yugoslavia.'

Macon dragged out his pipe paraphernalia and began reaming and peering into the bowl with his terrible nonchalence. He smiled solemnly as he reassembled the pipe. 'By the by, your friend Kohler will be dropping round soon with the latest word from on high.'

'That ought to make my day.'

★

There was no wind, yet as he stood at the focus of the empty bandshell there was something like a sound, eerily pressuring his ears, a machine throbbing miles beneath the earth, or the soft coaxing of something far too large to be seen. He moved sideways along the folding chairs, out of the sound focus, and the machine died away to leave the ordinary sounds of traffic drifting across the park. A bicycle whirred illegally down the path, its rider crackling in a clear plastic cover as he leaned into the mist. Before long they would be locking the park gates, and she hadn't come.

Sloane glanced at the trail of dead cigarettes he had left along the concrete. He counted nine. Almost half a pack in little more than an hour; the habit was back in spades. Come on, man, he told himself, she'll come. She got away from the inn.

She thinks they might recognize the car and she's waiting until pitch dark.

Or did someone steal the string off the fence? he worried for the tenth time. Some child trailed its fingers along the wire and plucked the signal loose with an idle twist. A zealous groundskeeper . . . He had to stop the tormenting nonsense. After they locked the gates, he would go down to New Oxford Street and wait at the umbrella shop in any case . . . Or perhaps the car had broken down and she had taken the train, was even now hurrying through the back streets from Finsbury Park Station. Perhaps the train was still ten miles south of London and she was beginning to panic, knowing she would be late. She was hiding out somewhere, waiting for him to contact Felicity. But he *had* called Felicity, and there was no message.

He caught himself reaching for another cigarette and snatched his hand away miserably with an exaggerated gesture of his loneliness. An old woman waddling along the path between two carrier bags had seen his pantomime; she fixed her eyes straight ahead of her, straining to be past the bandshell and away from the odd, dangerous man. A flasher in a cheap blue mac? A mugger signalling his confederates? As Sloane watched the woman, she glanced around furtively and caught his eyes on her. Now she was doubly alarmed, almost running down the path.

I did you a favour, madam, he thought idly. Acknowledge that fear, act on it. The world *is* as dangerous as you think. Every man you see is a Cutter waiting to invade your life and steal your peace of mind. Or if he's not a Cutter, a Sloane reluctantly but loyally spreading the poison the Cutters manufacture. Too weak to stand up to the pressure ourselves, we pass it along until our friends swallow pills. Run for home, bolt the door, arm yourself. Against us.

You hurt them.

He gave up the small battle and slid out the cigarette. He'd wait a little longer before the next one. A woman turned into the park through the gate on Green Lanes, a tiny brown figure a quarter mile away who hurried purposefully along the central path in a gait that was unmistakably not Sarah's. Her hair was right, and she had the same body, angular and fleshless as a heron, but Sarah had never moved with that intent step, stabbing at the sandy path with long busy thrusts of her legs. An executive's step. A head nurse in a hurry. Time had always been Sarah's lazy enemy, hovering in the corners of a room, each day heavy with a threat of leisure, of vacuum – and the night to lie awake. He ground the cigarette out, only half smoked, and watched the rain against a nearby lamp. The globe was haloed, with tiny sparkles drifting across the yellow glass.

As the woman approached the empty animal pens, Sloane toyed with the pretence that it was indeed Sarah and the waiting was over. He tested the shock of recognition, the easing of tension he would feel, the words he would use. Then he was loping across the grass toward her, clutching the unbuttoned raincoat at his chest.

She was tying a piece of yarn to the fence as he slid to a stop on the slick asphalt apron. 'Oh, *you*!' She had often called him *you* when she was annoyed. 'You gave me a start.'

She was in his arms, hugging him back around the damp coat, and there was no annoyance at all.

'Jeffrey, Jeffrey.'

'It's good to hold you.'

They kissed desperately, like lovers parted for months, and he felt her hips pressing against him. But his tension hadn't gone as he'd anticipated. When she set her temple against his jaw, he kissed the top of her head, tasting the familiar smell of her hair, and he saw himself standing there with her, someone else, someone better who could build her a decent life.

'It's good to be fancied,' she said. 'I missed you. Are you all right?'

He saw the strain in her eyes when she pulled back, but there was something else that he didn't recognize immediately; it was in her voice too, like the strange confident stride across the park. And what he saw frightened him, like the sight of a wild animal outside its cage.

'How are *you*? I called the inn and they said something about trouble in your room.'

She told him about it, made a joke of the poor old soldier she'd recruited to help her escape. 'Do you know what they wanted with me?'

'They didn't say?'

'I didn't stop there to ask.' She smiled momentarily, then it flickered and went out. 'Last night I slept in the car. Outside a village in the Downs. Lord, was it cold.'

'They were Cutter's altar-boys,' he said. 'I imagine they planned to hold you to put pressure on me. Where's the car now?'

217

'Don't worry. It's a mile away in Highbury. I walked and I'm wet and tired, and I'm stiff from the car.'

'Let's have a drink. The pubs are open.'

'In a minute. You still haven't told me about you.'

'It's almost over,' he said, and the words pleased him suddenly, inordinately, hearing them out loud like a promise of truce after years of siege. 'Almost. I've got what they want, and now I'm sure you're safe, I just have to pop down to the West End and deliver it.'

She pulled back and her eyes became very still. 'Haven't you seen the papers?'

He shook his head, alarmed by her alarm.

She dug through her large handbag, in the centre section with a bulky misfolded map and a lot of wadded-up tissue, and then the outer pocket, where she found the quartered *Mirror*. 'It's not going to be so simple.'

It was only a small article, boxed at the bottom of the second page and facing a bare-breasted woman who twined a string of pearls around her neck – *Maid Mary of Nottingham, our maiden of the hills and valleys* . . . There was his passport photo under a bold headline: *LONDON MANHUNT*. The article said next to nothing, only that the search was concentrated in the area of Soho and St Giles – which could certainly have been a discreet way of saying the Research office – and that Sloane, forty-seven, was wanted to assist the police in their enquiries concerning a recent crime. There was a flurry of journalistic indignation that the police had released so few details, and a snide reminder of a similar search a year earlier in which more than a dozen innocent tourists had been picked up in a hunt for a Provo bomb layer.

'That's where you need to go, isn't it?'

'I'd better have that drink.'

★

Kohler was dropped off at the corner by a dark blue Chrysler and he sauntered toward them in a short overcoat and an open-necked blue shirt, smiling like a schoolboy off on a field trip. Ross retreated some way from the others, hoping that Kohler would steer for the English policemen and leave him alone.

'Where's Calloway?' Macon asked a uniformed, middle-aged policeman who waited by the shop window with a hard air of authority.

'On his way. He's been putting up in Guildford it seems. With his aunt.'

'Hi there, Harvey. How's spying?'

'The aunt's taken sick. Never one for the do-this-by-yesterday orders, Calloway wasn't. Have we got new information?'

'His wife was driving a red Triumph, J reg. Her sister's.'

'You have a full share of mouth, Guy. It's a shame you couldn't reach Sparrow.'

'Stroud has the number of the car. You can circulate that to your lads, and her description. I imagine they'll be getting together.'

'Isn't it? I doubt if he'll call now. I suppose the whole thing will just have to run out to its destined conclusion.'

'I don't hold with spreading the focus of search like that. We've got a thousand men out there trying to remember his photograph.'

'I hope the Old Man has a steel jock. He just might catch a stray knee in this business.'

'Confuses the issue, adding the car and the woman.'

'I think it's best. The two together throw a different profile. One misses that watching for one man.'

'You've been undercutting him from the beginning. If this fucks up any worse, I'll see you remember it.'

'If you insist, I'll have it given out.'

'I followed the letter of my instructions.' Kohler spoke indignantly and then devoted himself to hunting for cigarettes in all his pockets.

'Whose, I wonder?' He was avoiding Ross's eyes, and Ross wondered what he was hiding.

Macon dismissed his policeman and noticed Kohler with a frown. 'There you are. You prepared to give us a fuller background?'

'What I know, you now.' Kohler fished out of his pocket what looked like an amber cigarette holder. It *was* an amber cigarette holder. Oh, God, Ross thought. One more affectation and the man would be a travelling museum of dandyism.

'Nothing new at all?'

'Not a lick, sorry.'

'If this turns into a shambles, it may be a trifle awkward for you people.'

'Someone will catch the can,' Kohler said amiably.

'Yes, and it'll be coming from a fair altitude, I promise. The Permanent Secretary is by way of having second thoughts, and he's demanding an explanation in private from one of your attachés.' Kohler's eyebrows went up with mocking concern. 'Hotting up, right, Harvey?'

'Ross said nothing. He could have strangled Kohler, but the man had to be there. Ross had no authority in London, and on his own he could do little more than observe, see that Kohler did at least the minimum – but mostly stand around with his hands in his pockets waiting to sweep up. To top it off, the rain was turning heavier, driving all three of them back into the cramped doorway where his stomach was wrenched by the cloying leathery cologne Kohler wore.

A squall of rain pelted down suddenly. All along the gloomy canyon the home-bound commuters sprinted toward the buses and trains, and shiny toe caps retreated conspicuously under awnings, doorways and window ledges. A cabaret, Ross thought, a Keystone Kops comedy at half speed. He had the sense of clinging to something gone out of control; the Abortionist watching helplessly as the haemorrhaging began.

★

Sarah arched her back against the wooden chair in a stately way and massaged her shoulder. 'Horses can sleep standing up; you'd suppose I could sleep sitting. I feel as if I've been beaten all night by cricket bats.'

'Reminds me of the night I slept on concrete, the floor of a cabin that hadn't been completed. I was at one of those give-a-poor-urban-child-a-week-in-the-country camps, and I thought the concrete slab would keep my borrowed sleeping bag clean. I killed the circulation in my leg so thoroughly, when I got up it wasn't there. I fell flat on my nose.'

She watched him in the dim pub light with a sudden domestic

concern. Between them a candle burned inside a blue glass sphere, someone's idea of adding character to the dreary pub. 'That's the very first story you've ever volunteered about your childhood,' she said. Her skin was as luminous as porcelain in the candlelight.

'We're still young lovers,' he said, trying to settle a light note on it. 'We've got a whole life ahead to look back.' He judged the moment and told her now about the Dalston flat.

Surprisingly she took it with a shrug. 'Not a thing there I treasured. I've never been able to care that much for things. It'll be good to start afresh.'

'You're bearing up all right, you know,' he said. It was all new, her confident walk, her stoicism, fresh mannerisms that lacked both timidity and haste, and again he found she troubled him. He wondered if the thin scream that had seemed to hang over the flat the past year had been his own after all. 'Better than I am.'

'Yes, I am, aren't I? You're not doing so badly. Felicity saw it as well. You're not the Jeffrey I knew a few months ago, nor even the hidden one I saw at Cuckfield.'

'Only at moments . . .'

The door banged open. Three young men jostled in with belligerent camaraderie, talking too loudly and elbowing for the free stool.

'Three pints, George, we're celebrating!'

'A short for me, twit.'

The tallest, with hair cropped close and hanging limp around a savage grey face, surveyed the room with a scornful eye. 'Not a young bird in the lot.'

'Just off wanking and already 'e's Errol fucking Flynn.'

'Keep it down, boys, please,' the barman bleated.

'That daft cunt won the pools, would you believe?'

'Mind, just a wee win.' One of them wandered to a slot machine and punched it aggressively.

Sarah gave the young rowdies a momentary glance. Then he saw her dismiss them from her mind. He thought: a month ago, a week even, the unpredictable menace they emanated would have left her on edge the rest of the evening.

'I know it sounds ridiculous, but in a peculiar way it's done me good to have those men after me. No, let me finish. I used to lie in

221

bed late at night wishing for an earthquake or a massive fire to sweep over the city. Something catastrophic, knocking down buildings. It wasn't anger or anything like that. I didn't want anyone hurt, that didn't enter into it. It's just, it would have validated all the strange dreads I had inside. Now it's come, in a way, and the world hasn't ended. Like the first time coming off a horse.'

She smiled and took his hand. 'Of course I knew we'd never get catastrophe, not here. The river just silts up, the bricks mildew, debris collects on the building sites, and the power dims out. Slow decay is what's so terrifying. It's like watching time go backwards.'

'And there I was, objectifying it all,' he said. 'Dimming out before your eyes.'

She laughed softly. 'You weren't as bad as all that. How are you going to make your delivery? They'll be on to you before you get close.'

'It's a big, busy city. I've got the edge on them. What I don't understand is what set off the fuss. What I have is penny ante; it'll be public record before very long. It's like tossing a firecracker and seeing the whole damn block blow up.'

'Seriously, I drove here through the West End and there were police cordons everywhere. It looked like . . . I don't know, would that be what a war zone looks like? Whatever it is, could I take it for you?'

'They'll know you, too. By now. We weren't exactly married in secret. After midnight, when everything grinds to a stop, there's a way.'

'I wish it didn't have to be then. That's the bad time.'

'You wait somewhere, and I'll pick you up in the morning.'

'Not on your life,' she said with sudden urgency. 'I'm not leaving you, not for a minute. Promise me.'

'And the tenner I owe!' came hoarsely from the bar.

'Never bloody well will!'

'Lads, lads.'

He felt her fingers grip tightly under his palm, and he was touched seeing such intense concern for him . . . while another part of him was strangely disturbed. It was an awesome change: the opacity she had always carried around herself like a wall of mirrors, reflecting her attention back inward, had cleared away. She saw him, she heard him, as she never had, he could see that. He didn't understand what had happened to her: it was a curious, perplexing feeling for him, like being left behind, like coming home from a trip to discover her using some new technique of love. It wasn't another man who had woken her – but it hadn't been him either. He had a sensation like jealousy. Had he been so very useless to her?

He could hear the voices of all the men he had been, how each of them would have responded to the Sarah watching him now – and he wasn't certain which of them this Sarah would have preferred. All this unsettled him more.

'No need to promise,' he said. 'I don't think I could bear being alone again. I missed you more than – ' His voice choked up with emotion.

'Come outside and give us a kiss.'

'I'll do better than that, I'll get us a hotel room for a while,' he said. He tried to smile. 'If you've got some money.'

'Both her hands closed around his, and she leaned so close he felt a stray hair tease his cheek. 'I want to make love like we've never done,' she said softly, with a directness that startled him anew.

'One phone call first,' he said with his eyes screwed shut.

★

Cutter fidgeted restlessly with a fly swatter, bringing it down on his desk now and then with a crack like a gunshot in the room. A child making noises maliciously, Downs thought, not for attention but just to impose his presence on a place. The bandage was off, leaving a small scar on his cheek. Crabb stalked from one end of the bank of windows to the other, parting the gauze curtains to peer down at the street. Di Santis, Mackey and two other Acolytes had shifted the cartons of printed reports off the largest desk to set up a poker table where they played sullenly, lobbing five- and ten-pence pieces into the kitty as they murmured their bets, obstinately calling the coins 'nickels' and 'dimes'.

Only Downs worked with any purpose, ferreting through his

desk to organize his clippings on Eastern Europe for the year. Someone was going to have to take over the files to prepare the monthly summaries, though he wondered who in the whole building would be capable. Cutter's impatience would wreck the files in minutes. He could picture Cutter flinging papers aside like a petulant child as he hunted for one immediate fact, heedless of the facts he would need to find a few minutes later. Di Santis might manage the summaries, if only someone could do rewrite. Mackey and the others were out of the question. He doubted whether, collectively, they could have named the capital cities of the Warsaw Pact countries. He glanced at Di Santis, wiping his palms on a baggy green corduroy suit as Mackey dealt the cards with flashy tosses that sent them just where he wanted. Yes, it would have to be Di Santis. Downs decided to give him a chance to prepare himself, to let him in on his departure before he told Cutter.

The phone rang, an angry burring that dropped into the tension like a hornet, and all eyes watched Cutter yank at the receiver with so much force that the body of the telephone bucked. Gently Downs lifted his extension.

Cutter announced the office number and waited.

'Cutter?' It was Sloane's voice, and Downs felt an electric shock of expectation.

'Here. Speak.'

'She's safe, no thanks to you. Don't interrupt me. I'll bring it to you tonight, there, after midnight.'

'The area is saturated with police.'

'I'll get it to you. Stay put. Your blunderers couldn't kidnap a frightened woman; they could hardly elude the police. What I need to know is who pulled the chain? What the hell did you do to call this down?'

'We don't know,' Cutter answered, and history was being made: for the first time, Downs heard something like a whine in his voice. 'It doesn't make any sense I can see. They've got everything but artillery outside.'

'You listen to me. When I deliver, I'm finished for good.'

'Yeah, yeah . . .'

'Your vicious stupidity drove Jannings over the edge. If I hear your voice after tonight, I'll kill you.'

Then he hung up, and Cutter set the phone down uncertainly. The alertness was gone from him, and he stared glumly out at the room, an active man denied recourse to action, like a large cat denied room to pace.

'Everyone stays put. He says he's coming.'

★

Outside, a policeman poked his head out of the van doors into the rain and called, 'Sir! They've just had a ring. I think you'll want to hear it, sir.'

19

Despite its pastoral name, Cambridge Heath Road trickled down the spine of southern Hackney like a muddy slough of urban decay. The street belonged to a London of gaslight and overworked horses; the tiny derelict shops were cramped together, walls buckled, paint rotted away, and a sullen cave people seemed to have emerged to carry on an alien civilization, selling broken machines under a faded grocer's sign or hammering out crude furniture on a butcher's tiled counter. Sparrow parked his black Opel up on the curb to wait. It was a place he often came to wait. It wasn't a question of his likes or dislikes; he simply belonged here, inconspicuous, a rag left by the ebb of a faraway empire.

Sparrow flicked the wipers once to clear the windshield and then switched off the key. From the first, as a small child, he had been remote and private, spurning even the overtures of the timid boys, the ugly girls: he wasn't a mouse and he wasn't second best. Only his mother had frightened him, not the bullies or the vice-principals who had tried to open him up with pain. When he grew older and became tougher than his mother, he could ignore her too. Much later still he had taught himself the final degrees of retreat: to see and yet not to feel. After the patrols: to hear and yet not to speak. His job had been to infiltrate, to crouch and watch, to identify cadres, couriers, porters, the doctors and teachers who visited from the North, and then kill. He had volunteered for it, a simple enough task in a world gone mad, its surface fuming under foot. Break the surface and you sink, but ignore the way the crust gave under your weight and everything remained sane. His dreams had known about black holes for decades.

'All stations. East End reports to now: nil from Stepney. No report yet from Mile End and south City. Bow and Millwall nil.' The bootleg police radio under his dashboard spoke once more, a word of temporary parting, and then it fell into brooding static. He could not pick up the five-watt car radios or the hand-held transceivers unless they were very near, but the base stations came in clearly.

He ate an apple very slowly in the dark. Sparrow's great secret as a hunter was his seamlessness; he had first driven out all human dependence and then almost all dependence on nature, until he was self-contained. He had no sense of time passing at all. He sat in limbo for hours, for whole days, almost stopping his bowels as he stared at a doorway or a telephone booth. The hands of his internal clock remained motionless until a particular face or a voice of a certain timbre set them moving again. One interminable moment hovered over him, uncluttered by human needs. The concept of boredom was meaningless: a crowded avenue or a noisy pub had no more interest for him than a blank, grey wall. The world had owed him for thirty-seven years, but he had learned long ago that it would never pay. And he didn't care.

The radio popped weakly and his second hand jerked to life. 'South central area in. Peckham and Camberwell nil . . .'

★

Raw cold gripped his ankle where his sock was still wet, but he hardly noticed the sensation against the burning ice of the pry-bar, just bought at a garage, that he carried down his pants leg as he walked. Very few people checked into a hotel in London with a two-foot wrecking bar and a tiny flashlight as their only luggage. He was tired and confused, apprehensive and quiet. He knew he should have been happy so near the end and back with Sarah, but something inside was ruining his happiness.

Sarah's arm was through his as they turned the corner onto Seven Sisters Road. Across from them was the dark hollow of Finsbury Park, stripped of trees against the muggers to become a flat wound in the city. He noticed the faint sweet scent of smokeless coal, washed downward by a fine mist that was no more than an eerie prickling on the skin. The smell reminded him of the early days with Sarah, as both of them had lain Sunday morning on the hearth, propped on elbows on their backs so the glowing coal embers would dry their hair. The smell clung for the rest of the day, but if you didn't find some way to dry your hair in the winter it stayed damp indefinitely. They hadn't talked much as the coal popped and shifted; a little about her fears, once in a while they had joked about one of the pompous writers in the Sunday papers: 'As I circled in over the battlefields of Bangladesh, I thought of my first O-level examinations . . .,' and they had touched occasionally. My God, what peace, he thought.

'I want a warm room,' he said softly. 'I want to be dry all through.' As he spoke, a police car cruised disapprovingly past on the broad road. They both watched in silence until it was gone.

'Let's invent a fantastic new way of making love that will leave us both with aching knees,' she prompted gaily. She had never talked like this, with such freedom, and he smiled uneasily.

They steered toward the row of small hotels that stretched away diagonally at the turning, each with a coachlight and an inflated name as badge of respectability.

'We should go and live where there's some sun . . . air, where people smile on the streets,' he said. 'We've been dead long enough. We've earned better.'

'Love, you just want my knickers off.'

'That, too.' But that wasn't it at all.

Arrathorne House was like the rest; with space for two cars in front, a white Greek portico, a metal crest so overpainted its outlines were blurred. In the tiny lobby, a woman in a grey turtleneck stifled a yawn as she eyed them with a policeman's practised scrutiny.

. 'A room,' Sloane said.

'Five quid the hour. Twelve the night.'

'The night,' he said, and Sarah counted out twelve pounds. She received a bent key on a white plastic fob.

'Eighteen-B, first floor. Toilet's down the hall. Two quid to bath. Any other services, you'll want to negotiate with . . .'

They were already moving away from the woman, mounting the narrow staircase. The flowered carpet quit at the landing, leaving only the worn wooden treads and a smell of disinfectant. They climbed clumsily with their arms around each other, clashing hips, like a single drunken animal. As she unlocked the door, he watched her in a moment of objectivity and saw how pretty she was, and how young. No, not young. She was older than *young*, in a glamorous way; she looked intimidatingly wise and self-possessed, a superior being as unapproachable as the women in films or fashion magazines. And as he went in behind, watching her small, high, firm buttocks, he was very, very frightened.

★

Even the Lucite soundshields seemed unable to muffle the irritable racket of the teletypes and code machines, clattering away like furious insects. The document hatch in the door rose. Dru's face peered into the room, caught sight of the Old Man leaning forward over a teletype and quickly withdrew, so that the hatch came down with the snap of a guillotine. Moore sat on the table where the old duty books were stored, his hands circling the warm coffee cup, and he imagined grabbing Dru's long hair to trap her face in the hatch and kiss her full on the mouth, forcing his tongue between her lips.

'Would you like some coffee?' he asked. 'It may be a long vigil.'

He could see the Old Man concentrating as he read, withdrawn privately into himself. 'Nothing,' the Old Man said with irritation.

Moore had recovered some of his confidence; he had decided that Ross, babysitting the operation in London, could keep Broken Back from tearing wide open if anyone could. But Dru had written her shrill memo and passed it along, *copies to Millie, Personnel and Directorate*, and she hadn't spoken to either of them for twenty-four hours. The operation probably wouldn't do anything for his career, even if it succeeded; it wasn't the sort of show they wrote up in the internal bulletin for a little pat on the back. But he told himself that disloyalty to the Old Man might easily look worse than carrying on conscientiously in a botched operation, even to the Old Man's enemies. Once you were seen to be disloyal . . . Dru, he thought with a hint of gloating insider's superiority, might just have bought herself a one-way ticket to the little grey trolleys of document folders that wheeled eternally down the library aisles.

'What time is it over there?' Moore asked.

The Old Man checked his watch. 'Ten tonight. I take it you've forgotten how to add the number five.'

'I wasn't sure when they end their Daylight Saving.'

'They call it Double Summer Time, or some such thing.'

'I haven't had the advantage of a British station. Like you and Ross.'

The Old Man tried to keep reading, but his concentration had been broken now, and he was very annoyed. 'You've had a lot of other advantages, haven't you, Jerry? Groton, sports cars, your own private tennis pro, trust funds, deb wife.'

'That's what we're fighting for, isn't it?' Moore put in lightly. 'Keeping up a certain standard. A world safe for privilege.'

'Be cynical on your own time.'

'What keeps you going then? You never had the silver spoon. They never even let you touch the hem.'

'Muscle,' the Old Man said, without looking up. 'It's a trick you learn on crutches. When everything else is gone, you can always keep your back straight on pure muscle.'

'And you call me cynical. Ross is right about Broken Back. It's too big a hunt for one poor Lumbago.'

The Old Man turned, and Moore saw something quite hard enter his eyes. 'Stop riding coattails. Stop drifting through life. It's quite possible to grow old without growing any wiser.'

'With an operation like Broken Back, I may not grow old at all.'

'Find yourself a parachute then. Like Dru.' Creaking across the room, the Old Man raised one crutch, and with the rubber tip he left a concentric target imprint of dust on the green wall. Moore had seen them at several places in the areas where the Old Man had stopped to meditate. Kilroy had been there. 'We have a cover story and two backups. Who knows, Lumbago may get himself killed.'

'Not in London. With all those cops around.'

'They'll stop him before he delivers, that's good enough. And we'll mop up afterwards. Ross is good at mopping up. He's got a fussy little suspicious mind that always finds the seams in a story.

That makes him good at inventing them.'

Moore sipped his coffee, grown lukewarm and bitter. 'We can hope.'

The Old Man shuffled out of the room. He had looked old and tired, except for a strange fire in his eyes, and Moore had a sudden vision of a man who had put aside his strength temporarily to bluff an enemy. He wondered who his enemies were.

★

They stood a little way from the junior policemen who were busy looking busy, earnestly prodding maps, leaning back in thought, consulting communications people in the van. Ross popped his last two aspirin into his mouth. He chewed the bitter pills with practised masochism; it was the only medication that came near controlling his fever. Macon stood beside him, angular and reflective, watching a young girl in an embroidered Moroccan coat walk an afghan.

'Dreadful dog,' Macon said sourly. 'Neurotic as a pop star. They kill cats, you know?'

Macon wanted something, and Ross replied with cautious neutrality. 'I've never had pets. They're impossible if you travel.'

'Ah. I love cats. You can learn all there is about police work in ten minutes watching a cat in the garden. The careful reconnaissance when there quarry is unaware, the suspicion and strict discipline, even that dangerous betraying eagerness toward the end when the haunches start to twitch. They're vindictive too, you see. Never forget a slight. They'll cut you dead for months. But fantastically loyal if you applaud their stalking. Few people realize that. One's told that it's only food that buys their loyalty, but it's simply not true. Oh, they'll come for food; they're not daft, and they'll make a bloody great show of appreciating it. But it only wants watching one of their stalks and letting them know you appreciated it, you've got an ally for life. The only thing they truly care about.'

Dear God, Ross thought, what does he want?

Macon looked around to where Kohler stood with the others,

grinning at some joke. Then he dismissed them all with one lift of his eyebrows. 'Perhaps it's a touch of that special quality, perhaps cats have it,' he said. 'At Lancing, they taught us a number of improbable truths. We absorbed them, actually; nothing was said openly. That would have been conceit, hubris; not done, you know.'

The old policeman appeared discomfitted, with an earnest shyness in his long military face, and the Atlantic gaped so wide between them that Ross had no idea what was going on. A helicopter passed overhead suddenly, hacking at the air and driving its thunder down into the narrow canyon. They both craned their necks to watch it.

'What we picked up – ' Macon began.

'Sorry, I couldn't hear.'

'We learned that at a certain level humanity divided into two types. The names were rather quaint but that's the schoolboy's disease, bear with me. We called them one-offs and compromisers. The first take what they want willy-nilly, and the other just make rules. One gets away with things, acts on instinct and impulse, and the other reasons and hedges and doubts and does the safe and sane. It's a fairly archaic notion, I expect, probably something to do with the gentry who once rode roughshod over the peasants' fields.

'These days, of course, that sort of thing, the general thing, is rather frowned upon. Or it's been debased into classless strivers and little cults of eccentricity. That's not what I mean at all.'

Ross was losing patience. 'What are you selling?'

Macon glanced at him and seemed disappointed. 'Our profession is one of the last where the one-offs survive honourably. Not police work. I mean the other, the bigger thing.'

He means *spying*, Ross thought, and he can't say the word.

'I suppose it's fitting since we're guardians of the past. This man you're serving was one of them. I don't imagine there's much left now, judging by the slackness of all this, but we learned to protect and make allowances.' His eyes filled with great earnestness, which Ross automatically discounted. 'We're allies, after all. Against the darkness, against those who break the rules *without the right*.' Macon fell silent, waiting for Ross to pick up on the suggestion behind his words.

'You'll help me smooth things over? Is that it? You'll protect the Old Man?'

'I have to know what's happening. I can't very well bolt the doors unless I know which doors. I have a thousand men out there trying to chase him up, and every one of them is in the dark because I am.'

Ross rocked on his heels. 'And you need to know . . .?'

'What's the purpose? What's he done?'

'Don't press,' Ross said. He moved away slowly and strolled up the road. The rain had cleared the air, and the gingerbread roofline was cut out of sheet tin and set against the threatening cloud. Trust was an art, he thought. It was a gentle art that rested – like the latest understanding of atoms – on nothing but probabilities. And the greatest obstacle to trust was thinking that there was a knowable, absolute integrity; that all hazard could be avoided if only you saw deep enough into character. Everyone who went into the field believed that at first. But no matter how deep you saw, the future always changed what had gone before, and today's absolute solid might become a gas when the atoms moved. Macon waited reflectively, sucking on his unlit pipe as Ross turned and started back.

'Research was set up,' Ross said. 'They were put on a false scent that should have discredited them for good. But the plan backfired.'

'How?' Macon's large powerful hands folded across the pipe, and Ross felt himself trapped by the inane metaphor.

'False scent, but there turned out to be a real fox. None of that can help now.'

'I suppose not.' Macon glanced again at Kohler, who was up the road at a dark Lincoln consulting one of his colleagues. 'Why is this man Sparrow out there?' Macon asked at last, grudgingly, like a small defeat.

So that was it, Ross thought. He knew a little, perhaps more than a little, and the whole oblique discourse . . . he'd been trying to talk around the fact that he'd tapped Kohler's phone or something similar. A cousin organization, that Special Relationship. But he hadn't been devious enough to steal that last fact he wanted, and he'd hoped Ross would spill it for him.

'He was watching Sloane, but he lost him.'

'There's more.'

'I put my finger in too late to stop the orders. He's to kill him if necessary.'

'Ah, I see,' Macon said gravely. 'We can't have that.'

'Pick up Sparrow if you can, but you won't be able to. Why worry? You've got a thousand men looking for Sloane; what chance does one man have?'

'We found the car his wife was driving, in North London. My guess is Sloane is up there somewhere, Hackney or Islington. It's his home territory. He was given out up there on the radio. Do you suppose Sparrow would have a police radio?'

'You can bank on it.'

Macon set his mouth primly, as if he'd overheard an unsavoury story. 'That will focus his search too, won't it? And he knows Sloane's habits. He was last to see him.'

'Can you flood the area with men? It would be good to pick Sloane up as far away from here as possible.'

'It's being done. And all the routes between. He won't get here, but let's keep him alive, shall we? We're already at sixes and sevens. We don't need an unsavoury murder to add to it.'

As opposed, Ross thought pedantically, to a savoury murder.

Stepping out a pace, Macon glanced up along the finicky vertical rhythms of the buildings toward the Research office 200 yards away. 'What do you think they make of all this?'

'Who knows? They're a third-rate little – '

'We know what they are. They're still yours.'

Ross shrugged. 'So was Three-mile Island.'

★

Breaking the office rules, Crabb had taken up a discreet collection and brought in several four-packs of beer, Carlsberg and the tall Longlifes. The lukewarm cans were set out haphazardly on the work table in the room downstairs, and even Cutter and Downs had acquiesced in the end, come down and tossed in their contributions for the next run. Cutter stood on a chair peering through the fanlight over the street door, sipping his beer with an uncharacteristic decorum.

'What have we done to deserve this?' he murmured for the

third time.

'Did you ever play kick-the-hat when you were a kid?' Mackey asked gleefully. 'Was that a great RF! You stick some old homburg out on the sidewalk waiting for your old man or one of the neighbours to come along. Nobody can hardly resist kicking an old hat. Then one day you stick a brick under it and someone breaks a toe.' He chuckled. 'That's what some shit did to us, stuck a brick under the hat.'

'The sense of humour of an amoeba,' Di Santis muttered.

'At least I know when I take it up the ass.'

'*Shut up*, morons. What was it like out there?' Cutter asked Crabb, who had braved the gauntlet to buy their beer.

'Boy oh boy, you'd think I was after the Queen,' Crabb hammed, unused to being the centre of attention and making the most of it. 'There must have been ten of them following me to the off-licence, and the minute I went out they were in there questioning the little Jew who sold me the beer.'

Set upon by conflicting moods, Downs waited near Cutter, trying to pry up a pop top that had broken off in his hand. Against his better judgment, Downs felt a protective urge toward the Cutter he saw now. Thwarted, the raging animal had turned into a bewildered child. 'Maybe you shouldn't have p-p-pushed Jannings so hard,' Downs suggested softly.

'He had it coming. Anyway, Sloane was playing him too loose. He wasn't going to do it, you could see that.' He stepped down heavily, his beer foaming out of the lid of the can. 'I don't think all of this is over one miserable suicide. There's something more important about that film. Why the maximum effort? Jesus, *why*?'

'Do you think the Russians complained?'

Cutter shook his head. 'I just can't dope it. We've got to get that film.'

'He said he'd deliver.'

'How? Over the roof? He can't fly, as far as I know. Disguise himself as a cop and drive here? If he doesn't make it, we'll never learn what it was about.'

'He'll come,' Downs said, and against all logic he really did expect Sloane to weasel through the largest manhunt in London since the Irish bombings. He liked Sloane and he wanted him to make it, if only to prove to Cutter – and himself – that nice guys don't always finish last.

★

She gave one taut cry in the dim, seedy room. It was exhilaration, it was the bleakest despair. It was the brief, brief abandonment to pleasure, or perhaps pain. Strange it had never occurred to him how ambiguous it sounded. He wasn't even certain now it was the same cry. But other times he had been concentrating on himself or on other things.

They lay twisted in the sheet, their hair stringy and damp. Sloane's cheek was on her belly, and he felt it still heaving lightly with muscle spasms. The steely flat band of muscle just under her skin. He heard gurglings inside. He had been impotent, despite all her efforts – and it worried him a little, but not inordinately. When he had been younger and far more romantic, many things that had happened to him seemed to be signs, and a bout of impotence had scared him so badly that he had read everything he could find on the subject; the worry alone perpetuating the condition for almost six months. It had cured itself only when something in him had changed, so that his maleness no longer seemed such a huge issue. Now, what he felt most was regret at a wasted opportunity – wondering deep inside how many more chances there would be. She loved him, but he had begun to worry if she still approved of what he was. Approval seemed terribly important.

He looked across her glistening skin and the fine dark pubic hair to a single item profoundly out of place in that room of commercial sex, of hurried illicit love: a cylindrical brass night-light with an old locomotive steaming across it, somehow hinting at immense innocence. Something inside rotated with the heat of the bulb to send a flickering out through slits in the design and suggest motion: smoke streamed back from the bulbous stack, and the gigantic cowcatcher swept along the rails. The child in him watched in fascination as the illusion reversed itself unexpectedly and the locomotive backed away, sucking in its steam. Take me back to the place where things went wrong, his mind said to the locomotive. If I can find that place, I can start

236

forward again along the right track. He couldn't be the master craftsman he had once wanted to be. But couldn't he lead another life altogether and work somewhere honestly in the sun with his hands?

Then he drifted off to sleep, though it couldn't have lasted more than a moment. He had been testing the end of a cantaloupe in the supermarket, and he had put his finger right through into rotting softness. The whole end of the fruit – he'd accidentally ripped it open. And now he was trying to put the cantaloupe back on to the pyramid so the end didn't show, but it kept slipping around to reveal the gaping orange hole he had made. He woke with her hand drifting through his damp hair.

'This is all there is – nothing more,' Sarah said gently.

'No world outside, no police. An island of peace.' She glanced down obliquely. 'Please . . .'

She touched his chin and he took the weight of his head off her belly. 'Are you all right? she asked with concern.

'Sorry. I guess I wasn't in the mood.'

She smiled. 'I didn't mean that. You just look so tired. *That* takes care of itself. You have no idea how many of these virile men have a little run of the limps.'

'Would you have known a statistically valid sample?' He tried to keep it light, knowing that the one emotion guaranteed to annoy her was jealousy, but he felt the nagging tone in his voice.

'Yes, I would have done,' she tossed back quickly. 'Twenty-thirty.'

'You've hardly ever mentioned them.'

'Because it makes you so tiresome. Don't do this.'

'But I've always wanted to know. It's part of you.' He thought, My God, she's beautiful. The thought was like a wound in him because he couldn't help imagining other men seeing her like this, seeing her body so slim and vulnerable and available, to hurt. What's happening to me? he thought. She was so far away. Too far to reach.

'You don't want to know, not in any way that makes sense.' There was still a gleam of annoyance in her eyes, and he felt stupid for prodding at her, childish. Things had begun to happen to him that he didn't understand, and he wanted desperately to keep her from noticing that anything was different. But he couldn't help himself – like the tip of his tongue going to a sore tooth.

'If it's in the past, what's the matter with me knowing now?' If he knew, they would take on ugly faces, bad habits, taints and sores and they wouldn't threaten him. Was that it?

'Because when I tell you, you'll watch me the way you're doing now. You'll be possessive and want to hurt. And it'll make me feel worthless.'

'I'm the one who broke down. I locked the doors for a year. How could I be judging you?'

'We all judge, don't we?' She showed the scars on her wrists. 'Can I hide these?'

'There's a different person in you right now, very different.'

'Perhaps. Who was it refused to show his scars? Coriolanus. He was too proud and aristocratic to display his battle scars to the rabble and he lost the election, or whatever. It's supposed to be a tragedy, but I could never feel anything for him. I always thought, "Sod you, Jack, if you think you're too good for the rest of us."' It was determined avoidance, talking of neutral things to divert him – as close as she ever came to lying.

He didn't know who Cariolanus was, and as he watched her he realized that he was afraid to admit it. Another gap in him. When you're self-educated, he thought, you leave a lot of gaps. Let it go, he decided. Let it all go. They had enough to worry about in the next few hours. With a great effort he put everything out of his mind and started chatting about Felicity.

'I'm happy for her and her house,' Sarah said. 'But she doesn't need my good wishes. She's a rock. She came through precisely the same mill, you know. With hardly a scar. That big country house in suburban nightmare Tudor down in West Sussex, where even the dogs are Tory. Atrophy the spirit in a day.'

There was a distant rumble of thunder, throaty and indignant, and he noticed the thumping on the window where the rain had picked up again. He wished their seclusion could go on and on. It was midnight and they would have to leave soon.

'We were outsiders,' she went on. 'Aliens from Mars. No one called round, no one invited us to visit . . . but Felicity laughed it off. You'd think I'd be the strong one, two years older. It's as if every family gets only so much to go round. So much was saved back in case there was a long string of us, and when Felicity came the gods realized those separate bedrooms meant the end of the line, so they gave everything left to her. She was happy. She was curious and inventive, fashioning games out in the peach orchard behind the house. Felicity, always pleased as Punch.

'And I just stared at things . . . as if it all belonged to her, or anyway to someone else, the whole world. I was the alien. I know this sounds maudlin. What's the opposite of sentimental?'

'I don't know.' He touched her shoulder tenderly.

'Blackly sentimental, I suppose. The only thing that's for real is punishment, so you punish yourself. For hating. Everything was so brittle. The last time I saw the house, they were cutting down the peach orchard. Like Chekhov. Talk about mixed feelings.'

He saw a moment of weakness and sadness in her, and he was appalled to find that now he loved her. Now he felt something. 'We'll go live somewhere sunny,' he said. 'We'll find a place where we fit.'

'We should do, but we won't.'

'I promise, and we'll survive.'

'Will we? I've always been certain I'd die young.'

'You're not so young,' he said quickly, sensing the opening.

'You *beast*.' She hammered his shoulder, and rose to tickle him. They wrestled across the creaking bed and ended up laughing.

Yes, now he loved her, now life was tolerable. 'We have to go soon.'

'How do you propose to transport us into Soho undetected?'

'Straight through the earth.'

20

A covered Scania lorry with Portuguese markings muttered grumpily up Caledonian Road, and the two policemen who hovered in front of a dark pub watched impassively. One was short and stocky and pugnacious-looking, a Londoner who had just come of age – a True Londoner, as he reminded his colleagues with tiresome regularity, born at St Bartholomew's Hospital, only half a mile from the chiming of the Bow Bells, in the very month they had been rehung after twenty-two years of silence. ''Urried the bloody job for my arrival, they did, guv. Toshed them up with a bit of rope just in time for Terrence Piggott's flaming debut.' The second policeman was older and taller, with a slight stoop and a habit of blinking both eyes with great purpose that made him appear grave and gentle. 'Huw Doughty, that's Huw with a double-u, you know. My mum fancied a Welshman. Holidayed at Colwyn Bay one year and got left with me.'

Across the road, a grey-haired stationmaster emerged from Caledonian Road station and drew the rusty accordion grate across the entrance with a screech like a stepped-on cat. Locking up, he waved once to the policemen and headed home, lofting a woman's transparent umbrella.

'Pinched that from the lost-and-found, 'e's done,' Piggott observed. 'Not such a bad job, you know? Stand at your 'atch selling tickets all day, no bloody aggro like them as are at the barrier. Hundred fifty quid a week and all found. And no bloody all-nights and specials, like us.'

'I like a change,' Doughty said. 'Do something different every day. I'd go right off my nut knowing tomorrow's just like yesterday. This job's spoilt us for ordinary work, and that's the truth.'

'You're right there. A good punch-up now and again. Get to put the boot in, right?'

Doughty frowned. Piggott had been on his case all evening, prodding and taunting. He hated fighting, as Piggott knew perfectly well. It was true he liked variety. He even liked stepping into a dispute with a throaty, 'What's this about, then?' to sort it out with tact and impartial authority. But he loathed actual human contact, even the touch of a handshake.

'Those niggers down by the chip shop, now, we should have shook them down,' Piggott complained.

Doughty blinked, keeping his blank, pale face diplomatically unreadable. Yes, that was it. He'd guessed Piggott might turn querulous for the rest of the night when he'd pulled rank and denied him his little pleasure. Lord knows, he wasn't particularly fond of West Indians, pulling their knit caps down tight to their ears and sucking their teeth at you in contempt, but something made him uneasy about picking them up for no better reason. It ran against the grain of a sense of fair play, deep and comforting, that Doughty had absorbed from his grammar school in rural Surrey. 'We're meant to be watching for this Sloane, not chasing off on our own.'

'I 'ear 'e's no terrorist at all, like they gave out. Nothing like it.'

'What's the rumour them?'

'Slipped into the Palace and slapped the Queen's bum, 'e's done. Had it away with one of the little waiting ladies.' Piggott gave a crass laugh.

This sort of humour puzzled Doughty. Why was disrespect meant to be so funny? 'I wish he'd chosen a dry night for it then,' he murmured. And they both watched the streaks of rain slant down out of the north like lines ruled across a photograph, real rain now, not the London drizzle. Both of them shuddered. They would have to trudge the pavements in it, wrapping up in the clammy black oilskins that fought every movement stiffly and obstinately refused to breathe.

'Absolutely bloody typical, it is. A duty night and it pisses down like Noah's ark.'

★

Three miles to the south, the surveillance team posted along Charing Cross retreated against the walls and watched one another stamp their feet in the cold. Occasional grey figures wandering home from the flesh shops of Soho found themselves funnelling down a gauntlet of eyes like a nightmare of bad conscience, and most of them scuttled quickly off the road to catch taxis for somewhere else. Two singing drunks crossed the road with their arms around each other, drawing stares, but they passed up a side street and the song sank under the rain without ever becoming intelligible.

Macon and Ross had crossed the street to shelter under a bracketed cornice, a spot that gave a better view of the Research office with its backlit curtains and single flat entrance beside a book shop. Ross lit a cigarette off the stub of an old one, and Macon's eyes rested thoughtfully on the turreted corner window where a human shape stood outlined like a pistol target.

'In an hour, he'll be the only thing moving in North London,' Macon said, his voice gently puzzled. 'If he's in North London at all, that is. He's chosen an odd time to deliver.'

'Maybe the phone call was a diversion.'

'He's not rung again, and they're all at home, restless as cats. *They* think he's coming.'

'We're all standing around waiting for Godot,' Ross mused. 'We're like a congregation of millenarians up on the roof in our white robes waiting for the bugle. It'd be a fine joke if he just grabs the next flight to Paraguay.'

'Jolly good luck to him,' Macon said.

★

'I'm glad you brought the sensible shoes,' he said. 'We've got five miles to walk.' They sat side by side on the bed, Sarah smoothing her hose and Sloane tugging at the knots on his shoelaces.

'I'll match you step for step,' she said briskly. 'Don't take a blind bit of notice.'

He rolled the film cannister thoughtfully in his palm and dropped it into his pocket, then slid the long crowbar down the sleeve of the blue coat, catching the hook over the armhole. He contemplated his feet, then his thin, gnarled hands. He was

242

uneasy, and his mind moved ponderously like a stick in syrup, anticipating the difficulties that rose now, far more real for their being immediate. He had a feeling that something terrible was waiting for them, just around the first corner. Whatever happened, nothing would ever be quite the same again.

She stood, hooking her skirt, and rotated it back to front on her hips with a grave energy. 'Through the earth.'

The blowzy woman was still at the front desk, still yawning, and she smiled woodenly as he turned in the key. 'That's it, then?'

'We'll be back in an hour or so.' In case anyone asked. But who would ask?

He waited at the door, watching in the glass as Sarah tied on a plastic bonnet, a beautiful, vulnerable woman he was driving into danger. But she seemed happy about it; not just resigned – happy. He watched her with incomprehension, then tugged on his shapeless tweed cap, dry inside where he had hung it over the radiator. They stepped out into the sharp, cold rain and he smelled the odour of decay brought alive by the wet. Arm in arm they hurried back the way they had come, sticking to the main roads to appear less conspicuous; a middle-aged couple without cab fare returning home late from a restaurant or from friends. From friends: he realized they had never had friends, not together. What did that say about them?

They turned at Blackstock Road, awash with light from the shopfronts, and skirted the burst trash bags at the gutter. A police car glided slowly across the lanes toward them, rain hammering off the windshield, and pale faces inside turned toward them. Sarah's hand tensed in the crook of his arm as the side window cranked ominously down.

Sloane raised two contemptuous fingers, backhand. 'Up the Provos!' he called, in as near a brogue as he could manage, and then began to sing to control the tremor he felt building up in his voice: 'We'll hurl the oppressors into the sea, don't you know, and send them to heaven in our own good time. Oh, won't Mother England be surprised.'

'. . . Sodding Irish drunk,' he heard.

A tiny beard under a pale, featureless moon wagged at him contemptuously through the car window as the glass started up.

'. . . Send the lot of you home!'

Sarah chuckled, clinging to his arm, as they turned onto Gillespie Road. 'Cool as charity,' she said.

'I damn near pissed in my pants.' He saw that he needed her there; the dependency was all on his side now.

Soon they reached the dark maw of Arsenal tube station, a long open frontage with a sliding grill to cage off the sinister, echoing hollow. The crowbar made a few desultory pecks at the heavy brass padlock without effect, and then one long tug that only scraped a mark into the rust of the hasp. It was so sturdy that he was afraid the whole idea would prove a bust. Past the station there was a blind corner, threatening an approaching car at any moment, and with anxious haste he slid the bar between the bottom of the grill and the shallow track in which it ran. Sarah put her weight onto the bar as well, and one link slowly deformed as they strained until it finally popped out of the track with a dull clank skittering away into the darkness. The next link was easier, and the next, until almost ten feet of the grate rattled loose at the bottom. He gestured, and lifting together they bent up a section of the metal. He crawled through first, Sarah unhitching his coat where it caught on a rusting rivet.

Then, hand in hand, they were swallowed up, running down the long, gloomy ramp away from the city light. They jostled at the turning, felt their way into the darkness, and collided breathlessly as the ramp turned back on itself. The collision knocked the crowbar out of his hand. The tiles still howled with echoes of the bar's fall as he patted around to reclaim it. He had forgotten the flashlight. He dug it out now, no more than a penlight, but the best he could find in the Indian shop. A pencil beam wavered ahead through the dust as they hurried on, picking out the meeting of two grey passages, the choice-point between platforms. One bore left, and the other descended sharply. The dark was taking its toll on his nerves. Up above, thinking about coming down here, he hadn't realized it would be like this (another failure of his imagination), hadn't realized how the eerie shadows and the feeling of helplessness would undermine his sense of purpose. As they reached the choice-point, their joined hands snapped taut and yanked them back toward each other. They had chosen different tunnels.

'This one goes south,' she complained.

He gave a small tug, and heard her laugh once at herself. He counted on a tiny extra margin of safety from going south along the wrong track. He wished he could laugh the way she had: she had found strength somewhere. They took the stairs quickly, following the fuzzy yellow spot that bobbed downward ahead of them, and soon they spilled out onto the platform under an arching roof that picked up a dim light from somewhere.

Sloane did a clumsy stutter-step, overcoming his automatic tendency to head in the same direction as the trains, and they ran to the lip of the concrete platform, almost four feet above the track. The long fluorescents overhead were out, but it appeared that every hundred yards or so down the tunnel a small bulb burned in a wire cage high on the wall. It gave just enough light to let them get their bearings, and enough to suggest menacing shapes beyond the pathetic beam of the flashlight. Fantastic animals crouched in the tunnel waiting for them; giant birds flew past, fanning his neck with the wind of their wings. The stagnant air was corrosive and smelled of mould. He heard a noise and swiveled in panic. Behind him, a scuttling and a tiny sound so shrill it hardly registered in his ears. The light shot back and forth, finding nothing.

'There,' Sarah said. 'Down there. Oh, God.' Her hand pressed the flashlight downward and he picked out a parade of rats the size of small cats scurrying along the tiled wall. One at the back stopped and reared up in the beam as if challenging an intruder.

'Not rats, anything but rats,' Sarah said, and clung to his arm. He felt her shiver.

He was near panic himself. For a moment his mind had shut down completely at the dreadful sound. 'They'll keep away from us. Come on.'

They lowered themselves to the concrete trench that ran between the rails and set off at a brisk walk toward Leicester Square station, four miles and seven stops to the south. On their left, the flashlight showed a rack of half a dozen sinuous signal cables like green and black snakes, and straight ahead three tiny bulbs retreated in a shallow leftward curve.

'One of the Leicester Square exits is across from Research,' he said aloud, like whistling past a graveyard. 'It's a ten-second sprint. The police won't have a chance to blink if we come out fast.' If we can get that far without dying of heart failure, he thought.

★

'This country needs a good shaking up, root and branch,' Quilter said. He was driving the patrol car, one hand loosely on the wheel, with the wipers lapping parallel arcs ahead of him. His hand massaged a small trim beard. 'Send off that Irish sot, show them all the red card. Bash the Trots into line for good measure. And the poofs. Bring back the rope, while we're at it. More monarchy and less grubby pandering after the levelers, I say.'

Jimmy Ely, riding beside him, sniffed and shrugged. He didn't trust Quilter's harangue and, anyway, he wasn't attracted by half-measures, no matter how strong they sounded. If he thought of the monarchy at all, he thought only of sterile ceremony with no effect at all against the corruption that he saw piling up everywhere and dragging his beautiful, eternally put-upon island deeper into the muck. The new broom he favoured was far less antiquated: they would march proudly up Whitehall in blue shirts and caps, put the boot to the lot of them, Queens, windy MPs and Cabinet, and usher in the rule of the true defenders of decency. He wanted Cromwell in a constable's hat, punishing the slack and unworthy with a terrible wrath that would last a thousand years. Cleanse the island down to the bone. Lacking Cromwell, Jimmy Ely had settled for joining the police's Special Patrol Group to slap down the long-haired protesters and wogs, but in six months he had been given little opportunity to get the boot in, and recently he had taken to attending National Front meetings in West Ham.

Still he was careful to say nothing in reply to Quilter's leading comments. He suspected the man of being a plant; internal vetting, set on him to draw his beliefs. There was no denying that enemies were everywhere, even inside the police.

'I was in the cinema last week,' Quilter went on. 'Some bloody foreign film, and not ten of those young anarchists sat through the National Anthem at the end. Laughing and rushing for the way out . . . even *kissing*. By God, I remember *singing* it as a lad, let alone just sitting there. No flaming respect.'

And to Ely's surprise he began to sing, booming it out in his deep voice: 'God save our gracious Queen, Long live our noble Queen, God save the Queen . . .'

The view out of the window was streaked with depressing rain, and Ely's eyes wandered to the metal clipboard riding on the parcel shelf. He picked it up idly and studied the photograph again. A chilly hand touched his neck.

'John . . .' He showed the driver the photograph. 'What do you think, eh?'

Quilter pulled to the side of the road and took the clipboard, sucking at his cheeks. 'It seems . . . thinner in the face. Not sure. We'd best have another look.'

The blue light on the roof went on, but not the siren, and the car U-turned and retraced its route, fast this time, up to sixty on the slick tarmac. Quilter took an illegal turn through the yellow cross-hatching, narrowly missing the curb, and the heavy Rover wallowed and hammered on its springs.

'On the right,' Ely said. 'That's the turning.'

Quilter was more cautious turning on to Gillespie Road, and they slowed to a purr, cruising the dark, deserted street past two-storey terraces of weatherbeaten brick. Ely rolled down his window but it was Quilter who spotted it out of the right side: a hump in the diamond shapes of the metal grill where someone had unmistakably broken into Arsenal Underground. Ely had the microphone in his hand before the car came to a stop.

'Easy on the detail, lad,' Quilter said softly. 'We never got a good look at him, remember that. Just a passing glance. We don't want to look a right pair of fools.'

★

Here and there water had collected in the channel where they walked, or rubbish, or cracks in the concrete filled with tar that humped up underfoot; and at their straining pace, with only the ball of weak light darting ahead of their feet, it was impossible to avoid an occasional stumble. Where the footing was worst, they stepped over the rail and walked to the outside of the tracks.

'I'll never have nightmares again, never,' Sarah said in a brave murmur, her voice enveloped in the hum it set off in the tunnel. Their hands clasped in a moment of superstitious fear: a robot shape had reached for them, but it was only an obsolete switching device with a long activating arm stretching away on rusty rollers along the wall.

One of the overhead bulbs approached, and for a moment they could make out the mist leaking into the tunnel through the great exhaust vents overhead, they could see each other dimly, and even the footing where they ran, iron springs clamping the rails to their concrete mounts. A third rail, the negative conductor, ran evilly down the centre of the track on concrete pylons and sooty ceramic insulators, and a fourth, the positive conductor, ran just outside the far rail. Neither would be carrying electric current in the dead of night, but he had a superstitious dread of the electric rails – and an eerie attraction: he was afraid he would test one of them with a touch, like the compulsion to draw a new razor against his thumb.

He saw his shadow swing ahead of them and then lengthen along the track in fits, as if grasping forward desperately. Before long, their shadows ebbed away into the meaningless dark. He could feel himself beginning to pant in the damp air. It was like being locked in a submarine, fighting along the narrow gangway, claustrophobic and obstructing, the outside pressure threatening to burst the walls and crush you. Then he was swatted off his feet and tumbling.

'Jeffrey!' Sarah's scream lanced down the tunnel, echoing. Something kicked him in the ribs, something else slammed sharply into his temple. Save the flashlight! was all he could think, but his right hand closed on empty space and it was gone. His body came to rest with a shock, and he felt pain like a bolt driven into his skull. Hands were all over him. He lay with panic surging through him like a dark wave: it's come, death comes like this. His ears roared, and he could taste bile in his throat. Then a bright light flared up in front of his eyes, and absurdly all his mind could fasten on was: They've dropped the bomb!

'God, God, you're *bleeding*!'

Blinded, he heard her sob once. The light flickered out, and another match scratched and glared painfully as she dabbed at his head with her skirt. His hand felt along the concrete, half his mind still desperate to find the flashlight, and his fingers came upon a flat piece of metal next to him. The metal shifted as he pressed, and like a universe without ordinary connections, the movement shot a pain through his opposite thigh. The metal had a welded lip on the side, and toward one end he could feel a rising slope and rivets. Then a thick wooden pole. As his racing heart began to slow, he realized what must have happened. He felt terribly foolish.

'I tripped,' he said angrily.'

'Don't *move*. Your head is bleeding.'

It was a spade, the handle lying between his legs. Someone had left it propped on the side wall of the tunnel and he had strode straight into it. Idiot accident, and panic had magnified it into a nuclear attack. He wanted to sleep where he lay – it seemed years since he had slept the way he wanted to – but he knew they had to be moving on. He heard her hands fumbling in the box for another match, and he reached out, found the hands and stopped their motion.

'Never mind my head. Use them to find the torch.' A show of bravery might take away the bad aftertaste of his panic.

'But . . .'

'Head cuts bleed a lot but they aren't dangerous. We need the torch.'

He was on his hands and knees now and when the match flared, they both hunted hastily along the dancing shadows, side by side to use what light there was.

'Try this way.'

It took three more matches, but finally he saw the fluted tin cylinder lying askew in a brick alcove in the wall. The flashlight was still in perfect shape, not even dented, except that the bulb was shattered.

'What do we do now?' she asked.

'It wasn't that much help anyway.' It had been more of a comfort than anything else, he thought, a little bit of the ordinary world he could impose at will on a small area of the tunnel and drive the spookiness back a few inches.

She helped him to his feet and the side of his head throbbed, with an ugly pressure near the eye. They held hands and talked dully as they walked, teaching each other how to set their feet and how to steer by the single faint bulb in the distance, reassuring each other with ordinary words as they picked their way into the dark. He touched his cheek and felt the blood beginning to harden over the tenderness beneath. His thoughts became formless, under immense control to hold back the invisible universe.

As they grew used to walking blind, they picked up the pace, and eventually they came on a brightening oasis. Vague, slow billows of mist emerged from the side of the tunnel. Tiles began along one wall, and they came out into a dim basilica with giant paper ikons along one wall: an immense bottle of Scotch, a sleepy redhead showing off her brassière, a gold cigarette box. At the far end of the station, off centre, a corbelled arch held a black mouth back into the earth. Every twenty feet a small square sign announced: HOLLOWAY ROAD.

'Six more stops,' he said. The glowing dots of his watch told him they had been going for only twenty minutes.

★

A uniformed policeman obsequiously held an umbrella over Macon's back as he leaned in the rear door of the van, listening to the amplified radio voices. Ross ducked like a small fullback going into the line and forced his way past Kohler and the others in the earnest circle, not bothering to apologize. The aspirin had worn off and he noticed with irritation that his forehead was percolating again, accompanied by the prickles of some deep inner loathing that swept in waves down his neck and arms.

The radio droned and crackled at full volume, and a weak voice fought up out of the static. 'The grating is definitely forced, prized open at the bottom. Should we follow? Over.'

Macon grabbed the microphone just as a loud, clear voice started to reply. 'This is Assistant Commissioner Macon, from Mobile Alpha. Tell those men not to enter the station, repeat, *not* to enter. They're to seal it off. Acknowledge. Over.'

The strong voice came back, 'Right you are. Any instructions, sir? Over.'

'Hang on.' Macon turned and pointed. 'Get me a tube map,' he snapped, and one of the aides foraged hastily in a pile of documents in the van. 'Come on, *come on.*'

The harassed man gave up in despair and plucked a tiny folding map out of his wallet.

'Will this do, sir? That's the Piccadilly Line they're on.'

'I know what line it's on, constable,' Macon said irritably. 'I just don't carry all the stops in my head.'

Ross peered around the musty overcoat at Macon's shoulder. The deep blue stripe of the Piccadilly Line slid down toward central London from the north-east – Arsenal, Holloway Road, Caledonian Road – then dived into the spaghetti at King's Cross, to escape due south and circle toward Leicester Square through three more stops, Russell Square, Holborn and Covent Garden.

Macon squeezed the trigger on the microphone. 'Have some of your cars knock the stationmasters out of bed, Holloway Road and Caledonian Road. Send teams into the stations as soon as you can, and get someone in from London Transport, someone who knows those tunnels.'

Ross reached over and tapped his finger on King's Cross.

'God forbid he gets that far,' Macon muttered. 'Five lines in and out, two tracks each, the service tunnels running out to the depot and all the connecting passages. We couldn't cover it effectively with an army.' He glanced at Ross and, annoyed at himself, bit off the complaint. 'Emerald Street, send everyone rattling round loose to King's Cross. That's a priority. Victoria Line depot's just behind the station, bound to be someone to let them in.'

'Absolutely, sir,' the voice replied with distaste. 'Please clear the line.' The radio man was annoyed; it wasn't often his instructions were observed so closely.

'My, my,' Kohler said from the edge of the small crowd. He was grinning vapidly. 'Aren't we all in an advanced state of pregnancy.'

Macon ignored him, and one of the policemen dug out a large plastic-coated map of north-central London and spread it on the floor of the van. Macon fumbled absent-mindedly in his coat pocket, staring intensely at the map, and brought out his briar pipe. 'Two hundred and fifty bloody tube stations. Get a man down there and then finding him is like fishing in ivy for a pin.'

★

Under the maplight from the glove compartment, Sparrow studied his own tube plan on the back cover of the *London A-Z*. The radio was spitting out orders for patrol cars, repeating names and addresses of stationmasters, but he already had what he needed and he wasn't listening. He traced routes with his stubby finger. With a little luck he felt he could beat the police to Sloane now.

He felt no special excitement at the prospect, no emotion at all. It would be the end of a job, that was all. And afterward, he would go back to the tiny bedsitter in Southwark to stare at the wall until the phone rang once again for him. He would go on answering one summons after another until some ordinary day the black hole swallowed him up. The single spark of curiosity remaining in his life concerned what that moment would it be like – would it be as bland and pointless as everything else?

He opened the cigar box he kept in the glove compartment and took out the .45 Colt automatic: nothing special, just an Army-issue sidearm bought from a crooked sergeant in Frankfurt, the tip of the barrel threaded for a hand-made silencer that he had had fashioned in a tiny workshop in Hackney Downs. There was no point in using a more expensive weapon since the silencer necessarily slowed a bullet to subsonic speed; even for a marksman, any shot over thirty yards with a subsonic round was largely a matter of luck. And once used, the pistol would be hurled off Tower Bridge into the deepest section of the ship channel at the Upper Pool, never to be seen again. The Colt slid easily into the break-front holster in his armpit, and he kept the fat, crudely machined silencer in his pocket.

In five minutes of fast driving across the dead streets of Shoreditch he was at Angel underground station. The Bank Line of the Northern, one stop west to King's Cross where he would cut off Sloane. He parked up a side street and carried the car's scissors jack to the side entrance of the station, facing a darkened row of shops. Fully compressed, the jack slid into one of the hollow diamonds of the grating, and he cranked the jack open until a rivet ripped from its hole. Three more times and he had a gap big enough for him to squeeze through.

Sparrow dropped the jack into a trash barrel just inside and took off at a trot down to the graffiti-ridden passage.

21

Piggott, squat and young and toughened by his weekends of soccer for the police second eleven, sprinted easily down Caledonian Road in the rain, his boots glinting in the lamplight and slapping spray off the pavement. Doughty, who had squeaked through the police physical training exam twelve years earlier, struggled along breathlessly a half block behind. Even the old stationmaster had a half step on him, jogging along wrapped in a long overcoat that flapped over maroon pyjamas.

'Sods!' Piggott reached the entrance and slapped the grating impatiently. 'Where the *'ell* are they?' He glared up the road for the car that was to meet them, but saw only Doughty splashing dizzily toward him.

'You don't half look knackered, Huw.'

Doughty set his hands on his knees to gulp air, and he heard the stationmaster open the grate. He swore to himself that he would go on a conditioning programme the very next week.

'Going in, are you?'

'We're to wait for the guv'nor. Bloody shirty, we knock ourselves out to fetch you – '

'There's not time,' Doughty panted, straightening with a hand in the small of his back. 'He may get by us. Here.' He handed his transceiver to the startled stationmaster. 'Lock up behind us and wait for the car. You can tell them we've gone down.'

Piggott had his heavy torch switched on before they hit the darkness that was waiting to pounce at the first turning. They took the steps two at a time, the wide circle of light bouncing ahead of them, and clattered out into a southbound chamber echoing with their descent. Piggott flashed his light through the arches into the northbound tunnel, catching the boots and spurs of a mounted cowboy on the wall. Then he knelt and leaned out over the lip of the platform to illuminate the tunnel where the train would arrive, if there were a train.

'Ahead of them, then,' he said.

'Shh,' Doughty cautioned, and they strained to listen over the rush of blood in their ears.

★

Fifty yards north of Caledonian Road station, Sarah had her arms wrapped hard around Sloane to hold them both still. Ahead, where the grey tiles of the station began, they could see light shifting on the wall. Now, unmistakably, the light went out and came back faintly, wavered, and went out again. They walked forward slowly, as if carrying cups of hot coffee, stepping carefully to avoid the scrape of their shoes. As they drew near the station, Sloane heard an elusive sighing sound that came and went like the rote of a tidepool . . . coaxing, as close as his hand.

'Christ, you're shagged. Look at you, gulping like a bloody terrier.'

'Hush.'

'We're ahead of them, I tell you. Not to worry.'

They're in the opposite tunnel, Sloane thought, against the sudden flutter in his chest. The vaulted roof continued to play its trick with sound, bringing it too close like the whispering gallery in St Paul's, so that he heard every rustle of their uniforms, every laboured breath. Through many of the stations a two-foot deep drainage trench ran between the rails. By hunching forward in the trench, they kept their heads well below the lip of the platform. Cautiously they picked their way forward through the cigarette butts, the crumpled candy wrappers and a single, stiff abandoned glove. Only a few yards from the men in the station, Sloane felt an unwilled scream building up inside him. He held it back with all his concentration.

There was a clatter from somewhere far away, and then the racket of several pairs of boots on concrete. Cautiously Sloane bent over further to unwrap a damp sheet of newspaper that clung to his foot, and then they moved with more haste. The wall over their backs glowed suddenly, showing a cowboy brandishing a pack of cigarettes. As suddenly, the light went out.

The footsteps hammered boldly, approaching, and they worried less about their own sounds now. The smaller archway grew ahead. At last it swallowed them and they were back in the train tunnel.

They held each other for a moment in the dark, their hearts racing, and he braced a hand against the tunnel wall for support. It was damp and rough, slimy. They were back to the three pinpricks of yellow ahead. Sarah touched his face gently, ran her fingers over the caked blood and kissed him softly. The footsteps behind, then a voice. They had to move. She tugged and they were hurrying on.

Now that they were past the immediate danger, his mind began to work, though absurdly; held by visions of the rubbish he had waded through, the torn wrappers, the glove, the newspaper that had clung. All the disorder seemed like warnings, signs of something dreadful that was coming. He suddenly felt disappointed in himself: all the wasted time; the squeamishness and cowardice, the pathetic muddle of his life locked away in Dalston. And he despaired at becoming someone else. He closed his eyes for a moment and opened them on darkness. The same yellow bulbs curving away gradually to the left. Why hadn't anything changed? Nothing seemed to have any importance, even the film in his pocket. What was happening to him? Gradually as he walked, his heart stopped pounding and fluttering.

'I think we're out of sight of the station,' she whispered.

'Not yet.'

They had found the torn grating at Arsenal, he thought. It was the only way they could have known, and he cursed himself for not taking the time to bend it back into place. Such a small thing. But once he and Sarah got to King's Cross, they would be home free. In his head he carried four alternate routes to Leicester Square from King's Cross, and even if those were blocked there were others, longer and more circuitous. And if all else failed, they could hide in the tunnels until morning and escape with the commuters to try again. If, he thought, spending the rest of the night hunted through the dark didn't drive him mad.

★

Police Sergeant Rutter found his two constables standing to attention, officiously guarding the southbound platform. He was a shrewd, ill-tempered man who wore a few strands of dark hair glued across the top of his scalp in a last stand against the inevitable, hidden now by the helmet. A length of twisted wire ran from a pink earpiece to a bakelite amplifier in his breast pocket, an obsolete hearing aid that left him looking like the last of a generation for whom making do was a kind of grim faith.

'You've checked the other line, have you?'

'They're coming south, aren't they, sergeant?' Doughty bleated, realizing just as he said it the dreadful flaw in his logic.

Rutter seemed to consider a number of replies, but settled for rolling his eyes away. He took a cumbersome electric searchlight from one of his men and strode through the connecting arch to the northbound platform. He pointed the powerful beam to the north for a moment, then walked briskly to the other end of the platform and aimed the light down the gracefully curving track to the south, toward King's Cross. The mist in the tunnel reflected back far too much of the light, but for just an instant he thought he had seen something – a teasing movement at the beam's limit.

Rutter turned to a stiff little policeman who waited beside him. 'I want absolute silence. Absolute, do you hear? Pass it through.'

The little policeman disappeared through the passage as the others froze in place on the platform. Soon the scrapes and whispers ebbed away, and Rutter heard only the hum he knew as the ordinary idling tone of the archaic hearing aid: G flat, a note he had grown to loathe. He lowered himself awkwardly to the track and walked a few yards up the tunnel, then swept his arm behind to reinforce the order for silence. He slid the rust-brown box out of his pocket, thumbed the volume wheel up to maximum and, swapping the earpiece to his good ear, he held the unit out at arms' length and screwed his eyes shut to concentrate. The throb of G flat was almost intolerable, but beneath it . . . It was doubled and quick, busy with sharp urgent tones – unmistakably footsteps. But why doubled, he wondered, and then he remembered there might be a woman with him. Rutter heard a stumble. Yes, footsteps.

★

'Milk and sugar?' she asked.

'Whatever,' Ross replied.

The young uniformed woman wore so much eye make-up that she had a permanently startled look, but she meted out the styrofoam cups coolly with an infallible instinct for protocol. Macon, straining to follow the voice on the radio, had waved his cup away, and the woman had glanced at two of Macon's aides, but seemed to conclude that Ross outranked them.

'Here you go, sir.'

Brake fluid, Ross thought, sipping. Boiled insecticide.

'They're definitely through Caledonian Road, sir, moving south in the outbound tunnel,' a voice said clearly on the radio. 'That would be Cockfosters side. Two of them, must be the woman with him. It's a long stretch to King's Cross, just over a mile. We should have a quarter hour to catch them up.'

'Dammit,' Macon blurted. 'Excuse me. Have you put any teams into King's Cross yet?'

'There's a frightful row with the night crew, sir. I don't mean to speak out of school, but the night officer in charge or whatever must be rather a Gorgon. He's sent away the first of our chaps who arrived, something about interfering with scheduled repair work. I ordered up someone senior and had him try to ring the man, but he appears to have been out of the building and no one could raise him. We have a number of men hanging fire for the minute we have permission to enter. It's all rather woolly. I haven't heard back yet whether they've managed it.' The voice oozed out of the loudspeaker in a steady complacency that seemed to drive Macon to distraction.

Macon stuck one finger into his ear and reamed with frustrated energy. 'Do what you must to get as many men as you can down there. *Quickly*, man, and contact London Transport operations. Find out how long it'll take to have a train running.'

'There's a man here, sir.' There was a pause, and they all tried to listen to a muttered conference off the microphone.

'Half an hour, possibly less. Normally they could go with a battery engine but the nearest ones are out at Hammersmith so they'll have to switch on the mains. And they'll need to collect the crews and switching teams. Shall we go ahead?'

'*Of course*, double time. And put some police on the trains.

Start up all the lines through King's Cross.'

'Hadn't we better warn the men down there, sir, to keep them away from the live rails, I mean? That's 600 volts. That's a frightful lot, and most of the men won't be expecting the line to be electrified. One of the sergeants called in, actually, wanting to double check whether it was safe, and I assured him on the best advice he could proceed. Over.'

'Yes,' Macon snapped, irritated beyond endurance. 'You'll want to warn them, yes. Go, man!' He tossed the microphone to the operator and fixed his dark, intense eyes on Ross. 'We're all dead, Harvey, that's what I think some days; dead of simple bloody inertia, and no one has noticed.' He stalked some distance away in anger, and Ross followed idly. Macon stopped and glared up at the ornate mock medieval knights high on the side of a building.

'Ever watched one of our chaps going for a loose ball, Harvey? I mean three runs behind the Rest of the World at half-past six on a Sunday afternoon and only half an over from Andy Roberts to go. If the chappie can't get down the pitch as comfortably as can be, he plays back. Off it goes gently into the hands of mid-on. Dignified, you see. Isn't done to be hasty, I mean, mustn't get into a tizz. Nurse saunters to a heart attack, cool as the proverbial cucumber, "Can I help, sir?" while the old chap turns blue on the carpet. No such condition as an emergency. Just muddle along nice and normal and the Huns'll never get across the Channel. That's how we won the war, you know. They say the Russians won it now, though.'

Ross let him run down, then handed him the coffee cup. 'Maybe over the long haul it's the best way. It saves going off half-cocked. My country seems to have become famous for impulsive fuck-ups.'

Macon sipped and pulled a face, then he nodded solemnly. 'True, we don't often stitch up the wrong ventricle, but the patient dies of old age waiting. *Elizabeth*,' he shouted. 'What is this substance?'

'It's from liquid concentrate, sir. I'm sorry.'

'Chicory,' Macon said mournfully. 'I *loathe* chicory.'

'If they get into that snake pit under King's Cross, we're in trouble,' Ross said.

'We're already in trouble. Rather, your man is. He's going to have quite a lot on his plate, I'm afraid.'

★

The noises had been behind them for ten minutes now, dozens of footsteps and an occasional oath or a scrap of talk lost in echoes. Once there had been a shrill whistle. The pursuers didn't seem to be gaining, and Sloane and Sarah hurried along the tunnel at their best pace. Their eyes had adjusted to the point where they could see a foot or two into the murk, make out a dozen tones of black grading into each other, even see their feet with a little imagination. From time to time, for assurance, he put out a hand to the rack of cables that ran monotonously to the left, dirty and rubbery. Each time, he pulled his hand away with a shudder of disgust. An apprehensive Sloane had risen inside him like a ghost of time past . . . hurrying down a shadowed corridor with voices crying out from the doorways. He stumbled and Sarah grabbed his arm.

Every once in a while along the tunnel there was a connecting passage for access to the opposite track, a horrible velvety black against the other blacks, and he couldn't help glancing sideways as he passed one of the gaps for confirmation that they were alone. It wasn't the police he feared there; it wasn't anything rational. Glowing eyes . . . yellow teeth.

'*Jeffrey.*' Her voice sounded shaken as she pointed ahead.

Sloane saw nothing and then a hand-held light burst out, flaring off the wall and sending reflections bounding down the tunnel. Taking her hand, he tugged her back to the nearest connecting cut. They stepped through along a short passage to the second track and saw light up the second tunnel as well, dim and diffuse, and then they heard a scratchy cough echoing from everywhere. Straight across the track was a narrow brick arch in the outer wall and they ran for it. He had no idea where it went, but there was no choice. A faint chilly breeze caught them head on from the arch, and concrete steps spiraled down steeply into the darkness without handrails. Constricted by the damp, sooty walls, they might have been descending an ancient passage through the fabric of a cathedral, down through the floor of the world. A drop of icy water shot down his neck, and grainy brick ripped at his elbows as the staircase spiralled to the right. They passed a low-wattage bulb in an alcove that lit the spiral for a few feet and revealed one mournful graffito on the wall: SOD ALL WEARY WORKING MEN.

The staircase was dark for another full spiral, perhaps more, and then ahead of them the walls gathered a visible grey substance. They emerged onto another track, indistinguishable from the one they had left.

'Can you tell what line this is?' he asked.

She shook her head quickly. 'It's deep. Perhaps Victoria.'

The staircase had twisted so much that there was no way of knowing whether the track ran east-west, or north-south, or something in between. He was lost and helpless, and he let her instinct work; she pulled him to the right. Before long there was a thickening of the mist that looked like a station platform.

★

Amrit Singh trotted away from the Victoria Line railmen's shed alongside a heavy policeman who grunted like an animal as he ran. The policeman wore a blue shirt too small for him, bulging between the buttons and threatening to burst open. Though the man lumbered awkwardly along the track now, he still carried an air of languid contempt, like an examining magistrate. At Singh's flat, and for the past ten minutes in the car, the policeman had maintained a massive, ominous slowness, eyeing him critically from time to time, and he reminded Singh of the line foreman who sat at his desk and peered searchingly over leathery hands that were always folded as if in prayer. Singh did not like the English very much better in England than he had back in Kampala, though here they were slower, a bit more polite, and – miracle of miracles – some of them worked alongside you and even took tea with you. Too many of them, though, seemed cool and sarcastic. Either they were profoundly uninterested in you, or they were waiting for one slip to damn all your people.

Rain pounded at Singh's turban and he was still only half awake in the freezing thin trousers he had thrown on in Camden

Town, hurrying to placate the policeman's obvious sense of urgency. Two more policemen waited beside the first train on the spur. The placard over the cab said Walthamstow Central, but they wanted to go south toward Brixton.

He climbed into the cab, followed by the fat policeman, and immediately worked the control for the air pump. Singh shrugged gently when nothing happened and said, 'Sorry, sirs. There is no electricity.'

'It's coming. Hold your bloody hat on.'

Ten miles to the south, on the far side of the Thames, in the Northern Line depot that nestled behind an embankment on the London Road, out of sight to the middle-class semi-detached homes of Merton Park and Morden, an old Irish driver waited in a battered Northern Line rail car, happy for the overtime though not knowing the purpose of his summons. Yet another driver waited idly in the Central Line depot, watching a truck crawl over the elevated West Cross Road that cut through Shepherd's Bush. And up on the northern rim of the city, at the edge of Trent Park, a cross and untidy young driver leaned back, smoking a cigarette, in his driver's box in the Piccadilly Line depot that spread between Oakwood and Cockfosters.

Once the despatcher was certain the men in the tunnels had been informed, he gave the signal. 'All systems go,' he said, mimicking a flat American accent. 'Switch on.'

Amrit Singh let the air pump chug away until there was enough pressure to release the brakes. He waved to the control shed, grasped the dead-man lever and worked the air controls to shunt power through the motors. With a jolt, the train nosed away from its brothers, and it gathered speed rapidly as it passed under York Road. The mouth of the tunnel raced toward them, and the train dived suddenly into the earth like a weasel after a rabbit. At almost the same moment, trains pulled out of Shepherd's Bush, Morden and Oakwood, all headed toward the heart of London.

★

Sparrow waited in the tiled connecting ramp at Euston, his eyes resting expressionlessly on a short stretch of passage that crossed his at a T-junction. Twice he had eluded the police pickets as he had made his way silently through the tunnels at King's Cross, but it hadn't been much of a challenge: they obviously hadn't expected anyone coming across on the Bank Branch. There had been so many policemen at King's Cross that it was obvious they hoped to capture Sloane there. Sparrow was betting that Sloane would get through. In any case, he couldn't deal with Sloane there, surrounded by police. This concourse was his best hope.

From King's Cross there were four routes to Leicester Square – not counting the ridiculous ones across half of London – and he was relying on an educated guess: a route no sane train-rider would choose since it involved an extra change. But on foot it would be the shortest. Sloane would abandon the Piccadilly Line and slip across to Euston to catch either the Northern Line or the Victoria one south. The Victoria tunnels were very deep, meaning a long climb up and down the dead escalators; so he had guessed the Northern – directly past where he stood.

Sparrow waited stolidly, his back to the tile wall and the pistol hanging limp by his right knee. His mind drifted in a void that was the negation of nervous energy. He had thought out his plans some time ago, and had mounted the silencer without haste. Once his plans were made, Sparrow never second-guessed, never worried the loose ends. He was not even that dedicated to completing his assignment; he would do it now, or he would do it later, or he would fail. X or Y or Z. It hardly mattered. As Kohler had explained to a colleague: 'Count on him to do as well as anyone can, but don't count on enthusiasm or that little extra push from trying to please his case officer. At first I thought it was a pose, but he actually doesn't give a shit. He's a fucking robot . . . no, a turnip. A fucking hundred-pound turnip.'

They would come up the dim passage from the right; he would hear their footsteps for at least ten seconds before they emerged into the open. That, too, he had decided some time ago, and then filed away and pushed out of his consciousness. He was perfectly lucid, but the wheels of his mind were at rest. Like a yogi in mental suspension, like a car sitting at idle, like a hundred-pound turnip, Sparrow waited.

★

There was just enough light to make out the huge arrow on the sign, the tick marks representing stations and the open circle at the bottom: *EUSTON*. They were in Euston, Sloane thought. On the Victoria level. The side of his head throbbed every time he moved.

'Where now?' he said. Something had broken in him. It wasn't just pain from the fall. He felt incapable of making a decision, incapable of following a line of argument to its conclusion, though he knew perfectly well the two choices that they had: change to the Northern Line now or at the next stop south.

'Northern Line,' she said. 'It's easier here. This way.' He let himself be led, enjoyed it. He thought of all the fighting and arguing that went on in the world. Was it really necessary? All you had to do was follow, as he was doing. It was so simple. Yes, Northern Line. His mind fastened on a comforting image of one of the old Northern cars, scarred and boxy, rattling out of a station. His first ever tube ride had been on a Northern, from Charing Cross up to Camden Town, to see about a job. How long ago? Fifteen years? Twenty? What had happened in those years? Fighting and arguing. So unnecessary.

'Help me, Jeffrey.' He heard the faintest hint of annoyance in her voice. He broke his reverie and hurried to boost her on to the platform, climbed himself, and then they made for the connecting stairs toward the Northern Line.

★

A whisper came first, then the footsteps, approaching. The world was back in motion. In an instant, Sparrow's feet were planted square to the opening where the passages met. The pistol was raised and the knuckles of his right hand were pressed into the hollow of his left, elbows slightly bent, the classic Weaver hold they taught for handguns. The safety was down, off, the external hammer back, and his finger just nudged the trigger.

Time stretched out, divided into infinitely tiny segments. A woman appeared first; he had seen her briefly in Sussex. She drifted ahead, dragging the man along by the hand. Something had happened to the man. His head was covered with congealed blood. He wore a loose blue raincoat and a sweater stained with the blood; it was definitely the man. They looked confused and nervous, both as grave as children. It was a clear shot, a perfect shot, impossible to miss even in the dim light, and he began to squeeze evenly, like drawing his finger through soft clay. He felt the sear slip away and the hammer tripped.

For a good ten seconds after, Sparrow stood in the same pose, unmoving, remembering the clear sharp snap of the hammer striking the tail of the firing pin. Even astonishment had difficulty poking up through the numbness inside him. The man had hurried forward to slip his arm around the woman. Then they were gone. Nothing had happened, nothing. Only the sad metallic ping like a canary driving its beak into a tiny anvil. He came to life finally and pulled the magazine, then ejected the round and caught it smartly in mid air to hold it before his eyes in the dimness. There was a tiny indentation on the faintly shinier brass of the percussion cap in the middle of the shell; the firing pin had struck, but the round hadn't fired. He locked the receiver back, inserted the round again and tripped the heavy receiver so that it slammed forward and chambered the round. Choosing at random, he aimed at a direction sign back the way he had come: *NORTHERN LINE – VIA BANK*, and an arrow.

There was a dull concussion from the silencer, and almost instantaneously the ringing of the metal sign. A fat oblong hole rested in the crotch of the V. Sparrow slid the magazine back into the grip, hit it once with the heel of his small hand and released the receiver to reload. Charles Hollingwood had sold him unjacketed dull lead reloads, old and unreliable. Still, the odds were almost impossibly against another misfire.

Sparrow turned and jogged along the passage, toward his quarry. A grey rat that was feeding on a candy wrapper in the shallow gutter beside the walkway panicked at the sound of feet pelting toward him and scurried off into the darkness.

22

Amrit Singh throttled the train back to a crawl and coasted past the policemen, each of whom was pressed into a man-sized emergency alcove in the wall. He knew there would be at least an eighteen-inch clearance between them and the train, but at speed he would probably have given three of them heart attacks and ripped at least one away from the wall with the suction. An older man in a suit curtly urged on the train. The headlamp picked out a station ahead, Euston it would be, and Singh nodded to a policeman on the platform and gave himself a little thrill in accelerating through without a stop. If only he could do that once or twice a day, whenever he felt low, leaving the smug Englishmen waving their umbrellas in comic outrage. Oh, it would almost be worth getting the sack.

'As far as Oxford Circus,' the fat policeman said beside him. 'Then come back the other side.'

'There is a crossover at Victoria,' he said in the high-pitched sing-song that he knew irritated so many of them. 'It will not be possible to reverse the train's course before that point.'

'Sure, sure. Slower now, man. Let the lads in back sniff round.'

Singh's train approached Warren Street station in the deep Victoria tunnel. Fifty feet nearer the surface of the earth, but still well beneath the deserted precincts of London University, Sloane and Sarah hurried along in the same direction through the Northern Line tunnel. Six miles to the south, just across the Thames, an old Northern Line train rattled at full speed toward them along the track they walked on.

★

They had felt the rumble under their feet a few minutes back, and Sloane had guessed what it meant. He glanced over his shoulder at the green signal lights that had come on just after they had left the Euston platform. A few of the overheads were on as well. Undoubtedly the electric rails were live too, and he walked to the far side of the trench, making sure Sarah was across the track from the danger. He could do that much for her, though his mind seemed to have lost its power to act decisively. How could he ever have considered making her wait and coming down here alone? Of the two of them, she was the one who could deliver alone; he was the handicap, the fifth wheel. He felt queasy, and the floor of the tunnel seemed to slope downward in all directions. A band of iron ran around his head, squeezing at each step. He forced his mind back to the present, forced it to stop rebelling.

They were facing the approach of a train as they walked, and he decided – actually decided – to stay on this track. There was little chance of being trapped since there were frequent crossover tunnels and this way they would see it coming. He hoped they would be able to pick out the headlight long before anyone on the train saw them.

He thought of squatting down with his ear to the rail, like an Indian scout in the movies, but he dared not stop. What worried him more than any train was the hint of footsteps that he picked up from time to time behind them. Only one set of footsteps, masked and careful. He saw nothing when he glanced back into the gloom. But whenever they stopped for a breather, the single echo behind them stopped too, perhaps an instant later. Overactive imagination, he thought – a trick of their own footsteps.

He could see Sarah labouring beside him with shallow cat's breaths, her hair damp and stringy. Part obstinate determination, and part something else . . . more furtive. He didn't recognize what it was, and he wondered if it was something as simple as courage. He felt a powerful loyalty to her, a feeling that would overwhelm him in a surge of tenderness if he gave it its head.

Abruptly something seemed to strike a pillar near his head, like a small hammer, and sing off into the distance. It woke him,

266

a chill of apprehension touching his shoulders and bringing him instantly into the present.

'What . . .?' Sarah cried and glanced at him, but neither of them stopped. He shook his head once, curtly. It couldn't be. The police wouldn't, Komarovsky wouldn't . . . but things hadn't made sense for some time now. Could there be someone else? Who was the little dark man he had seen on the train?

'Expansion,' he said unconvincingly. 'Like the sounds of a house at night.' If it wasn't, they would know soon enough. There was a sharp scrape behind him, unmistakable, and then the echoing steps died abruptly. The centre of Sloane's back tingled in anticipation.

'Jeff.' Open-mouthed, Sarah was pointing ahead.

★

As they neared the station, the two rail tunnels ran side by side, separated only by a row of green steel girders and a web of signal cables. Sparrow braced himself and lined up his second shot, standing not in Sloane's tunnel but across the girders so that his outline wouldn't show against the lights – as far as he knew, Sloane was still armed. The oblique line of fire gave him his aiming point: he had the spot picked out between two girders where they would come into his sights as they ran. But once again something extraordinary happened. They crossed his line of aim in the wrong place. Instead of continuing down their tunnel, they had ducked suddenly into his. Holding hands they stepped quickly over the electric rail, and then slipped into a large alcove behind a pile of sand. He hadn't fired; he had always refused to act in haste, against plan. Had they seen him? Was that it?

Then he heard what his concentration had blotted out. From all around him came an organic throbbing, louder and louder, as if a giant had struck the earth above the tunnel with his fist. Wires began to sing in sympathy, and a curious whine scurried along the roof. He recognized what it was just as he saw the pinprick of light far along the tunnel, flickering behind the girders. He glanced around for somewhere to hide. Calmly, without urgency, his mind ticked off the possibilities. It was ludicrous to try flattening himself behind one of the girders, no more than eight inches wide. Lying prone against a live rail was out of the question. The emergency alcoves were simply scallops in the walls, offering no cover. A steel air duct crossed the tunnel overhead, knobby with rivets, but there was no way to climb to it. And it was too far to run to the blind where the other two hid. He could shoot out the overhead bulb, but the train carried along its own bright ghost: the glow from its windows swept toward him up his own track, with a flutter off the walls like a film at the wrong speed.

★

Kneeling beside him, Sarah watched the train approach with a still intensity he had never seen in her before. There seemed nothing restless in her. She was totally unselfconscious, all her attention directed outward, like an old soldier standing on a hill overlooking a winning battle far below. Half of her was another person, and yet she was the Sarah he knew – which made it all the more frightening and disturbing. He felt the rumbling clearly under him, and as the headlamp drew nearer they both settled lower against the gritty sand. She turned her head as she pressed flat to the sand pile, and he looked into her eyes, so deeply at peace that he wondered if she had fallen into a trance. Then she smiled at him from far away. He felt a dam break inside and panic at her calm smile rose, tumultuous, through him. Suddenly he began to sweat and he felt dizzy. He shut his eyes, everything gone red. Who was she? It was like his fingers tearing loose from the last handhold on the face of a cliff; he was falling through the unfamiliar, straight into the underside of the universe. Had she been no more than a mirror for him for so long? And now she wasn't? There was strength there, more than he had' ever imagined in himself at his best. He knew now that she would make it. And he knew that he would not. He was too broken.

She still loved him; her smile from far away said that too, but with a terrible promise. He looked into the future and saw that she would insist on staying with him out of that love. But gradually the love would turn into patronizing concern, and eventually the concern too would change, would wear away to quiet resentment. Even then, she would stay beside him, unable to hide the resentment, honesty running so deep that she would find it impossible to lie to him. She would only retreat farther, to save him the pain. In that future, he saw a young vital woman who was watched hungrily by an old man across the room. It was a long way down, the abyss, and he had looked for a moment.

★

If the policeman standing in the open doorway of the train had had sharper eyes, he might have noticed a truly remarkable feat of acrobatics. Drifting past at the level of his knees he might just have seen the toe of a brown shoe thrust between two of the signal cables. Sparrow was stretched out horizontally behind the running band of cables, five feet off the ground, suspended by one shoe and by his fists clamped implacably to the upright iron stanchion, his arms stretched straight out and shuddering with the effort.

By the time Sparrow dropped to the ground in the sudden dark, kneading his forearms, Sloane and Sarah were a hundred yards ahead, entering Tottenham Court Road station, the last stop before their destination. Sparrow started running. It was only a quarter mile to Leicester Square, a quarter mile to catch up again.

★

'Still reading your Reds?' Kohler enquired.

Ross nodded indifferently. They sat side by side on a low window ledge not far from the van. A tenuous peace seemed to have descended on the small army of policemen as the rain died away to leave a crisp, clean night, alive with small sounds.

'I read mysteries,' Kohler said with bravado. 'Not those unreal British ones, with all the clues and governesses and drawing rooms, whatever the hell a drawing room is. The tough-guy mysteries. Chandler and that ilk – determined men digging out the truth with a sense of style.'

Ross grunted.

'I don't like spy stories, though. Ironic, isn't it?'

Kohler flicked his hair back with three fingers cocked like a garden rake, an actorish mannerism that Ross found pathetic and characteristic. And his reading tastes as well, that he insisted on inflicting on anyone who would listen. The mystery *noire*, Ross thought, so classically American and sentimental, with one bold man digging up the facts in a world where loyalty was ultimately certain. If Ross had had to chose, he would have chosen spy novels – so archetypally European, with their puzzled, wounded men searching for loyalty in a world where only the bare facts were certain any longer. Certain and meaningless.

'The Old Man is the original hard-boiled egg, isn't he?'

'For Christ's sake . . .'

'How come he never married? Okay, okay, don't bite. Balls shot off in the war or something like it, but brave as hell, toughing it out. Throwing his energy into his work.'

Ross stood up. 'That's enough, Guy.'

'He's not Jesus Christ. For your own good, Harvey. He's not the Holy Grail of Langley. This mess isn't going to come out in the wash.'

'When you reach your sixties after a long career,' Ross said, feeling his face colour, 'I hope your friends gather with the same touching show of support.'

'I'll be damned, true love for fellow man. I'm moved, I really am.'

Ross said nothing more, but stared across toward Macon at the van, suppressing the rage that crept up through his weariness. Kohler had a brain like whipped cream, and nothing anyone could say would leave an imprint for more than a few seconds. If life held no ambiguities beyond 'who done it', how could he ever appreciate the need to find something, someone to be loyal to – and the risk of error. And, he thought now, damn the risk.

He felt the teasing earthquake from one of the search trains passing underneath. Then he abandoned Kohler and walked to the van.

'Something on the wireless,' Macon said with fatigue. He got up from the rear bumper, and the young radio operator cranked up the volume.

'. . . And Victoria south, nil as far as Victoria. That's the lot. They'll make another pass now. Out.'

The radio operator stretched back on his tiny stool. 'We must

270

have them isolated outside the central ring, sir.'

'Unless they got over and past Euston somehow,' Macon said. 'It would be a straight run down the Northern.'

Ross glanced up Charing Cross Road. Diagonally across from the door of the Research headquarters there was a dark tube exit with a blue glass sign: LEICESTER SQUARE – NORTHERN & PICCADILLY LINES. Two policemen lounged near the exit, careful not to stray too close to Research. Ross plucked at Macon's coat. 'Shouldn't you send some men inside?'

Following Ross's gaze, Macon's eyes rested on the grating locked across the darkness like a denial of some primitive disturbing force. 'It's hardly credible, but . . . Cowley.'

'Sir?'

'Put two men directly onto each way out, I believe there are four. Keep the gates locked up just at present.'

'Sir, Right away.'

23

They were running now, awkwardly; throwing their arms about for balance so that he had to let her run a pace ahead. She had left him in any case, gone into another world where he couldn't follow. Did she know he was still there? Would she even look back if he stopped?

He had never in his life felt more lonely and miserable. He carried on mechanically, drawn forward by pure momentum, like a man riding home after seeing the shadow of doom on an X-ray. Everything was strange now and had lost its validity. The future offered nothing and his mind recoiled from it. A tiny corner of him still whispered that everything might turn out all right after all, but he knew he was kidding himself. She had been rising and he was falling, and they had touched hands for a few moments as they passed. He wondered if any of this showed on him, but she didn't look around.

As he ran he sensed the tremendous weight above him, department stores, six-storey flats, buses and trucks, all pressing down to crush the tunnel and them with it. Ahead the roof seemed to bow under the pressure. He felt the avalanche of rock, the cells in his body crushing to nothing. Catastrophe, let it come. For the first time he understood her half-wish for the disaster that would make sense of her dreads.

The Leicester Square station was visible as a growing aura in the mist, with four fluorescents left on in the vaulting, brighter but more diffuse than the incandescents in the tunnel. From time to time he heard the sounds of the third, sounds that had grown steadily behind them for several minutes. Superstitiously, neither he nor Sarah mentioned the presence aloud.

He felt a pressing need to reach the safety of the platform, a desperate pull toward the lights. Someone was back there, and he hardly cared what would happen. He was certain now that there had been a shot. He felt dull and stupid in the face of something that obstinately refused to fall into place. Who would be after them with such fanaticism? Nothing about the job made sense, least of all the innocuous data on the film he carried. Though he had seen the paper for only a moment through the finder, he remembered it clearly: France had purchased 260 metric tons of gold, newly released by the Soviet Union. It was a large buy, a very large one, but not astonishing when you consider the French obsession with gold. West Germany had purchased twelve metric tons and Great Britain nine. Was that it? Was it something in those other figures, something the British were doing with gold? Within a month the figures would be known to the IMF, declared as part of the purchaser's gold reserves. Where was the urgency? Had things just gone wrong somewhere, some freelancer stepping unexpectedly onto a field like a spectator running on to give the ball a quick kick the way it ought to have gone? He tried to imagine a friend of Jannings's, enraged at the men who had driven him to suicide. But if anyone filled that role it was he, himself, friend and enemy at once, and remorse stirred uncomfortably. *You hurt them.*

Revenge: he played with the idea momentarily, but it wouldn't come alive for him. It was a conceit for someone who believed in justice, attainable, standing calmly above the world and sorting out the loose ends. A Stranger riding into town to gun down the Corrupt Sheriff. In the name of those too weak to fight. In a way, he admired the certainty he had seen in Komarovsky: justice and history and his place in it all. The old soldier had kept his word. No, justice was an idea for children: who the hell had ever promised anyone justice? That way lay a universe of turmoil and mad vanity. The Cutters would go on bullying, and the Jannings's and Sloanes being bullied. He had given up the idea of justice years ago for a bare promise of peace, but even that seemed to have gone now. Barren loneliness was not peace.

They reached the lip of the concrete platform, and Sarah took his hand confidently. 'Up we go.'

★

He would make certain this time. Sparrow had run hard to bring himself close enough, stretching his short legs to vault piles of rubbish in the trench, no longer caring about the noises he made. He had nearly caught up as they entered the brighter light and made for the platform. It was now. He set his feet and drew the automatic, twisting on the silencer in one quick motion. This time he would make certain. This time there was no train to interrupt, and if the pistol misfired he was prepared to thumb back the hammer and trip it once more within a fraction of a second.

Again time altered, drawing out to a crawl in which every instant and every detail registered vividly. Sloane was boosting himself up the platform, kicking for purchase with his knee. The woman's skirt kept her from lifting a leg, and she tried to slither up on her belly. No, he held back his trigger finger . . . if Sloane leaned forward to help her, an edge of the girder would block a clear shot. Sparrow took a step closer and to the side, the pistol still raised, then one more step across the rail for the angle. He almost had it. The woman slid back to the track bed and Sloane squatted quickly to offer his hand as Sparrow had anticipated. She hiked up her skirt to the waist, revealing the darker amber where her hose became a panty, and she launched a knee over the lip of the platform. Frail legs, Sparrow thought without a trace of sexual desire. He couldn't use the blade sight, hidden below the dark bulk of the silencer, but at twenty yards aiming was unnecessary, he had only to point. Both eyes open, one clear on the whole scene and the other behind the partial eclipse of the fat silencer. He saw the dull blood-stained sweater where Sloane's coat fell open as he squatted. All Sparrow's prodigious concentration was focused on the loose weave of that sweater where any instant there would be a small implosion, a fresh red stain. One more step to remove the distraction of the girder.

The woman cried out softly in pain as her knee tore loose on the concrete, and the man's face crumpled in sympathy. Sparrow never heard the comforting words Sloane whispered. There was a horrible dull crackle at Sparrow's ankle. All his muscles tensed and a shot squeezed off, rising well over Sloane's head. The bullet flew uselessly through an arch and down a connecting passage, ricocheting twice off the tile walls before sliding to rest in the gutter beside a discarded Kit-Kat wrapper.

Trousers soggy with the perspiration of Sparrow's last run formed a near perfect conductor to the polished metal negative rail. The rail carried 600 volts of direct current, but the voltage, the driving force pushing the electrons forward, was immaterial. It is the current, the sheer bulk of electricity, that kills: even twenty amperes through the heart will kill, and an underground train accelerating out of a station draws several thousand amps from the rail. With only one train running on the Northern Line that morning, the current available to circuit up Sparrow's left leg, through his groin and down his right leg to earth in the running rail was for all practical purposes infinite. His body drew as much amperage as its tissue, blood and bone could carry.

It is unlikely that Sparrow knew what was happening. His mouth ripped open in a purely mechanical grin as his facial muscles contracted, and there was certainly little time for him to think: *this* is what it's like. His grey world probably just snuffed out too quickly for thought, but it is impossible to know for certain. Perhaps one corner of his mind was protected from the raging storm of electrons for an instant, an instant in which he might have seen with something like pleasure that his waiting was finally over.

By the time the man-sized cinder toppled forward and rolled on to its side next to the rail, Sloane and Sarah were hurrying toward the steep escalator. They had heard nothing over Sarah's fall and cry of pain. Breathlessly, they climbed the motionless steps and emerged into the large ring of the underground station, hemmed in by shuttered shops. Grey ticket machines stood in ranks in the centre like parading soldiers, and four stairways led up to the street off the outside of the ring.

'How do we get out?' she whispered.

He motioned to wait and crept warily up one of the stairways. As his eyes came level with the small, chilly lobby at the street, he saw a newspaper kiosk rolled tight with green canvas for the night, and then the dark grating to the night outside, with a tiny red glow beyond. The glow moved, drifted sideways. Two policemen passed a cigarette silently on the other side of the bars. Sloane retreated, toe and heel, down the steps.

Making a hushing gesture to Sarah, he found the phones along the lower ring. His pocket yielded only a twenty-pence and a fifty-pence piece. He waved at her urgently.

'Sarah,' he hissed. '10p.'

She dug a 10p piece from the pocket of her blouse and handed it to him with a wry pride. 'For emergencies.'

Cutter answered immediately, announcing the office number in an impatient slur.

'This is Sloane. Sloane,' he repeated painstakingly. 'Send someone outside. Onto the street.'

'Where are you?' Cutter snapped in his bullying voice, a voice full of stage drama and self-importance. Sloane could picture him at his desk, one fist on the telephone and the other restlessly clenching.

'Where have you been for the last two days? I'm not taking a goddamn step until you answer some questions. Remember, we can still find your wife if we want to . . .'

Sloane screwed his eyes shut as a tiny panic of frustration rose within him. Cutter was going to make his last try at salvaging success on his own terms: what good was the prize if he hadn't hammered it, unwilling, out of a victim?

'Is this a trick, Sloane? You're poison. Speak to me! Are you part of some lousy decoy trick? You shot at me! Where are you?'

The aggravation came near pricking Sloane's eyes with tears.

'We're not doing a goddamn thing until you explain what you've been – '

'Onto the street,' Sloane said evenly, and then his voice broke. 'For *once* in your life, do something right!' He hung up, just stopping himself from slamming the receiver on to its hooks with enough force to alert half London. It took some time for him to stop trembling, staring blindly at a closed ticket window.

'What is it?' Sarah asked with concern. 'You've gone red as beetroot.'

He shook his head slowly, back and forth, back and forth. He had to get control to explain what they were to do.

★

The walkie-talkie shrilled and the policeman handed it to Macon as if it might burn his hand.

'Macon. Yes?'

'He's just rung them up! He's out here somewhere!'

'Nothing else, man?'

'No, nothing. They're to send a man outside, onto the road. That's all.'

Macon rose from his seat on the front bumper of the van and glanced toward Research. Somewhere a dog was howling. Ross was already strolling thoughtfully up the middle of the deserted road. Moonlight lay at his feet in cut ribbons. Where, where? Behind him he heard a scuffling of activity, but to what purpose? Ross checked the far rooftops, sharp against a clear patch of sky, checked the shadowed dead doorways, glanced twice at moving shadows in the distance that turned out to be restless policemen. The night had grown much colder after the clearing, and few of them could stand still for long. Between each investigating glance, his eyes returned to the tube station and the two policemen standing against the locked grating. Then out of the corner of his eyes, he saw a sliver of light as the Research door came open, and he looked over to see a small man slip diffidently out into the night.

★

Hand in hand they climbed the steps, clinging flat to the inner wall, she ahead of him. She nodded as the tiny lobby dropped into view, and she felt one firm, pleading squeeze on her hand before he let go. She pressed even tighter to the tiles, feeling their chill through her hips, and then climbed the rest of the way quickly and silently. She took the three exposed steps to the kiosk, and flattened into the space behind it, her heart thumping so hard it felt like an animal trying to burst out of her chest. She wondered why the policemen a few yards away didn't hear it. Jeffrey retreated a few steps, then gathered himself together and offered her a wan grimace. This was it: it was all in her hands. She had no idea where the new strength had come from but she was proud of it, and she would be worthy – if only the hot flush riding behind her eyes didn't cause her to faint dead away behind the kiosk like a Victorian maiden.

The new strength hadn't just come tonight. Three – no, two – days earlier in a little beech wood near Cuckfield, bundled up for her aimless stroll, she had felt an extraordinary stillness come over her as she watched a small patch of sun lazily warming a drift of brown leaves. The restlessness had been ebbing away from her for a few days, never completely and never so predictably that she could count on her moods, but her mind had become still enough so that for the first time in years she found herself studying the world around her – a blotchy plate of fungus on a stump, a row of hanged, gutted stoats left dangling from a limb by a gamekeeper (a warning? she had wondered; a demonstration of his industriousness to some local landlord?) – surveying things without watching herself through them, and that was the point: the extra presence was gone. She had always been two people, one inside to act and another, hiding in the walls or the furniture or the hedges, to judge how the action appeared. Now the watcher was gone. Perhaps it had been the days of silence in her refuge, or the days with no one to lean on. She was suddenly neutral to her surroundings; they were just things in their own right, and it was like landing clean on another planet, in a world that demanded nothing from her.

A minute later, coming upon a small emerald bed of wild garlic on a stream, the air soaked with the garlic's cloying scent, she had had a thought: what you do can change you . . . utterly. Change you forever. For that moment, she no longer felt ruled by the past.

A half hour later still, after picking her way down the streamlet's course to the sluggish Ouse, the thought had come to seem terribly prosaic; she had run it through her mind so many times that it had lost everything but the most literal meaning and given up its magic. Still she knew she had once thought it. Sarah St Jores Sloane, whose future had never stretched ahead as anything more than a shallow cave – she had believed for an instant in possibility.

She had smiled to herself by the river. Even the possibility of possibility was so strange and so charming that it seemed you could live on it for days. It had been a long, long time since something had carried such a sense of cheer for her. For too many years she had vegetated in the big melancholy house in Sussex or lain awake in some London bed rerunning the daily events of an affair with the most recent Peter or Derek (a relationship

278

destined to be as unsatisfying and short-lived as all the others), and something had eroded gradually, perceptibly, inside her until, finally, in the face of the emptiness, deep unused capacities had collapsed like a limestone cave tunnelled away by an underground river. And once the walls had collapsed it was impossible to say what she might have stored in them. Love? Hopes for the future? Selfless compassion . . . for whom? How did others build their self-respect? It was too late: she was idle and worthless. And she had grown accustomed to the feeling of self-disgust. Jeffrey had come along as a convenience, a comfort – child and caretaker both. He had prodded her into staying alive, but he hadn't brought back anything essential. Now something had stirred, and she was afraid to look too closely for fear it was all an illusion.

She fidgeted behind the kiosk. Only five minutes earlier, listening to Jeffrey outline his plan, she had been delighted. She had felt clever and capable. But as he retreated out of sight on the stairs, the uneasiness came back: if she stopped concentrating for even a moment, the trick of strength would escape her and inertia would win; she would never move from the comfortable shelter. She glanced down and saw that her knuckles were white where she clutched the film cannister.

Then he came running up the steps noisily, flailing his arms for balance, and she heard a rattle from the grating as the policemen turned to look. He slid to a stop a few feet from the grating as if he had just seen them. His eyes widened and he stood frozen in place for a moment in a convincing display of panic.

'Hello, here he is!'

A whistle blew, and the night outside filled with sounds: shouting, another whistle, an engine starting up.

Jeffrey took off down the stairs. She had just caught his whisper as he passed: 'It's Downs.'

'Going to ground!'

'Over here, sir!'

The lock squeaked and snapped, and she heard the grating slide open. One after another, two policemen barrelled past and down the steps, trailing brass glints from their uniforms.

This was the moment. *Now.* But she found that her feet were glued to the floor. What if there were others just outside? They would grab her as she emerged. She tried to imagine herself a fictional heroine, bold and impetuous, but the second-hand image was useless. Stage fright had turned her insides to water.

Finally she ripped her feet up and thrust herself out of the niche behind the kiosk. As she forced herself toward the dark opening, she was hit by a cold breeze sweeping in from the street. Then she was outside, taking in too much commotion in an instant: to her right a half dozen policemen ran toward her, heavy coats flying against the rhythmic blue light of a police car. None was within fifty yards. It was to her left that they were closer, and closest of all was a stocky, red-faced man who wore a horrible narrow-lapelled American coat that whipped open with each straining pace. A few steps behind him was a taller, gaunt man with a moustache who looked as British as the Raj and as awkward as only a running upper-class Englishman could look.

'Downs?' she called.

'Here, here.' It was a very small man, diagonally across the road, semaphoring desperately with his arms.

'No, here. I'm Downs!' Narrow-lapels called quickly as he ran. 'Come this way. You're safe now.'

She was frozen by indecision. Both had spoken in the flat, nasal American that she knew so well. Which was it?

'For G-g-god's sake! *I'm* Downs.' The man across the road seemed to try to move toward her, but he couldn't break his own restraints.

'Not him! *Me*! Here!'

Taking pity on the stutter, and on his own immobile fear – for no better reason, she pushed off straight into the road.

'This way!'

'No, you'll ruin everything. I'm Downs!'

It was almost academic now. *You waited too long*, she reproached herself as she ran. Narrow-lapels was only a few feet away, angling to cut her off and gaining. A powerful lamp came on, filling the air instantly with silver dust and turning the rain-wet pavement into a river. Impossibly long shadows stretched away against the buildings, tilting and hurtling like giants. She dodged, but a hand took her upper arm and another scraped for her free hand with the film. Their arms jabbed and feinted like swords in the tiny contest until she felt herself grow desperate, and simple panic at being held and constricted made her kick out. The man shouted hoarsely as her toe caught his shin. She tore her arm free and, holding to her instincts, she hurled the film can clumsily in the direction of the stutterer. But not straight to him. She stumbled and went down on one knee, tearing her hose. The can shone like a meteor, arcing through the light. Narrow-lapels left her and made, limping, toward it. Several policemen did the same, and she knew she had chosen right.

The stutterer ran two steps to set himself beneath the film can, bobbled it, knocked it into the air in his own panic, and nearly went down on the slick pavement himself as he lurched to grab it again. Then he had it. He fought with a door behind him, tugged it open and slammed it as he went in.

Delivered. She had done her duty. She felt a satisfied smile grow across her face. She hadn't let herself down – that thought first; then – she hadn't let Jeffrey down. It was all true; she was stronger. And then a hand more powerful than she had ever felt closed on her arm and raised her to her feet in the middle of the road.

★

The policeman had one hand on the Research door and his long truncheon drawn back ready to break the frosted glass at a signal. Ross, staring up at the fanlight as he wheezed, shook his head dumbly. Then Macon arrived at a trot, breathless himself.

'Shall we go in?'

Ross mumbled something, his mind already somewhere else, already beginning to make plans to sweep up the mess. The Abortionist had not cut properly, but he could still bury the corpse.

'What was that?'

'We've been told not to interfere directly with Research personnel.'

'That's it then,' Macon said. 'The Old Man's for it, is he?'

'We'll do what we can.' Ross's eyes swept around toward Macon's. 'Won't we?'

Macon's expression was non-committal, counting his own chances. Across the street behind him two policemen frog-marched Sloane out of the tube station, his blue raincoat pulled half-way down his back to pinion his arms.

★

Sloane's eyes found Sarah standing in the middle of the road, her face side-lit by a searchlight and her arm pinned by a gigantic policeman. She smiled and nodded to him, and he made a strange sound that the policeman on his right interpreted as a laugh.

'Here now, what's this?'

A faster pace along the road punished him for the levity. As he was thrust down Charing Cross Road toward the grey false dawn that gathered under the clouds to the south-east, he saw the first milk float of the morning heading toward them. The small electric van filled with milk crates whirred contentedly beside the curb like a messenger from a tidier, more innocent world.

24

'. . . I proceeded to follow suspect into Leicester Square station. He didn't run no farther than the first level, whereupon suspect turned on myself and Constable Waters.'

The constable stood rigidly to attention at the cell door as he recited in sing-song from a small pad. A tall English official of some kind with a tidy moustache like a caterpillar on his lip stood by the door as well, contemplating something along the corridor, seeming totally uninterested in the catalogue of crimes. A stocky man was inside the cell, not far from Sloane. His forehead was covered with a film of sweat and he held a stiff finger under his nose, pressing hard. This man too seemed oblivious to the dreary chant. Then he gave a tiny sneeze, quick and soft like an animal's.

Sloane felt poisoned by weariness as he sat on the stiff cot. Space had been cut out to fit him, and their voices had difficulty penetrating the vacuum. He had been marched away from Sarah, thrust into a top-heavy black van and driven straight down Whitehall and up Victoria to New Scotland Yard, where he had been deposited without ceremony in an isolated holding cell that seemed miles from any other rooms in the building. These three had come later.

'Sorry,' the stocky man said. His sneeze had stopped the performance.

'We clearly identified ourselves as from the Metropolitan Police, but suspect ignored our statements and, crying out, "Take that, you rascals!", suspect struck a blow upon Constable Waters' chest, causing grievous injury . . .'

It was difficult for Sloane to work out that the droning young man was speaking about him and his capture. The story was so unlike his simple surrender at the foot of the motionless escalator that his mind found nothing to grip and slid off into disjointed speculation.

The stocky man had picked up a tan water jug from a small concrete shelf, and he was holding it upside down, intent on reading something written on the base.

'Suspect then turned to myself and delivered a blow upon the ear what aggravated an injury received some years earlier in the line of duty . . .'

The official raised his palm to the man and offered Sloane a small, insincere tut-tut shake of his head. 'Assault upon a police officer. A very serious charge, indeed, unless you should prove unfit to plead. I rather think that may be the case.'

'Don't stop him,' Sloane heard himself say. 'I want to hear the part where I shoot the nuns.' Who had found the strength for sarcasm? Surely not himself. Maybe he hadn't spoken at all.

Maybe he hadn't. The officer merely gave the constable a wave. 'That's all. Thank you.'

The man saluted like a toy soldier, trembling with the vehemence.

'I'm not in uniform, lad.'

'Yes, sir. Sorry sir.' The policeman turned on his heel and disappeared with a smart marching step. The stocky man set down the jug and dragged a filthy handkerchief across his forehead while they waited. Finally they heard a heavy door open and shut along the hall.

'Unfit to plead,' the officer repeated, and his boredom seemed to deepen. 'It's not altogether the worst possibility for you. I gather you've spent time in hospital before now. Fancy, now, a nice rest, a room to yourself, all the mod cons, up to a point.'

'With my wife?'

'Perhaps after a year or so . . .' As he let the sentence hang, he turned in place, surveying Sloane. Sloane read a dangerous quality in his expression, distant and commanding, another trump to play yet. A grey light filled Sloane's mind, and he was so tired he couldn't fight through it, couldn't think.

'I don't know. I don't know what that would do. It might just kill one of us.' Kill *me*, he thought. She was much too tough now for anything like that.

'Then there would be three,' the officer said, with a dark

knowing look at the stocky man. 'Let's not be melodramatic,' he said. 'We don't want this in the *News of the World*; you don't want to spend time in prison. Believe me, you don't.'

'Three?' Sloane said vacuously.

'A man was killed in the underground tonight . . . this morning, rather. Unfortunate, very. Electrocuted. He appears to have been after you, poor chap. It makes the whole situation rather more . . . over-wrought.'

Who could it possibly have been? Maybe I am mad, Sloane thought. Maybe that was the only way it all made sense. The one fixed idea he clung to in his fog was that of not letting himself be separated from Sarah.

'In any case, you might wish some time to consider your position. The hospital would have its perks.' The officer spoke in a drawl that emphasized the indifference and disdain Sloane had heard so often from Englishmen of his class. 'We'll give you the opportunity to rest.'

He turned and walked away silently. The stocky man lingered beside the cot, fingering the scratchy grey blanket as if deciding whether to buy it. Sloane had heard him speak once in a brusque American accent. He did not know precisely who he was, but he knew clearly enough what he was.

'You're in trouble of some sort,' Sloane said.

'Publicity could be unfortunate for us,' he confessed. 'If you were British we'd have you sign the Official Secrets Acts, and put out a notice to the papers. They have very convenient laws here for situations like this, for all concerned. But you're not, of course. Whatever you promised us, you might feel you have to tell your side later, to protect yourself. It's a shame, really.'

The man glanced at him and shrugged. He took to wiping his forehead again. 'You should realize that people's careers, the prestige of whole departments . . . rest on what you choose. Some of these people play golf with presidents,' he added with a faint contempt. 'We'll make it easy for you; we'll make it comfortable for you. I promise that your wife will be able to join you in a year or two.'

'I've done nothing wrong.'

'Do you really believe that? My God, there's one innocent man in the universe.'

'Go away,' Sloane said.

'I'll let you rest, but you mustn't force my hand.'

Abruptly the man was gone. The barred door remained open until another door shut heavily along the corridor, and then a motor whirred and the cell door ran quickly into a slot in the far wall. It snapped home with a taunting finality. The cell smelled of bread mould and urine, and Sloane lay back and drifted off to sleep almost immediately.

★

'It's all quite voluntary,' the man with the moustache confided as he slid the paper round to face her. 'I assure you, in a few months you'll both be removed to the same institution.'

Until he had come into the cell, she had been doing quite well prolonging the feeling of calm strength. She knew she needed it now for both of them. Perhaps it was the unused courage of a mother who had never had children, she thought. Protecting Jeffrey with all the fury she would have used to save a son from the bullies, a daughter from the snobs and users.

She was still rather pleased with herself for delivering the film, though now an unmerited guilt crept through her at being put in the wrong by so many people in official positions. First there had been the giant constable, gripping her shoulder in the road and reproaching her with quiet ticks of his tongue. Then the young, acne-scarred policewoman who had led her to the cell with a volley of practised East End taunts. The woman waited on a hard chair now, doing her nails vigorously, as the tall man beseiged her with his unctuous smugness and his blank medical form.

'I want to see a solicitor,' Sarah insisted again.

'There's no question of that, Mrs Sloane. Nor of seeing your husband just at present.'

Her voice quivered, but she got it out: 'I despise people who have power over people.'

'Don't be impertinent, luv,' the policewoman said, glancing up and pointing her emery board like a dagger.

'There's rather a lot of it about,' Sarah snapped, and she could tell by the malice that burned in the woman's eye that she would be made to pay for that in some way.

286

'Do you have any idea what happens in prisons, Mrs Sloane? They can be rather bitter places for someone unused to their rigours. For anyone, I daresay. At his age, I shouldn't like to spend very much time in prison.'

As long as she remained obdurate, she knew she left them nowhere to go but over the same ground. 'I would like to see a solicitor.'

'A comfortable rest in a clean hospital . . . or quite the other thing, in prison. You can save him a great deal of discomfort, perhaps worse. All it needs is your signature as authorizing relation. We have the doctors submit their observations, and your consent will seal a voluntary commitment, until the automatic review in six months. There's nothing definitive about it all, you see. The choice will come round again.'

'No.'

'This is all there is, I promise you. The whistle's gone.'

She shook her head.

'I'll leave this with you, shall I? Give you time to consider. I'm sure by this afternoon you'll see what is in his best interest.'

She refused him any complicity, not even acknowledging the form he left on the small table before walking away. She listened hard, hoping to hear him speak to Jeffrey, but as his footsteps died out there were no other noises in the building.

The policewoman watched her now with a gluttonous interest. 'La, aren't we 'igh and mighty. There's some as changes their tune, I can tell you, when the world's not so smooth and jolly for 'em.'

'*Cow*,' Sarah said.

★

'Alternatively, we can come to our understanding,' Macon said blandly. He had his teacup resting on an electric hotplate in the corner of the office, and he was pressing it gently with his large hands as if driving the warmth back into the ceramic. Sloane had learned his name off the door: *Dep. Supt. P. A. Macon*. The office was deathly cold in the morning, with a pale directionless light filtering in through the wall of glass from the outside world. As he had the night before, the stocky American hovered in a corner, quiet and patient, examining a few pressed olive leaves under a glass in a small gilt frame. Somewhere a radio was playing slow morning music.

Sloane sat facing the desk, trying to ignore the emptiness inside himself whenever he tried to imagine living with Sarah again. He had slept badly, and they had waked him after only a few hours. He could still feel the stiff cot in his bones, and his blood felt slow and thick, hardly flowing.

'From the sacred tree of Athena in front of the Erechtion,' Macon said in an aside to the American. 'I was going to be a Hellenist, you know . . . but I got sidetracked. A shame really. Perhaps it was the parallel that drew me to this work; playing Greece to your Rome. The old power keeps a few embers of the culture alight as the former colony carves out its new empire.'

'Marx said the first time it was tragedy, the second time farce. Seems fair enough.'

'I thought that was Lord Acton.'

'It's from the *Eighteenth Brumaire*.' Without changing his tone and without looking up, the American began speaking to Sloane. 'We'll make you both as happy as we can. You'll have decent rooms and we'll make the doctors leave you alone as long as you behave. You've been there before, and you know it's not half bad.' He glanced at Sloane, keeping his eyes flat and bored, but Sloane thought he sensed a hint of eagerness, a need. 'What are you objecting to? To putting her inside? We'll use the very best places. It might do her some good.'

There was so much chaos inside him. It was hard to listen. He kept picturing Sarah and wondering where she was. Spangles darted in front of his eyes, and the scum above the radiator on the large window made him sick to his stomach. He felt his brain was made of some brittle cheese, cracking and falling to bits. His legs seemed jointed wrongly and he made a great effort to arrange them naturally in front of the chair.

Sloane thought of the contagion of his life, and in contrast the sturdy look he had seen in Sarah's eyes. How had she come through it all? Without knowing it, he might have been dragging that look down for years. And would again.

'Here's my offer,' Sloane said. 'Take me and let her go. Send me to prison or whatever you want. Let her stay outside. She's young.'

'No good,' the American said. 'Would she keep quiet with her husband taken by the police and then vanished? This isn't exactly Chile.'

'If you explained . . .'

'It's not even on the table, Sloane. It's our hand or nothing.'

He sat for a while, saying nothing. For some reason, he had a furious impulse to smash the Englishman's teacup. 'What happens to poor Research?' Sloane asked.

The American shrugged. Macon walked to the desk with his teacup and sat. 'Most probably they'll be given a commendation by your President. But they won't receive it here. Home Office are requesting their removal from the United Kingdom immediately. There seem to be irregularities in their rebuilding permit for the Charing Cross offices. Makes them unwelcome.'

Sloane watched the American carefully. 'And you people?'

'If you must know, we'll be eating crow for some time. Yes, Sloane, in this version everyone loses.'

'I don't like it.'

'Send him back and let him sleep properly,' Macon said with abrupt solicitude. He's playing 'good cop', Sloane thought. 'It'll clear his mind. I'll send round some food from the cafeteria.'

They were as good as their word. He was marched back to the cell and this time given a second scratchy blanket against the chill. Within a minute a plastic tray arrived with three small cellophane parcels containing sandwiches that were indistinguishable from British Rail catering. He knew those sandwiches. There would be acrid margarine on the soggy white bread. One would have a gristly slice of ham, another a slab of cheese tasting like old socks, and the third would contain only wilted lettuce and a thin slice of tomato, known maliciously as 'salad sandwich'. He fell asleep with only one bite gone from the first, and the ham slice fell out into his chest as he began to snore.

★

It was odd that he had never noticed it in the office before. He wondered where it had hung. Moore squatted to look closer at the framed black-and-white photograph that leaned back on the rug against a large carton filled haphazardly with books. He recognized the twin-bodied airplane that sat rakishly on the runway as a World War II P-38. It was painted black as a night fighter, or, anyway, for night work of some kind. The men who stood casually and rather self-consciously in a semi-circle in the foreground wore no badges of rank on their uniforms, and two had their faces blacked out with crisp rectangles that had been cut through the negative. Slightly apart at one end was a man supporting himself on one crutch. Despite that giveaway, it took quite an act of imagination for Moore to see the Old Man there on the runway. He couldn't have been much over twenty. The young man looked grave and burdened but very alive, a junior officer forced by circumstances to take on a field command and knowing he was doing it well. There was none of the flat resignation he saw in the Old Man now, the wounded quiet and the middle-aged bitterness. What had Ross said? Competence without satisfaction.

'The Aylesham Group?' Moore asked.

'I'm surprised you've heard of it.' The Old Man rooted through his desk drawers, sorting personal items into a small suitcase. There wasn't much personal: a gold pen, the chest ribbons to a forgotten group of medals, a cheap portable radio, a spool of thread, German beer mats, a screwdriver kit.

'Don't be silly. It's a damn legend,' Moore said.

'Just a bad job.'

'Bad job, hell. That was real cowboy stuff. Your faces smeared with burnt cork, jumping into Germany. I read the book as a kid.'

'The book was lies. Most of the men died.'

'No one blames you for not going again.' He could have said: for not dying.

The Old Man stopped his rummaging and stared flatly across the room toward Moore. 'Blame is never the point. You ought to learn that much. Success doesn't make something right, but nothing can ever be right without success. Aylesham was a flop. Thirty-seven alumni dead. Fourteen were recovered with little more intelligence than we could have gotten from aerial photos.'

'It must have been worth something,' Moore said with a dogged optimism that seemed to annoy the Old Man further.

'The intangibles. Serendipity, you know. There's always the hidden results – like that report on Czecho machine tools that Ross found in the old clip files last winter. There's always something.' And in Moore's universe, there always *was* something. Though he could not quite visualize the physical laws involved, the mere fact that he played golf so gracefully or that he drove his Ferrari so effortlessly well was bound to spread outward in ripples of some good effect on other people.

The Old Man shrugged. 'You know what Napoleon said about espionage?'

'Mm?' Moore didn't.

'If you're winning, you don't need it, and if you're losing, it won't do you any damn good.'

'Napoleon lost,' Moore said amiably.

The Old Man took a deep breath of self-dramatized tolerance. 'Not through faulty intelligence.' He seemed to begin a line of thought and then drop it. 'He's the one European I admire, dragging that whole continent kicking and screaming into the modern world.'

'Are you so fond of the modern world?' Moore said with unusual insight.

There was a fleeting animation to the Old Man's face. 'Touché. But I never knew anything else.' He closed the suitcase without locking it; the guards would want to check inside. The act ended their conversation, and he was suddenly deep in his own thoughts. 'Anyway, it hasn't been the intelligence business for thirty years now. Deception is what it's been about. Deceiving people into thinking they're happy with one tattered corner of the blanket; deceiving people into supporting what they don't want so that one of your relatives can pick their pocket. I did my duty to your world. Now it's all yours. It was always yours.'

After the valediction he fumbled behind him for his crutches.

'I'll carry some of the boxes out for you,' Moore offered. 'Retirement won't be so bad. God knows, you've earned it.'

'Touch one of my boxes and I'll break your hand.' The Old Man raised one crutch, meaning it. He looked very angry.

★

291

He must have slept well, for he found himself back in Macon's office feeling almost human. Diffuse afternoon light beat at him from the window, and both Macon and the American seemed defeated in some indefinable way.

'You appear to have won,' Macon said with distaste from his desk. 'If you were willing to say nothing, nothing at all about the last week, if we could work out a binding contract, something with a bite in it, your people would be prepared to play a different hand.'

Sloane glanced at the American, with the question large in his eyes.

'Yes, it's true. We'll fly you out to Australia. I imagine that's far enough away for us. With your wife, of course. We'll set you up in a suburb out there under a different name, the way the FBI do it with informers. It's the best arrangement we can offer. And it's a damn good one.'

He wondered if it could be different. He had a vision of recreating for Sarah the same walled-in life as before, the same non-life. Or trying to, and making her that much more resentful. It was inconceivable that he would ever again look at her and not feel the horror of her confidence and independence – though that was precisely what the better part of him had always wished for her. The irony was that they were now offering him a new life just as a future no longer seemed possible. They were offering him nothing less than redemption.

'For pity's sake, Sloane. Your horse has come home. Don't tear up the ticket.'

What was he playing at, he thought. Of course he was going to accept. He only held back now as a kind of delicious self-denial. The acceptance would be so sweet that he was rehearsing his feelings, savouring what he would feel.

'Throw in a new Mercedes?' Sloane asked.

'There would be a financial arrangement as well. Within reason.'

As soon as he made his decision, the turmoil of sudden good fortune denied him the full taste of the victory he had antici-pated. He shook the American's hand, and things began to move too fast, to overlap and skip transitions, like a dream. The next thing he truly noticed was the bright sun outside the small oval window. Sarah leaned close to watch too, and the sky was unnaturally lucid above the clouds. It seemed the first sun he had seen in a lifetime. He didn't even remember climbing up the ramp, or the takeoff.

Sarah touched his shoulder and it was electric, like that very first touch with a new woman. His eyes followed the trail of a tiny jet that scooted past beneath them, seemingly just skimming the fluffy cloud bank on its way down toward Heathrow. Turn back, his mind told the airliner. Down below the siege is still on. And the wounded and lost stand there and accept the shells that fall among them without complaint, resigned to it all. If you have to land, he thought, land as outlaws. Come down that ramp with your guns drawn. Fight. I couldn't; I'm running.

'It'll be warm there,' he said. 'Sunny. Clean.'

'We'll have peace, won't we? Real lives?' Her head pressed wearily into his shoulder, the old Sarah that he knew. 'We'll try?'

'All we've got is our own devils to beat,' he said. 'We'll make it.'

And now he relaxed, touched Sarah's thin dark hair and let the tenderness fill him.

★

What was it so near his eye? A small triangular wound in the darkness. He sniffed. It was ham, and there it lay on the blanket, a slice of soggy bread beside it. He crushed his eyes shut, hoping that the ham would disappear when he reopened them and the airplane come back, but when he looked, nothing was different. All the horror and disappointment in the world seemed concentrated in that ugly piece of meat. A black spot moved, a cockroach scurrying along the cot. And a chill told him he had come awake for a reason: there was someone in the cell with him. Without turning his head, his eyes picked out the bulk against the barred door that now stood ominously open. The bulk shifted slowly, working at something unseen.

Slowly he curled his legs upward to defend himself. But against what? The cot creaked under him, and the shape seemed to turn. Someone was watching him now, and he tried to keep his eyes slitted, keep his breathing regular.

'So you're awake,' the shape said mildly. It was the voice of the stocky American. 'There's nothing to be afraid of.'

The man came a step closer, blotting out more of the dim light from the corridor, and Sloane drew himself back on the cot. He's going to kill me, Sloane thought. Final defeat was there in the room, breathing softly.

'No, I won't kill you,' the man said.

Sloane started at the echo of his thought and he wondered if he had spoken aloud. Am I mad? I mustn't show weakness, Sloane thought. Whatever was about to happen, he sensed that it would be definitive. He had to take the offensive in some way, but how? He was so exhausted that he had to struggle against a bitter current for every clear idea. The shape came in and out of focus. There was a tiny sound, metallic and abrasive. Sloane fought desperately to identify the sound, but it was something just at the boundary of recollection – not a weapon, not a tool he could identify; a slow grating noise, repetitive and in some way circular, like a fingernail drawing loops on a fine rough surface.

'I'll kill you,' Sloane said, sitting half up. He felt stupid, like a child jumping into a karate pose he'd learned in the movies, without the least real training. He firmed his jaw absurdly, trying to make himself appear formidable.

The tiny sounds had stopped, but the hands kept on working, now pressing together as if assembling a small toy. 'Yes, it's sometimes the broken ones who cause the most trouble,' the man said with clinical indifference, and then he chuckled softly to himself. 'I had a friend – in school he went out only with the unpopular girls, the homely and fat and broken-spirited. He thought they'd be easy. I think he actually expected them to be grateful.' He chuckled again, and set something down beside him. 'Inevitably they were shrill and demanding. "Hell," he told me, "they won't even wash the fucking dishes. It isn't fair." He didn't know the first thing about the integrity we all feel toward our situation. Do you see what I mean?'

Sloane watched the hands carefully, looking for some signal to strike out and protect himself. 'You have to kill me. By your logic.'

The same soft, sad, tolerant voice: 'I don't think the British would appreciate that. Anyway . . . the laws of civilization assert

294

themselves. There has to be a certain level of urgency.'

He took a definite step forward, and Sloane pulled back and set his arm hard against the chilly wall for leverage.

'This'll be simpler if you don't struggle.' The man began to speak about his friend again, and Sloane could see that the talk was just a way of covering his glacial progress toward the cot. There would be no sign, no sudden increase in the level of danger. Sloane counted three and pushed off, his fist hurtling toward where the man's head would be. He was completely unprepared for the agility with which the stocky man stepped aside, and then a quick blow caught him behind the ear and he was on his hands and knees on the floor, dazed. He could feel warm blood trickling down his ear as his wound reopened, and his insides filled with nausea.

'This won't hurt at all. With any luck, in a few months this whole nightmare week of yours will have vanished from your mind.'

Blood ran around his chin as he turned his head. He saw a syringe, the needle glinting faintly in the light from the corridor. The glass body was filled with a yellow liquid. All the terror he had ever known was concentrated in that needle. The needle that would penetrate his flesh.

'It's a psychoactive agent,' the man said. 'You'll be free of worries for a while.'

They were going to make certain he went into the hospital without a fight. An arc of pinkish light appeared from somewhere over the man's head.

'You know my mind is already half gone. What you're doing won't be temporary.'

'Permanent consequences are very rare.'

The syringe wavered. Inside, he would be changed, against his will. The idea frightened him to the core. Sarah, help me. He imagined her beside him, helping him to his feet as he had in the tunnel, and his weakness shamed him even deeper than the fear.

What good was he to her? In a flash of insight, he saw that the needle would free Sarah. It was what he had asked: take me, leave her. He would be gone. He knew it would be no brief holiday when that liquid disruption entered the guilt and fear and confusion already swimming through him. *Men like you* . . . The

295

long, long sleep of unreason. A marriage of a year wouldn't leave that large a hole in her life, and she could pick up the pieces, marry again. Do one selfless thing, he thought. Before you lose the will to it. *You hurt them.*

'You'll remember who you are, more or less. Don't worry.'

'I doubt it,' Sloane said, and he ripped his shirt down from the collar to bare his arm. 'Hurry.'

The needle plunged like a fiery splint. He felt the burning pressure inside his arm, nothing else for a few moments. Then his ears began to hiss, building toward a scream. His eyes went wide, the pupils dilating, and very soon the room started tearing into fragments and drawing away from him, faster and faster. A pair of giant inky wings folded over him.

Ross watched as the man's breathing slowed after the initial panic, and his limbs went into small fits like a cat running in its sleep. He wondered why Sloane had submitted so freely at the end, but he didn't wonder for long. The Abortionist had buried what he had come to bury.

Epilogue

There was little rejoicing in the Playpen when Ross returned. They were pleased that he had kept the disaster under wraps, but his efforts had not saved the Old Man, who was now vegetating in a run-down bungalow in the Florida Keys. And a tarnish would cling to all their records from Operation Broken Back.

Ross was even quieter and more withdrawn when he came back for real after a brief vacation. He busied himself with the chores of taking over the department, all the little adjustments of transition: deciding who would get which office, noting carefully the many tacit alterations in the ways authority, daily work and plain gossip moved through the section. He had Dru transferred immediately – out, anywhere. He wouldn't have disloyalty serving under him. And he moved Moore sideways to a slot where he could do less harm. In his place, he brought in as deputy an old friend who had been languishing in Personnel.

In reality, these were only the superficial activities, and underneath, Ross was beginning his long vigil for signs and clues that would lead to the Old Man's enemies. Like the last wild Commanche crouching just on the rim of the hated reservation, he would spy out the braves who had trafficked with the Cavalry scouts and cost them the big battle. He knew eventually he would identify those who had paid out the rope, who had given Kohler the instructions that had subtly undermined Broken Back. And when he found them, a cherished operation would turn itself inside out suddenly and calamitously, a bomb would go off in the coffee pot, a trap door would spring on the third floor and someone would twist slowly, slowly in the wind. Ross was not a forgiving person, and now he had an object for his deep inner need for revenge.

★

Sarah fought her way out of the induced psychosis in just over a month, to find herself in a small hospital in the north near Darlington. After six months of playing stoic possum for the doctors and the quiet visitors who came from some government ministry, cherishing the strength she still found in herself, she won her release. Her sister took her in, and she lived in Hove for almost a year, nursing a cold fury that she could not batter her way through the official doors that were closed to her as only British official doors could be closed. No one could find Jeffrey and no one seemed inclined to try very hard. She spent a lot of her sister's savings hiring confidential investigators who only repeated the story they were given again and again at the end of the line: *in confidence and off the record*, Jeffrey Sloane had died of a heart attack that first morning, within minutes of receiving a massive tranquilliser to calm some uncontrollable seizure, the precise nature of which the doctors could not diagnose later. But there were no death papers, no physical proofs. Eventually she accepted his death – or told herself that she accepted it in order to carry on – and the fury ebbed. Her curiosity receded as well; she would never know what it had all been about.

At the end of the year, at a Brighton dinner party, she met an old friend from university, slept with him and, as Felicity had suggested, he soon found her a position as a fashion buyer for Peter Lyle's, a chain of suburban department stores. For a year she enjoyed her new life as a professional woman, well paid and independent, with a semi-detached house in south London. When someone in the government finally released a document that was acceptable proof of Sloane's death, she was able to marry an accountant at Lyle's, a quiet man several years younger than herself. Soon, perhaps a little too soon, she had a son. She was tempted to name the boy Jeffrey, even with the American J, but in the end she chose Colin instead. The marriage never quite took. As the boy grew, he watched with a grave remote apprehension as his parents became bored with each other and backed away step by step into their own pursuits. When they separated, he went with his mother and was seen to grow much happier. The boy too was disappointed in his natural father, so tediously ordinary, and he always carried a seed of curiosity about his 'first father', as he inaccurately thought of Sloane.

298

Deep inside, Sarah felt that Jeffrey had not died. He had only been spirited away somewhere. But how could a lone woman fight her way through all the official barriers to find out where? And then a disturbing scrap of information reached her from an unexpected source. Eight years after *that week*, in a chemist's shop in the West End, she ran into her old neighbour Mrs Granby from Richmond Road. Mrs Granby told her about a small, timid man she had confronted acting suspiciously in front of the house, peering, then turning away in some inner hesitation. He was American, spoke with a stammer and said he was a schoolteacher on holiday. He told Mrs Granby he knew something about a man who had once lived in No. 16 and was now confined in a small asylum hidden in an arid range of hills in Eastern Oregon. It was important in some undefined way that someone in the neighbourhood know that the man was alive and might be in need of help. He said the man was carried on the records of the asylum as John Slocum, and his treatment for acute schizophrenia was being underwritten by a secret bank account in Virginia. The source of all this information he refused to reveal.

Immediately Sarah took a leave of absence and flew to Oregon to investigate for herself. Rather, she flew to Seattle and hired a car which she drove south-east across what seemed hundreds of miles of hostile, virtually unpopulated land to the asylum. A stiff administrator in a pale blue coat barred her way in and told her pugnaciously that no one of that name or any similar name or description had ever been treated there. Unsatisfied, she sat in the car for an hour staring at the tiled Spanish building nestling into the hills. Then she made her way to a windswept town called Pendleton nearby. The town reminded her far more of a Texas cow-town than of her mental picture of Oregon.

On one of the back streets she found Colfax Investigations, up a flight of wooden stairs to the upper floor of an old frame house. There was only a single desk in the office, and only a single investigator under a welter of signs, *Walter Colfax, Licensed and Bonded, Day or Night, Strictly Confidential, Civil and Criminal, Surveillance, No Credit Work Please*. He was a gaunt, grey-haired man who gulped a lot and drawled an odd sort of language that seemed distilled from old films and comic books.

'Well, ma'am, seeing it isn't a case of . . . uh . . . voluntary disappearance, you know, if he's ever been in these parts, I reckon I can find out in seventy-two hours. There's a flat rate of $250 and . . . uh . . . expenses.'

'That seems like quite a lot.'

'No, ma'am, I'll be taking you on exclusive-like for the time, and I got to cover incidentals and lost office time and . . . uh . . . the like. I know we don't look much' – (*We?* she thought) – 'but you couldn't do better with one of them big out-a-town outfits like the Pinks. I been in business here for twenty-two years, and it's indispensable in this line of work to know whose axe is being gored, like.'

Reluctantly she paid half in advance and took a room in an antiseptic motel overlooking a vacant rodeo ground that howled with wind at night. She had never felt more foolish and alien, and she longed to be in a more comprehensible country, or even just a bigger city, where she would know better how to go about things. It was Jeffrey's country, she knew, but she wondered if he would have felt comfortable here any longer. Everything seemed to be on the surface, with no roots underneath; no consciousness stirring under the oddly open, intimate, impertinent words that were spoken from the tongue, not the mind. So many of the people seemed like children playing in a toy house they had built; all their actions calculated to deny any meanings except the most obvious and banal. Even the money sneered at her, so smug, inward and self-sufficient that the smallest, thinnest coin was labelled just 'one dime' without a hint to tell you its relation to the dollar.

Two days passed, and Walter Colfax's daily reports listed nothing but dead-end inquiries – spelled with that hostile American 'i' – many of which she suspected he had fabricated or at least embellished for the expense sheet. On the third night he arrived in a state of agitation and insisted on driving her across town.

He parked his huge battered car in front of a stucco bungalow where yellow weeds fought up through an abandoned boat trailer. The screen door hung askew on its hinges. 'This is truly amazing,' he kept repeating. 'People are sure something, you know? In all my years tracing, this just about beats the cake, you better believe it.'

She'd better? What if she didn't? she wondered. A shrivelled woman waited for them inside, clutching a glass of red wine, and Sarah didn't catch her name when she was introduced. They sat on overstuffed chairs leaking their padding onto a hooked rug and waited as the woman paced from an empty fireplace to a china cabinet filled with pamphlets of some kind.

'I shouldn't oughtta tell you, cause you'll laugh at me like some of the others, but I know this for God's own fact.'

Sarah was leaning forward, growing agitated herself, and she wanted to cry out to the woman to stand still and speak plainly, but she held her tongue.

The woman stated a precise hour of the night and a date, some weeks before. With her eyes roving and frightened, she explained that at the very aforementioned hour, a large glowing object had landed outside the town with a hissing noise like a Hoover over a wooden floor. The thing had taken aboard her nephew, Tommy, his two children and several other people. Among those kidnapped were several patients from the asylum. 'Undoubtedly for the purpose of their scientific study of mental disease in earth creatures. They don't have things like mental disease and they must be curious about us.' John Slocum was one of the patients taken aboard, but it had all been hushed up by the authorities.

Sarah remained as polite as she could, though inside she felt a mixture of rage, helplessness, and deep mortification. Driving back to the motel, Colfax seemed hurt that she didn't show more appreciation of his amazing discovery, and in her head she tried out and abandoned a number of indignant, sarcastic replies. Early the next morning she checked out and drove straight west on Highway 80 toward the airport in Portland. As she left town, she looked back once at the streets and buildings spreading like a stain between the low furry hills, and the bare vulgarity of the place overwhelmed her. She had a sense that in a town like this, even the highest forms of tragedy wouldn't ennoble people; victims would be left grovelling and ugly in the dust. The thought made her feel petty and mean, but she couldn't help it and she hoped if Jeffrey had ever been there he had gone on somewhere else to live and die.

The nerve of the detective! she thought, allowing herself a small rage as she drove over the last rise, and Pendleton dropped out of sight for good. For just an instant, she wondered if one of those dollar-rich American intelligence agencies might actually whisk people off in secret flying machines. Or was there some hidden message for her in this bizarre American obsession with pseudo-science mysticism? The woman was obviously a True Believer; she had seen enough of them on television. In a way you couldn't blame them: look at the flat and hollow world they lived in. There had to be something better.

They were always convinced that the Celestial Visitors brought news of a world that was more rational, better ordered, more advanced, more joyous, and more just. But Sarah had always wondered, what if it's *worse*?

The flight home was uneventful, and the low sky was dark and drizzling when she emerged from the tube at Clapham South.

OTHER BOOKS FROM PLUTO

WATCHING THE DETECTIVES
JULIAN RATHBONE

In Brabt, trains run on time and the bags you lose end up at the lost-and-found. Suddenly, the clockwork state is interrupted – by police brutality and terrorist violence. Headlines and news bulletins put the blame on 'left-wing violence committed to the overthrow of the state'. Commissioner Jan Argand agrees, until an anti-nuclear demonstration turns into a near massacre and Argand himself narrowly escapes an attempt on his life.

'Julian Rathbone is a highly original artist who uses the thriller form to comment on the increasing violence and absurdity of the post-industrial world we live in.' *Literary Review*

240 pages
0 7453 0011 1 £2.50 paperback

NOT A THROUGH STREET
ERNEST LARSEN

Emma Hobart drives a New York taxi. Her
lover, Hoyt, is investigating a mysterious death.
Emma's cab is involved in an accident that
causes Hoyt's death. Student anti-war politics
and political corruption block her search for the
killers. One question too many and Emma is
driving for her life.

A feminist cabbie invades the Chandler
tradition – the result is stunning.

Ernest Larsen was born in Chicago and went
to Columbia University. Since then he has
worked at a variety of jobs, including being a
house painter, a department-store Santa Claus
and a taxi driver. He is currently Editor of the
film journal *Jump Cut*. He lives in California.

'Something decidedly new in the author's style,
which is sensitive, compassionate and even
poetic.' *New York Times*

240 pages
0 7453 0039 1 £2.50 paperback
0 7453 0041 3 £7.95 hardback

DANCE HALL OF THE DEAD
TONY HILLERMAN

A young Zuni Indian Fire God disappears – and is then found murdered. His Navajo friend is running for his life. Lt Joe Leaphorn, also a Navajo, stalks a killer whose trail is crossed by archaeologists on the make, a Federal narcotics agent and hippy dropouts.

'Hillerman has created an altogether believable set of characters… He knows his background well.' *New York Times.*

The reputation of Tony Hillerman's Indian reservation thrillers is growing fast. *Dance Hall of the Dead* won the prestigious Edgar 'Mystery Novel of the Year' when published in the US. This is its first publication in the UK and Australia.

0 86104 692 7 £2.25 paperback
0 86104 693 5 £7.95 hardback

FRISCO BLUES
GORDON DeMARCO

It's 1947. San Francisco. The war is over and the boys are coming home. America is changing. Jackie Robinson has just broken the colour bar in the national game and baseball has been 'integrated'. Or has it?

Chet Jones, a promising young black baseball player in the negro leagues, has fallen to his death in a racially troubled shipyard. Was it an accident, as the company claims, or murder? Riley Kovachs finds himself in work once again.

Gordon DeMarco lives in San Francisco. Before becoming a full-time writer, he was a student striker, a dishwasher, a chauffeur and a docker. His hero, Riley Kovachs, also appears in *The Canvas Prison* and *October Heat* (Pluto Press).

'Mr DeMarco makes his points without sacrificing his excitements in what must be the most innovative publishing experiment of the crime-story year.' *Guardian*, reviewing Gordon DeMarco's *October Heat*

128 pages
0 7453 0040 5 £2.25 paperback
0 7453 0042 1 £7.50 hardback

JUNK ON THE HILL
JEREMY PIKSER

To avoid being a customs officer, Joe Posner
was prepared to do a lot of things – including
becoming a private eye and moving to New
Jersey.

Business is slow. So slow that Posner is
reluctant to turn down sixteen-year-old Melanie
Gold's offer of work. Gold later turns up dead,
and Posner is left without a client but with a lot
of unanswered questions. His search for the
answers takes him to the affluent suburbs – 'the
human potential movement', therapy, and
heroin consumption. For sure, Posner's New
Jersey looks nothing like the covers of *Time,
Life* and the *Saturday Evening Post*. Still, what
can one expect of a state where the delis run
out of strudel.

'Crude vitality.' *Guardian*
'Slickly written, ironically humourous.'
Tribune

224 pages
0 86104 786 9 £3.50 paperback
0 86104 787 7 £8.95 hardback

THE ANVIL AGREEMENT
KEN BEGG

Cytogerm is a miracle drug with deadly side effects. Its manufacturers are intent on eliminating everyone connected with it. Its discoverer, Dr Sean MacLean, is on the run. He attempts suicide. His failure has terrifying consequences. A medical thriller of *Coma* standards.

Ken Begg works for the Medical Research Council of Great Britain at Edinburgh University.

160 pages
0 7453 0030 8 £2.50 paperback
0 7453 0031 6 £7.95 hardback

MURDER IN THE CENTRAL COMMITTEE
MANUEL VAZQUEZ MONTALBAN

The first appearance in English of a Spanish writer whose crime novels are international best sellers and have won both the Planeta Prize (the Spanish Booker) and the Grand Prix of detective fiction in France. Set in the fratricidal world of the Spanish Communist Party, this is the perfect political thriller.

   'At last a thriller worthy of the name; a taut, intelligent tour de force set in the shadowy minefield of post-Franco Spanish politics.' Julie Birchill

224 pages
0 86104 747 8 £3.50 **paperback**
0 86104 771 0 £7.95 **hardback**